GUARDIAN

STAR

Lorna Brockway Lieske

Seven Sisters Publishing

Reading is heavenly . . .

Guardian Star
Copyright © 2017 Lorna Brockway Lieske
2nd Edition 2025
All rights reserved.
ISBN: 0692973788
ISBN-13: 9780692973783

Surely one of life's most treasured blessings
is having someone special travel the road with you.

…I am counted among those thus blessed.

And in the shelter of that blessing,
I gratefully dedicate this novel to my husband, Richard.

For some unfathomable reason,
this brilliant, talented man
loves me in spite of my myriad flaws and failings,
still seeing the girl I was;
in his eyes unmarred by life's travail.

…Yes, truly I am blessed.

CONTENTS

PROLOGUE

Cold air gushed up from out of the inky blackness. It drove her hair away from her face and caused tiny chill bumps to erupt on every inch of exposed flesh as she leaned forward, straining to see into the expansive void below her.

She shivered involuntarily.

From deep within the black, the rhythmic thrumming of a mechanized heartbeat pulsed continuously. A derisive counterpoint to the rush of icy air, it reverberated through the frigid metal against which she braced herself and filled the silence with menacing emptiness.

She was alone.

It seemed to her—as she took stock of her present situation—that "aloneness" was the defining characteristic of her life. Every relationship she could recall had offered little more than an embryonic sense of belonging and she wondered anew if belonging was what she had ever really wanted.

With a sardonic smirk at her momentary lapse into philosophizing about the meaning of life, she realized that what she *really* wanted was a cigarette—badly.

What a time—and what a place—for a nicotine attack!

Cautiously shifting her weight so as not to relinquish the rather precarious hold she maintained on her balance, she once again peered into the blackness below the ledge on which she crouched; a blackness that seemed as vast as eternity.

It returned her stare with insolent confidence. . .

Government is not reason;

it is not eloquence;

it is force.

Like fire, it is a dangerous servant. . .

. . .or a fearful master.

~ George Washington

CHAPTER ONE
Borders Settlement #4
In the former state of Missouri

I.

Valaria Thorpe was caught between the proverbial rock and a hard place. Her nicotine-starved brain was crying out for a cigarette. In fact, it wasn't just crying out, it was wailing like a colicky infant. This was the nexus of what had become a precipice-ridden dilemma for the Borders resident.

The rocky part of Thorpe's predicament was the fact that it was hours after curfew and the consequences if caught outside would be significant. The hard place was the reality that cigarettes were illegal and the lingering smell of burnt tobacco would be a dead giveaway if she smoked inside. Either way she could land in some deeply serious shit.

She hesitated—rock or hard place?

The last thing Valaria needed was another smoking violation on her record—one more and the Health Enforcement Agency would swoop down, talons bared, and subtract yet another ten health credits. At this rate, by the time she was 50 she wouldn't qualify for a box of tissues!

The hard place won.

Snatching the pouch of freshly rolled smokes from her stash under the bar, Thorpe crossed the pub and headed for the steps leading from the door up to the surface, the omnipresent mutt who had adopted her some three weeks earlier matching her stride for stride. She and the dog paused in the shadows at the bottom of the stairwell before committing themselves to the dusty expanse at ground level. Valaria was defiant by nature but even her nicotine-induced desperation recognized the wisdom of acquiescing to at least a degree of post-curfew caution.

"Hold up, bud," she said, palm outstretched in front of the dog's snout when he moved toward the stairs.

Attention focused heavenward, Valaria scanned the night sky in the direction of the distant cluster of lights forming an artificial constellation atop the mile-high Guardian Star tower twelve miles to the northwest. Anticipating the arrival of a Tactical Observation Drone—her late night nemesis—she stood in the dark and listened for its familiar low-pitched hum. Called TOD for short, the low-flying surveillance drones were constant companions and their purportedly random flight patterns should bring one within range any time now.

She scratched the dog's head and waited.

Nothing but the familiar symphony of crickets and bullfrogs serenaded the sleeping settlement. Thorpe's vigilance eased but she lingered in the shadows a moment longer anxiously fingering the drawstring pouch that cradled the contraband smokes.

She could almost taste the heavenly bite of tobacco.

Growing confident that the drone was still out of range—and driven by a need for nicotine that was coercing her like a schoolyard bully—Valaria climbed the steps and emerged from the shadows into a bath of icy-white moonlight.

The circular base of the decrepit geodesic dome under which she had both lived and worked for almost thirty years curved away behind her. Its tall, sloping surface threw a shadow across the moonlit ground that offered refuge from the lunar spotlight. Slipping into the dark silhouette's embrace, she glanced down at the dog.

"Anything on radar, or are we're good to go?"

He responded with a look of adoration and a wagging tail.

"Good to go it is then," she murmured.

Slinking along the curve of the dome's base, Thorpe headed for a small, dilapidated storage shed some 50 yards to the west and the ragged canvas awning drooping mournfully across the entrance. The dog—a black and white Border Collie mix—tagged along devotedly, creating a canine version of Valaria's well-practiced slink. Just short of the shed she stopped dead in her tracks and with a snap of her fingers brought the dog to her side as she darted beneath the limp awning.

A barely audible low-pitched hum heralded the approach of the 3 a.m. TOD.

As it flew overhead the drone's wide-angle NightSight lens swept the barren terrain with a slow, repetitive arc, its sleek, aerodynamic fuselage basking in the reflective glow of the full moon. Valaria pressed herself back into the dappled shadow cast by the ragged canvas—throwing a hand gesture TOD's way that she hoped was appropriately insulting should her presence be detected by the analyst at the receiving end of the drone's telemetry.

"Good morning, Dawson," she muttered under her breath, assuming that Hayes would be at his post dutifully scanning and analyzing the data being relayed from the drone to the Guardian Star.

"Gotta light?" she asked as a sarcastic exclamation point to punctuate the rude gesture she prolonged in upward fashion. A self-satisfied chortle gurgled up and she glanced around, half expecting to find someone other than herself as the source. Once more assured of her solitude, Valaria directed her attention to the drawstring pouch and, with a level of reverence usually reserved for something sacred, extracted a somewhat crumpled, hand-rolled cigarette.

With the gentleness of a kiss, she placed it between her lips.

If detected, she knew Dawson would turn her in. The fact that she let him drink after hours wouldn't protect her. It made her pause... for about as long as a child hesitates before snatching a cookie from an unguarded plate. Pulling a small lighter from the back pocket of her jeans she hesitated just a moment longer, thumb poised over the small tab that would activate the heating element and bring the torch to life.

"Aw, what the hell?" she asked the dog.

Yancy—as she had dubbed the mutt after realizing he had decided to stay—offered no response other than a broad canine grin and a tail that wagged with the enthusiastic approval of a co-conspirator.

Thus encouraged, Valaria flicked the tab and drew nicotine deep into her grateful lungs.

Luxuriating in repeated draws on the cigarette, she heaved a contented sigh and lowered her guard as the observation drone evaporated into the inky blanket of the early morning sky.

This was her favorite time of day. Most residents of the settlement respected curfew—or at least violated it as inconspicuously as possible—and once the wee hours of the morning rolled around she usually was the only one who ventured outside. It was something that gave Thorpe an almost proprietary sense of ownership over the grouping of twenty geodesic domes and adjacent domed farm that comprised the settlement. Despite the fact that maintaining the skeletal framework supporting the farm's covering had long ago passed from routine to critical, and 'showing their age' was a polite euphemism for the deterioration taking hold of their dwellings, this was home and, like most residents of Settlement #4, Valaria had grown accustomed to the bleak sameness of her world.

Her thoughts snagged on the adjective as she took a brooding draw on the cigarette.

Bleak... a physical appearance, an emotional perspective, an anticipated future. This was the word she cynically associated with her surroundings and with her life.

The settlement she called home was dusty, drab, and decaying.

Her outlook on life was tainted by years spent in the shadow of regimented routine.

The future was a dirt road meandering across the desolate five-mile circumference of her world.

Scoffing at her momentary lapse into tedious philosophizing and shaking her head in self-disdain, Thorpe absently flicked a length of ash off the end of the cigarette. She stepped somewhat cautiously to the front of the shed and lowered herself to sit cross-legged on the ground just under the shelter of the awning. Actually, in spite of its bland sameness and the mercurial mood swings of the regime under whose thumb they toiled, life in the Borders had its advantages; she doubted if a city dweller could even *find* a cigarette let alone think lighting up was worth the risk.

"Poor bastards," she mused.

Staring up at the chaos of stars that peppered the night sky Valaria continued to smoke, squinting as the exhaust expelled from each satisfying draw wafted into her eyes. Yancy settled himself contentedly at her side as she blinked the smoke away, listened to the quiet and took stock of her world.

The cluster of domes scattered across the empty landscape looked more like a family of turtles basking on a sun-drenched beach than a group of dwellings glistening in moonlight. The metaphor was intensified by five long-abandoned wind turbines silhouetted on the distant horizon. Her grandfather had always called the turbines "bird blenders"—derisively dismissing them as inefficient energy sources and nothing more than visual pollution—but they reminded Valaria of the simple pinwheels he had fashioned for her from broad-leafed reeds when they sat along the shore of a tiny lake just inside their 5-mile limit and she inhaled bittersweet memory along with her next draw on the cigarette.

Her grandfather.

Thoughts of Otis brought the trace of a wry smile to Valaria's face, momentarily softening her cynical outlook on the world.

A master carpenter and something of a recluse, her grandfather had been less than enthusiastic when faced with the prospect of raising his 5-year-old granddaughter following the death of Valaria's parents. The elder Thorpe had been in the Borders just over four years by then so hadn't seen Valaria since before she could walk. He was a silent, brooding man and the word reticent barely covered his feelings about taking responsibility for a child he barely knew. But when news had finally reached him that his son and daughter-in-law were dead Otis had been determined that the child not be raised by the state and was willing to do whatever it took to gain her transfer to the austere hinterland that defined his exile.

And so Valaria Thorpe had become a so-called Pioneer.

Created after The Revanche, the Borders was a 400-mile-wide buffer zone formed by the Reorganized States of America's dual border system. It stood between two defunct north-south interstate highways—I-55, running some 850 miles from Lake Michigan down into southern Louisiana and, farther west, I-35 extending 1,400 miles from the southwestern shore of Lake Superior to the Republic of Texas. As its name implied, the Borders was intended to protect the RSA, to insulate it from the vast unreclaimed western territory. Over the decades since The Revanche, it had done that and more, becoming the locus of a lopsided symbiotic relationship between the ostracized misfits confined there and their more compliant counterparts living in the Safe Zones east of the Mississippi River.

Otis Thorpe had always thought the insulation worked both ways and had sought the Borders's anonymity for the orphaned child he reluctantly took under his wing.

Valaria couldn't help smiling. Her earliest memory of her grandfather was looking up into unsmiling eyes in a gaunt, weathered face. He was tall and angular, and when he reached out his hand to take hers it seemed to emerge from a very great distance above her. The fingers were gnarled, skin sun-browned and papery, the top of his hand dappled with dark spots and crisscrossed with protruding blue veins. But when those fingers had closed around hers a surge of kinship passed between them and the little girl knew she was safe. She had never asked how Otis procured her release from the State Primary Academy and although the 5-year-old girl had been apprehensive about leaving the familiar routine of school and dormitory life, there was something about the old man towering above her that, in the mind of a child, seemed heroic even if he was a total stranger.

Valaria took one last drag on the cigarette's dwindling stub, singeing her fingertips in the process before letting it fall to the ground. She pulled Yancy to her and scratched the dog behind his alert ears, rose and snuffed out the smoldering butt with the sole of her shoe.

"Come on, bud, let's not press our luck."

Thoughts of family dogged Thorpe's heels alongside her canine companion as they walked the short distance back to the dome's entrance.

It wasn't as if her father and grandfather had been estranged exactly. It was just that Otis was a fiercely independent person willing to leave the relative security of the Safe Zones for the increased autonomy he believed was available in the Borders—however marginal that increase might be. Unlike him, Valaria's parents had been city dwellers through and through. Computer engineers selected for government service, they had opted to stay where they were rather than follow the family patriarch on what they perceived to be a foolish, misguided quest for something that no longer existed. The few times it had been referenced over the years, Otis had characterized the separation as a simple parting of the ways with no strong emotion attached to it one way or the other but, as she matured, Valaria had grown to suspect the old man of guarding wounded pride—and a lonely heart.

Vincent and Mara Thorpe had been assigned to the so-called "NAB'D" project, the **N**orth **A**merican **B**order **D**efense initiative intended to "nab" illegals and terrorists. Working on NAB'D had been a plum assignment—bringing better housing and increased rations—and Valaria's parents had considered themselves lucky to be chosen. Otis had never talked much about his son but Valaria had gleaned that her parents' work focused on maintaining and upgrading the computerized network that was the heart and soul of the border defense web—a physical barrier and technological security grid created after The Revanche to prevent penetration of what had just proven to be tragically porous national borders.

Because of his son's status Otis could have stayed in the RSA but, as someone who worked with his hands, his skills were virtually unmarketable there and his independent, Luddite-leaning philosophy veered dramatically away from popular dogma—he walked an extremely fine line between what was acceptable and what very definitely was not. As a result, Thorpe's grandfather had, quite logically, opted for relocation to the hinterland where his "deviance" would be less noticeable and less of a potential problem for his family. His more conventional son was not inclined to follow and, if truth be told, had been relieved to see his father go.

As time passed and the years with her grandfather gave color and dimension to her life, Valaria often wondered whether—if her parents had lived—she would even have visited the old man let alone been the recipient of his unorthodox influence. In light of the physical and philosophical distance between father and son—and since travel passes were virtually impossible to obtain—it was likely that Otis would have been nothing more than a familial footnote had her parents not died. And in spite of that traumatic loss, she was very glad the fates had deigned to bring the old man and the little girl together.

Lights blinked on as Valaria and Yancy reentered the dome, unpredictable sensors having suddenly detected their presence. The dog trotted ahead, tongue lolling and tail wagging in anticipation of the late night—or rather early morning—snack that usually followed their clandestine treks.

"Yeah, OK," she said to the dog as he cast an expectant glance back her way, "just give me a minute."

Thorpe wove her way through the tables and chairs of the pub, following in Yancy's wake as he made a beeline for the bar at the rear.

Still adrift in thoughts of Otis, Valaria slid her fingers reverently along the top of each wooden chair as she walked, appreciating the velvety smooth surfaces and enjoying the strong smell of the beeswax polish she still made according to her grandfather's directions and diligently applied to the wood. There was no metal or recycled plastic in Otis's pub. Each table and chair was a tribute to the skill of her grandfather, made from various woods and in various styles as supply and inspiration had dictated over the years. This was his legacy—hers now—and she was determined it would stand the test of time and continue to offer patrons what Otis always believed to be a more natural and quality atmosphere in which to unwind and enjoy their libations.

"Here you go, Yance," she said to the dog. His plaintive whine had shaken her from her reverie as she stood behind the bar for a moment, smiling into the memory of her beloved curmudgeon. She tossed him a broken piece of the seasoned dry toast that passed for snack food in the pub.

"But don't think you're getting any beer, dude," she added sardonically in response to his imploring look. "It's way past curfew."

II.

Dawson Hayes was tired. It was his last night on the month long graveyard shift and he could hardly wait to be relieved. He dreaded the duty roster inevitably bringing this overnight stint his way; seemed he would just be getting his sleep cycle back on track when his name would come up again and he'd be right back where he started from.

Surreptitiously rotating his stiff shoulders first left and then right, Hayes stifled a yawn and hoped his three comrades didn't notice. Of course, they probably were just as tired as he was and growing just as restless from monitoring their own TOD as it surveyed the monotonous, overgrown tangle of trees, weeds, and decayed structures that extended in every direction from the deforested 2-mile perimeter surrounding the tower.

Dawson chuffed quietly. He knew his colleagues only too well. As elite members of the Guardians none of them would take the risk of admitting fatigue, not even to one of their peers. They were the brightest and best of the Corps, selected because of their physical and mental prowess. Any sign of weakness could result in demotion and reassignment; a fate worse than death in the status-conscious RSA.

As if validating his thoughts, Hayes noticed that, although effectively stifled, his yawn seemed to be contagious as Cooper Hendricks, the officer to his right, did an exaggerated throat clearing that barely masked his cavernous maw.

He caught Hendrick's eye and raised a conspiratorial eyebrow. Cooper shrugged in diffident acknowledgement of their mutual fatigue but said nothing.

They rarely spoke while on duty, each officer focusing on the 3D screens hovering at eye level as their ever-vigilant drone relayed visuals and data for them to interpret, catalog, or act upon. Even though the drones rarely detected anything more sinister than the occasional curfew violation or black market transaction—Freebooters being less accommodating when robbing and pillaging—their tactical observations were an integral part of homeland security and Hayes was good at his job. He had a sharp eye and was particularly adept at maneuvering TOD's cameras by means of the optical interface embedded in his right temple, directly connecting him to the drone.

Dawson refocused his attention on the screens in front of him. TOD was continuing along its programmed flight pattern and, in a moment, the unmistakable humps of settlement domes emerged across the moonlit horizon.

"Right on time," he smirked to himself, *"let's see what the 'warts' are up to tonight."*

He shifted position, directed his attention to the middle screen and, moving his eyes ever so slightly, flew his TOD in for a closer look at Settlement #4.

There were twenty geodesic domes in #4, the maximum allowed. Each curved roofline crested at a height of no more than 15 feet since much of the structure was below ground. An architectural anomaly that enjoyed fleeting popularity during the previous century, they were an excellent example of form following function. Simple and elegant in design, as well as being relatively easy to assemble and maintain, the domes had the added feature of being able to withstand an F-5 tornado—an ideal characteristic for life on the frontier. But as a result of emerging as little more than squat bumps on the flat Borders landscape, some Guardian long ago had referred to them as warts and the nickname stuck.

As TOD made its final approach, Dawson refined its NightSight lens for a careful sweep of the settlement.

The trace of a sardonic smile creased his face as he scanned the barren terrain. Although he wouldn't have called them warts to their faces, since the Borders was populated by people the government publicly referred to as 'Pioneers' but officially categorized as 'Deviants' the term seemed apropos.

Here society's potentially troublesome nonconformists were contained. Ever since the Borders's inception, those who espoused unacceptable beliefs, asked the wrong questions, or simply proved unable to adapt to modern life were given the choice of re-education programs designed to enhance conformity or relocation to the hinterland's work camps. For many people there was really only one viable option. And although Borders settlements fell somewhere between an 1800's Indian reservation and a 20th century Soviet gulag, as long as one adhered to the strictures of resettlement and obeyed the regime's draconian laws, government intervention was minimal. It was a situation acceptable to most residents, especially since the consequence of violation was *mandatory* re-education. In reality, being sent to the Borders was a type of exile, but it was a banishment of generally like-minded souls who grew accustomed to limited conveniences and came to rely on their wits and one another for survival.

In addition to providing a dumping ground for society's discards—one deemed acceptably humane by the Triumvirate—each Borders settlement was assigned a specific industry that benefitted the Safe Zones and every resident was required to provide the labor needed to meet their community's quota.

Settlement #4 was an agricultural posting.

Located just south of the residential area Dawson Hayes currently scanned were three long, domed greenhouses divided into climate-controlled sections where crops and fish with similar needs were grown and monitored. The pavilion took up a fraction of the space needed by traditional farming for each section was designed to facilitate maximum yield with a minimal footprint. Under the first elongated dome, vertical walls grew kale and spinach, in front of which plants that typically sit on the soil—squash, broccoli, and tomatoes—flourished in rot-resistant nets suspended in rows several feet off the ground. The second dome was dedicated to corn, wheat, and soybeans that had been genetically modified to provide multiple harvests each year. And in the third, a fish farm raised high-protein salmon.

Once harvested, the bulk of #4's yields were transported to the Safe Zones in return for manufactured goods produced in Borders settlements assigned to industry. Although shortages abounded it was, purportedly, a mutually beneficial relationship referred to as the 'Symbiosis System' and intended to meet the needs of Exiles as well as city dwellers. The irony of the name wasn't lost on Guardian Hayes. As a member of the vanguard tasked with keeping the exiles in line, he knew the reality of their existence was more like host to leech than the symbiotic bond touted by the government in Columbus.

As his TOD approached the western edge of the settlement, Hayes dipped its left wing slightly, glimpsing a pinpoint of light as the drone banked into a slow turn.

Just beyond the last dome there was a small shed that had been the workshop of the carpenter who had lived there until his death about a year ago. If Dawson's suspicions were correct, it was more than a flash of reflected moonlight that had caught his eye.

Someone was breaking curfew.

The dome that had grabbed his attention housed a pub called *The Shoe and Gear* of which the carpenter had been proprietor. Since his passing, the carpenter's granddaughter had taken over.

Dawson shook his head at the thought of Valaria Thorpe.

She was a real piece of work. Her tall, almost regal bearing definitely was contradicted by the mouth and attitude she had inherited from her grandfather. It was a rare thing for an exile to be accepted back into the Zones—and there was no way in hell Valaria Thorpe would ever be among them!

Focusing his concentration on the screen's image, Dawson blinked slowly to enhance resolution. There was slight movement barely noticeable at the edge of the shed's awning.

It was the wagging of a dog's tail.

"Got ya," he whispered with a satisfied smirk. "Just had to have that last smoke, didn't you, Valaria? God, what a disgusting habit!"

Feeling rather smug as a result of earning a point in the one-sided game of Drone Tag he played with her, Dawson readjusted TOD's camera and flew on.

III.

One of the few advantages of living in the Borders was that, as long as you did your assigned work, no one told you when you had to get up in the morning—no one, that is, unless you had a restless dog living with you who wasn't averse to hiking his leg on your furniture if you didn't supply a tree quickly enough.

Valaria stretched languidly, emerging from deep sleep into the abrupt realization that there was a dog's moist nose about a millimeter from her face.

"Holy crap, Yancy," she blurted out, startled into alertness and bumping her head on the curved wall above her as she bolted upright.

Because of living in a dome, flat walls were rare since they created useless space behind them due to the curved bones of the structure. The bunk in Valaria's bedroom was inserted into one of those rare flat surfaces in order to utilize the void the wall produced and maximize the room's floor space. As a result, however, the curve grew more pronounced the farther into bed she nestled and even sleeping there for 30 years was no guarantee against the occasional head-on collision.

"You nearly made me pee my pants," Valaria scolded the dog, plopping back onto her pillow and gingerly touching her forehead. "Shit, how am I going to explain a bruise on my face? My dog beats me?"

Yancy's tail began happily sweeping the floor where he sat and his face, resting against the edge of the bed directly next to her pillow, sprang to life in an expression of pure canine joy.

"OK, OK, you win," she moaned, pulling herself up to a sitting position and swinging her legs over the side of the bunk. "God, you're a royal pain in the ass sometimes."

She sat there for a moment, absently scratching the dog behind his ears and waiting for her body, still leadened by sleep, to catch up to her dog-induced wakefulness. Yancy gave her a rather stricken look of urinary urgency. He pulled away from her touch, trotted over to the bedroom door and started doing what she had come to call the piddle-prance—a series of low bows, tight spins, and throaty chuffs that was as entertaining as it was insistent.

Triggered by the dog's movement, the lighting began its automatic transition from a dawn-like glow to what Valaria bemoaned as a more intrusive wake-up call.

"Yeah, Yeah, I'm coming," she said to the light. To the dog she added, "You can just wait a minute or two—at least you better, butt-head!"

She slid out of the bunk and straightened the oversized t-shirt she wore for sleeping. Pulling on a pair of jeans, she headed toward the door. Automatic lighting continued to acknowledge them as the pair made their way through her small living quarters, crossed the pub, and headed toward the main entrance to the dome.

Yancy was out the door and up the stairs almost before Valaria had a chance to lean into the retinal scan that released the door lock. She followed at a decidedly slower and less-than-enthusiastic pace.

Not being a morning person, the painfully perfect blue sky that greeted them was far too virtuous for Valaria to handle so soon after waking. She left the dog to his morning ablutions and, with the front door ajar so he could return when he wanted, headed back into the welcoming embrace of the dimly lit pub.

Just as she reached the doorway to her rooms a familiar voice called out from the dome's entrance.

"You open for business?"

Turning, Valaria smiled at the heavyset woman who had entered the pub.

"Not for drinking," she replied, "but I'll put the coffee on if you want a cup."

Mavis Pope returned the smile gratefully. "That's just what I was hoping for; as long as you've still got some of the real stuff and not any of that rancid crap the feds palm off on us. God, that stuff tastes like piss!"

"Make up your mind," Valaria said with a smile. "Is it crap or piss?"

Mavis smiled broadly, displaying an ample amount of pink gum above teeth that seemed too small for her mouth. "Take your pick."

Bearing the distinction of being the Settlement's only newcomer in more than five years, Mavis Pope was a flamboyant young woman who was almost as broad as she was tall. She blamed her size on a genetic predisposition to corpulence—regardless of the fact that such things were supposed to be detected during embryonic screenings—and an appetite for all foods deemed decadent. Valaria sometimes wondered if Mavis also was genetically predisposed to wear the most garish caftans she could tailor for herself from the scraps of cloth she hoarded as obsessively as a magpie collects anything shiny.

Opting for resettlement when her lack of dietary compliance and increasing girth brought her to the attention of the authorities, Mavis ended up in Settlement #4 when the death of Valaria's grandfather left an opening in the strictly controlled population. At first Valaria had found the woman's presence disconcerting if not actually insulting, coming as it did on the heels of the greatest personal loss of her life. But such was the reality of the ebb and flow of settlement existence; there were very few births but people died and eventually someone came along and took their place. Valaria knew her distaste for the new arrival was irrational and the young woman's gregarious personality—and perseverance—eventually had won her over.

Mavis made her way through the labyrinth of tables and joined Valaria at the back of the pub, presenting her with two ruddy eggs and another gum-displaying smile. "I'll provide breakfast if you provide the caffeine."

"You've got yourself a deal," Valaria replied as the two women entered her quarters.

Allotted only about one-quarter of the overall space, the private portion of the dome was divided into three sections. There was a small bedroom and an even smaller bathroom at the back, complemented by a larger living, dining, and kitchen area directly behind the pub.

As a result of her grandfather's skills as a carpenter, their quarters were furnished with unique pieces of his own design; the main area outfitted with an oak dining table and four chairs, a compact futon that had served as Otis's bed once Valaria had joined him, and two matching side chairs. Ingenious cabinets and shelving units added storage versatility as well as visual appeal to the kitchenette and periphery of the small living area. Like the tables and chairs in the pub, each piece of furniture was beautifully crafted, but these personal items were augmented with the carpenter's signature engraving either on their surface or around their legs—intricate geometric designs that had always intrigued and mystified the child living there. Otis had described his style as 'Frank Lloyd Wright Meets Primary School Math' and had shown Valaria an antique publication from long before The Revanche containing hundreds of pictures of the revered Mr. Wright's work.

That musty old book was now one of her greatest treasures.

"Wish I had known your grandfather," Mavis was saying somewhat wistfully. She had taken a seat at the dining table and was running her fingers along the geometric pattern enhancing its edge. "No one does work like this anymore."

"That was Otis in a nutshell," Valaria replied, coming over to the table to get the eggs. "He definitely was one of a kind; liked to use his hands and definitely was stuck in the past."

Mavis looked up at her host as she handed over the eggs. "Damn, Valaria, what happened to your head?"

Valaria paused for a moment, throwing an "*I told you so*" look in the direction of the absent dog.

"…Yancy beats me."

If you love security greater than liberty, the tranquility of servitude greater than the animating contest for freedom, go home from us in peace. We seek not your counsel, nor your help. Crouch down and lick the hand that feeds you; may your chains set lightly upon you, and may posterity forget that you were our countrymen.

~ Sam Adams

CHAPTER TWO

I.

Living in the Safe Zones of the R.S.A.—the Reorganized States of America—was a privilege not to be taken lightly. Christopher Damon couldn't imagine anyone even questioning the validity of that statement but there were times when he wished more would in order to reduce the burden he shouldered as a low-level government functionary. For him the bottom line was clear—the more people they could ship to the Borders, the better off those remaining would be.

Years of crisis had followed the plague and only five metropolitan areas had fully recovered—all located west of the contamination from decaying nuclear facilities that had turned the eastern seaboard into a virtual wasteland. The country's infrastructure had been shattered in the wake of the deadly pandemic, the innumerable cities and towns that defined America's past lying empty and deserted as the remnant of a once vast population was relocated to five protected urban centers. Over the ensuing decades, the fragile system that finally emerged from the rubble faced seemingly endless shortages of everything except suspicion and despair.

Vigorously scratching his itchy head—an itch that seemed to grow in direct proportion to his stress level—but oblivious to the flurry of snowy dandruff showering onto his shoulders as a result, Damon stared intently at the computer screen projected before him. The agile fingers of his free hand continued to access data as he scratched, a knot of anxiety growing in the pit of his stomach as a series of production and delivery delays paraded across the translucent 3D panel.

"Good god," he muttered bitterly. "At this rate, there won't be enough of anything by the end of the month!"

Acutely aware of the consequences of being too free with one's opinion, Damon refrained from openly criticizing the government but privately felt the Triumvirate in Columbus was totally clueless in many ways. Their vaunted claims of successfully balancing the post-Revanche dilemma of supply vs. demand saturated the media. The program—referred to as 'Equilibrium'—was lauded everywhere. Everything from omnipresent public holograms to broadcasts in every hallway, workplace, and residence touted the skills and accomplishments of the Neoterics in Columbus.   Regardless of what they claimed, however, lower level bureaucrats like Christopher Damon knew the reality of life in the trenches—*there simply wasn't enough to go around.*

Even after population constraints had been established nationwide—strictly enforcing the Population Protocols that had been merely a topic for debate prior to the pandemic—Damon's workload at the Production Planning Department seemed to grow exponentially.   He sometimes wondered how the P.P.D.'s Czar, Treva Howard, maintained her sanity; there were days when he definitely felt he was losing the grip on his own. But perhaps she was high enough on the political food chain that the strain of responsibility nibbled rather than gnawed at her sense of well-being.

His lip curled into a sneer at the thought of those above him.

That was where Christopher Damon ultimately intended to be; high enough to look down at this maelstrom from the safe and secure realm of those with the power to delegate.   Nothing—and no one—was going to prevent him from achieving that kind of protection for himself and his family.

Thoughts of delegating responsibility brought Damon back to the stark reality of the data projected at eye level in front of him.   "Quinn," he bellowed toward the open door of his office. "Get in here."

Almost before the words were out of Damon's mouth, Gideon Quinn stood before him.   A tall and commanding presence, Quinn even made the bland grey uniform identifying them as civil servants look good. He wasn't an exceptionally handsome man, Damon was sure of that, but there was something about Gideon Quinn that demanded one's attention; all the women in the department certainly knew who he was.

Christopher Damon *loathed* Gideon Quinn.

When Damon shouted, Quinn spoke quietly.   When Damon was agitated, Quinn was calm. When Damon was sure the worst was going to happen, Quinn was optimistic that a solution would be found.   He was just the type of person Damon saw thwarting his plans for upward mobility—he was just the type of person Damon would love to see shipped to the Borders! In fact, his favorite daydream was that Gideon Quinn would prove to be a deviant or a subversive.   He had even considered manufacturing evidence against his colleague and denouncing him to the authorities but had gotten cold feet, certain that something would happen to turn the tables and *he'd* end up being the one banished. That was the type of luck a person like Quinn would have. Quietly confident, quietly competent he never drew attention to himself but was impossible to miss—a real smooth operator. There were times when Damon was sure Gideon Quinn had to be a government plant. How else could you explain the fact that he was always there, always ready, and always willing to do the job at hand?

"Is there something I can do for you, sir?"

The question shattered Damon's momentary lapse of concentration and he scowled fiercely at his subordinate as if Quinn had distracted him from the data he studied.

"Last week's discontinuity—have you finished the analysis?"

"Yes sir, I have," Quinn replied, reaching across the desk toward the projection hovering between them. "If I may?"

With a light tap to the upper edge of the screen, the entire projection reversed to face him. Saying nothing further, he began to tap and drag information into view. In just a moment, he again reversed the screen.

"As you can see," he began, "the breakdown wasn't at the production end; overall, there actually was a slight surplus last week. The problem was along the distribution route. AmTrak's southern magnarail broke down again and transport had to be redirected, or was cancelled entirely. That affected supplies in Atlanta. There's just no way to avoid some disgruntled people when transport is so unpredictable. And this problem isn't going away, sir, it's only getting worse."

An apoplectic flush began creeping up Christopher Damon's neck as he reviewed Quinn's data. He tugged at the neckline of his uniform as if it were the culprit.

"This is totally unacceptable," he sputtered. "What are the imbeciles over at Logistics thinking? I can promise you one thing—this will *not* go down as a black mark against my office!"

He had stopped scratching his head when Quinn came in, now he ran a hand through his disheveled mop in a futile attempt at grooming. "My god, just what we need is for Columbus to start looking over our shoulder, questioning every time we take a crap."

There was a momentary pause as Damon continued to scan the data. Suddenly, he threw a sly look Quinn's way and the flush began to visibly recede.

"You've done a fine job on this, Gideon," he observed, his voice dripping with superficial collegiality. "Why don't you take lead and submit our findings to Columbus?"

II.

Quinn shook his head stoically as he recalled the smug look of satisfaction on Christopher Damon's face when their meeting had drawn to a close and his boss had released him with a curt nod and a dismissive gesture. Gideon harbored no illusions where his supervisor was concerned. Damon's suggestion that he take the lead reporting ongoing distribution problems was in no way meant as recognition of a job well done. He was insulating himself. What was the old saying—*don't kill the messenger?* Well, in this case, Quinn was certain that that was precisely what Christopher Damon was hoping would happen. Let the proverbial hammer fall on his detested underling with all the force a report likely to be perceived as insubordinate could muster. If the black mark didn't fall squarely on the shoulders of their colleagues at Logistics and Infrastructure, then let the blame fall on the man filing the report. Let the blame fall on Gideon Quinn.

Quinn couldn't suppress a smug smile of his own. Christopher Damon might sleep the sleep of the innocents tonight, weighed down by nothing more than shoulders laden with the snow of nervous eczema, but tomorrow would be another story entirely.

At the end of his shift, Quinn took a last look around. He had double-checked that all the tech feeds at his station were wiped clean—physically as well as electronically. His cubicle was spotless, as always, and the data he wanted to take with him was encrypted and secure.

He was ready.

After spending five months playing the role of the loyal civil servant, being subjected to the labyrinthine inefficiencies of a heavily regulated bureaucracy—not to mention the erratic, sometimes paranoid ranting of his direct superior—this stage of his mission was finally complete. One final security scan and he'd never have to darken their door again.

"You look like the cat that swallowed the canary," the Guardian manning the security monitor observed as Gideon approached. "You just hit the housing lottery?"

"I should be so lucky," Quinn replied. "No, just anticipating a few cold ones down on the Strip. When are you off, Murphy? You should join me."

"On that score, I'm the one who could use some luck; afraid I'm stuck here overnight."

He gestured Quinn onto the scanner.

"And anyway, you know the rules," he added in a friendly imitation of a reprimand. "Guardians don't fraternize with the public."

"Sorry, Officer Murphy," Quinn quipped, raising three fingers to the side of his brow in a mock salute, "lost my mind there for a minute."

Gideon stepped onto the pad as indicated, carefully controlling his breathing and concentrating on his favorite watering hole down on the Strip as the scan relayed heart rate, respiration, pupil dilation, and even sweat secretion to the virtual display Murphy scrutinized. When he switched from internal to external mode, he paused and gave Quinn a quizzical, mildly suspicious look.

"There's a minor burr in your departmental I.D. chip. It keeps jumping between error codes; probably just needs to be recalibrated but might need replacing."

He studied the affable bureaucrat for a moment and then smiled. "Better have it checked out. You'll keep getting stopped if it's not fixed."

Quinn nodded in agreement and Murphy continued pleasantly. "It's OK for now—don't want to keep you from those cold ones."

Gideon thanked him and left the building, grateful it had been Murphy on duty this last evening; most of the other Guardians were real hard-asses and might have insisted that he have the 'malfunction' checked out immediately. Murphy was a good man and he felt a twinge of guilt that he'd be the Guardian held responsible if Quinn's true role came to light and it was revealed that the burr detected had actually been the data he was taking with him.

III.

Valaria and Mavis lingered over their scant breakfast, pushing aside the detritus and savoring another cup of weak coffee while talking about everything from the recent blight that had almost wiped out Mavis's bees to Valaria's latest experiment brewing ale from the honey Mavis contributed to the settlement's barter system. As the smell of food lured him back inside from less compelling pursuits, Yancy added his amiable canine presence and unique form of bartering to the mix—brown-eyed adoration offered up in exchange for scraps of food.

Settling in next to Mavis, the exuberant mutt plopped a heavy paw on her ample thigh and looked up pathetically.

"Good grief," she observed, wincing a bit under the weight of his devotion. "It's no wonder you've got bruises; this beast's foot alone weighs a ton!"

Valaria directed her attention to the dog. "Yancy, *off*."

In response to her commanding voice, Yancy reluctantly relinquished his claim to Mavis's leg and reestablished his bartering from the dejected posture he assumed, chin and belly flat against the floor, eyes riveted to her face, back legs splayed to either side in a lumpy impression of a bearskin rug.

"Stop mooching, you cretin," Valaria said, nudging the dog with her foot as she picked up their coffee mugs for a final refill. "You're not half as cute as you think you are."

After setting the steaming mugs back on the table, she turned and opened the bank of octagonal windows above the kitchen countertop, folding each insulated glass panel onto the panel next to it, three each to the left and right of the center latch, until they looked like a matching pair of accordions snuggly compressed against the curve of the dome. With six screened octagons now open to the morning breeze, their idyllic oasis soon was sweetened by birdsong drifting in from a coppice of adjacent apple trees.

Mavis rested her elbows companionably on the table, nestling her mug of steaming coffee between both hands and looking across at Valaria and then down at the dog. "God, I hate to leave but I've got deliveries to make."

"You're not in the Zone anymore," Valaria reminded her. "No one's going to report you for making your rounds a little later than usual."

"I know," she replied. "Old habits die hard, I guess."

She smiled somewhat wistfully and drained her coffee mug. "You know, sometimes I just like to slow down and *listen*. The birds in the morning and the frogs and crickets at night are nothing short of amazing; a little overwhelming when I first got here but now I can't seem to get enough of them."

"Don't tell me all the critters have been banished to the Borders, too," Valaria said, making no attempt to mask her sarcasm. "I suppose they're just too unpredictable and messy for the Triumvirate to deal with—*literally* subversive shit, is that it?"

"Now come on," Mavis retorted with a gum-displaying smile, "you're a city girl, too. Weren't you a little intimidated by the quiet when you first got here?"

"But you just said yourself it's *not* quiet."

"True, but it's different from city noise. This is *empty* noise; the kind you never hear in the Zones. You should remember. You were, what, six years old when your grandfather brought you here?"

"Five. Afraid my memories of living in the city are pretty vague, though. I remember the school and dormitory mostly, a few of my teachers and classmates... that's about it."

Valaria gathered up their empty mugs and egg-smeared plates and put them in the sink.

"I don't remember telling you about my grandfather bringing me here," she added, returning to her seat at the table.

"Haven't we thoroughly shared back-stories?" Mavis asked. "Well, I picked it up from somebody. What else have we got to talk about except each other," she added with a contrite shrug.

"That's truer than I like to admit. People around here are like a bunch of old women with nothing better to do than gossip."

"And you *live* in 'Gossip Central,'" Mavis pointed out. "You may not join in but—running the only pub in town—you're bound to hear everybody's story sooner or later."

"Now *that*," Valaria agreed with a wry smile, "is only too true— sometimes waaay more information than I want. God, you can't imagine some of the shit people tell their bartender!"

"Well, personally, I think it's great," Mavis replied. "And most of the time it's not really gossip."

She rose from the table, pushed the chair in, and ran her fingers aimlessly along the intricate pattern that graced the backrest. "Geez, Valaria, you don't know what you've got here; nobody talks this freely in the city. There's nothing like sitting around here at night drinking and listening to everybody. . . once you all stopped being freaked out by my presence and turning to stone whenever I walked in, that is."

"Well shit, Mavis, you were the first newcomer we'd had in years. You couldn't have stood out more if you'd come dancing in stark naked."

"Oh my God," her friend laughed, indicating her girth. "Don't visualize that; you'll be permanently traumatized!"

"It's true. Other than the occasional black market shyster, we don't see many unfamiliar faces; makes you pretty skittish around strangers."

Abandoning the breakfast dishes, the two women left the private portion of the dome and reentered the pub.

"I know it was hard on you but who can blame us," Valaria continued. "Most people here know firsthand what can happen if you're too free with your opinion. But now that they've gotten to know you it's OK, isn't it—not that we've got a helluva lot of choice in the matter."

Mavis acknowledged Valaria's points and turned to leave. Promising to stop by later with a fresh supply of raw honey, she headed for the door.

Valaria watched as her bulky, caftan-clad friend swayed gracefully through the tables on her way to the stairs leading to the surface. Mavis was an interesting person and, having lived in a Safe Zone more recently than anyone else in the settlement, she offered insights and information no one could match. The only downside was her tendency to pry—like talking to people about her childhood with Otis.

Thorpe liked the flamboyant newcomer but felt just a tad exposed.

IV.

By the time the evening crowd began wandering into the pub—the twenty-some regulars Valaria saw on a daily basis—she had spent most of the afternoon in the shed behind the dome monitoring her latest batch of apple ale. When Otis was alive the shed had served as his workshop and brewing had monopolized their small kitchen area. In the months following his passing, Valaria had struggled with the idea of emancipating her living quarters and transforming the now-defunct workshop into her brewery. It was a difficult decision and one that had her stymied for a while as it smacked of blatant disloyalty to his memory. In the end, practicality won out and Valaria had lovingly boxed up Otis's tools and what remained of his supplies and plans and stacked them reverently off in a corner of the shed. Even more than a year later—and after scrupulous cleaning—she was convinced the smell of oak, hickory, and maple lingered and added a unique undertone of flavor to whatever she brewed in her grandfather's former sanctum.

Although the location had changed, afternoons spent in the company of ale and cider was a well-established routine that varied little. After putting in her required time at the settlement's farm each day, Valaria would putter around the pub, dealing with any locals who came by to trade or visit, and then head for the shed to work on the ale and hard cider she served the pub's clientele as well as the non-alcoholic juice that rounded out her barter currency. Even though her homemade brewery might have been a bit kludgy, Otis had shown real creativity in cobbling together the makeshift parts needed to create the system. Valaria enjoyed the work of brewing and had become something of a master distiller in her own right. She had grown adept at creating spirits from almost anything that became available but apples were her mainstay. The task of peeling them wasn't the most enjoyable part of the process (she'd been doing it since old enough to be trusted with a knife!) but the smell of the fruit was always clean and pleasing, and the solitude of her little brewery gave her ample time to think... and smoke; something she was wishing she could do at that very moment as she stood behind the bar listening to the pub's evensong.

Yancy was making the rounds of their regular patrons and a comfortable murmur of conversation had settled over the group when Valaria looked up from thoughts of cigarettes to see a stranger standing in the pub's doorway. He was tall and lean, unshaven, with dark, shaggy hair brushing the collar of the calf-length suede duster he wore over blue jeans and a black turtleneck sweater. Yancy bounded gleefully toward the newcomer, greeting him with his customary front-paws-to-chest version of a handshake and dislodging the large rucksack casually slung over the stranger's shoulder in the process. It fell to the floor with an audible thud, drawing attention to the fact that an unknown entity had just been added to the mix.

As if on cue, the bar fell silent.

Subduing the rowdy dog with some friendly tousling of canine ears, the stranger took his time evaluating the group of weary-eyed men and women scattered around the pub, nodding respectfully toward two octogenarians playing chess at a table near the bar and smiling kindly at old Miss Baxter who quickly glanced down while absently adjusting the frayed shawl she wore over a badly-pilled cardigan sweater.

Accurately perceiving his status—and with a touch of deference—the man accepted the group stare that created a wall of suspicion between regulars and outsider. Retrieving his rucksack from the floor, he slowly made his way to the bar where the tall, stately barmaid was openly assessing him.

"Evening," he said to Valaria, taking a seat on one of the stools.

"Hey," she replied evenly, with just the trace of a noncommittal, rather tight-lipped smile. "What can I get you?"

"Beer would hit the spot."

Valaria pulled the tap and set a dripping glass of apple ale in front of the stranger.

"You're a real event," she observed, stating the obvious. "What brings you to our little corner of Heaven?"

He turned on the stool and looked out across the pub. "I'm looking for someone and hoped you might be able to help me."

"This is the Borders, mister," she said with a mordant smirk. "If they've been assigned here you won't have much trouble finding them—they've got nowhere else to go."

The stranger redirected his attention to his host and began slowly turning the glass of ale between hands protected by gloves that ended halfway up his fingers.

"Well, to tell the truth, I expected to see him where you're standing so may actually need some help. I'm looking for a man called Otis Thorpe. Have I come to the right place?"

Valaria paused, once again taking measure of the stranger. "Right place but you're about a year late."

His gloved hands froze in mid-turn, piercing brown eyes pinning her where she stood.

"Oh Christ," he breathed. "Are you telling me he's dead?"

"Yes," Valaria replied slowly, nodding with sardonic irony. "I'm telling you he's dead."

She had begun wiping the bar's glossy surface and his next words brought her up short.

"Well then, what about his grandson Larry? Do you know where he is?"

When she was little, Valaria had gone by the nickname Lari. It literally had been decades since anyone had called her that and she was instantly wary of a *stranger* knowing that childhood moniker. The two old men playing chess adjacent the bar—longtime residents and friends of her grandfather—also were instantly alert at the sound of a name no stranger should know and the time between moves grew longer.

"Don't know where you got your information, mister, but Otis Thorpe didn't have a grandson."

The man looked genuinely puzzled. "Are you sure?"

"Pretty sure, yeah," she replied, throwing a wry smile toward the chess players.

One of the men choked back a laugh, drawing the stranger's attention.

"She's right," he volunteered. "Otis didn't have no grandson."

The stranger fell silent, drumming the bar with the fingers of his left hand and staring into the glass he cradled with his right.

Not known for her tact, Valaria openly evaluated him. He was quite handsome in his own way; tall and broad-shouldered with thick, shaggy hair and a shadow of whiskers dusting his jaw line—she rather liked the scruffy look—and amazing brown eyes that seemed to look into your soul. Her own eyes came to rest on the large rucksack at his feet.

"Why'd you want to see Otis Thorpe?" she asked bluntly. "If you've got supplies to sell, then deal with me. But you better do it quick and be on your way; this is a regular watering hole for the local Guardians and they don't ignore the black market."

The man heaved a sigh and turned his strong gaze her way. "Yes, I wanted to do business with Mr. Thorpe. I just don't understand how my information could be so wrong. Records show that Otis Thorpe had one child—Vincent—and that Vincent also had one child."

"Records," the chess player asked, his suspicions heightened. "You come from the Zones?" He turned to his partner with undisguised anxiety. "He's from the *Zones*, Jasper."

"I've spent some time there recently, yes. I've been trying to track down Otis Thorpe and his family."

Shortly after the stranger came on the scene, the more skittish among the regulars had begun slipping into the night. When he admitted coming from the Zones something resembling an exodus ensued.

In just a moment the pub was almost empty.

"Your honesty is refreshing, mister," the chess player called Jasper chimed in with undisguised suspicion. "But just who the hell are you? You're obviously not with the black market and I can't believe you'd think admitting you've been in the Zones is gonna make things easier for you here."

"My name is Gideon Quinn and you're right, I'm not with the black market."

"You a Freebooter?" the first chess player demanded.

"A *Freebooter*," Jasper said incredulously. "What's the matter with you, Pete; you gone loony or something? I swear you're getting senile. Since when do Freebooters come into town bold as brass—or stalk without their pack, as far as that goes?"

"I'm not black market and I'm no Freebooter. And I'm honest about having been in the Zones because I figure out here there's really no reason to lie. Am I wrong?"

"No, mister," Valaria responded, "you're not wrong... We're not the liars."

"But we've learned not to volunteer information and we protect our own," Jasper interjected. "Gideon Quinn, did you say?"

Quinn nodded.

"All right; so I ask you again Mr. Quinn—what are you doing here?"

"The liberties of our country are worth defending at all hazards; and it is our duty to defend them against all attacks... It will bring an everlasting mark of infamy on the present generation, enlightened as it is, if we should suffer them to be wrested from us without a struggle, or to be cheated out of them by the artifices of false and designing men."

~ Sam Adams

CHAPTER THREE

I.

Gideon Quinn took a lengthy sip of ale, scanning the pub over the lip of the glass as he studied the handful of people who remained and considered possible responses to Jasper Hahn's demand that he identify himself.

"You ever hear of the Sons of Liberty?" he asked quietly, setting the glass on the bar and wiping it down with the gloved portion of his hands.

Jasper snorted sharply and disdain colored his words. "The ones on the history discs or the foolish dreamers who have taken to using the name?"

Gideon took careful measure of the man before replying. "Both."

"Don't tell us you're one of those misguided knights in shining armor, riding off to joust with the windmill of government," Valaria interjected scornfully.

Gideon turned his dark, steady gaze on her. "Don Quixote wasn't exactly a knight in shining armor, and I don't think any of the Sons would appreciate their efforts to restore our freedoms being compared to his hapless quest."

"Maybe so, but I'd say challenging an entrenched government that's had control over the country for forty years isn't just *hapless*, it's downright *insane!*"

Quinn's gaze grew darker. "It wasn't insane in the 1700s and it's not insane now."

"You're delusional, buddy," Valaria replied sharply. "The ale's on the house—drink up and get out."

Quinn drained his glass as instructed but instead of heading for the door moved from the bar to the table where the chess players sat.

"Listen," he said firmly, sitting down with the elderly men, "it took me months to get the information that brought me here. I'm not giving up so easily."

"Just what information are you referring to?" Valaria demanded of his back. "Regardless of what you think you know about Otis Thorpe, I can assure you he wouldn't have wanted anything to do with your little rebellion."

"How can you be so sure," Quinn challenged, turning to face her in his chair. "Just how long did you know him?"

Before she could catch herself Valaria spat out her response. "All my life—he was my grandfather."

Now it was Quinn's turn to sputter. "Your *grandfather?*" He turned back to the men at the table. "But you said he didn't..."

"We said he didn't have a grand*son*," Jasper interrupted evenly, "and he didn't."

Quinn refocused his attention on the woman at the bar, really taking her in for the first time. She appeared to be in her mid-thirties; every nuance of her posture a virtual porcupine of challenge and defiance, just waiting for an excuse to throw a barb. Tall, and slender to the point of skinny, she was all angry angles and truculent glares—almost pretty if one could get past the glower.

"You're Otis Thorpe's granddaughter?" he asked, just to verify what he had heard.

"Yes," she replied, adding rather smugly, "I'm Lari Thorpe."

"*You're* Larry Thorpe?"

"That's right; short for Valaria."

He wasn't sure he believed her—Thorpe's grandson was a grand*daughter?*

"Vuh–LAIR–ee–uh," she pronounced slowly when he didn't respond, exaggerating each syllabic break of her name. "Get it—Valaria... *Lari?*"

"Yes," he mused quietly, more to himself than to the small group that had slowly migrated to the table. Riding the crest of an epiphany, he continued. "I wondered why the records on Otis Thorpe were so sketchy and hard to dig out. He must have pulled some major strings to accomplish that level of redaction. He was protecting you."

Valaria balked—loudly.

"Otis pulling strings? Protecting me? Protecting me from what? You've really got your wires crossed, mister. Listen, to everyone except us Otis Thorpe was a *nobody;* just a crazy old carpenter banished to the Borders because he didn't measure up to city standards. And I'll say it again—he never would have gotten involved in any rebellion. He bitched about society all the time but he wasn't the type to stir things up."

"True enough," Jasper assured him. "Otis believed living here in the Borders was the best people like us could hope for under the circumstances."

"And how long did you know Mr. Thorpe?"

Jasper heaved a sigh. "Well, I was relocated twenty-two years ago. Pete's been here about twenty-five." He gestured toward an elderly couple who had pulled chairs up behind them. "Hector and Mary have been here the longest."

"That's right," Mary said, joining the conversation. "We knew Otis before he went and got Valaria after her folks died."

"What does it matter how long anybody knew my grandfather?" Valaria interjected, bristling. "The point is, if you're looking for someone to help the Sons of Liberty, you've come to the wrong place."

"Mr. Quinn," Jasper said, gesturing Valaria over to the table and putting a gentling hand on her arm as she sat down beside him, "there have been rumblings of discontent ever since Reorganization in the years following the plague." His voice was calm and he exuded a wisdom and authority that became the focus of the room. "The Borders settlements were the Triumvirate's solution to the problem. We 'pioneers' as they like to call us are really their *discards*—widely dispersed and successfully isolated so we don't rock the boat, but still useful to them through each settlement's work assignment. It's not what we might've chosen but it's all we've got. And if we ever had any revolutionary fervor I'm afraid it fizzled out a long time ago."

Quinn ran his fingers through his shaggy hair in a gesture of exasperation.

"OK," he said, heaving a sigh, "cards on the table. Obviously I'm with the Sons of Liberty and obviously I've been sent here on a mission."

"Ooo, a *mission*..." Valaria said sarcastically.

"Yes, Miss Thorpe, a mission—to find your grandfather; as far as we knew, he was the last one still living. And with all due respect, sir, I don't believe revolutionary fervor has been extinguished in everybody out here."

Mary edged her way into the conversation.

"That may be true, Mr. Quinn," she said quietly, "but what Jasper says is spot-on. The Borders settlements are intentionally spread out and isolated from one another. There's no contact, no communication between us. We don't even know just how many settlements there actually are or where they're located. There's no way we could organize even if we wanted to—without jeopardizing what little we have, that is. And with Freebooters out there it's suicidal to go exploring."

"And groups like yours are likely to bring the full force of the government crashing down on our heads," added her husband, his voice dark and ominous. "They can shut off vital supplies and medical care whenever they want—not to mention taking away what little freedom and autonomy we do have if we ever end up with a full-blown Guardian occupation!"

"Organizing the Borders is already happening, I can assure you of that," Gideon replied firmly, addressing Mary's comment. "And as far as the freedom and autonomy you speak of is concerned," he said to her husband, "I also can assure you that what you've got out here is only an *illusion* of freedom. The way things are now, you have only as much liberty as the government allows at any point in time. You said it yourself—they can take it away whenever they want through deprivation or the use of force. But what you don't seem to realize is that they need *you* just as much as you need *them*. Hell, they need you more. Some of the nation's brightest and best ended up in the Borders." He turned pointedly to Valaria. "People like your grandfather."

She shook her head and smiled sardonically. "I'll say it again, mister—you are *delusional*. The government shipped my grandfather out here because he didn't have anything they wanted."

"They put him here because he had *everything* they wanted."

"What the hell does that mean? They threw him away just like they did the rest of us. He was a cultural throwback who hated technology and could be a major pain in the ass. Out here he was just another worker drone placated by being allowed to practice his trade in his spare time and spit his Luddite philosophy into the wind... And what the hell did you mean when you said Otis was the last one still living?"

Quinn was about to respond when one of the men at the periphery of the group interrupted to point out the time.

"Oh, Geez," Valaria hissed, "the Guardians." She looked around the pub. "And the place is almost empty."

"What about the Guardians?" Gideon asked.

Ignoring his question, Valaria directed her attention to the regulars. "Hector, you and Mary contact some of the others and get them back in here. Marcus, you, Geoff, and Tully get the vids cranked up; Pete and Jasper, how about another game? Let's get things back to normal."

"What's the problem?" Gideon asked again as Valaria resumed her place behind the bar.

She glowered in silence for a moment before responding. "Since we're so close to the Guardian Star, they come in after their shift. They're suspicious by nature and it's never this empty when they come down—I don't think we want them wondering about what's been going on in here tonight, do we?"

"No, I suppose not," he conceded.

"What about him?" Jasper asked, gesturing at Quinn.

"I don't think we want them wondering about *you*, either," she said to Gideon before adding, "Crap, what are we going to do with him?"

"Well, whatever we do, we better be quick about it," Jasper replied, directing their attention to the return of several locals.

"Bloody hell, I guess you'll have to wait in my quarters until the pub closes and I can get rid of everybody."

"What a charming invitation," Gideon said, rewarding her reluctant hospitality with sarcasm of his own. "How could I refuse?"

"Charming my ass," she retorted, ushering him toward the door and indicating her living area. "Just sit there, and don't even *think* about getting into my stuff."

He settled on the futon and put his feet on the low table in front of it.

Valaria rolled her eyes heavenward. "Yeah, this is just great. I'd turn you over the Guardians myself if it didn't mean we'd all probably be remanded. Thanks a lot. You Sons of Liberty are sons of *bitches* as far as I'm concerned!"

She slipped back out the door after pushing Yancy inside and ordering him to guard—a totally useless gesture since the dog basically did whatever it wanted but one she hoped might at least give Quinn a moment's pause in case he was inclined to snoop.

In just a few minutes the electric whir of a ground transport was clearly audible and moments later a large group of Guardians noisily entered the pub.

Valaria's nemesis, Dawson Hayes, was in the lead.

"Light crowd tonight," Dawson observed good-naturedly. "What happened, Valaria; they find out you spit in the ale?"

"Naw," she responded with a sneer, "I only do that to yours."

He gave her the finger and looked around the pub as his companions assumed their usual tables adjacent the bar.

"Hey, your shadow's missing; where's Yancy?"

She threw him an acidic smirk. "He's guarding the strange man I've got hiding in my quarters."

II.

It seemed to take forever but finally the notoriously unreliable automated timer announced last call and the pub slowly began to empty. Eager to send the Guardians packing, Valaria had just about been ready to announce closing time herself when the capricious technology kicked in and she was spared the argument that typically ensued whenever the no-nonsense electronic voice failed to announce curfew.

The shank of the evening had been blissfully uneventful. The size of the crowd seemed to go unnoticed, except for Dawson's rude comment upon arrival, and other than that nothing seemed out of the ordinary; nothing, that is, except for Valaria's sweaty palms—a condition she suspected was shared by everyone in the room who knew a dissident was hiding in her quarters.

Mavis Pope had added her bulky presence to the tableau about an hour after the Guardians came on the scene, her size and flamboyant caftan garnering disapproving looks and a few derogatory comments from the government's image-conscious enforcers. Valaria took note of the fact that it was Dawson Hayes, the senior officer present, who put an end to their lewd ridicule... probably hoping for a free beer.

As a result of their blatant derision, Mavis never stayed long when Guardians were around and tonight was no exception. She had been keeping her distance, sitting at a table near the door, and dispensed a wave and salute to the bar before making an inconspicuous early departure. Valaria was relieved. She didn't think it wise for too many people to know what was going on and Mavis's ability to ferret things out was uncanny—she also didn't have the best poker face when it came to keeping information to herself.

As always, the Guardians were the last to leave, loitering under the pretence of making sure everyone obeyed curfew but ending up indulging in some after-hours drinking. Eventually, Hayes sent the others out for a final check of the settlement.

Looking less than official and far from intimidating, he leaned nonchalantly against the main entrance doorframe with his arms folded across this chest. He appeared to have something on his mind and Valaria's heart lurched as she feared someone had mentioned the presence of a stranger in their midst.

"Look here," he began, "I was serious when I asked about Yancy. Is he all right?"

"Didn't know you were a dog-lover," she replied, basking in his question's reprieve. "Yeah, he's all right. He's just wandered off someplace. Knowing my luck he'll probably come back with something bloody and dead and drop it triumphantly at my feet."

"Hey, don't complain, you're lucky to have him. He's obviously devoted to you and he's the perfect friend; doesn't drink your beer—or mooch your smokes."

"My *smokes*?" she interrupted with exaggerated shock. "Cigarettes are illegal, Guardian Hayes... And how do you know Yancy doesn't drink beer?"

Dawson laughed more genuinely than she thought possible for a Guardian—he surely must be breaking some kind of regulation—and for a fleeting moment she almost wished she could ask his advice about the dilemma lurking just a few feet away, dirty boots resting on her grandfather's carefully crafted furniture.

When Dawson finally climbed the stairs to the surface, Valaria leaned into the optical security scanner and shut things down. She didn't think she'd ever been more relieved to come to the end of a day and hear the dome's automated locks slide into place. She stood for a moment, back resting against the door, eyes staring across the dimly lit pub without really seeing anything. It was after curfew and, with Guardians making the rounds, she knew everybody had to go home but she felt deserted and mildly betrayed nonetheless; left on her own to deal with what surely had to be the epitome of contraband.

Heaving a sigh so heavy she would have struggled if required to carry it, Valaria headed toward the back of the pub.

There hadn't been time for an optical scan when she and Jasper had hustled Gideon Quinn into her quarters so the door was unlocked, opening without the low hum of the scan's intrusive beam and the subsequent fanfare of sliding bolts.

Valaria leaned against the door after locking herself in and stared blankly into the darkness. It took just a heartbeat for her mind to come back into sharp focus, however, quickly reminding her that there was an irrepressible, unpredictable dog somewhere in the room and she found herself hoping Yancy wouldn't suddenly decide a greeting was in order and knock her noisily off her feet! She stood still and listened to the quiet a moment longer, her presence not yet having triggered the lighting. The only sound was the deep, rhythmic breathing of her uninvited guest who had fallen asleep on the futon.

He'd better have taken off his goddamn boots!

Stepping forward in order to bring up the lights, Valaria stopped in her tracks as the subdued glow revealed that more than one transient lay sprawled on the futon. Not even an eyelash twitched on either derelict—canine or human—as she directed a stormy glower in their direction. Dislodging them hardly seemed worth the effort so she didn't even try.

"Traitor!" she murmured at the dog as she shuffled off to bed.

III.

Valaria woke earlier than usual the next morning. She had crawled gratefully into her bunk fully clothed the night before, too tired to tolerate even the most basic of bedtime ablutions and acutely aware that—regardless of the fact that her disloyal dog had welcomed him into the pack—a strange man slept in her living room. Now alert and awake, if not particularly rested, she hastily changed into fresh blue jeans and a clean shirt, running a damp comb through her unruly hair before quietly opening the bedroom door.

Yancy lay at the threshold, looking up at her adoringly. Beyond the dog, she could see the stranger's boots under the bottom edge of the futon. Why hadn't he had the good sense to slip out sometime in the night?

"So," she said accusingly to the dog, "have you come to your senses about which side of the bread your butter's on or do you just want something to eat?"

Yancy responded with an enthusiastically wagging tail.

"Aw, just as I thought—it's the food, isn't it?"

She reached down and scratched the dog behind his ears. "You're an ungrateful cur. You realize that, don't you?"

"...Well, I'm afraid sometimes I do lack an appropriate level of gratitude—although I don't recall ever having been called a *cur* before."

Receiving a response to her question caught her off guard.

"Oh, you're still here," she managed blandly, addressing the back of the futon.

Quinn swung his legs to the floor and stood in one fluid movement.

"Well, since I don't have the requisite *eyeball*," he pointed out, gesturing to the security panel, "I don't see how I could have accomplished an early departure."

"Oh, right. Guess I did kind of lock you in."

"Yes, you did. And regardless of my status as a cur, I *am* grateful and definitely appreciate a good night's sleep." He gestured toward the dog. "Yancy was particularly accommodating."

She took it as a good sign that he had his gloves on and had immediately begun lacing up his boots; surely his departure must be imminent.

"Yeah," she observed. "My so-called guard dog."

Both directed their attention to the dog who wagged all over, giving them his most endearing canine grin.

"I know this is a huge inconvenience," Gideon said, coming forward and taking a turn at scratching Yancy's ears, "and you've already been incredibly kind to a stranger who—I admit—sounds pretty off the wall sometimes... but I'd really appreciate one more kindness if you wouldn't mind terribly. Could I take a shower before leaving? I've been on the road almost a month now and have been living rough most of the time."

Valaria didn't answer his question, wondering instead just how he could have stayed out of the government's line of sight for a month—even their peripheral vision had peripheral vision.

"How can you move around like that?" she asked. "Doesn't your tag give you away?"

There was a significant pause before he responded.

"I'm not tagged," he said quietly.

Valaria started to express her disbelief but Quinn continued.

"That's not all that unusual, you know. There are probably thousands of untagged people."

She looked at him like a cow encountering a new gate. "But what about population control? Your parents had to pass all the screenings before being allowed to conceive, so wouldn't registration be automatic?"

"Not every pregnancy is sanctioned under the Population Protocols; contraceptive implants fail once in a while, you know. Believe me the government's not as omniscient as they'd like us to think."

Having lived most of her life in the shadow of the Guardians, Valaria seriously doubted that but managed to keep her opinion to herself for once.

"Come on," Quinn persisted, "why should you have to terminate a pregnancy just because the government hasn't given you permission to have a kid..." He stopped short. "Do you even know what the so-called Population Protocols really are?"

"Sure I do. It's the government program that's protected the country from over-population during recovery."

"Oh my God Valaria, stop spouting the Party line. The Protocols are all about *eugenics*. And eugenics isn't about controlling the country's population growth—it's about controlling *who* populates it."

Valaria gave him a look somewhere between quizzical and dismissive.

"No, seriously," he continued. "The Protocols were developed by Party members who believe one way to improve society is by making sure only the 'desirables' have kids. It's a Neoteric tenet Naomi Blanchard toyed with long before she became president; the plague just gave her the opportunity to turn it into policy. And this shit's been around forever. It was first popularized during the so-called Progressive Movement of the early 1900s—a time that saw the eradication of lots of ugly shit like child labor but one that also had a seriously dark side. Two of Blanchard's presidential role models—Teddy Roosevelt and Woodrow Wilson—were stars of the Era; but they were also eugenicists. Roosevelt actually said since we control the breeding of *cattle*, doing the same with humans was only logical—can you believe that? Hell, back then there was even one bastard who went so far as to say that not only should there be controls on who has kids but that even *after* we're born we should have to go before a panel each year and justify our continued existence!"

Quinn was launching into his well-worn tirade on the subject but, adept at reading an audience, scaled things back. "Listen, I don't want to turn this into a lecture..."

"Too late," Valaria observed with a lopsided smirk.

"The bottom line is pretty simple. The Triumvirate is using their Population Protocols—using eugenics—for a helluva lot more than just managing population growth during their so-called recovery. Think about it, under the guise of controlling the birthrate, what the government's really controlling is who *can* and who *can't* have kids. That's what eugenics is really all about and it's exactly what they're using it to accomplish. *Pioneers* sure as hell aren't being given permission to reproduce!"

"But the Protocols prevent birth defects and screen out all kinds of future medical problems."

"Yeah, right, Blanchard and her cronies are such grand humanitarians. Open your eyes, Valaria. Based on a set of standards determined by them, the government's violating one of the most basic privacy rights—whether or not to have kids."

He paused to let his words sink in before continuing. "Why should they be able to stick their noses into our families like that—into our most fundamental rights? And I'm telling you, their rabid control of reproduction has led to a slow but steady decline of population in the Safe Zones—just like what happened in China before the plague—while population out here is slowly rising despite their best efforts."

"Population in the Zones isn't declining," Valaria chuffed. "The cities are thriving."

"Who'd you hear *that* from?"

"The people who move here come from the Zones, you know," she replied tartly, recalling how the settlement had welcomed Mavis Pope's updates long before they actually accepted her presence. "When was the last time *you* were there?"

"Trust me," he said, fully aware of the irony imbued in those words. "The government can *say* anything it wants; the Safe Zones are *not* thriving."

She ignored his statement, chalking it up to what Otis would have called "drinking the Kool-Aid," his favorite dismissal of anyone he deemed too devoted to the absurd—a reference to a centuries-old tragedy where followers of a charismatic cult leader drank poison-laced juice as a result of their misguided devotion to a maniac. Instead, she pursued her query as to his status.

"But if you're not tagged that means you don't qualify for government services."

"It means I'm off their radar and can go where I want, when I want, with whomever I want. And, please, don't tell me you believe being tagged means we're the beneficiaries of the government's largesse. All it really means is that they can keep track of us more easily."

Valaria exhaled sharply.

"Well, on *that* score you and Otis would've totally seen eye to eye." Referring back to his question about showering, she gestured somewhat less than graciously toward the bathroom and added, "...Be my guest."

The incongruity of her words was lost on neither of them and Quinn smiled sheepishly as he picked up his rucksack and headed for the shower.

"There are towels on the shelf above the toilet," Valaria said as he walked away. "Help yourself," she muttered under her breath, shaking her head in tight-lipped appraisal of an increasingly surreal situation.

By the time Quinn returned, hair still damp and curling slightly where it lay on his collar, Valaria had decided she might as well feed him before ridding herself of the compromising intrusion he presented. As she laid the table for breakfast she realized there wasn't much to offer; half a loaf of bread and Mavis's honey as well as an ample supply of apple juice being all she had on hand.

She didn't offer to brew any coffee from her dwindling stash.

"Wow, now you've really gone above and beyond," Quinn said, observing the two place settings at the table. "I've got some coffee in my pack, if you'd like to brew some."

He smiled as he offered up the small packet retrieved from his rucksack. She accepted his peace offering with a tentative half-smile, noticing as she did so that he had shaved, not completely but enough to tame the dark stubble that shadowed his lower face and jaw line without completely erasing his rather scruffy appearance.

It was a good look for him.

The two strangers soon sat at table, munching on toasted bread and honey while trying to ignore the awkward silence that filled the room almost beyond capacity, like a balloon inflated to tautness just short of bursting.

"This is really good coffee," Valaria observed, deflating the balloon a bit by taking a stab at civilized chitchat. "Thanks for sharing."

"It's the least I could do," he replied. "I'm glad you like it."

They lapsed into silence once again until both suddenly began talking simultaneously.

"Look, I know I've put you in a really weird position..."

"I've been thinking about what you said last night..."

Quinn stopped midsentence and gestured that Valaria should continue.

"...about my grandfather. Listen, if it really is a Thorpe you're looking for—and I'm far from convinced that it is—then it's probably my father or mother you're interested in; they're the ones who worked for the government." She paused for a response but Quinn just blew into his steaming coffee so she continued. "They were involved in the NAB'D project—border defense, you know?"

Dipping a spoon into the honey, she drizzled the sweet, golden goo onto another piece of bread. Musing to herself about honey's uncanny ability to migrate, she stopped to lick her sticky fingers before going on.

"...They were computer engineers, I think; something to do with computers. Anyway, that's what my grandfather told me. So if anybody did some redacting of our family information like you said, it must have been them, don't you see—cutting ties with Otis, I suppose. My grandfather wouldn't have had those kinds of skills—didn't *want* them— but that kind of thing easily would have been in my parents' skill set."

She looked across the table at him with an expression that struck him as a cross between defiance and dejection. Feeling slightly overwhelmed by another growing silence, she offered her final observation, hoping to inspire his departure.

"Unfortunately, they're gone, too. They died thirty years ago during a flu epidemic. I don't have any more information about them so I'm afraid you've come to a dead end."

"Listen, Valaria," Quinn began almost gently. "I can understand why you might want to explain away my sudden appearance by rationalizing that it's a case of mistaken identity that brought me here. But trust me we're well-acquainted with your parents and their work for the government. Researching them was an integral step in the process of tracking down your grandfather. I can assure you it's not their skill set we're interested in; it's your grandfather's."

"But that just doesn't make any sense," she replied, defiance reasserting itself. "I keep telling you—my grandfather was a *carpenter*."

She gestured to the furniture gracing her living quarters.

"Look around you; *this* was his skill set. He thought technology had ruined our lives and tolerated it only as far as absolutely necessary."

"What about the technology I see all around me," Quinn pointed out. "Gotta tell you, it's more than unusual for a Borders settlement to enjoy the automatic lighting and security systems you people have."

"And just how would you know that?"

Quinn sighed before deciding to dig himself in even deeper. "This isn't the first settlement I've been to, Valaria."

She made no attempt to conceal a more than mildly suspicious scowl and only slightly toned down the disbelief that colored her response. "Yeah, right; you just hopped in your car and took the grand tour, right?"

When he didn't respond, she heaved a sigh of surrender and shook her head. "Jasper—one of the old guys you met last night—loves to tinker. He and Otis wanted the people here to be as comfortable and safe as possible. Unfortunately, since Otis died, their hodgepodge has been growing increasingly unreliable; probably won't be long before we're reduced to candles and truncheons."

"Since *Otis* died," Quinn observed, his emphasis conveying the 'touché' behind his simple statement.

"Oh shit," she sputtered, throwing him a dubious glower, "now I suppose you're going to tell me that that's evidence of the mystical 'skill set' you attribute to my grandfather."

"I said it last night Valaria, a lot of the country's brightest and best ended up out here."

"And I've said it before—you are one delusional son-of-a-bitch!"

"Tell me about your grandfather," he urged, taking her invective in stride.

She bridled a bit, her voice growing icy. "Why?"

"Well, if I'm ever going to convince you that we're talking about the same man, I think I need to start by getting acquainted with *your* Otis Thorpe."

Valaria looked at Quinn steadily across the table and fell silent for a moment. The predicament she currently found herself in was unreal and unnerving—not to mention seriously irritating. But, as with cleaning and feeding him, she decided a few insights into her grandfather was probably the best way to get Gideon Quinn to leave.

Divulging personal information wasn't Valaria's forte, however. She was an almost obsessively private person with serious trust issues—undoubtedly the result of being raised by a man about whom the term curmudgeon would have been a compliment. Otis Thorpe had felt betrayed by society, finding some degree of respite in the Borders and instilling in his granddaughter the same distrust and defiant cynicism that made him an unlikely candidate for success in the Safe Zones.

"I think Otis felt more than just a little betrayed by society," she began uneasily. "Are you familiar with the term 'Luddite'?"

Quinn shook his head. "I remember you using it last night in reference to your grandfather but I've never heard it before."

"It's a really old word; comes from 19th century Europe, actually. I looked it up when I was a kid since Otis used it a lot. It's a name for someone opposed to change—especially someone against technology—first used in England after a group of workers protested losing their jobs to machines by trying to destroy them. I think they threw shoes into the gears, or something like that."

"I wondered where the pub's name came from."

"*The Shoe and Gear*—Otis's tribute to 19th century lunacy," Valaria observed.

Quinn smiled and sipped his coffee.

"Yeah, I know," she continued, "sounds really stupid, doesn't it? But Luddite pretty much sums up my grandfather—opposed to technology and thrilled to whip a shoe in its face if given the chance. He believed our reliance on tech was dehumanizing us. God, if I had a credit for every time I heard him say that!"

She went over to the stove to refill their coffee mugs. As she sat back down, she again gestured around the room. "Otis loved working with his hands. Almost everybody in the settlement has something he made. He loved the entire process—design, production, finishing; perhaps especially the finishing as that's when he added his unique geometric signature to each piece. He did most of the engraving completely by hand, but did use a laser for the really intricate carving. And *that* was about the extent of his use of technology, by the way."

"Except for building automatic lighting and security systems," Quinn added with a '*you've-got-to-be-kidding-me*' smirk.

Valaria ignored the barb.

"I was admiring his work before falling asleep last night," Gideon continued, running his fingers along the engraved outer edge of the round table top. "This is unlike anything I've ever seen; the pedestal is especially striking."

The round oak table was supported by a pedestal consisting of three five-foot lengths of gracefully curving wood about two inches thick with flat surfaces six inches across. Each length curved up and in from opposing directions on the floor, touching one another in the center and then curving out again to form the base upon which the tabletop rested—the flat surface of each length intricately carved with a different geometric pattern. It gave the solid wood table a very stately and elegant appearance.

"This was one of his favorites," Valaria said, "made me promise never to sell it—as if I would. 'This old table could hold up the world,' he used to say. Just a dash of hyperbole but he made it clear how much it meant to him; drummed it into my head ever since I was a kid."

"I take it he made that, too," Gideon observed, indicating the simple wooden crucifix hanging on the wall by the door."

Valaria nodded. "Another indication of Otis's disconnect from society. As a Christian he balked at the government initiating their bland state-sanctioned churches after the plague."

"And you? Where do you stand on that?"

Valaria considered her response carefully. "I guess I believe that faith—like everything else that really counts—should be a matter of personal conscience, not something dictated by the state."

Quinn smiled and relaxed a bit. "I assume your grandfather made the tables and chairs out in the pub, too?"

"As well as the bar. Otis felt people couldn't truly relax sitting on plastic chairs at metal tables, no matter how ergonomic their design. According to him, the stark, utilitarian stuff produced by the government was further evidence of how we were living in a dehumanized, sterile world. Otis always said wood has a connection to the soul. He wanted the pub to provide an environment conducive to relaxation and quality conversation; he believed wood did that."

As she spoke, Quinn's eyes came to rest on a beautifully maintained cello leaning with elegant nonchalance against the side of a shelving unit opposite the futon. "What about that? Did Otis play or are you the musician in the family?"

"No," she replied. "That belonged to my grandmother. She died before I was born."

Valaria swirled the dregs of cold coffee around the bottom of her mug for a moment and drained it before speaking again.

"OK, enough about the Otis Thorpe I grew up with," she said sharply. "It's your turn. Tell me about yours."

Quinn heaved a sigh.

"I don't know if what I have to say will be convincing," he began. "Will you try to keep an open mind and listen all the way through?"

"On my honor," she replied, crossing her heart with feigned sheepishness.

Her somewhat disingenuous gesture wasn't lost on Quinn, but he made no acknowledgement other than to swirl his own coffee for a moment while gathering his thoughts. "Long before the plague and The Revanche, a lot of attention was already being given to the problem of national security. I can tell by the way you talk that Otis didn't shirk when it came to your education so I assume you're well-versed in history—undoubtedly more *accurately* than the indoctrination kids in the Zones get!"

He paused for a beat, directing himself back to topic. "Anyway, you probably remember at least the high points—or should I say *low* points— of what led up to The Revanche's final act of retribution: beginning with the airliner attacks here in the U.S. in 2001 all the way through the establishment of the Mid-East Caliphate; not to mention the acts of terrorism around the world preceding and following those major events."

"Yeah, I suppose you can say I'm well-educated—especially for an exile. That was Mary's contribution. She was a professor of some sort before being banished. Together, she and Otis made sure I was well-versed in history's litany of tyranny and terrorism—no player was spared their brutal honesty; regardless of creed or color."

Quinn smiled slightly, as if her statement confirmed something for him. "OK, now don't fly off the handle at me, but I take that as evidence in my favor. I believe your grandfather wanted to be sure you knew the *truth* about what led up to and what followed The Revanche."

"So I'd be sure to follow in his Luddite footsteps," she assured him emphatically.

"I think there's more to it than that. Valaria, how did your grandfather die? Was it from natural causes?"

She raised her hands slightly in mild exasperation at the segue. "He was killed in a Freebooter raid."

"Freebooters attacked the *settlement?*" Quinn asked in disbelief. "That's really weird; seems like being so close to the Guardian Star would scare them off. Freebooters are *marauders*—scum of the earth, yes, but they sure aren't known for coordinated assaults against established enclaves and, for obvious reasons, want to keep a seriously-low profile around Guardians.

I'm surprised they'd bother you at all since you've got Guardians living in your back pocket."

"Well, it didn't take place in town."

She stared off into the distance of memory.

"Otis was in the habit of walking the 5-mile limit trying to find wood for his projects. The last time he went out he didn't come back."

Her voice grew increasingly bitter; her eyes alight with anger and pain. "We found him unconscious about three miles out, barely alive. I'll never understand why they hurt him. He wouldn't have resisted being robbed; didn't have anything worth taking other than the cart and a few tools he had with him and they left those."

She ran her fingers absently through her hair. It seemed to steady her. "Unfortunately, at his age—and being an exile—I knew treatment wouldn't be approved. Euthanasia would have been the only option offered by the Health Administration so I didn't even contact them; took care of him here at home until he passed. He never even regained consciousness."

"Valaria, if he never regained consciousness, don't you think it's at least possible he simply died before telling you about his past? I bet he would have filled you in eventually. He just waited too long."

His host bristled. "There you go again implying that Otis led some kind of double life—which is just a load of absolute crap!"

"Sorry. I really don't mean to antagonize you and it sucks that you had to lose him like that." Quinn's voice had softened considerably. "It's bad enough to lose someone we love when we're expecting it, but at least that gives us time to come to terms with the loss, to a certain extent anyway. Your loss was stark and brutal. That's gotta be the worst."

A silence stretched between them that felt much longer than it actually was; the porcupine sitting across from him bristling with quills of anger and grief.

In that brief moment, Gideon found himself wondering if it really had been Freebooters who killed Otis Thorpe. Had the government realized the potential threat he posed as a possible resource for the resistance and taken action to silence him? After all, everybody he'd worked with was dead, too.

He decided that that was a possibility best explored at another time.

"Are you still interested in hearing me out?" he asked instead.

Valaria gave him a withering look but didn't follow up on her inclination to kick him out on his ass.

"As best we can tell," Gideon said, continuing to present his case. "at least two or three years before The Revanche—at about the same time as the last Arab/Israeli war—a small cadre of computer and engineering experts was given the task of strengthening our defenses against acts of terrorism, both physical and cyber. The long-standing viewpoint that equated national borders with bigotry was more controversial than ever and really beginning to erode as terrorists, drug cartels, and human traffickers took advantage of President Porterfield's 'Citizens of the World' policy. Your grandfather would have been around forty-five at that time; idealistic, patriotic—and an incredibly gifted engineer."

"Sounds like a great guy," Valaria observed sardonically, regaining her equilibrium, "I'm sure I would have liked him."

Ignoring her sarcasm, Quinn slowly pulled off his fingerless gloves.

"With all due respect to your grandfather's opinions," he said, "we need to access some tech in order to complete the picture."

He moved his chair closer to hers, licked his right index finger and laid it on the surface of an elaborate tattoo on the back of his left hand. In response to the DNA in his saliva, a small 3D screen coalesced above his hand.

Valaria was openly dumbfounded.

"Oh my God," she blurted, "there's *tech* embedded in your *tattoo*?"

"What have I been telling you," Quinn pointed out with a smile.

"Here we go again," she replied, rolling her eyes heavenward and raising her hands in surrender. "'The brightest and best'…"

Gideon's smile broadened as he keyed in a series of decryption commands with his free hand. In a moment the logo of the Sons of Liberty appeared—a stylized tree with spreading limbs. 'The Liberty Tree' was emblazoned across the trunk but Gideon had opened a file before Valaria had time to read the motto at its base.

Over the next half hour, Quinn proceeded to take Valaria on a tour of the documentation the Sons had been able to accumulate on the men and women who had comprised that elite cadre of engineers and computer programmers. From curriculum vitae and background checks to work orders and pay vouchers, a picture slowly developed—albeit sketchy and with substantial gaps—in which the name Otis Thorpe appeared prominently.

"OK, I'll admit you've gathered some significant information and have at least piqued my curiosity," Valaria conceded when he was finished. "But how do I know you haven't manufactured all the shit you just showed me? Even we ignorant exiles know data can be manipulated."

"Why would we do that?" Quinn asked. "What possible benefit could there be in creating a background for your grandfather that didn't actually exist?"

Valaria shrugged. "I don't know... but you've gotta realize it's not easy for me to reconcile the Otis Thorpe you present here with the one who raised me; they're diametrically opposed to one another."

She stood and moved to the windows over the kitchen sink, turning her back on Quinn and seemingly lost in the barren terrain beyond the settlement.

In a moment she turned to face him.

"So let's say, just for the sake of argument, I'm convinced that Otis was part of this secret cadre of yours," she proposed, rolling her eyes slightly at the words 'secret cadre.' "Just what did he do back then that makes him so important to the Sons of Liberty more than forty years later?"

Quinn paused, not for effect but because her continued sarcasm made it obvious he hadn't really convinced her. Perhaps he should wait to play this final card.

"Well?" she demanded.

"Valaria," he began quietly, trying to smooth the edges of what he was about to tell her. "Otis Thorpe was the engineer who designed the Guardian Star."

People who are willing to give up freedom for security deserve neither and usually end up losing both."

~ Benjamin Franklin

CHAPTER FOUR

THE REVANCHE
Washington, D.C.

I.

It was bitterly cold that 20th day of January. Removing her gloved hand from the Bible held by her nineteen-year-old son, Micah, the newly-inaugurated president smiled benignly at the Chief Justice who had just administered the Oath of Office, touched her precious son's wind-pinked cheek and turned toward the adjacent podium.

The sea of faces before her, stretching beyond the Capitol's temporary inaugural platform toward the distant Washington Memorial, was far smaller than it should have been—a result of the weather, no doubt, but her opponents would point it out ad nauseam nonetheless and attribute it to the fractional popular vote difference that had helped her cross the finish line ahead of the incumbent.

"Should have cited the cold and held the damn ceremony indoors," she mused in silent hindsight while waving to the crowd. *"These optics are crap."*

The assembled hoi polloi who had braved the cold—along with the select seated behind the new Chief Executive—all awaited her highly anticipated first speech as president huddled into their heavy winter gear and wishing they'd had the foresight to put heat-packs in their socks. Framed by U.S. flags and patriotic bunting that was also being assaulted by the icy winter wind, their applause for the woman who stood waving from center stage was muffled by gloves and mittens; some in their midst chilled as much by the woman's politics as by the freezing temperature. But none of that mattered to Naomi Blanchard. Benign smile intact, she began her carefully-crafted Inaugural Address, relaxing into the heat that radiated from the podium and fully believing her words marked the first steps into a future she saw as her legacy.

"Since the day we first began to walk upright," she read from a teleprompter only she could see, "humanity has seemed to be fulfilling a destiny characterized by expansion, confrontation, assimilation, and—to our great shame—annihilation. As a result, the story of humankind is a contradictory saga of honor and deceit, heroism and treachery. It is a chronicle rife with moments of glory and triumph as well as the crushing reality of tragedy and atrocity."

Playing to the cameras that were catching every nuance of her words and body language, Blanchard shot a condescendingly sympathetic glance toward her New Liberal predecessor before continuing. An equally adept player of the game of politics, there was no tell, no crack in the outgoing president's poker face even as his gut constricted at his opponent's obvious reference to the diplomatic fiasco that had occurred on his watch and the subsequent ill-fated rescue mission Blanchard successfully exploited in her campaign against him—what historians would undoubtedly call his 'Jimmy Carter Moment.'

"It is in the wake of that epic story," the new president was saying, "that the seeds of distrust and hatred have been sown; seeds that often bear fruit for generations as suppressed cultures fester under the thumb of perceived or actual oppression. For many of those cultures, such as India under British imperialism and Eastern Europe under communism, periods of subjugation ultimately led to an awakening, a Renaissance of potential once the oppressed were freed from their shackles. But for others, perceived or actual domination led only to an outlook on the world that ultimately became gangrenous and, as a result, tragically susceptible to the doctrine of extremism. That is the stark reality of our world today as the continuing litany of terrorism bears witness. But, my fellow Americans, *it is also our greatest opportunity*."

She gestured to the multiethnic group of school children sitting in a row in front of the podium who moments before had presented a pitch-perfect a cappella rendition of *No Man is an Island*.

"Let these beautiful young faces ever remind us that we are on the threshold not only of a new presidential administration but of a new era of possibility for this great nation."

Pausing as the crowd before her broke into applause—enthusiastic from those who supported her ideals, merely polite from other quadrants—she once again displayed her beneficent, confident smile for the cameras.

"As promised in my campaign, the Neoteric Party's agenda—an agenda built on the promise of modernity and change—not only will bridge the gap between the haves and have-nots within our own nation but will heal the rift between those among our extended global family who feel debased and disenfranchised by the rest of the world. This is our *challenge*... this is our *opportunity*... *this is our ultimate destiny*."

As if on cue, applause once again erupted from the audience.

Basking in the crowd's approval, the newly-inaugurated Chief Executive stood silent for a moment, striking what her teenage daughter had sarcastically dubbed 'The Mount Rushmore pose' of her campaign photos; shoulders back, chin slightly elevated, eyes directed forward into her vision of the future. She let the applause wash over her, gesturing for silence just a beat ahead of its natural decrescendo.

"Yes, my fellow Americans, the new ideas, the modernization inherent in my party's name, the Neoteric reforms we begin today, truly are the doorway to our ultimate destiny but they are even more than that; they are also a *moral imperative*. We cannot—we *must* not—be satisfied with the status quo. We cannot—we *must* not—be lulled into complacency by our own success at the expense of the less fortunate all around us. We cannot—and we *will* not—be the willing accomplices of decades of blatant disregard of the deadly schism growing between the satisfied and dissatisfied within our own nation and around the world. Those who are successful are *morally obligated* to bridge the gap between rich and poor. Those who are empowered are *morally obligated* to engage the disenfranchised. Those who are safe within these borders are *morally obligated* to offer the hand of welcome to others."

Heady with their first major political victory, Blanchard was interrupted once again by a fierce and prolonged outpouring of applause from the Neoterics dominating the audience.

From where he sat behind his successor, a fleeting trace of the disdain he harbored for the woman now standing on the threshold of the Oval Office creased the brow of its departing occupant as he waited for the applause to subside. The barely discernible grimace eloquently conveyed the chasm that lay between the two politicians—one, a moderate seeking to strike a balance between entitlement programs and personal responsibility, the other a dedicated champion of what her critics called the 'Nanny State.'

"And beginning this very day," his adversary continued, "changes will be made across this great land, changes that will ensure authentic progress; systemic change that will usher in the Neoteric Era..."

II.

Otis Thorpe had heard enough.

"Viewer off," he barked in the direction of the 3D panel dominating the eastern wall of his living room.

Slumping back into the cushioned recesses of his favorite chair, his eyes moved from the now translucent screen to the small data pad on the low table before him.

"*Systemic change,*" he muttered to himself as he picked up the pad and reviewed the numbers he had entered. "Well, they elected her; hope we're not getting a pig-in-a-poke."

The fact that the voting public truly was a 'they' revealed something of an irony in the life of Otis Thorpe. He long ago had divorced himself from the political process and yet now was involved in a project teeming with political potentialities. Unlike the blatantly intrusive goals of the new Chief Executive, however, Otis Thorpe believed *his* legacy—if it ever actually was built—would be something truly of service to his fellows; a monument to the triumph of technology and a tribute to the problem-solving potential of the human spirit akin to victories like the safe return to earth of Apollo 13 in the second half of the twentieth century... or the introduction of 'Space Tag' at the beginning of his own era.

The trace of a satisfied smile brightened his face for a moment at the juxtaposing of a *true* conquest of space with a virtual-reality game everyone under the age of 30 seemed addicted to. He made a mental note to share the joke with Charlotte.

Thorpe leaned forward to pick up the stylus lying on the table and began jotting equations onto one of the numerous data pads that littered the surface. With so many problems and ideas dancing among the neurons in his brain his thought processes often were more cacophonous than symphonic; having separate tablets around facilitated recording those thoughts in a way that kept as many as possible simultaneously visible. The hint of a smile creased his face again. Hell, he'd still be using pencil and paper if his colleagues hadn't balked at the idea of having to shuffle through random sheaves and not have immediate, *electronic* access to his work!

He re-submerged into the bliss of mathematical proofs only to be interrupted a moment later by the disembodied voice of the InfoMinder.

"Dr. Thorpe—you have a meeting at the Institute in one hour."

"Yeah, yeah, yeah," he replied vacantly, twirling the stylus nimbly between the fingers of his left hand and continuing to focus on the work before him.

After two additional, equally futile, attempts to get him to surface from the cognitive depths, the InfoMinder—having correctly surmised that it was essentially being ignored—switched from standard to familial mode.

"Otis?"

It was Charlotte's velvety southern drawl that now filled the quiet room.

"Don't forget you have a meeting in less than an hour, hon."

The stylus slipped from his fingers and clattered to the floor.

Although he would be eternally grateful that it had been Charlotte's voice they had chosen to use for the familial mode of the InfoMinder, it also was an ever-present reminder that she was lost to him and that only a reproduction of her voice could now forestall his tendency toward procrastination; she never again would nudge him from his intellectual stupors or chuckle lovingly at his lame jokes.

Running a hand through his unkempt, graying hair, Otis replied somewhat wistfully.

"Yes, my love, it's time to go."

III.

Just outside Falls Church, Virginia—almost completely obscured from view by a stand of centuries-old trees—stood a brick and stucco building bearing an inconspicuous brass plate engraved with the innocuous-sounding title, 'The Telliman Institute.' The building housed the Telliman Think Tank, a cadre of some of the country's most capable minds—a fact which, although it did its best to remain inconspicuous, made the think tank far from innocuous. A skillfully vetted group of physicists, engineers, mathematicians—and even a small sampling of the best computer hackers the country had to offer—the Triple-T (as they had been dubbed by those aware of their existence) was tasked with applying their expansive intellects to the myriad security challenges facing the United States as it headed toward the dawn of a new century.

Otis Thorpe had never been much of a joiner and as he arrived at the Institute on that fateful January afternoon, he was struck anew by the uncanny circumstances surrounding his decision to add his expertise to the group. When first approached about joining, Thorpe had inwardly scoffed while outwardly declining with what he hoped was an appropriate level of civility. As destiny would have it, however, he had been offered the position again a few months later—shortly after the most traumatic loss of his life, the death of his wife, Charlotte. A cellist with the Washington Symphony, Thorpe's wife had been one of the victims of a small scale terrorist attack while en route home on the D.C. metro after a rehearsal.

Otis still winced at the memory.

'Small scale' may have been how it was described by the media but it was anything *but* small in the lives of those directly affected. Seated near the epicenter of a blast that ripped through the transit car as if it had been made of paper mache, Charlotte Conti Thorpe had been virtually obliterated; nothing remaining but burned and bloody fragments intermingled with other victims sitting closest to the IED. In a grotesquely macabre gesture, fate had seen fit to take his wife but return virtually unscathed the cello upon which she created the magic that had brought them together thirty years earlier. Lost and alone in the quagmire of grief—and intensely aware of the irony of the moment—Thorpe had responded to the Think Tank's second invitation as anyone might if offered the chance to make a difference after having been shattered by the stark reality of terrorism. Still reeling from the barbaric insanity of such acts, he said yes.

But now, three years later, the double-edged nature of his current situation was becoming increasingly clear. On one hand, his professional life had never been more fulfilling but on the other his work—in concert with that of his Triple T colleagues—had the potential of fundamentally altering the international playing field, something that gave him pause. And in light of the newest blip on the American political radar—and the intrusive nature of its promised 'systemic change'—Thorpe was beginning to consider ways of extricating himself from the think tank's grasp and returning to his reclusive separatism. As a result, he arrived at the Institute in the throes of conflicting emotions.

Pausing in front of the steps leading up to the entrance, he was about to backtrack when the automated security system detected his presence.

"Good afternoon, Dr. Thorpe," the electronic voice said evenly, no trace of automation in its intonation (if anything, Thorpe thought he detected a faint reprimand for tardiness!). "Your arrival is anticipated in the Engineering Section. Your colleagues are waiting."

Doorknobs being an archaic anachronism by the Institute's standards, the security system released with a gentle hum when Otis came within range and the heavy front door automatically swung open before him.

He entered the wide vestibule and paused for a moment, taking in his surroundings as if seeing them for the first time. The entryway was elegantly appointed with thick oriental rugs accenting large slabs of white marble flooring. It looked more like the lobby of a prestigious law firm than the home of an unorthodox group of brilliant geeks playing games that could change the world.

Continuing on through a warren of empty hallways, Thorpe's footfall was a noisy counterpoint to the thoughts cluttering his mind and darkening his mood.

"Ah, here he is at last," announced Carson Telliman, Director of the Institute, as Otis entered the Engineering Section's main office.

Telliman was brandishing a bottle of Dom Perignon and filled a crystal champagne flute almost to the rim before handing it to Thorpe.

"What's all this?" Otis asked, taking the glass from his boss and looking around the room at his smiling colleagues. "Someone's birthday?"

Telliman was draining his own flute and almost choked on the effervescent wine.

"We're celebrating," he crowed. "And *you*, my friend, are the man of the hour!"

Not comfortable in the spotlight, Thorpe instinctively backed away from the Director and tried to blend into the group.

"I don't understand," he said quietly.

"It's the L.A.S.S. project, Otis," Preston Sinclair replied as Thorpe stopped next to him. "The Blanchard administration has promised approval— *The government is going to build the tower!*"

Sinclair was the closest thing to a friend Otis had and he clapped Thorpe on the shoulder while simultaneously clinking his champagne flute against that of his perplexed compatriot.

"And not just one," Telliman interjected. "The prototype will be the first of many security stations around the country, I promise you that."

Still holding the champagne bottle with which he'd just refilled his glass, he made a sweeping motion toward the small group of men and women before him. "This truly is a triumph for the Institute and I congratulate each of you and applaud you for your contribution."

He refocused on Otis. "But in a very real sense, we couldn't have done it without you, Dr. Thorpe. Ultimately it was your insights, your designs that got us across the finish line and we are so very fortunate that you finally accepted our invitation to join us."

Champagne glasses around the room were raised toward Otis in recognition of the Director's words; most with sincerity.

Standing at Telliman's elbow, his second in command, Regina Agnew, also raised her glass in tribute. A handsome young woman already obsessed with keeping the approach of middle age at bay, Agnew's sleek, sophisticated appearance was a testimony to recent advances in cosmetic enhancements. Her raised glass seemed genuine but the accompanying smile didn't make it past her lips. Otis never felt completely comfortable around her, never quite certain of her purpose or the means she applied to achieve it. As a trusted steward of the Institute's goals, Regina Agnew was responsible for keeping it well-funded and ably-staffed. She did her job adeptly and with enthusiasm, often employing tactics others would have termed unsavory at best had they come to light.

She was poised, polished, and utterly poisonous.

During its renewed attempt to recruit Otis, Ms. Agnew had been the Institute's emissary, appearing at Charlotte's memorial service with Mr. Telliman and then following up with personal condolences and visits to the Thorpe home, trying again to convince the newly grieving widower to join them. Solicitous and caring, she was darkly sexual, her kind and flattering words shadowed by a subtext focused solely on her own agenda. But at that point—Charlotte's death at the hands of terrorists being a gaping emotional wound—Agnew's homeland security sales pitch bore an effective resonance with the sought-after engineer and, coupled with the encouragement of his son Vincent (who saw the Institute as the ideal anodyne for his father's grief), the rest, as they say, was history—

But being part of the Telliman Think Tank was one thing; he could walk away from that. What made Otis wince was the government's interest in their tower—concerned that the new president somehow saw it as a means to accomplishing her so-called 'systemic change.'

While Thorpe's thoughts drifted, Director Telliman was acknowledging the group's tribute to their chief engineer by raising his own glass.

"Here's to *all* of you," he said proudly. "The brightest and best of the Institute… Hell, the brightest and best of the whole goddamn *country!*"

IV.

To the less-than-enthusiastic observer of the nation's first Chief Executive from the Neoteric Party, 'systemic change' began to happen with alarming speed once Naomi Blanchard was comfortably ensconced in the Oval Office; to those who shared her world view, it couldn't happen quickly enough.

Like her presidential idol, Woodrow Wilson, who had abhorred the system of checks and balances built into the document Naomi Blanchard had sworn to "preserve, protect, and defend," the new president saw the strictures of the Constitution's first three Articles as inconveniences to master. Commenting on the Founding Fathers' separation of power into three branches, Wilson had argued that "leadership and control must be lodged *somewhere*" and had thought the president should be in charge of the entire nation rather than leading one of three equally-important parts of a carefully balanced national government as originally intended by the Founders. Taking her cue from her progressive hero—as well as walking in the footsteps of notoriously imperious presidents like Donald Trump and Elizabeth Porterfield—lodging power in the executive became President Blanchard's endgame and playing that game would become a source of great personal satisfaction.

As originally designed, the law-making process in the United States was a perfect example of balanced government in action, elegantly constructed with multiple layers of overlapping authority intended to ensure that only carefully crafted, truly necessary laws were superimposed on the lives of the American people. Once introduced in either chamber of Congress, a bill must make its way through committee hearings and floor votes in both the House and the Senate before passing through a joint Conference Committee and final congressional vote on its way to the Chief Executive's desk—facing 'death' time and time again before finally encountering the president's pen. Over the years, however, this balancing of power within the legislative branch itself and between it and the executive slowly devolved into a morass of political gambits as temporary alliances were forged and favors were brokered, all in the name of getting a preferred or detested piece of legislation to go one's way. And with the president as the final player—pen poised to sign or veto—the pendulum of power could be a highly vexing thing indeed; the Chief Executive with an over-eager pen perceiving the system as unwieldy at best and onerous at worst.

As a result, from the nation's infancy presidents attempted to circumvent the system through the use of what many critics would come to identify as a Constitutional loophole—the Executive Order.

Beginning their life as presidential policy directives intended to facilitate *implementation* of the laws passed by Congress, the Executive Order slowly transmogrified into presidential *fiat*. Leap-frogging over Congress, EOs essentially emasculated the legislative branch—and eventually created a perilously domineering Chief Executive that stretched the boundaries of Constitutional intent to the breaking point.

Becoming a common way to evade Congressional oversight, Executive Orders surged during the New Deal Era (Franklin Roosevelt setting a record for the time with 3,721) and became particularly contentious during the administrations of Richard Nixon in the late-twentieth century when he froze wages and prices, and Barak Obama in the early years of the 21st century when he hobbled the coal industry with the stroke of a pen and conferred amnesty upon millions of illegal immigrants. Two administrations later, assisted by controversial appointees his opponents called 'The Clown Car Cabinet,' Donald Trump careened down the already slippery slope of executive fiat, reveling in immunity conferred upon him by a renegade Supreme Court and issuing an all-time record number of Executive Orders (52 in his first two weeks alone!) in an effort to accomplish goals such as immigration sweeps and mass deportations, dismantling the country's primary international aid agency, firing tens of thousands of experienced government employees, freezing funding to federal programs, and even attempting to nullify the Fourteenth Amendment's unambiguous creation of birthright citizenship. Earning the dubious distinction of being history's most divisive president, the inflationary effect of Trump's radical tariffs and the consequences of his policies horrified the 50% of the population that had voted against him and eventually disillusioned large swaths of even his Dunning-Kruger effected followers. A populist-driven Left/Right presidential rollercoaster ensued, with the Progressive Party's Elizabeth Porterfield eventually turning the tables on remnants of conservative extremism, using every means at her disposal to sweep away the political crumbs of what she saw as the xenophobic zealotry of Trump's 'MAGA' era through her 'MAFA' (Make America Free Again) *Citizens of the World* initiatives—

...Proving that Executive Orders could be wielded by the *left* just as potently as by the *right*.

It was in the imperious presidencies of the likes of Woodrow Wilson, Donald Trump, and Elizabeth Porterfield that Naomi Blanchard found her political validation. And although she was an ultra-*progressive* she nonetheless took a page out Trump's ultra-*conservative* playbook, using his 'muzzle velocity' approach to bombard the country with Executive Orders at a pace that made it difficult for Congress, the Courts, and even the media to keep up.

The newly-elected Neoteric president definitely shared Mr. Trump's decidedly autocratic obsession with EOs—despite finding the demagogue's pandering to full-fledged dictators like history's notorious Vladimir Putin and Viktor Orban more than a bridge too far. And in addition to being cut from the same autocratic cloth as her infamous progenitor, Naomi Blanchard also shared his drive to humiliate and destroy anyone who got in his way, especially perceived 'enemies'—as typified by Trump's desire to imprison those who had the temerity to investigate him (like fellow Republican Liz Chaney), and the very public, vitriolic ambush of Ukraine's President Vladymr Zelenskyy during the 21st century's Russian invasion of their small democratic neighbor—a shared appetite to which many of Blanchard's battered and abused colleagues and nay-sayers could attest!

Believing she could employ Trump's tactics without her administration imploding like his ultimately did, Blanchard created a Trumpian kakistocracy; a fealty-based administration filled with unqualified, kowtowing 'yes-men' (once the troublesome Speaker of the House, James McFarland, resigned, that is). With them at her beck and call, Naomi Blanchard would wield executive fiat like no Oval Office resident before her.

Her presidential role models would have been proud.

V.

By the end of her first year in office, President Blanchard felt she had pretty much mastered the whole governing thing. Having surrounded herself with a cadre of kowtowing yes-men, she was managing to outmaneuver an intractable Congress most of the time and was turning the use of executive orders into an art form. There was an aura of smug confidence about her that infuriated her detractors and, if truth be told, at times even unnerved her closest allies.

She simply believed she knew what was best and that she should be allowed to do it.

Early on in her watch, Blanchard had built upon the 'borders-are-bigotry' philosophy of Elizabeth Porterfield. Adeptly co-opting the anti-union 'right-to-work' mantra of her conservative adversaries, President Blanchard broadened the concept into a corruption of their stand that they found uniquely odious—an administrative policy statement that effectively opened the borders between the U.S. and its nearest neighbors. Proponents marketed the change as not only humanitarian but the logical extension of the conservatives' right-to-work platform—why shouldn't the right-to-work extend to our Mexican and Canadian neighbors, they asked with self-congratulatory pride in what they saw as a victory over archaic notions of isolationism. Surprisingly, an unlikely alliance against the new policy sprang up between conservatives, who saw the move as a serious threat to national security, and unions, who opposed it on economic grounds, but their ad hoc détente soon collapsed under the weight of their inherent philosophical differences and no successful opposition was ever mounted. Working tirelessly to widen the gap between the two disparate allies, the Blanchard administration placated the unions with promises of more government contracts while openly scoffing at those who claimed fluid borders compromised national security.

Quick to point out that there hadn't been a successful large-scale terrorist attack on American soil in more than 15 years, President Blanchard assured the nation that her administration was actively developing plans that would continue to keep the American people safe. Consequently, in her first State of the Union Address—a speech that would change the lives of those at the Telliman Institute forever—Blanchard introduced the world to Otis Thorpe's legacy.

"And lastly, my fellow Americans," she continued with grave authority. "Let us address the issue of homeland security."

She had been speaking for almost forty-five minutes; allies and adversaries alike among the joint Houses of Congress were growing restive but ears on both sides of the aisle perked up at her words.

"Over the past decade, our great nation has experienced a time of safety and security. The agencies of this government have been vigilant and the American people have slept easier as a result. This is not, however, a time to rest on our success. Even as we increasingly reach out to the global community with the hand of tolerance and encouragement, even as we greet our neighbors with open arms, we must also be realistic about the continuing threat posed by those trapped by self-destructive fanaticism. It is in light of that ongoing reality that I stand before you this evening not only with the *promise* of continuing success against fanaticism but the means by which to *secure* it."

She was interrupted by a surge of applause from the floor.

"As the twentieth century's Cold War drew to a close, President Ronald Reagan proposed the creation of a fleet of security satellites; the so-called 'Star Wars' initiative. That proposal—far too costly and far too aggressive from a global perspective—could never have been realized. But I stand before you now with a plan that *can* and *will* become reality; a star for the night sky that will be a beacon of hope and security for the American people."

Another eruption of applause momentarily broke her rhythm but it took only a beat for her to regain her poise.

"We will build not a satellite system that could be misconstrued as an act of aggression by the global community, but a series of security stations—homeland security *towers* from which we will monitor our land and protect all within her borders. And those towers will be manned by a corps of specialists—the country's 'guardians' if you will—whose sole purpose will be to use their expertise to identify and neutralize threats to this great nation and her most precious natural resource, her people."

VI.

Watching the president's speech from his living room, Otis Thorpe couldn't help feeling proud that his dream for enhancing the security of the nation was going to become a reality. His rather tight-lipped smile was fleeting, however, since implementation of the plan had abruptly been given to the Department of Homeland Security the week before and no one from the Telliman Institute was to have any further input.

As a result he didn't know whether to celebrate or immigrate.

The Low Altitude Security Stations (referred to simply as "L.A.S.S.") were designed to be a series of mile-high towers strategically located across the United States. Each would be equipped with monitoring, detection, and response capabilities for its portion of a geographic patchwork quilt that would divide the contiguous states into overlapping grids. The site for the prototype had been selected long before the L.A.S.S. project was officially given the green light. Located in Missouri approximately half way between St. Louis and Kansas City, the first tower's skeletal framework began to sprout from the expansive landscape within a surprisingly short time after jurisdiction over the project passed from the Telliman Institute to Homeland Security.

It was an exciting time for the Blanchard administration. Thanks to the L.A.S.S. project, national security nay-sayers were at least temporarily silenced as public opinion modulated upward at the prospect of the towers' capacity to increase the nation's ability to reduce the threat of terrorism. Major unions simultaneously were mollified as they contentedly suckled at the teat of government contracts that accompanied construction of the mile-high monolith.

At ground-breaking ceremonies for the first station, President Blanchard and the Director of Homeland Security shared the honor of removing symbolic shovelfuls of earth, taking turns posing for the cameras as they leaned into the task with a red-white-and-blue beribboned spade. There were hearty congratulations all around and Blanchard could barely contain the elation she felt in anticipation of the ways in which this one feat would enhance her ability to move the nation forward.

She was to find that elation tragically short-lived.

Seven months into the tower's construction—in a synchronized strike of myopic insanity—Islamic fanatics marked the anniversary of the most infamous of all terrorist attacks—September 11, 2001—with a global gesture they expected to be the denouement of their efforts to extend the Mid-Asian Caliphate, what they referred to as 'The Cleansing.' Taking advantage of borders that had become tragically porous, they crossed into virtually every major western nation unchallenged. But it wasn't explosives wired to a dead man's switch with which they were armed. Their chosen weapon of mass destruction was both simple and unremarkable—a slightly elevated fever. Using the most basic weapon of all—themselves—they methodically exposed the world's innocents to a genetically modified version of one of the most dreaded biological agents, y. pestis, better known as pneumonic plague.

The more virulent of the diseases caused by Yersina pestis since it spreads person-to-person rather than requiring primary infection like its notorious bubonic cousin, the Caliphate's 'new-and-improved' version of the plague was particularly virulent and wielded the potential of a 100% fatality rate! Despotic regimes like the old Soviet Union had toyed with the idea of weaponizing y. pestis but had focused on an aerosolized release—a nominally effective delivery system since airborne bacilli would remain viable only for about an hour. Utilizing the ongoing incubation of a human host, however, their modern Islamic counterparts overcame the limits of viability—if not morality—that had prevented y. pestis from achieving the status of biological weapon and unleashed it on an unsuspecting world with the smug conceit of an overconfident dilettante.

The terrorists who laid death on the world's doorstep manifested early stages of the disease within a few days of being infected—fever, headache, and cough—and immediately began a race against time to accomplish their mission before the illness overtook them and overwhelming weakness, raging fever, difficulty breathing and a bloody cough incapacitated them. It was the cough that became their primary weapon as person-to-person transmission of y. pestis occurred through respiratory droplets expelled when the terrorists instinctively tried to clear their increasingly compromised respiratory system. With hearts grown icy by a warped devotion to fanaticism, their goal was to personally encounter as many Westerners as possible in the short time available to them before the rapid progression of the disease made their illness unmistakable.

Doomsday scenarios of global Armageddon—including the possibility of a worldwide plague—had been fodder for popular fiction since the dawn of the twentieth century's Cold War and governments around the world spent billions of dollars playing the game of ultimate destruction in an effort to stay one step ahead of the demonic portion of the globe that played the game for real. But decades of apocalyptic simulations had produced little more than voices crying in the wilderness—no one was anywhere close to being prepared when the unthinkable actually happened.

As sickness spread and the horror began to be identified worldwide, borders were slammed shut. But as a consequence of the political mindset of the majority of western nations—equating diversity with open, or at least porous, borders—the closing of those borders was more easily *ordered* than *accomplished*; security long since having become more a matter of gathering intelligence and managing public perception than controlling the global interdependence that ultimately played into the hands of fanaticism. For days the world went about its ordinary routine, the disease spreading exponentially before any government realized that the ultimate terrorist attack had boarded random means of mass transportation and simply sat down beside them.

In a sudden frenzy to protect themselves nations scrambled to procure the antibiotics necessary to try to treat the ill and attempt to stem the tide.

But that tide too quickly became a tsunami and demand for the precious pharmaceuticals—medicines that were only marginally affective against the new strain—tragically outstripped supply. Within a few months the worldwide death toll began climbing into the tens of millions.

Infrastructures fractured.

Public services failed.

Governments fell.

The stench of death was everywhere and the world wept.

VII.

By December, Congress had been adjourned as a result of the plague and, except for a strong military presence, Washington D.C. was a virtual ghost town. On a Christmas Eve unlike any other, Naomi Blanchard summoned the Speaker of the House, the Director of the FBI, and the Chairman of the Joint Chiefs to the Oval Office. All had been fortified by a prophylaxis regimen of seven antibiotic injections—the best anyone had to offer against this new version of the plague—and they had the sore arms to prove it.

Blanchard greeted the Speaker, the Director, and her senior military advisor with a grim handshake, directing them in turn to the comfortable sitting area before a crackling fire. In spite of the homey ambiance of flickering firelight, the atmosphere was bleak. All had lost family, friends and acquaintances to the plague, but the woman before them had lost her favorite child. Micah Blanchard, a Rhodes Scholar traveling Western Europe between terms at Oxford, had succumbed to the pandemic and had been cremated and buried with hundreds of others before news of his death had even reached the United States. The men now seated with his mother wisely withheld the words of condolence that would have flowed under less extraordinary circumstances.

Dark shadows under the president's eyes betrayed her grief but her voice was steady.

"The Vice-President died this morning," she informed them slowly, sitting down in the wing chair closest to the fire and absently touching her sore arm; prophylaxis injections had done little to protect many of her colleagues. "We've lost five Supreme Court Justices, more than a hundred members of Congress, and God-only-knows how many among the general public."

"Yes, ma'am," General David Kramer, Chairman of the Joint Chiefs, replied. "We've lost a staggering number among all branches of the military as well."

Nodding gravely, she poured him a cup of tea.

"And there are reports of utter mayhem in the streets, Madam President," the Speaker of the House, James McFarland, interjected. "People are terrified. Basic provisions are beginning to run low... looting and violence have become commonplace. Police across the country are overwhelmed—and they've been decimated by the plague just like everyone else. Hospitals, of course, are completely overrun and supplies of antibiotics are totally exhausted. I don't think there's a bottle of *aspirin* left in the country, let alone any streptomycin."

"Yes," she replied evenly, nodding toward the expanse of windows beside her. "There are times when it sounds like a warzone out there."

Turning an icy resolve toward the solemn trio before her, the president continued.

"It stops *now*. I don't see how anyone could disagree that we've reached a point where the only way to restore even a modicum of control is through Executive intervention. And as far as I'm concerned, we have no choice but to institute martial law for the duration of this emergency."

A murmur of agreement circled the room but they waited for the president to continue.

Blanchard leaned forward and picked up the data tablet lying next to an incongruous plate of Christmas cookies sitting untouched on the low table between them. Without speaking, she accessed the desired document and entered the keystrokes necessary to send it to the tablets the others had brought with them. She gave the trio a few moments to scan its content.

"I believe these establish logical protocols," she said at last. "Responsibility for the nation's food resources—livestock, fruits and vegetables, domestic distribution and the like—will be delegated to the Secretary of Agriculture. The Department of Energy will be responsible for prioritizing power usage across the country. Health and Human Services will administer health resources, and overseeing all forms of civil infrastructure will fall to the Transportation Department. I'm delegating management of the nation's water resources to the Secretary of Defense since that would be a prime target for further terrorist action; and the Secretary of Commerce will monitor all other materials, services, and facilities. You, General Kramer, will oversee domestic security in cooperation with Director Anderson and the FBI. And all, of course, will be directly accountable to this office."

"...For the duration of the emergency," the Speaker of the House added pointedly. Not a presidential appointee, James McFarland was in many ways odd-man-out in the room and was beginning to think he might also be the sole voice of reason.

"Yes, Mr. Speaker," President Blanchard replied in a tone usually reserved for a child, "for the duration of the emergency."

The president lapsed into silence. She obviously had more on her mind and, once again, they waited until she was ready to continue.

"Gentlemen, we are more vulnerable at this moment than at any other point in the history of the nation. God only knows what the Caliphate may yet have planned, or what we might expect from other rogue elements or—God forbid—North Korea if they decide to take advantage of the situation. Basic services are almost nonexistent... there are corpses in the street going unburied! We don't even know exactly what's left standing within our own country let alone what the rest of the world is doing."

Her voice had turned to cold steel and a deafening silence filled the room. It was clear she wasn't finished.

General Kramer glanced at his colleagues before speaking for them all. "Ma'am?"

"Gentlemen, I've called you together this evening not only for the purpose of initiating martial law. You are here to discuss The Revanche."

Caught off guard, the Speaker of the House, a colleague from Blanchard's days in Congress, almost dropped the tea cup he held; he did drop the pretence of presidential protocol.

"Holy shit, Naomi, do you realize what you're suggesting?"

The president exhaled sharply, throwing a look of incredulity his way. "Yes, James, I can assure you I do."

"The President's right, Mr. Speaker," Director Anderson said. "This is already a worst case scenario. It would be utter insanity *not* to take whatever measures are left open to us to try to assure that it stops here."

"But you're talking about a weapon of mass destruction," Speaker McFarland retorted vehemently. "You're talking about the *United States* using a weapon of mass destruction!"

"Not a WMD in the conventional sense," General Kramer said. "The Revanche is a means to *cripple* an adversary without *obliterating* him."

"Detonating a high-power microwave device in the atmosphere rather than a thermonuclear device on the ground is a distinction without much of a difference in my mind."

"There's a huge difference," the general replied emphatically. "The HPM's electromagnetic pulse will cripple their infrastructure—it'll corrupt computer data and fry electronics across the region without annihilating millions. Buildings will still stand. Lives will be spared. And the EMP will incapacitate their bunker system. It'll pass through the ground, knocking out the bunkers' lights, ventilation, communications. Their bunkers will be completely uninhabitable. It'll stop them in their tracks."

"*Lives will be spared...*" McFarland repeated in a stunned hush. "What about the people in hospitals? What will the entire population do when medical treatment is suddenly limited to stethoscopes and thermometers? What about the millions who will suddenly be without light, heat, refrigeration, clean water and sanitation?"

"What about the millions dead and dying all around the world right *now?*" Director Anderson asked pointedly.

McFarland looked at the president. "Please don't do this, Naomi."

It was then that Naomi Blanchard—grieving mother—uttered words the Neoteric reformer never would have believed possible just a few months previous.

"It will send them back to the Stone Age... right where they belong."

"Gentlemen may cry, 'Peace, peace'—but there is no peace. The war is actually begun! Our brethren are already in the field! Why stand we here idle? Is life so dear, or peace so sweet, as to be purchased at the price of chains and slavery? Forbid it, Almighty God! I know not what course others may take; but as for me, give me liberty or give me death!"

~ Patrick Henry

CHAPTER FIVE

Guardian Star #1

I.

When Dawson Hayes arrived for the morning briefing, he could tell immediately that something was up. He took his place standing in rigid formation among the other Guardian crew chiefs gathering in the briefing theater, noting as he did so that Colonel Mertens, pasty and pale at the front of the room, looked even more skewered by constipation than usual—although previously he would have doubted the possibility of that. Mertens was accompanied by an extremely grim-faced twig of a man whose austere black suit was a clear indication of upper level government status—and undoubtedly the cause of the escalated twisting of Mertens's colon.

Strict discipline being one of the hallmarks of the Guardian code, there was no talking among the men and women as they gathered. Like Hayes, however, each was acutely aware of the increased tension that was practically sucking the air out of the room and the government presence that surely was its cause.

"Guardians, attention," Mertens barked officiously after a harsh, computerized tone indicated it was time to begin.

With all the originality of well-programmed automatons, the collected officers sharply responded "Guardians attention!" stamping their feet in thundering unity as each pulled themselves up to full height, standing even more rigidly, arms behind them, right hand clasping left wrist. They would remain in this formation for the duration of the briefing; a taxing demonstration of discipline and control that sometimes proved counterproductive as their minds inevitably began struggling for purchase on the slippery slope of concentration, distracted by muscles growing taut with fatigue.

Intending to impress his superior with a display of the power he wielded, Mertens glowered menacingly at his underlings. After a lengthy pause, he began. "As you can see, a government representative joins us this morning. Mr. Lucas Clifton comes to us directly from Columbus."

After another pause pregnant with the intoxication of power, Mertens once again sought to flaunt his superiority and control over the Guardians standing rigidly before him by adding in an ominous voice, "You will give him your full attention." He gestured the other man forward. "Mr. Clifton..."

As the brittle-looking man replaced Mertens at the front of the briefing platform, Dawson was struck by the thought that a stiff wind or a hearty sneeze would probably snap him in two. He smiled to himself and swallowed the impulse to share the observation with the Guardians within earshot.

Clifton regarded Colonel Mertens with a dismissive and slightly derisive smirk, turning his attention to the officers assembled before him.

"I'm sure you are wondering what an emissary from Columbus is doing in your midst today. Our Honorable Triumvirate has entrusted a very special mission to me. They have dispatched me specifically to address the fine officers of our Guardian Corps; coming first to you, the center—the *linchpin*—of Homeland security."

He smiled beneficently and began walking back and forth across the platform, his steps precise and stiff. "You men and women who have dedicated your life to the service of your country are called upon not only to *physically* protect the 55th," he observed, referring to the closer of the two defunct north/south interstate highways that formed the RSA's double western border. "You are our best defense against those who seek to undermine it *philosophically* as well as physically."

His smile turned predatory. "I refer, of course, to the so-called Sons of Liberty, although Sons of Sedition would be a far more appropriate appellation."

He let his words sink in for a beat before continuing, starting quite softly but adeptly plaiting his message with an energizing magnetism that stirred the hearts of the faithful before him.

"No nation will ever be totally free from discontent. No matter how stalwart and dedicated the national government, there will always be those who seek to undermine what it stands for and what it seeks to achieve; the troublesome gnats who buzz around us leaving dissent, distrust, and destruction in their wake. We must, as a result, be ever vigilant—*and thus we are.*"

With a generous sweep of his hand, he offered the Guardians symbolic inclusion in his ubiquitous "we."

"That vigilance is reaping a bounty that will insure the future success of this great nation. Over the past few months, we have learned that these dissidents are not content to sow the seeds of discontent only among their fellows. No, these agitators now seek to spread their venomous ideology into the Borders! They seek to destroy all that the Triumvirate has achieved—all that our leaders have selflessly dedicated themselves to on our behalf. They seek to undermine all that we stand for as a people. They seek to prey upon the weak and uneducated among the Pioneers in their quest to inflate their ranks. They seek to gain a foothold in the destiny of this great nation and lead us away from the bright future the Triumvirate foresees for us. These maladjusted malcontents would have us turn our backs on all the progress we have made and would happily see us collapse once again into the uncertainty and chaos that followed the plague!"

Clifton had reached fever pitch; his voice as loud and brittle as his cadaverous frame, his protruding forehead glistening with perspiration.

"That is why I come to you today. You are our first line of defense, our ever-watchful eyes and ears. And, on behalf of the Triumvirate, I therefore charge you with a vital mission—not only to *maintain* our border, but to *secure* it by being ever more alert, ever more watchful, ever more the dedicated Guardians our Triumvirate—and our *people*—need you to be. The Sons of Liberty must be apprehended and their diabolical, destructive plans thwarted, no matter the cost!"

Clifton continued his bombastic monologue for what seemed an eternity to Dawson Hayes—and to any others among the Guardians who were discovering to their dismay and discomfort that they seriously needed to pee. The terrain of his speech became well travelled—generous praise heaped upon the Triumvirate and strengthening vitriol for the Sons of Liberty.

He finally concluded by outlining four new policies intended to tighten security and thwart the insurrectionists. In an effort to curtail the movement of dissidents who seemed increasingly able to come and go virtually undetected, additional checkpoints and identity sweeps were to be initiated. To assure the populace that the government was in control, unannounced searches of homes and public places would be established in hopes of apprehending agitators. In order to enhance the government's ability to monitor the broader scene, additional observational drone flights were to be scheduled, and finally, in addition to the TODs, tactical *attack* drones (TADs)—which hadn't been broadly used in almost a generation—would be directed against the Sons of Liberty without mercy whenever and wherever they were detected.

II.

Valaria laughed. It was a genuine, cathartic laugh that bubbled up from the depths, bringing tears to her eyes and easing the tension that had begun to manifest itself as stiffness stretching from the base of her neck into her lower back.

Yancy threw a look of canine wonder toward his human, a woman not known for mirth.

Gideon Quinn waited in silence.

"Oh my God," she said at last from where she leaned against the kitchen countertop, considering him anew and wiping her eyes with her sleeve. "Sorry, don't mean to insult you but that's got to be the most hilarious thing I've ever heard. *Otis designed the Guardian Star?"*

She choked back another fit of laughter but couldn't subdue the sarcasm. "Yeah, right and I'm secretly a member of the Triumvirate, out here rubbing elbows with the little people so I can better relate to them!"

Quinn sat motionless and stone-faced.

With a renewed effort to be civil, Valaria resumed her place at the table, crossing her forearms and resting them on the smooth surface. She leaned forward, clenching the edge of her lower lip between her teeth and biting down hard in order to focus before speaking. "Seriously, Quinn, what would the designer of the Guardian Star be doing living as a carpenter here in the Borders?"

"That's partly what I'm here to find out. Don't think for a minute we didn't have a similar reaction when we finally traced him here. How did one of the government's wunderkind end up as a Borders exile?"

Adrift in the imponderable, he ran a restless hand through his shaggy hair. "You see, the problem of 'drumhead' flooring in SuperTalls had been surmounted a few years before your grandfather's team came on the scene—couldn't keep heading for the clouds if the same building materials that allowed additional height made people feel like they were walking on a trampoline at the highest elevations."

"Yeah, right; that ol' mushy-floor issue was a real bugger," Valaria interjected with a disdainful smirk. "Definitely had *me* stumped."

Quinn ignored the sarcasm. "But even with the flooring issue resolved, there still was the dilemma of primary structural support as well as the challenge of moving people up and down the SuperTalls. Magnetic levitation had already moved from rail transport into elevators but there was still the issue of *speed*... We believe your grandfather was the engineer who overcame some final structural issues as well as developing the system that made it possible for elevators to transport people quickly up and down the tower without making them sick and blowing out their eardrums."

He again directed Valaria's attention to the virtual screen still projected just above the surface of his tat. "Look here, it's definitely your grandfather's name that shows up repeatedly in connection with the low altitude security station project..." He pointed to the L.A.S.S. acronym appearing on several documents. "They called it LASS back then; the term Guardian Star wasn't used until the government actually built one."

The smirk disappeared from her face as Valaria stiffened involuntarily, visibly taken aback by his words.

Quinn cocked his head slightly, eyes narrowing.

"OK, now play fair," he said pointedly, reading her body language. "That obviously rings a bell. What did you just remember?"

She was silent for a beat before once again leaning forward and resting her arms on the tabletop.

"Only a weird coincidence," she assured him with a dismissive gesture and then falling silent.

"Yeah... *so?*"

When Valaria gave no indication she intended to respond, Quinn also fell silent and stared at her expectantly, eyes resolute.

"Oh, all right," she said with an exasperated glare. "It's undoubtedly nothing; just a weird coincidence like I said." She paused again, her certainty wavering slightly. "...It's just that whenever I asked Otis why he left the city, he'd scoff and say it was to get away from a lass. I'm sure he just meant some widow trying to snag him after Grandma Charlotte died."

Now it was Quinn's turn to laugh.

"You're kidding, right?" he asked with undisguised delight. "Come on, Valaria—'get away from a lass'? That's gotta mean the tower.

Together with everything else I've got, it's obviously not a coincidence he said it that way. He was getting away from the L.A.S.S. *project* not some woman. Doesn't that finally convinced you?"

She had grown subdued, thoughtful, and completely serious.

"Maybe," she conceded, her unintentionally furrowed brow giving testimony to the effect his evidence was having on her. "But even if it's true, what difference does it make if Otis used to be an engineer? That part of his life obviously ended—and ended badly if winding up here is any indication."

She fell silent again, shaking her head solemnly. "Just why did you come here anyway? What were you hoping to accomplish?"

"Well, I was hoping to talk to your grandfather. We were hoping he'd be willing to help us."

"Help you do *what*?"

Quinn considered his options for a moment, deciding there was little harm in divulging what undoubtedly was general knowledge in Columbus anyway.

"The government's line is that we want to bring them down and accomplish a coup of some sort," he began. "That's really just propaganda and fear-mongering as our message begins to resonate with more and more people. We don't want to bring them down. What we want is a return to constitutional democracy."

"*Constitutional democracy*—what are you talking about? We've got a constitution; the same one written in the 1700s, for God's sake!"

"That document may still exist in a sealed vault somewhere, but we're definitely not living under its precepts."

"But we've got the same three branches of government. We've got the same Bill of Rights."

Quinn exhaled sharply. "Yes, we've got three branches, but *not* as set out in the Constitution. We've got the Speaker, the President, and the Chief Justice—our venerated Triumvirate—but if you read the Constitution, you'd see that the branches are supposed to be more than just three people and a dictatorial system of elites empowered to enforce their edicts. Each branch should have *hundreds* of people working in it—and the core of those people should be there as a result of regularly held elections so they're accountable to the people they're supposed to be serving."

"I know all that; every kid learns that stuff in school. But everything changed after the plague. The Triumvirate was all that was left."

"So, why are they *still* all that's left almost 40 years later? And why are we still living under martial law? I'll tell you why, because by declaring and sustaining martial law, Naomi Blanchard was able to close the 'Overton Window.'"

"The *what?*"

"The 'Overton Window.' It's a term from the twentieth century used to describe the political process. If a politician wanted to be re-elected—and that's what they lived for!—they had to be careful not to alienate the voters, right? Well, as a result, they didn't really *create* political change, they *responded* to social change. As something became acceptable to a broad cross-section of the population, then politicians were likely to absorb it into their political stand and, ultimately, transform it into policy. Take something like euthanasia. The issue was debated for years but politicians didn't begin backing legalization until the idea had become widely acceptable to the general public. That's the 'window' they had to stay within in order to be re-elected. It was a rare politician who was able to open the window themselves; even the most skilled manipulator had to be patient enough to wait for the public to get on board."

Valaria's stare—dim or disinterested, he couldn't tell—inspired a different approach.

"You watch baseball, right?"

"Yeah..."

"OK, think of it this way—what happens to a pitcher who can't keep his pitches inside the strike zone? He gets pulled from the game, right? Well, the strike zone is his Overton Window. And that's exactly what would happen to a politician who strayed too far outside the 'strike zone' of what was socially supportable—the voters would take him out of the game and elect somebody else next time around."

"So you're saying the voters were the umpire—calling strikes and balls?"

"Something like that, yes."

"And martial law closed the window by ending the game."

"It's not a perfect analogy, but it works pretty well. If President Blanchard had been around 100 years ago and advocated her 'cross-border worker' program she never would have been elected. But the window had been opened little by little long before she came along and ultimately we ended up letting terrorists literally walk right in. I'm not saying she wanted the terrorists to attack us—of course she didn't—but once Blanchard and the Neoterics were in the Oval Office that act of terrorism—the plague—actually gave them the opportunity to close the window by initiating martial law which then allowed her to shift her political agenda into high gear. Even expanding implementation of martial law to include the Speaker and Chief Justice—creating the Triumvirate—still *kept* the window closed since the voter is out of the picture."

He let Valaria digest that for a moment before continuing. "But we don't expect to see a rebirth of the American republic here in the RSA. The Neoterics are slowly dying from within and are just as tragically myopic as the terrorists who brought the system down in the first place and the world leaders whose obsession with openness and appeasement who unintentionally allowed it to happen. What we want is for the Borders settlements to be allowed to break away and form a new United States."

Valaria regarded him darkly, again convinced that he and his compatriots were more than a few bricks short of a load.

"The *Borders settlements* form a new United States?" she asked dubiously. "How could an unconnected string of small settlements form a *country*? Hell, they couldn't even form a decent *conga line!*"

Undeterred by her skepticism, Quinn continued. "Come on, Valaria, think about it. Do you honestly believe the government's rhetoric that their handful of Safe Zones and the Borders settlements are all that remains of the original country? We were a nation of more than five hundred *million* before the plague. Isn't it only logical to believe that more survived than what's officially recognized by the Triumvirate? It's to their advantage—and part of their self-destructive navel-gazing—to at best deny and at worst attempt to destroy anything that serves to undermine their control…"

Intensity had driven Quinn to his feet and he stood behind his chair, clutching the backrest as a preacher might his pulpit. "Believe me, there are pockets of survivors all over the western territory and some are quietly thriving. If we could organize and unite with them we could slowly rebuild the *real* United States."

He paused again, once more considering just how much he should disclose. "And we'd like to do that with as little bloodshed as possible. If we can take down the Guardian Star, we figure the Triumvirate will be more likely to let us go."

"*Take down the Guardian Star*," Valaria repeated flatly, her voice almost a whisper as an epiphany dawned. "So that's why you wanted to find Otis. If he helped designed the damn thing, he should be able to take it down, right?"

Quinn resumed his seat.

"Put simply, yes. But we also were interested in just *talking* to him," he said, seeking to assure her of their motives. "Remember, he was one of the chosen and yet he ended up out here."

Valaria found herself bridling once again at Quinn's depiction of her grandfather. "God, you are one insane bastard. And just who is this 'we' you keep referring to?"

Ignoring the insult and taking her curiosity as a good sign Quinn let it go unchallenged.

"I'll show you," he offered with no small measure of satisfaction.

The tech layered into his tattoo had automatically returned to dormancy while they talked. Gideon once again went through the decryption sequence that brought the virtual screen to life. In a moment the Sons of Liberty logo reappeared—a stylized tree with the group's motto sheltered beneath its spreading limbs:

Those who expect to reap the blessings of freedom
must undergo the fatigue of supporting it.

Gideon noticed Valaria had focused on the quote.

"Thomas Payne said that," he explained. "It's proven to be a rather sobering truism."

He paused a moment, almost in tribute, before continuing. "This tree isn't just our logo it's also the encryption portal through which we communicate. Would you like to meet some of the others?"

Valaria checked the time. She had missed her shift at the farm, but it wasn't like that had never happened before so no one was likely to have taken much notice. But with only an hour or so left before the pub should open, she figured they were cutting it close in terms of being safe from interruption so declined Quinn's offer…

She also wasn't sure just how deeply she wanted to explore this alternate version of her grandfather—or the organization that seemed so eager to claim him.

III.

Most of the day's farm work was finished—most private enterprise as well—and people began making their daily pilgrimage to *The Shoe and Gear*. It was, after all, the only game in town and, although located on the settlement's western edge, had long since become the figurative center of the community. Residents came not only to imbibe but also to interact, try their luck at the vids, and take in a movie or sporting event on the widescreen monitor that was used as much as a vehicle for government propaganda as for distracting the masses. Since large scale public gatherings were unheard of after The Revanche, and professional sports and Hollywood a thing of the past, government entertainment broadcasts consisted of games and movies featuring athletes and stars who were moldering in their graves. Tonight a baseball game was on the schedule. They were up to the 1974 season and fans were no less enthralled by 'The Big Red Machine' out of Cincinnati and the likes of Reggie Jackson and Johnny Bench than when blood had coursed through their heroes' now virtual veins.

Broadcasts always made the pub even more popular than usual. Not only the regulars drifted in but a number of individuals and families arrived, bringing food for an informal potluck. Valaria had grudgingly invited Quinn to stay another night but trying to explain his presence would be problematic at best so she once again stashed him in her quarters so as not to unsettle her neighbors.

Jasper and Pete were among the first to arrive, settling in at their regular table for their nightly game of chess. It wasn't the game they had on their minds, however, when Valaria delivered the first round of drinks.

"So," Jasper said in hushed tones, "since the Guardians came and went without incident last night, I take it your guest made it out of town all right."

Valaria hesitated a moment, debating whether the truth or a lie was best under the circumstances. "My *guest*, as you call him, is still sitting in my living room."

Knowing she had just instigated what undoubtedly would be a lengthy conversation she pulled out one of the extra chairs and sat down.

"*What?*" Pete demanded overly loud and nearly choking on his ale.

Jasper and Valaria responded in stereo with a stern "Shhhh," defusing the curious glances of those nearby with rather insipid smiles.

Jasper put his hand on his partner's arm before the other man could speak again but directed his attention to Valaria. "Just what do you mean, he's still here?"

"I mean just what I said. He's still here; sitting in my living room with Yancy serving as babysitter. It's déjà vu all over again."

"Good god, Valaria, why haven't you gotten rid of him? You're endangering not only yourself but the entire community!"

The reprimand stung but she bit back a retort.

"True enough, I suppose," was all she had to say.

"Is that all you've got to say," Pete squeaked. "For Christ's sake, Valaria, you want to get us all killed?"

"That's not going to happen," she replied tartly.

"They could cut off supplies," he countered. "Deliveries are sporadic enough as it is."

"That's not the government, that's Freebooters."

"How can you be so sure? I say the government's just as likely to be keeping things for themselves and then claim our shipments have been hijacked—and harboring a fugitive would give them an excuse to cut us off even more!"

"He's not a fugitive," she insisted.

"He's a member of a subversive organization," he hissed, "that makes him a wanted man!"

Jasper again put his hand on Pete's arm and edged his way back into the conversation. "He's got a point, Valaria. 'Symbiosis' isn't as tidy and fair a system as the government claims. It's tidy and fair for *them* but not necessarily for us exiles. We sure as hell don't want to give them an excuse to cut off supplies."

"We do OK."

"For the most part, yes, but largely because we're agricultural and don't rely on them for food." He raised his palms toward them in a gesture of focus. "Let's get back to the problem at hand—why is Quinn still here?"

"He's still here because I want to hear more of what he has to say."

"Now *that* is going to take some explaining," Jasper said, genuinely perplexed. "Last night you were calling him delusional and wanted to turn him over to the Guardians yourself."

The broadcast had begun and although most patrons were thoroughly focused on the game—or mesmerized by the unbelievable number of people in the stadium—Valaria lowered her voice even more.

"Jasper, you and Otis were friends forever; just what did he tell you about his background?"

"What do you mean?" he asked warily.

Valaria leaned in and, while her neighbors complained about a call at the plate and Reggie Jackson hit another homerun, she filled her grandfather's friends in on the disconcerting education she had received that day at the hands of Gideon Quinn.

"How can you believe all that," Pete sputtered in disbelief when she had finished, looking like he'd just bitten into something rotten.

"His arguments and the evidence are pretty compelling."

Pete waved her comment off and took a healthy swig of ale, washing away the metaphorical foul taste in his mouth.

Valaria directed her attention to Jasper. "What about it?"

"I think this is a conversation that needs to continue in the presence of the man himself," Jasper observed. "Can we slip away or do we wait until closing?"

Valaria opened her mouth to respond but before her reply could take form everyone's attention was drawn to a commotion at the pub's entrance.

A company of Guardians—replete with helmets, body shields, and StunStix—was pouring through the doorway like a human version of pyroclastic flow. In eerie silence, they took up position, shoulder to shoulder, around the curved periphery of the pub.

Suddenly, the only sounds were those of a long-dead baseball announcer and the ubiquitous background noise emanating from the vids.

Dawson Hayes approached their table.

"Valaria," he said almost apologetically, "you need to shut everything off."

In a moment the pub was as silent as a tomb.

A man known by sight as the unit commander pushed his way through the Guardians closest to the door in a caricature of the grand entrance, swatting his gloved left hand theatrically with the riding crop clasped in his right.

"Geez, could he look any more ridiculous," Valaria whispered with a smirk in the direction of Jasper and Pete.

"Pioneers," the commander shouted even though he had the unwavering attention of everyone in the room, "you will present yourselves for identification purposes forthwith. Failure to comply will result in your immediate detention and remand for further interrogation. You are also hereby notified that your domiciles are currently being subjected to scrutiny and any contraband will be confiscated and may also result in your detention and remand."

Everyone in the pub was deathly still.

Jasper had turned a rather cadaverous shade of grey and Pete looked about ready to projectile vomit in the direction of the approaching officers.

"*And that's that,*" Valaria thought—so much for learning more from Gideon Quinn.

Anticipation of what would happen next was the stuff of dread and an overactive imagination—what would be the penalty for giving safe harbor to someone from the Sons of Liberty? Would she be thrown into prison and left to rot? Would the government lobotomize her and ship her off to some kind of gulag? Would she be turned into *Soylent Green* as in the contraband video she had fixated on as a teen?

Being turned into foodstuff was temporarily forestalled as the Guardians prepared to check the identity code—or "tag"—layered into the skin on the back of the residents' necks.

Increasingly incensed at this violation of their rights and beginning to seethe, Valaria drew her lower lip between her teeth and bit down firmly, her long-standing way of reining herself in; even she realized that what they *didn't* need right then was a public display of sarcastic indignation.

Acutely aware of her internal struggle, Jasper laid a somewhat clammy hand on her arm.

In a gesture obviously intended to instill a healthy measure of fear, as well as quell any potential resistance, the exiles gathered in front of the baseball game were roughly separated into groups of four and shoved into chairs at the nearby tables. In the process, Miss Baxter—one of the more elderly residents—stumbled and fell noisily to the floor, beginning to weep quietly as she steadied herself on hands and knees. Intending to rescue their fallen neighbor, two younger exiles wrenched themselves free of the Guardians clutching their arms but almost immediately found themselves writhing on the floor, subdued by StunStix thrust into the nearest available soft tissue. As the Stix crackled menacingly one of the three children who had been herded unceremoniously off to the side shrieked in fear and another began crying loudly for her mother.

While directing one of the women to go quiet the children, Dawson Hayes helped Miss Baxter to her feet and onto a chair. Valaria was certain he shot a subtly cautioning glance her way in the process.

As a child of the Borders, Valaria was accustomed to the presence of Guardians. A ubiquitous dark and menacing counterpoint to the rhythm and flow of 'normal,' they were known for bullying but had never been overtly violent or so outrageously intrusive before. Struggling to curb the anger now surging within, Valaria surveyed her neighbors. Many faces were ashen with fear, but a few were almost apoplectic with barely contained rage.

There were no further outbursts, however, and once order had been restored, the Guardians began systematically scanning each person.

Although still seething, this part of the process didn't overly concern Valaria as she knew for a fact that there were no untagged residents in Settlement #4—except, of course, for the man currently relaxing blissfully unaware in her quarters! Regardless of the fact that it hardly mattered who scanned them, she nonetheless found herself feeling inordinately relieved when Dawson Hayes was the Guardian who approached their table.

Scanning first Jasper and then Pete, Hayes turned the scanner toward Valaria. His voice was formal and flat. "Turn away from me and lift your hair."

She was about to launch the relatively neutral barb that this intrusion was going to significantly jeopardize his drinking privileges when Dawson stopped mid-scan to visually scrutinize the small circular disk embedded in the back of her neck.

"I get no reading off your tag," he said quietly. "It's malfunctioning— although I've never heard of such a thing before."

"Must be your scanner; government quality control at its best."

Hayes moved to the next table and successfully scanned the quartet sitting there.

"No," he said, coming back to Valaria and trying again. "It's just you. Something's deactivated your tag."

"Well, shit, Dawson, you know who I am," she said curtly.

"Yeah, I know who you are—you're a royal pain in the ass."

"But I'm the royal pain in the ass who runs the pub so if I'm remanded it shuts down," she reminded him quietly.

Hayes rolled his eyes. She was right; everyone knew who she was and—although annoying in the extreme—there was no reason to suspect her of subversion, and he had to admit that the prospect of the pub closing was dismal at best.

Caught in the quintessential 'damned-if-you-do-damned-if-you-don't' dilemma, he moved on to another table.

IV.

It was more than two hours later when the Guardians finally left the settlement; the most surprising result of their sweep being the fact that the proprietor of *The Shoe and Gear*—currently the reluctant host of a wanted subversive—hadn't been among those they took with them.

No one was more surprised by that fact than Valaria Thorpe herself.

When the officers assigned to search her quarters entered the private portion of the dome all that had greeted them was an enthusiastic black and white dog. Since Yancy was always with his owner, the Guardians initially were suspicious about the reason for his incarceration but Valaria's glib lie that he had gotten into something rancid and she didn't want him puking in front of her customers struck them as plausible and they said nothing more before beginning their search with grim determination.

Distracted in equal measure by anger and bewilderment, Valaria's heart was in her throat as the Guardians proceeded to open drawers and doors and scrutinize her personal property. When they finally were finished, she and Yancy followed the blank-faced officers back through the pub—their search of cupboards and closets miraculously having yielded no evidence of contraband... *or dissidents.*

Shadowing the Guardians' steps as they returned to the surface, Valaria watched as they melted into the darkness and became one with the night. Nearly overwhelmed by a sense of relief to see them go, she swatted Yancy on the rump as he dashed past her in his urgent quest to find an obliging tree. He always had a calming effect on her. She heaved a long, cleansing sigh and steadied herself against the cool surface of the dome, concentrating on slowing her thundering heart and convincing it to return to its proper location.

She was utterly baffled—*not only hadn't they found Gideon Quinn, they hadn't even found her illegal smokes!* Valaria had no idea how he had accomplished the feat, but she was undeniably indebted to the man for somehow managing to get out of the dome—and for taking her cigarettes with him.

Having successfully convinced her heart that the danger had passed, and knowing that Yancy was likely to be out all night, Valaria wiped her sweaty palms on her jeans and slowly descended the stairs leading back into the dome.

The empty pub yawned before her, shrouded in unfamiliar shadows cast by tables and chairs strewn carelessly about and filled with the eerie quiet of a violent storm's aftermath. Although that metaphorical storm had left her largely unscathed, Valaria considered through new eyes the detritus of overturned chairs and interrupted meals left in its wake. She leaned gratefully into the retinal scan that would secure the front door for the night feeling violated and vulnerable as a result of what had transpired.

Maybe Quinn was right. Maybe it was time to stand up and say enough is enough.

With nascent thoughts of rebellion bubbling just beneath the surface of her natural defiance, she turned from the scanner to find herself face to face with the man who inspired them.

"Where the *hell* did you come from," she sputtered as a jolt of adrenaline shot through her.

"I never left."

She looked at him slightly agog. "Yeah, right; they searched the pub and my quarters—you weren't here. Are the Sons of Liberty imbued with super *powers* as well as super *bullshit*?"

"You're kidding, right?" he asked.

Valaria looked at him blankly.

He obviously was enjoying himself.

"You mean to tell me I know something about your home that you don't?" He smiled and took her wrist. "Come on, I'll show you."

With his free hand he tossed her the cigarette pouch. "Here, thought it might be best if they didn't find these."

"Or *you*," she added caustically.

As they entered her quarters, Quinn continued. "I had the windows open and heard the sound of engines in the distance. Since you people don't have any vehicles I knew it had to be Guardians—and more than just a handful of off-duty apes coming into town to get wasted. I hit the lights; couldn't see much of anything but began hearing the sound of people being rousted and knew I had to do something, and do it quick. This was a bad situation for both of us, Valaria. I can*not* afford to be captured and I sure as hell don't want to be responsible for getting you in trouble."

"How magnanimous of you," she chuffed.

Tiring of her sarcasm, he heaved a sharp sigh before continuing. "Anyway, I knew I couldn't get out but I had faith in your grandfather."

They had entered her bedroom.

"Voila," he crowed, gesturing toward a panel lying on her bed and an exposed opening into the void between her bunk and the circular foundation of the dome.

"It's a pretty cool cubby. I'm surprised you didn't find it when you were a kid."

He pulled a small flashlight out of his pocket and shone it into the empty space. "Not a lot of room but the spiders were reasonably accommodating—think they're subversives?"

He was having way too much fun at her expense.

"You're really enjoying this, aren't you?"

"Well... yeah, guess I am."

"If they had found you here you wouldn't be so jovial, now would you?"

"No, but thanks to your grandfather they didn't."

He slid the panel back into place, making sure Valaria saw the ingenious mechanism that secured it. "All kidding aside, Valaria, this cubby makes me think there may be other hiding places around the dome. That means there's a good chance Otis kept the information I'm looking for and hid it here someplace."

Valaria was dubious—and more than a little suspicious of his intentions. "And just how long do you intend to hang around looking for it?"

"Bringing down the Guardian Star is Plan A," Quinn said soberly. "And there really isn't much of a Plan B. I can't give up so easily. I can't give up just because your grandfather is dead."

He looked at her almost imploringly. "But I promise I won't stay any longer than absolutely necessary. I don't want to put you or your neighbors in jeopardy."

"Again, how magnanimous of you," she interjected.

Gideon ignored her. "I don't expect you to put me up. You're on the edge of the settlement so it'll be relatively easy for me to come and go as needed."

"I guess I really don't have much choice in the matter, do I?"

"You could always turn me in," he replied, trusting she wouldn't take the suggestion seriously. "Valaria, this is *freedom* we're talking about." As he continued, his voice became charged with hope and idealism. "We're talking about rebuilding what we've lost—*really* rebuilding it this time, not creating a cheap imitation that ends up being a façade that masks something more like fascism than democracy."

Unimpressed by his surge of patriotism, Valaria couldn't resist a bit of wheedling. "Geez, is that a fife and drum I hear in the background?" She was finding it difficult to abandon her sarcasm—and her solitude—to embrace his vision. "Listen, I'll give you three days. If you haven't found what you're looking for by then, you're gone. Got it?"

Quinn smiled. "I can live with that."

They had re-entered the living area and Valaria slumped moodily into one of the side chairs, gesturing for Gideon to take the futon.

"You might as well sleep here again tonight," she offered without enthusiasm. "It's pretty late to be heading off into the woods and trying to set up camp. And God only knows how many Guardians may still be lurking around. They're exceptionally good at lurking."

"Thanks, Valaria, I appreciate that. You know, when you round off those edges you're actually a pretty decent person."

She gave him her best expressionless expression.

"Anybody hurt out there?" he asked, refocusing on the raid and gesturing toward the pub.

"They used StunStix on a couple guys who got out of line. I think they just wanted to scare the shit out of us for some reason. They checked our identity tags—which is ridiculous since they know everybody in the settlement."

She looked mildly perplexed and involuntarily touched the back of her neck.

Quinn raised a quizzical eyebrow. "And?"

"...Mine didn't register."

"A scanner malfunction?"

"Dunno; everybody else showed up. It was just me."

"And they didn't take you in?"

"The Guardian who scanned me likes drinking here too much."

A slow smile creased Quinn's face. "Wait a minute. You're telling me that you were tagged as a kid but it's not working anymore?"

"Yeah."

"Oh come on, Valaria, that is so unlikely it's virtually not possible. Tags don't wear out. Don't you see? Yours has been *deactivated*—and we both know the only person who could've done that is your grandfather! Wow, how cool is that? Way to go, Otis!"

"Don't start that crap again," Valaria sputtered defensively. "It was just a damn malfunction with no cosmic significance attached."

"OK, OK, sorry I suggested it," Quinn replied with a smug grin, obviously satisfied that he had scored another point in their debate about her grandfather. Since he was walking the tightrope of Valaria's largesse, however, he decided not to pursue the matter.

"Do you play?" he asked instead, taking a stab at normalcy and indicating the chessboard holding pride of place on the low table in front of the futon.

He picked up the thick board and studied it closely. The dark and light squares across which the chess pieces would move were delineated by blocks of white birch and black walnut, but here again it was Otis's signature engraving that took center stage and gave the piece its soul as the entire surface of the board was covered with a beautifully rendered, intricate geometric pattern.

"This detail is amazing," he said, placing the board back on the table. "So, do you play?"

Valaria heaved a long, cathartic sigh, relieved at the change in subject. "Couldn't have survived being raised by Otis without learning to play chess. That was his mantra—'*Chess is the key to everything.*'"

Too wired to even consider calling it a day, she picked up the black king and waggled it in Quinn's direction.

"Ready to get your ass kicked?"

What country can preserve its liberties if their

rulers are not reminded from time to time that

their people retain the spirit of resistance?

~Thomas Jefferson

CHAPTER SIX

I.

By noon on the third day after the Guardian raid residents of the settlement were growing increasingly anxious about the fate of those taken in for questioning—while Gideon Quinn was simultaneously becoming increasingly anxious about his chances of finding any information left behind by Valaria's grandfather before his reluctant host sent him packing.

In total, five people had been taken into custody the night the Guardians had descended on the pub. Trevor Schmidt and Carlos Rivera were obvious targets for remand after physically clashing with Guardians over the shoving of old Miss Baxter. Chloe Jennings, whose open secret was her regular contact with the black market, also was arrested as was Sam Gleason, a hothead even more combustible than Valaria Thorpe who had eagerly told the Guardians exactly what he thought of their unjustified incursion. If anyone actually had foreseen the raid, it undoubtedly would have been Thorpe and Gleason they would have expected to see dragged away, both being more than willing to bestow their opinion in no uncertain terms upon anyone within earshot; Sam Gleason being hoisted on his own petard with some degree of regularity. As a result, after coming to terms with the harsh reality of the raid itself, the only truly surprising outcome was that Valaria Thorpe had managed to keep her mouth shut and that *Mavis Pope*—who didn't seem to have any opinions at all—had been taken instead.

Joining the ranks of the exiled less than a year ago, Pope was still something of a Borders virgin, adhering to government-imposed rules and regulations more like a rigidly monitored city dweller than one of its largely forgotten discards. What she possibly could have done to warrant investigation was instantly a focal point of conversation. She never spoke openly against the government, never missed a shift at the farm, and bemoaned her lot in life far less than many of her neighbors. As a result, it quickly was agreed that her size and flamboyancy must be the culprits since she had been the target of Guardian derision from the moment of her arrival; the 'era of tolerance' ushered in by the Neoteric revolution just prior to the plague apparently extending only to those who met their narrow definition of acceptable. It seemed there was little room for a gaudy, corpulent beekeeper in the Reorganized States of America, exiled or otherwise.

As they waited for the return of their neighbors—or word of their fate—life for the residents of Settlement #4 inevitably returned to a semblance of normalcy. Although at times rather mindless toil, the farm required daily attention from everyone and the repetitive tasks associated with maintaining the three dilapidated farming domes and caring for the various crops and fish nurtured within gave them something to focus on other than the dramatic underscoring the raid had just given to their precarious living situation. In addition to that long-accepted routine, however, a new normal quickly became evident—when the day's work was finished most residents hurried home and were understandably reluctant to venture beyond their own door for fear of being swept up in whatever Guardian maelstrom might next befall them. As a result, the settlement's dusty streets were quieter and emptier than Valaria had ever seen them—as was her pub.

The fear that now draped itself across the settlement like a thick low-lying fog was almost palpable and Gideon Quinn felt mildly guilty about finding some measure of satisfaction in the wake-up call the raid had provided—and the fact that empty streets and a deserted pub made his remaining time among them much easier.

True to his word, Quinn had gone back to living rough somewhere nearby and no longer sprawled awkwardly across Valaria's futon at night. Aided by those virtually deserted streets, he had become adept at slipping into town unnoticed shortly before dawn, lurking restlessly in the shadows at the bottom of the stairwell leading to the pub until Valaria, still groggy and disheveled from sleep, would grudgingly grant him entry.

She had given him three days within which to find the illusive key to the Guardian Star he felt certain Otis Thorpe had left behind; a deadline she almost gleefully reminded him of with untiring regularity as the hours marched inexorably forward.

Having found the hiding place where he had taken refuge during the Guardian raid—ingeniously nestled into the curve of the dome behind Valaria's bed—Quinn had been convinced that her grandfather had put his engineering skills to work and incorporated other secret places into the meticulous finishing work he had invested in their home.

When they found a *second* hidden cubby shortly after his quest began on the first of his three days, Gideon was doubly-certain Otis Thorpe had planned ahead after being exiled, and refused to be discouraged by the fact that it, like the first, was devoid of any information relating to the Guardian Star.

After discovering a *third* hiding place shortly before stopping for a break at six in the evening of the third—and final—day, Quinn nearly crowed with delight.

"I don't see what you're so damned excited about," Valaria stated pointedly as she handed him a flashlight so he could scan the small void they had just revealed under the shelving beneath the pub's bar. "It's gonna be just as empty as the others."

She moved from where she had been squatting next to him to sit cross-legged on the floor and leaned back against the smooth end panel of the bar's enclosure. "This is a royal waste of time and a shitload of bother."

Lying flat on his belly beneath the bar, his head and shoulders thrust under the storage shelves in the dusty corner and his legs and feet extending back into Valaria's proprietary space, Quinn clenched the EverLight firmly between his teeth so to free his hands for exploring.

"It's not a waste of time," he replied tersely, his words slightly garbled by the flashlight currently residing in his mouth. "And I've still got six hours," he reminded her, refusing to be deflated by his host's pessimism.

"And that's *all* you've got, asshole," Valaria muttered under her breath.

She was about to repeat her imperative at an appropriately authoritative volume when an outburst from Quinn brought her up short.

"Holy crap, Valaria," he shouted. "There's something in this one!"

In an instant she had joined him, belly flat against the floor, looking like a misshapen earthworm as she wriggled her way closer to the small cubbyhole under the far corner of the shelving beneath the bar.

Quinn rolled to his side to make room for her, holding out a rectangular container roughly 10 by 12 inches and an inch deep. The lightweight metal from which the box was constructed balanced easily in one hand as he displayed it.

"What have you got there," she croaked, inhaling a cobweb. "Geez, somebody should clean under here!"

"You got me," he replied as he examined the container to see how it opened.

As they slowly began to extricate themselves from the dusty labyrinth of shelves under the bar so to inspect their find in better lighting, their exit suddenly was barred by a wet nose and fifty pounds of canine exuberance.

"Hey, Yance, where did you come from?" Valaria asked, draping an arm across the dog's shoulders as he joined them on the floor.

"I let him in," a familiar voice called out from across the pub. "What the hell are you doing under there?"

In the heartbeat it took her to identify the voice as that of Dawson Hayes, Valaria's life flashed before her eyes—albeit an abbreviated version where she once again saw herself permanently confined in the bowels of a government gulag.

Gideon pulled his legs to his chest and tried to completely disappear under the bar while Valaria scooted back and lurched upward, smacking her head soundly on the bartop's rolled edge in the process.

"*Shit*," she exclaimed as she rose to a standing position.

Gingerly touching the top of her head, Valaria's gut constricted as the last thing in the world she needed to see right then greeted her eyes; five Guardians, with Dawson Hayes in the lead, stood—armed and unsmiling—just inside the door of the pub.

Hayes crossed the room, an expression somewhere between concern and suspicion on his face. "You OK?"

Catching herself just a beat before sharing the disdainful retort any expression of concern from a Guardian inspired, Valaria bit her lower lip and ignored the question.

"What can I do for you, Guardian Hayes?" she asked coolly and deliberately, composure regained. "Is there a problem?"

"No, nothing's wrong. Yancy was getting in the way of our patrol; didn't want him to get hurt so brought him home."

She repaid his act of kindness with a cold, withering look.

"Your '*patrol*,'" she repeated quietly. "Gosh, such an innocuous name for something that's anything but; just how often are we going to be honored by your presence—your '*patrols*'—Guardian Hayes?"

Dawson glanced over his shoulder and gestured the others forward before replying.

"How about dropping the sarcasm and just getting us something to drink," he said sternly. "Nonalcoholic; we're on duty."

Valaria moved farther along the open side of the bar as Hayes and the others approached. Quinn's feet were still clearly visible and she gave him what she hoped was a successfully surreptitious kick as the Guardians made themselves at home on the other side.

Taking a pitcher of apple cider out of the cooler, Valaria fell silent and tried to envision positive endgame scenarios for a situation that seemed almost cosmically hopeless; a life sentence in a gulag instantly becoming more appealing when measured against the possibility of being sliced and diced by StunStix set on kill.

She found herself wondering what must be going through Gideon Quinn's mind right then. Was he up to taking on five Guardians if it came to that? She didn't even know if he was armed. If he carried a weapon, was he likely to go on the offensive or play it safe and remain quietly huddled under the bar? Several old movie heroes flashed through her mind as she filled five glasses with cold cider. Even though one of the Guardians currently scowling at her was female, the testosterone quotient went off the charts whenever the government's swaggering, black-clad enforcers showed up. God, how she hoped Quinn didn't decide now was a good time to prove his manhood by pulling a Clint Eastwood and emerging from under the bar with guns blazing!

Although she could only imagine what her seditious guest was thinking at the moment, there suddenly was no doubt about what was going through Yancy's mind. Out of the blue, the dog decided Quinn should either be joined under the bar or convinced to join those standing in front it. Without warning, a hurricane of black and white fur pushed its way behind Valaria, dipped into a low play-bow and yapped delightedly in the direction of the subversive struggling to keep his towering frame compacted under the bar directly beneath his adversaries.

"What's up with the dog?" Hayes' second-in-command demanded, his hand automatically hovering above his StunStic.

"Wants something to eat but knows he's not supposed to be behind the bar," she replied, grabbing Yancy by the scruff of the neck and hauling him away from Quinn. "Sometimes he is such a goddamn pain in the ass," she added, almost dislocating her left hip as she shoved the dog out from behind the bar with a determined sideways thrust.

In a moment, the Guardians had drained their glasses and Hayes gave a curt gesture toward the door. With a derisive glance at their host, they moved away.

In spite of being inordinately relieved to be looking at their backs, Valaria couldn't resist a parting shot. "Leaving so soon?"

Dawson Hayes stopped in his tracks, turned, and retraced his steps to the bar.

"Get a clue, Valaria," he hissed. "Things are going from bad to worse out there. As long as the Sons of Liberty are stirring things up, the government's gonna do its best to shut things down. So, yeah, you better get used to seeing us around."

"And we exiles are always gonna be prime targets for the fascists in Columbus, aren't we?"

"Watch your mouth," Hayes replied forcefully. "You know as well as I do that exiles are always suspects as far as the government's concerned. But they're cracking down *everywhere*—increased identify checks, random searches, more drones, you name it. Be forewarned, Valaria; keep your head down... and your mouth shut."

The bar having just vividly taught her a lesson about the value of keepings one's head down, she digested the wisdom of his words for a moment. The collision with her grandfather's handiwork had given her a headache and she again touched a finger to the point of impact. It came away tinged in red.

"You sure you're OK?" Hayes asked, mellowing slightly. "Just what were you doing under there anyway?"

She paused for a moment before responding.

"I've been trying to get rid of a big *rat* for the past few days," she said with a smirk, "thought I saw it under the bar."

II.

Valaria slumped to the floor and wrapped her arms around Yancy's neck, burying her face in his soft fur.

"Oh my God," she muttered quietly in disbelief. "*Oh... my... God!*"

She emerged from her canine cocoon and glared at the dissident kneeling beside her. "Do you realize how close we just came to utter and complete *disaster?*"

Although the Guardians hadn't come into the pub looking to roust revolutionaries but truly had just needed a drink—and in spite of the fact that it actually had taken a blessedly short time for them to move on— every second had seemed like an hour to Valaria and she once again was livid with herself for putting her entire community at risk by allowing Quinn to stay.

Her guest rose to his feet and offered her his hand. "The price of patriotism, I'm afraid."

"*The price of patriotism*," she repeated angrily as he pulled her up. "Holy shit, do you *ever* stop talking in platitudes?"

With metaphorical thunder clouds gathering all around her, Valaria left him standing by the bar and stormed to the door of the pub to lock up, then stormed past him on the way to her living quarters.

He found her sitting at the dining table, head in her hands.

"Sorry if that sounds like a platitude to you," he said, taking the chair across from her and laying the dusty container between them. "But I'm totally serious. If things are going to change—if things are going to get better—people have to be willing to stand up and make a difference. People like you and me, Valaria... People like your grandfather."

"People like my *grandfather?* According to you he's one of the geniuses who designed the goddamn Star. Doesn't that make him one of the bad guys?"

"Their original intent was honorable—the Tower was meant to protect not oppress. It's because I believe that that I also believe your grandfather was one of the good guys. And *that's* why I continue to believe he left something behind for us. By the time he moved here I think he knew the day would come when we'd have to bring the Star down."

He reached out and brushed some of the dust off the box. "Wanna take a look at his message in a bottle?"

"Might as well," she replied with a deep sigh, leaning back in the chair and running her fingers through her hair.

Quinn picked up the box and wiped most of the remaining dust off the surface, exposing eight shallow divots along the edge of the top as he did so.

"The metal this baby's made of hardly weighs anything," he observed almost to himself.

He handed the box across the table as an awareness seemed to dawn. "Valaria, I think this is made from the same stuff as the Tower!"

She, too, was surprised by the almost weightless nature of the box but, unlike Quinn, felt more annoyance than wonder. "Well, there better be a trick to getting this puppy open, 'cuz I sure don't see a clasp or anything."

She slid the box back across the table.

"And if I'm right about it being made from the same metal as the Tower," Gideon added quietly, "there's no way in hell we're gonna be able to break it open."

"That's just great," Valaria said, her voice dripping with frustration. "So, you actually turn out to be right—which I can't believe I'm saying! Otis really did leave something behind but he's so goddamn paranoid it's a frickin' puzzle box that we've got no clue how to open!"

Encouraged rather than daunted by her words, Quinn smiled. "I'm glad you're beginning to see things my way."

"Well, shit, Quinn, it's not like he'd use a box made out of the same crap as the Tower to store a butterfly collection. And why hide it under the bar? How likely was it somebody would ever find it there?"

Quinn pondered her words for a moment and then smiled. "You said it yourself earlier—somebody should *clean* under there. I'll bet your grandfather assumed *you'd* find it if he didn't need it during his lifetime."

He had stepped over to the sink as he spoke. Returning with a damp cloth, he carefully wiped every exposed surface of the box.

"These divots have got to be the key," he mused, wiping them gently.

Valaria's voice was bitter. "Then that's no help at all! There are *eight* of them," she nearly hissed. "You don't have to be a genius to know that means there's a mind-blowing number of possibilities if it's some kind of pattern lock."

Quinn conceded her point and they sat in silence, both staring at the mysterious container until an audible rumbling from Valaria's stomach broke the spell.

"Let's take a break and get something to eat," she suggested. "I can't think when I'm hungry."

It wasn't the most companionable of meals. Despite the fact that Valaria had finally come to accept Quinn's portrayal of her grandfather as something far more complex than a simple Borders carpenter—and no longer found his presence about as appealing as a bout of diarrhea—she continued to be uncomfortable around the man. He just seemed like such a *decent* person—the word "honorable" actually came to mind but tasted so sour she managed to choke it back down. And she had to admit his idealism and intelligence made it difficult to dismiss him out of hand... and made what he stood for and what he said increasingly challenging.

Both of which facts were forcing Valaria far out of her comfort zone; terrain she assiduously avoided.

When they had finished eating and cleaned away the debris, Quinn picked up the box once again, gliding his fingers over the smooth surface in wonder.

"God, this is amazing stuff," he observed.

"This is amazing *shit*," Valaria countered. "Get your head out of your ass and focus on the problem, Quinn."

Gideon looked at her and smiled. "And here I thought you were learning to play nice."

"This *is* me playing nice."

In spite of her words, Quinn noted her tone had softened considerably.

"OK," he replied. "Let's review what we know. First of all, this box must've been left behind by Otis since no one else has ever had that kind of access to the pub. Am I right?"

"I suppose."

"Good. Second, the stuff the box is made from is utterly unique—it has to be the same fiber-metal as the Tower."

"Since you know more about the Tower than I do, I'll have to trust you on that one; it's certainly different from anything I've seen."

Gideon smiled but didn't point out that Valaria had just granted him a measure of trust without any conditions or sarcasm attached.

"So, we've got a box made from the same material as the Tower, left behind by Otis."

"Which takes us absolutely no further than we were before."

"I disagree. Based on those facts, I think it's fairly logical to deduce that *you* are the common denominator in all this."

She shot him a dubious look but said nothing.

"Come on, Valaria, Otis knew the pub would be your home long after he was gone. I also imagine he thought you'd *clean* it from time to time. Like I said, you're the only logical person he intended to find the box if he didn't need what's inside before he passed."

Valaria shook her head and gave him a mordant—albeit reasonably friendly—smirk. "I think I'm going back to my original opinion that you're delusional. If I'm the intended recipient of the box, just how did he *intend* for me to get inside? This is just a tad more complicated than opening a Christmas gift. And he sure as hell didn't leave a printout of any directions."

"No... no printout."

"Then what?"

She picked up the box and gave it a shake. "We can't even be sure there's anything inside the damn thing."

She tossed it down on the table.

"Oh my God, Valaria, that's it!"

"*What's* it? The box is empty?"

"No, what you said about a printout."

"But there isn't one."

"Right, there's no printout," Quinn sputtered dismissively. "That's not it. Not print*out—prints!* The eight divots…"

He held up his hands and waggled his fingers at her. "The divots represent *fingers!* And I'd bet the house they represent *your* fingers."

"What makes you think they're fingers? Last time I looked we had *five* on each hand. That means there should be *ten* divots—where're the *thumbs?*"

Gideon arched his fingers slightly and placed them in the divots, thumbs failing to reach the surface.

"The pattern doesn't accommodate thumbs," he conceded, "but the other fingers sure fit. And ten divots would have looked a lot more like hands than eight anyway; too easy to figure out."

He pushed the box toward her. "This may be the best 'Christmas gift' ever, Valaria." Dipping his head slightly in encouragement, he nudged the box closer to her. "Go ahead, give it a try."

III.

There were fewer than twelve miles lying between Settlement #4 and the Guardian Star tower but the only route connecting the two was the deteriorated remnant of an old highway that hadn't been resurfaced since The Revanche. All across the unreclaimed portion of the former United States the situation was the same—the arteries of a sophisticated interstate highway system and the smaller veins and capillaries of state roads and city streets having long since been corrupted by weeds and saplings thrusting skyward through increasingly compromising cracks in dry, decaying asphalt; their unrelenting progress complimented by plants of every description encroaching with equal zeal from the sidelines. It was a scenario repeated in myriad ways across the country—and around the world—the footprint of humankind slowly being obliterated by the firm hand of nature.

As a result of the condition of the roads—or the complete lack thereof in some places—the trip back to the settlement from where they had been incarcerated at the Guardian Star was almost as unsettling for those arrested during the raid as their time in confinement had been. Especially since they weren't entirely certain they were, in fact, being taken home.

Mavis Pope sat in the back of the Guardian transport vehicle looking straight ahead and keeping her distance from the others. She had nothing to say to these people and, as she sat there unobtrusively watching them, she wondered whether they were, indeed, anything other than what they all claimed. The transport was almost stiflingly hot, the ventilation system sputtering and coughing noisily above their heads as it struggled to provide fresh air. Deep in contemplation, however, Mavis barely noticed the temperature or the constant jarring to which they were subjected as the vehicle traveled east over a route that at times was nothing more than ruts worn into the earth by repeated Guardian traffic.

Sitting across from Pope on one of the metal benches attached to the long interior walls, Trevor Schmidt also was silent, welts and bruises on his face clear evidence of the nature of his treatment at the hands of the Guardians. His face dappled with beads of sweat, Schmidt sat with arms folded firmly across his chest protecting what Mavis suspected were cracked or broken ribs, grimacing in tight-lipped pain with every jolt that rocked the transport.

Farther down the bench Carlos Rivera sat with his arm around the shoulders of Chloe Jennings. She leaned into the protective circle he provided, laying her head against his chest and crying softly. Rivera was murmuring quiet assurances in Spanish and Mavis wondered vaguely if Chloe understood a word he was saying. If nothing else, the gentle cadence of his voice was undoubtedly soothing. For some reason, Mavis found the tableau inordinately annoying and if Miss Jennings didn't soon demonstrate a little backbone, she was afraid she might find herself compelled to "give her something to cry about," as Pope's father had often threatened his young daughter when frustrated by what he perceived as unwarranted displays of emotion.

Mavis leaned her head back against the wall of the transport, her thoughts turning to Sam Gleason, the only detainee from the Settlement missing from this return trip. They all showed physical evidence of the interrogations to which they had been subjected, but Mavis had overheard two Guardians referring to Gleason in the *past tense* as they talked about his sessions with Colonel Mertens and she had assumed the worst. Mavis had encountered Seth Mertens only once during her time at the Tower and she hadn't been impressed; he struck her as a coward and a thug. His caricaturish buffoonery when leading the raid on the settlement—making the grand entrance brandishing a riding crop—made her believe it was entirely possible he had gone too far while questioning Gleason and had actually beaten the man to death. The fact that Gleason might have been the only detainee who actually had ties to the Sons of Liberty made that thought doubly troubling.

She needed to see Valaria Thorpe.

IV.

Valaria's hands betrayed her.

She reached out to pick up the metal box only to discover a distinct tremor as she did so. She immediately sat back in her chair, tucking her ice cold fingers under her thighs.

Give it a try? Easy enough for Quinn to say; *she* was the one whose genetic reputation was on the line. If her fingertips weren't the key to Otis's puzzle box then she wasn't the linchpin of her grandfather's life that Quinn believed her to be, this wasn't Otis's tribute gift to her, and they truly were screwed. If her fingers *did* prove to be the proverbial 'Open Sesame,' everything Gideon Quinn claimed might actually be true and the contents of the box would be the next piece of the larger puzzle that was Otis Thorpe.

Both possibilities were paralyzing.

Quinn said nothing as Valaria sat and stared at the box.

She leaned forward, resting her elbows on the table and pressing tented fingers against her lips, chin resting on her thumbs.

Sensing his human's distress, Yancy came and sat next to her, looking up adoringly. She reached down and scratched him behind the ears.

Suddenly taking control of the moment—and her trepidation—she pulled the box closer and placed her fingertips on the divots.

The lid slid away with a barely audible "whoosh" as air rushed in.

Quinn smiled broadly.

"Merry Christmas, Valaria."

"Tyranny like hell is not easily conquered yet we have this consolation with us, the harder the conflict, the more glorious the triumph. What we obtain too cheaply, we esteem too lightly; it is dearness only that gives everything its value."

~Thomas Paine

CHAPTER SEVEN

I.

It was one of those moments that sends a rush of adrenaline surging through your body and literally takes your breath away. As the box slid open at her touch, Valaria's hands jerked away from the surface as if it was molten.

"Holy crap," she sputtered, fingers frozen in midair.

"Holy *something*," Quinn agreed. "My God, Valaria, I've been telling you your grandfather was a genius!"

"Runs in the family," she mused in a whisper, folding her hands in her lap like a child freshly scolded to be quiet in church.

Gideon looked at her and smiled. "I wouldn't be at all surprised."

He gave her a beat or two to catch her breath, his own level of hopeful expectancy simultaneously ratcheting skyward as he waited. "So, is there anything in there?"

She was almost afraid to look but pulled the box closer as Gideon moved from across the table to the chair next to hers. With some degree of hesitancy, they both peered into the opening that had been exposed when the lid slid away on its invisible track.

There were papers inside, held together by a clip.

When Valaria made no move to do so, Quinn extracted them with a degree of caution that made her realize he feared they might disintegrate at his touch.

"They're not *that* old," she assured him.

Regaining his equilibrium, Quinn shrugged rather sheepishly, removed the clip and spread seven sheets of paper out in front of them so each was clearly visible.

"Any idea what these are?" he asked. "Is that your grandfather's handwriting?"

Quinn leaned forward, carefully scrutinizing the intricate diagram meticulously drawn on each piece of paper. They were similar but each had its own unique pattern.

Valaria had slumped back in her chair and folded her arms across her chest.

Gideon appraised her quizzically.

"Any idea what these are?" he asked again.

"Oh yeah, I know what they are," she replied morosely. "They're a lot of *nothing*, that's what they are!"

"A lot of nothing? What do you mean?"

"I mean just what I said—they're a lot of nothing. They're worthless."

"How do you know?"

Valaria pushed her chair noisily away from the table and went to stand by the windows over the sink, staring angrily out at the darkness.

"Valaria?"

She turned back to him.

"They're just a bunch of *chess games*," she barked, gesturing angrily toward the papers on the table. "That's how Otis diagramed his goddamn games; how he kept a record of his favorite matches. So, like I said, they're a bunch of nothing. You've wasted your time on a wild goose chase—and found nothing but goose *crap* for your trouble!"

She ran a hand through her hair, looking vacantly down at Yancy who—recognizing her distress—had glued himself to her side, doing his canine best to make everything OK.

"Don't be so quick to give up," Quinn replied calmly. "You sure these are games? I've seen chess diagrams before and they don't look like this."

"Of course I'm sure! Otis had his own way of recording games; that's his system."

"So, why would he hide them?"

Valaria came back to the table and slumped into her chair. "I'll tell you why. Otis was an old man..." She glanced over at her grandmother's cello. "He'd been through a lot of shit in his life. Maybe after everything he'd seen and everything that happened to him he was just a few bricks short of a load."

"You don't believe that," Quinn stated flatly, "and neither do I."

"How would *you* know? You never even met the man."

"True, but after all the research I've done and the time I've spent here with you, I feel like I've gotten to know him pretty well."

He placed a hand reassuringly on Valaria's arm. "Let's take a careful look at these. Maybe there's more to them than meets the eye."

"You sure are one optimistic son-of-a-bitch," she said drearily, shaking her head.

"Hey, in my line of work, if you're not optimistic the bad guys win."

Without giving her time to formulate a retort, Gideon organized the papers into two rows in front of her. "OK, take a look at each of these. Do you notice anything unique; anything special?"

Valaria took a slow, deep breath before visually dissecting each diagram. "Well, this one's from a match he played with Jasper a few weeks before he died."

"How can you be so sure?"

"Trust me," she assured him. "You learn the game from Otis you learn this shit along the way."

She picked up three other sheets. "These are older; matches Otis lost— must have wanted to remember how he was outmaneuvered. The rest I don't recognize."

She started to shove the papers away from her but stopped short.

"Oh, cool," she said quietly.

"What?"

She singled out a lone piece of paper and pushed it toward him. "I didn't notice right off—this one's the first game *I* ever won. God, that's so long ago now; never realized Otis was sentimental."

Quinn studied the diagram in silence for what seemed an inordinately long time to Valaria, glancing through the others again as well before speaking.

"Maybe it's more than sentimentality," he said at last. "Remember, Valaria, you're the common denominator in all this. Your fingers opened the box and he hid it where you were the only person likely to find it."

"Yeah, so what?"

"So, what if these other games are only window dressing? What if *this* game..." He picked up the diagram of her win. "Your first victory, is the one he really wanted you to find? He must have known it would stand out to you—just like it did."

"OK, so it stands out. I'll say it again— so what?"

"Yeah," he agreed quietly. "So what?"

Another long silence stretched tautly between them; Quinn deep in thought about the possible significance of the diagram, Valaria quietly musing about her surprisingly sentimental old Luddite.

"Where'd you play that game?" Gideon asked suddenly.

"Whaddaya mean, where did we play it? We played it here."

"Out in the pub or here in your living quarters?"

"Here," she replied, gesturing toward the low table in front of the futon, "on Otis's board."

Clutching the diagram, Quinn grabbed her by the wrist, pulled her to her feet, and ushered her over to the living area.

"Come on," he said firmly. "Show me."

"Show you what?" she asked, slouching down into a chair adjacent the futon, her voice a mixture of incredulity and petulance. "Show you the *game*?"

"Yes," he replied with growing confidence. "Show me the game."

He sat on the futon and handed her the diagram.

Spreading the now rather crumpled piece of paper out on the table, Valaria pulled the chessboard toward her.

The petulance had gone but the incredulity remained.

"I think I know where you're going with this," she said. "If I re-enact my winning game, it'll be 'Open Sesame' time again and the top of the chessboard will pop off." She wiggled her fingers at him. "Just like my magical little fingers opened the box. That *is* what you're thinking, isn't it?"

"Something like that, yeah."

She started to speak but before she could launch the sarcastic barb he knew was coming, Quinn cut her off.

"Your grandfather was a genius, Valaria. That box is *amazing*! He possessed the key to the Guardian Star and I still believe he left that key behind for you to find. Remember what you told me the other day? Otis always said '*chess is the key to everything.*'"

"So? What are you saying?" she asked with a snarky smirk. "Otis was embedding some kind of subliminal message in my brain pointing me to the chessboard?"

With another sheepish shrug, Quinn acknowledged that that was pretty much exactly what he'd been thinking.

"And I suppose the only way to prove you wrong is to replay the damn game."

"Or the only way to prove me *right*," he countered. "I know this is difficult for you. I know you find it tough to accept the fact that you're a major player in all this, but I'm afraid that's right where your grandfather put you—intentionally or not."

Valaria heaved a long, slow sigh. "Geez, this is all just so weird."

Without further commentary, she began to re-enact the game.

It hadn't been the most sophisticated match; as Valaria grew older she sometimes wondered if Otis had let her win. Nevertheless, she had contributed a few intelligent variations along the way that had proven his young opponent had promise.

Neither Quinn nor Valaria spoke while she played. When her black queen had forced Otis into check for the third time, she paused and looked at Quinn with a shrug.

"What?" he asked. "That's 'check,' not 'checkmate.'"

"There are only three moves left," she explained. "Don't you think if something's gonna happen it would have happened by now?"

"You know what they say, 'it's not over 'til the fat lady sings.'" He gave her an encouraging nod. "Finish the game."

With some degree of reluctance—and seriously concentrating on keeping her fingers from trembling—Valaria completed the last few moves.

Nothing happened.

The chess pieces remained as they were. The board remained flat and inert.

"*Shit,*" Quinn muttered in disappointment, leaning back against the futon and sounding defeated for the first time.

Valaria's voice became almost sympathetic. "I tried to tell you..." But as she spoke, the chessboard began emitting a low, slow thrum.

The duo looked across the table at one another, each too dumbfounded to speak.

Quinn leaned in, crossing his arms and resting them on his knees, not wanting to miss what came next. Valaria leaned away, looking as if she half expected the board to detonate.

The thrumming continued and neither spoke.

Although barely audible, it seemed to be picking up speed. Quinn reached out and gingerly touched the chessboard.

"It's vibrating," he observed almost reverently. "I think you triggered an energy source of some kind—something's powering up."

Quinn's words had barely had time to register with Valaria when the chessboard began to divulge its secrets.

As Gideon watched in awe and Valaria looked on in utter disbelief, Otis's intricate geometric designs—previously thought to be purely artistic augmentation—gradually came to life as rivers of energy flowed into them.

An electronic schematic began to rise in three-dimensional relief from the surface of the board.

Suddenly fascinated—and exceedingly grateful it hadn't exploded in their faces!—Valaria unintentionally mimicked Quinn's posture, leaning in with crossed arms resting on her knees.

"Any idea what we're looking at?" she asked in a hush.

"Yeah, as a matter of fact, I think I know exactly what this is."

As they watched, the schematic continued to coalesce above the surface of the board. The designs Otis had layered into the overall pattern were separating into different colors, each representing a particular component of the plan taking form before them.

"*Beautiful,*" Quinn breathed in awe when the completed three-dimensional diagram finally stood proudly above the chessboard.

Valaria smiled involuntarily, recognizing the level of concentration Gideon directed toward the schematic—she had seen it hundreds of times on her grandfather's face as he worked and knew Quinn was no longer remotely aware of her presence.

With a level of respect in her voice to which he undoubtedly was oblivious, she nudged her way back into his consciousness. "So, is that what I think it is?"

"Oh yeah," he replied, reaching across and clutching her arm triumphantly. "Otis left you a blueprint for the whole damn Star!"

Quinn released her arm and she leaned back into the recesses of her deeply cushioned chair, heaving a long sigh and assessing him with tight-lipped concentration while absently picking at one of the fraying patches on the seat cushion.

"So what do you do now?" she asked at last. "You can't quite go around with a chessboard tucked under your arm, replaying an old game every time you want to access the diagram."

"Hardly," he agreed. "It's also impossible to know just how long the energy source powering the display will last. I've got to figure out a way to store this puppy."

He pulled off his fingerless gloves and once again accessed the technology embedded in the tattoo adorning the top of his hand.

"Don't think I'll ever get used to that," Valaria observed from her adjacent vantage point.

His own computerized wizardry had risen above his hand and he began entering code and assessing possibilities as he spoke.

"Even with all our encryption protocols," he explained, "I don't want to upload your grandfather's schematic to the Liberty Tree. Unfortunately, there's not a lot of memory in this embed. I'm hoping there's enough."

"How are you going to get it off the board?"

Quinn flashed a confident smile. "I've got a few tricks up my sleeve—or in my tat, I should say."

He refocused his attention on his work, diving into the bowels of the programming layered onto his hand determined to create a connection between the two disparate technologies. More than half an hour passed—accompanied by more than a few choice expletives along the way—before he stopped abruptly and looked at Valaria with smug satisfaction.

"Got it!"

"You stored it in your tat? Damn, how'd you do that?"

He gave her a hesitant, self-deprecating shrug. "Well, I designed the thing," he admitted almost apologetically.

"Bloody hell, you're as bad as Otis—a man of unknown talents."

He smiled so innocently she decided to let him off the hook of the sarcastic line she felt more than justified to reel in.

"So, is that it?" she asked instead. "Mission accomplished?"

"Hard to say," he admitted honestly. "I'm gonna need time to study this and see just what we've got but, since this *is* the end of the third day..."

He looked at her expectantly with what he hoped were the same mournful puppy-dog eyes that made Yancy so irresistible.

With no small measure of resignation in her voice, she smiled weakly, lifted her hands in a gesture of surrender and said rather dourly, "See you in the morning."

II.

After Quinn finally slipped away into the dark and barren emptiness stretching west beyond Valaria's dome, she collapsed gratefully onto her bunk—taking time only to stash the now invaluable chessboard in the hiding place Gideon had discovered behind her bed. As often happens when in the throes of utter exhaustion, however, a sound night's sleep proved elusive. Tossing and turning her way into the wee hours of morning, Valaria's restless sleep was riddled with troubling dreams in which she tried to unravel clues to an endless scavenger hunt that kept leading her blindly back to the Guardian Star. Typical of the contradictory nature of nightmares, Otis, Quinn—and even Dawson Hayes and Miss Baxter—appeared and disappeared as she thrashed; sometimes taunting, sometimes encouraging her to persevere.

Surfacing just before dawn, Valaria shuffled to the door of the pub and once again allowed Gideon Quinn to usher her into an only slightly less surreal version of the dreams that had left her groggy and grumpy.

Quinn appeared to have slept no better than she but was in decidedly better spirits, taking over duties in the kitchenette while Valaria led Yancy back through the pub so he could greet the morning from the unfathomable depths of his boundless enthusiasm—and pee on his favorite tree.

"I've been wondering," Gideon began as Valaria reentered her living quarters, "if you'd like to take a closer look at the Liberty Tree."

When Valaria's only response was to slump into the nearest available dining chair and rub her sleep-encrusted eyes with the heels of her palms, he continued.

"I offered before, if you remember, but you needed to open the pub so there wasn't time."

He placed a plate bearing a single fried egg and piece of toast in front of her, taking nothing for himself.

"Your larder's almost bare," he explained. "I'll get something later."

"Supplies are overdue—*long* overdue," she replied. "Think it's part of the Triumvirate's fascist formula to keep the peons in line?"

"If you want an honest answer—yes. You guys are lucky you're an agricultural settlement and not industrial; those folks are in deep shit if the government decides to use Symbiosis as a weapon instead of just a way to keep exiles in line. Your settlement can survive without toilet tissue, the ones *making* the TP'll be hard pressed to go without a regular source of food."

Not feeling up to another political science lecture, Valaria took advantage of Quinn's reference to her settlement's function and redirected the conversation. "Speaking of the farm, I've really got to put in an appearance there today. Everybody's been pretty much staying home since the raid, but we still have to fulfill our work allotment—and I've missed two days in a row now. You can stay here and work on the diagram. Yancy'll keep you company."

He smiled at her mention of the dog. It was obvious she still wasn't completely comfortable with his presence and considered it best to leave him at least somewhat supervised when she wasn't around. That realization led him back to his original line of thought.

"You didn't answer my question," he observed. "Do you want to explore the Liberty Tree?"

She responded with a question of her own. "You're pretty trusting, aren't you? Isn't that the key to the Sons? You sure you want me poking around?"

"I'm offering you more than the opportunity to poke around," he replied solemnly, "I'm asking if you want to join."

"Are you the Sons' recruitment officer as well as their head techno-spy?"

Her portrayal of him as a spy made Quinn smile. "Not necessarily; although we had been hopeful your grandfather might join us."

"And since he's dead I'm his proxy, right?"

"Not at all," he assured her. "You're your own person—no one in his right mind could ever doubt that! I just thought you might be interested after all you've learned."

"I guess I *am* curious," she admitted hesitantly.

Taking that as the go-ahead, Quinn reactivated the Liberty Tree portal.

Each leaf on the stylized tree that emerged in three-dimensional relief above Quinn's hand represented a ranking member of the Sons of Liberty, referring to themselves in generic form as 'Sons.' Valaria was amazed at how many there were; it was no surprise the Triumvirate was growing increasingly nervous regarding their potential impact—and equally determined to track them down. Remaining anonymous through the use of Revolutionary War pseudonyms, everyone from famous patriots like Patrick Henry and Paul Revere to less known heroes like the teenaged Sybil Ludington and the African slave James Armistead were represented. And when the leaves were accessed the tree seamlessly connected whoever needed to communicate. In spite of her scant knowledge of technology, Valaria realized that the firewall required to protect such a complex system must be extraordinary and found herself wondering what role Quinn might have played in its creation.

"So, am I allowed to know who *you* are?"

Gideon considered her question carefully.

"Sharing that is no small thing," he replied. "Even though it would be almost impossible for someone to access the Tree with that information alone, there's always a risk of the firewall being breeched; the government's undoubtedly drooling at the prospect and have their hackers actively hunting us 24/7."

"I understand," she said, accepting his refusal with a graciousness that surprised him. "Thanks for the introduction but I think I'll pass on signing up."

As Quinn restored the Liberty Tree to its dormant state, Valaria continued.

"So, is George Washington the Sons' head-honcho?"

Gideon blanched slightly. "Sam Adams is who you'd call the head-honcho. He's the guy who created the original Sons of Liberty so his name was claimed early on by whoever got our version going."

Valaria was struck by his use of the word 'whoever' in reference to Adams. "You don't know who he is?"

"Hardly anybody knows who he is—or *where* he is," Quinn explained. "Information like that is divulged strictly on a need-to-know basis."

He smiled and shrugged. "And I'm not high enough up the tree to need to know."

Valaria was about to challenge his claim that he wasn't very important when they were interrupted by someone pounding on the windows over the sink.

"*Shit*," she sputtered, her voice instantly dropping to a hoarse whisper. "You better head for the bedroom—might want to get in the hiding place; the chessboard's already there. I'll take care of this."

Without comment, Quinn did as she suggested.

When he had left the room, Valaria opened the windows—with a suitable expletive for the intruder—only to find Mavis Pope standing a few feet back from the dome waving at her.

"Geez, Mavis, what the hell are you doing here? And why are you pounding on my windows so frickin' early?"

Mavis looked hurt. "I saw your lights on but couldn't get your attention out front. Thought you'd want to know the Guardians finally let us go."

Feeling appropriately ashamed of her insensitivity, Valaria took a mental step back.

"You're right. Of course I want to know," she replied contritely. "Meet me at the door; I'll let you in."

As she would during any visit, Mavis headed for Valaria's living quarters immediately upon entering the pub. This, however, was anything but an ordinary morning and, having once again locked the front door, Valaria followed in her wake trying to focus on her chatter while simultaneously struggling to come up with a way to get rid of her.

Mavis deposited her ample backside on the futon and waited for Valaria to join her.

"So, are you all right?" Valaria asked in genuine concern as she sat down across from her corpulent friend. "Did they hurt you?"

"To tell you the truth, I was scared shitless the whole time," Mavis admitted. "But other than not being allowed to sleep—and being bombarded by endless questions and insults—I think I got off pretty easy. There was a lot of yelling and intimidation but other than bruises, nothing that did any permanent damage."

"What about the others?"

"Chloe Jennings looked like she got pretty much the same treatment as me—some bruises and a lot of bullying. I'm afraid the bastards beat Schmidt and Rivera pretty bad."

When she showed no signs of continuing, Valaria stepped in. "What about Sam Gleason?"

Mavis paused and licked her lips, weighing her next words carefully. "I don't think he'll be coming back."

"Are you telling me he's *dead?*"

Mavis shrugged noncommittally. "Wasn't on the truck."

"God, this is a nightmare," Valaria muttered. "Why are they doing this? What do they want? We've never given them any trouble."

"They kept asking the same questions over and over—who's speaking out against the government; is anybody acting different lately; have there been any strangers around? I don't think they were just fishing, either. I think they're expecting trouble."

Valaria nodded in agreement.

"*Have* any strangers come around lately?" Mavis asked pointedly. "I figure if anybody knows the answer to that, you would."

Valaria paused just a beat; a beat that didn't go unnoticed.

"What is it, Valaria?" her friend asked eagerly.

"It's nothing. I haven't seen anybody I don't know."

"Are you sure?" she prodded. "If there've been any strangers around, we've got to get ahead of this as quick as possible. My god, Valaria, these bastards are serious! They weren't rousting us just for the hell of it—*they're looking for somebody!*"

The urgency coloring Mavis's words was understandable—after all *she* had been detained, Valaria hadn't. Nonetheless, the forcefulness of her questions made it clear Mavis could never be trusted with knowledge of Gideon Quinn's presence—and in no way could she be told about the unbelievable discovery they had made.

Without warning, Mavis stood and headed for the dining table. "I'm famished," she said, shifting gears abruptly. "What's for breakfast?"

Valaria also rose but once again Mavis was a beat ahead of her—noticing Quinn's gloves lying on the table just a fleeting moment before Valaria could snatch them up.

Her voice more suspicious now than urgent, Mavis turned on Valaria.

"What're those?" she all but demanded.

While silently screaming '*shit*' at the top of her lungs, Valaria's brain scrambled for a response.

"These?" she asked, picking up the gloves and playing for time. "They're nothing. They belonged to Otis. Found them this morning while cleaning out a drawer; made me feel kinda sentimental so I thought I might wear them."

As lies go, not bad, she assured herself.

"You've been cleaning out drawers already this morning," Mavis pressed with blatant skepticism.

"Couldn't sleep; do some of my best cleaning in the throes of insomnia," Valaria lied glibly. "Anyway," she added, going on offense. "Why should you give a damn about when I clean out a drawer?"

Mavis's face reddened.

"You're right, of course," she said quickly. "Guess I'm just hyper-sensitive right now after all I've been through."

Valaria couldn't stop an uncharitable thought. "*Yeah, right 'after all you've been through'—at least you came back.*

III.

Gideon Quinn once again sat at the dining table, this time making sure he had possession of the gloves that had almost betrayed him to Mavis.

"I don't trust that woman," he stated flatly.

Taking Valaria's advice only to the point of retreating into her bedroom when Mavis Pope appeared on the scene that morning, Quinn had stayed by the door listening intently to the conversation taking place not more than ten feet away from him.

Just returned from her shift at the farm—the excuse she had used to finally send Mavis on her way—it was now Valaria's turn to lurk behind that same door as they talked, quickly changing into clean jeans and a sweatshirt that didn't smell like manure.

"She's harmless," Valaria assured him. "A pain in the ass and a bit of a snoop, but just another outcast like the rest of us."

"She sure asked a lot of questions."

"You think she's a government plant," Valaria scoffed, joining him at the table. "Since when is obesity a Guardian prerequisite?"

"Be one helluva disguise," he observed, warming to the idea. "Take on the role of something they despise. Haven't you ever heard of hiding in plain sight?"

"She's just scared. Hell, we're *all* scared!"

"You going to tell her about this?" Gideon asked, indicating the chessboard sitting in front of them on the table.

"No. I haven't even decided if I'm going to tell Jasper and Pete so I'm damn-sure not going to bare my soul to somebody I hardly know. You heard our conversation this morning; I lied my ass off avoiding her questions. Just because I'm an exile doesn't mean I'm a moron."

"No, of course not. But when it comes right down to it, Valaria, it would be ideal if I could get out of here without *anyone* ever knowing what we found."

"Yeah, that might be best," she conceded glumly. "You do realize, don't you, that you've just robbed me of years of conversations for the pub. But then, you know what they say," she added with no small measure of satisfaction, "*'patriotism has its price.'*"

His easy laugh brought a smile to her face. "So, just what *have* we found? You've had all day to play with it."

"Well, there's no doubt about it being the blueprint to the Guardian Star. In addition to the basic floor plan, each color represents a different element of construction—plumbing, ventilation, electrical, you name it. But there seems to be one glaring omission and I've been trying to think all day where Otis might have hidden it."

"What's missing?"

"There's nothing here about the *elevator*. And you can't very well storm a SuperTall without an understanding of how people are transported up and down the thing."

"Makes sense," she agreed. "So, where'd Otis put it? I suppose he might have left something with Jasper."

"Actually, talking about your friend Mavis just now got me thinking."

"Mavis? What's she got to do with any of this?"

"Something's been niggling at my brain ever since I made that comment about a government spy hiding in plain sight. The chessboard was certainly in plain sight and I think it just hit me."

"OK, so enlighten me. What else is hiding right in front of us?"

Quinn was running his fingers along the ornate edge of the dining table.

"I'm trying to remember what you told me your grandfather said about this table. Didn't he always tell you it would save the world? His observation about chess being the key to everything definitely was intended to point you to the board so I'm thinking his comment about the table might be another clue and *this*..." he indicated the table with a flourish, "could be waiting to tell us the rest of the story."

Valaria was shaking her head. "He said the table could *support* the world, not save it."

"Pretty much the same thing," Quinn observed, leaning over to inspect the patterns carved into the flat surface of the gracefully curved leg closest to him. "These engravings look an awful lot like the kind of designs layered into the chessboard. There could be more data right here."

"Don't tell me you think there's another latent power source in there, just waiting for my DNA to bring it to life. What do you suggest I do this time? Spit on it? ...*Pee* on it?"

Having grown impervious to her sarcasm, Quinn continued. "No, this is different."

He squatted down and began carefully inspecting the three curved legs supporting the tabletop. The flat lengths of wood forming the table's pedestal were about five feet long and six inches across but only about two inches thick. Each curved up and in from opposing directions on the floor, touching one another in the center and then curving out again to form three horizontal supports upon which the tabletop rested. Otis's signature geometric embellishments ran down the long, flat, six-inch wide surface of each leg.

What gave the table it's graceful, elegant appearance now struck Quinn as another way the Luddite-version of Otis might have tried to preserve the knowledge of the disillusioned engineer.

"These are way too similar to the style of the engravings on the chessboard to just be a coincidence," he said hopefully.

Yancy had already joined Quinn under the table—getting a friendly scratch behind the ears for his trouble. Valaria decided to make it a trio.

"Unless they're intentionally similar so the chessboard wouldn't stand out as totally unique," she suggested. "'Window dressing' like the other game diagrams we found in the box."

"I suppose that's possible," he admitted.

He obviously didn't believe that to be the case, however, for as he spoke he also was reactivating his tech-tat and suddenly ran a small scanning beam down each leg while Valaria looked on in wonder.

"What're you doing?"

"If I can upload these images," he explained, moving from the floor to sit at the table once again, "maybe I can figure out if it's data or just designs."

Three long, narrow bars—the curved legs now extended and digitized—appeared on the virtual screen in front of him as Valaria sat down on an adjacent chair and Yancy curled contentedly at her feet.

"Good luck with that," she said skeptically, glancing at the clock. "I suppose I better go open the pub. There haven't been many people around lately, but they might start coming back now that the hostages have been released. Don't want anyone else to come pounding on the windows."

"Good idea," Quinn agreed. "I'll keep working."

He paused for a moment as if considering his next step but, instead of continuing to study the screen, reached into a pocket and pulled out a small conical object.

"Here," he said, handing it to Valaria. "You should take this. It's a communicator. The range isn't great but it should let you warn me if any unwanted guests stop in for a drink. Just put it in your ear."

"How do I use it?"

"Squeeze it gently before putting it in, that'll turn it on. After that, just talk naturally if you need to tell me something."

"Well, call me James Bond and I'll call you Q," Valaria said lightly.

"James *who*?"

"Never mind," she replied with a smirk, tucking the communicator into her ear, "just my way of saying this is pretty damn cool."

IV.

Valaria was correct in her belief that, with the return of the hostages, things were likely to start getting back to normal. For the first time since the raid most of the pub's regulars began filtering in shortly after she unlocked the door and turned on the sign.

As usual, first on the scene were Jasper and Pete, the former of which sang out a cheerfully innocuous greeting as the two strolled in and headed for their regular table adjacent the bar.

"Evenin' bar-keep."

Pete punctuated his partner's salutation with a mock salute as the men settled in for their nightly game of chess.

Without missing a beat, Valaria grabbed two large glasses, pulled the tap, and delivered the first round.

"It's good to see you guys," she said earnestly.

"Good to be seen," Jasper replied with a wink.

"It's good to see things getting back to normal, *that's* what's good," Pete added.

"*Is* everything back to normal?" Jasper asked pointedly.

There was no mistaking his meaning. He wanted to know if Gideon Quinn was still around—and Quinn had made it clear that, as far as he was concerned, the best course of action was to let those aware of his presence believe he had just disappeared into the upheaval left behind by the Guardian raid.

For the first time in her life, Valaria lied to her grandfather's best friend.

"Yup, everything's hunky-dory," she said simply and strode back to the bar. The look of utter relief that washed over the two old men's faces made her realize how much she wanted to protect them and went a long way toward easing her feelings of guilt about lying to them.

Jasper and Pete weren't the only ones looking to the pub for evidence of normalcy. It didn't take long for the dome once again to come alive with the rumble and hum of conversation, the periodic outburst of dismay or triumph from the gamers clustered around the vids, and the occasional group greeting shouted from the door by the latest arrival.

And they were right; it was all comfortably normal and routine.

But as Valaria stood behind the bar, vacantly wiping the surface while watching her neighbors, she was struck by the abject incongruity of it all. Everyone seemed tragically eager for things to be as they were before the raid. Even when Carlos Rivera came on the scene—still bruised and limping from his interrogations at the hands of the Guardians—other than greeting him warmly it was as if no one even noticed. No one was willing to burst the bubble of the fragile illusion that everything was OK.

Valaria silently shook her head at the vacuous montage being played out in front of her, a scene more bitterly surreal than the dreams that had plagued her the night before because it was actually happening. As far as she was concerned, it didn't matter how much ale they drank, how many vids they played, or how assiduously they avoided the reality of their situation, nothing was ever going to be the same. Life had been precarious enough prior to the raid; they now knew the stark reality of living on the razor's edge—whether they wanted to admit it or not. And even as she was filled with genuine empathy for these people she had called neighbor as long as she could remember—these people who so desperately wanted nothing more than to be left alone—Valaria found empathy being supplanted by indignation that they would actually be willing to settle for nothing more than an illusion; so willing, in fact, that they unwittingly were playing right into the Triumvirate's hands.

Quinn was right; it was time to stand up.

"Are you there, Gideon?" she asked quietly, trying to move her lips as little as possible.

The response in her ear was so clear, for a moment she thought he must have joined her at the bar. "*Is everything all right?*"

"Yeah, everything's fine... if you like watching a bunch of automatons going through the motions of being alive, that is."

"*What?*"

"God, Quinn, you should see these people," she hissed. "They're acting as if nothing's happened."

"*Understandable. They probably don't feel they've got much choice.*"

"You're a helluva lot more charitable than I'm feeling right now."

He started to say something, but a distinct crackle of interference made his words unintelligible.

"What'd you say?" she asked, smiling insipidly at Jasper who was glancing her way with a mildly perplexed look on his face. "You're breaking up."

"You're breaking up, too," Gideon responded. *"Something's interfering with the signal."*

As Valaria paused in hopes the interference would pass, its cause was suddenly all too obvious as a small cohort of off-duty Guardians noisily entered the pub, the wireless electronics that were a ubiquitous part of their gear undoubtedly the source of the competing signal that was wreaking havoc on Valaria and Quinn's short range connection.

"Oh shit," she said, enunciating as clearly as she could while keeping her lips as still as possible. "We've got company."

"Guardians?"

"Yup."

The illusion of normalcy Valaria silently decried quickly began to erode in the presence of the government's black-clad enforcers. Signaling Valaria for a round of drinks, the five men strode boldly over to the vids, laughing loudly and slapping the current players on the backs as if they were all old friends. The reality of the situation was as clear as their intentions, however, as the residents who had been enjoying the distraction of the games quickly dispersed and the Guardians took over.

The bubble had burst and within moments the pub was almost empty.

"Want us to stay?" Jasper asked when Valaria began wiping down the recently vacated tables near them.

"Naw," she replied earnestly. "If you guys want to head out don't worry about it. I totally understand."

She gestured toward the group of men laughing overly-loud as they played the vids. "These guys are no problem. Anyway, last call is only an hour or so away. I can handle things 'til then."

If Pete hadn't looked so frightened, Jasper probably would have insisted on staying. But his partner had aged considerably in the past week—looking and acting far more elderly than before—and Jasper wanted to see him safely home.

With an apologetic smile and a final wave from the door, the two men left Valaria alone with the Guardians.

"How's it going?" Gideon's voice crackled in her ear again.

"Everybody's gone except our friends."

"I'm only a few steps away if you need help," he reminded her.

"I'm fine," she assured him.

"Hey babe," Roger Trineer, one of the few Guardians she knew by name, called out. "How about another round?"

"You got it," she replied.

Trineer ran his hungry eyes over Valaria as she worked behind the bar, consuming her almost as rapaciously as he did the apple ale he swigged. Avoiding eye contact, she turned away in an effort to deflect the unwelcome suggestions that always accompanied his leering.

"Let Yancy out, will you," she murmured under her breath to Quinn. "I don't think these guys are gonna give me any trouble, but if he's around they're less likely to mess with me."

Quinn didn't respond but a moment later the dog was assuming an instinctively protective stance at her side.

She smiled down at her canine bouncer. "Hey, Yance. Howya doin' bud?"

"What about those drinks," another Guardian barked angrily.

She bit back a retort and saluted smartly. "Comin' up."

They immediately refocused on the game and she was struck by the thought that, individually, these men were as insignificant as everyone else on the planet. But arm them, put them in a group, and dress them in ominous black uniforms, and somehow they transmogrified into an effectively menacing force that found it frighteningly easy to bully and intimidate people who otherwise were just like them.

Adrift in her musing, Valaria took fresh glasses down from the shelf behind her.

"Why is it the bad guy's minions always wear black?" she asked Quinn quietly. "I mean, why black? Why not stripes? Or polka dots?"

"*Polka dots*," he repeated incredulously.

"Yeah, polka dots; now *that* would add a splash of drama."

She threw a derisive glance toward the Guardians while pulling the tap to dispense their ale.

"Geez, they're so lame they don't even realize they're a laughable cliché!"

"*They may be a cliché, but they sure as hell aren't laughable.*"

"No," she conceded. "I suppose this whole situation is too damn tragic to be laughable."

She tossed his disembodied voice a mordant smirk.

"But I still think polka dots would add a little panache.

"America stands armed with resolution and virtue; but she still recoils at the idea of drawing the sword against the nation from whence she derived her origin. Yet Britain, like an unnatural parent, is ready to plunge her dagger into the bosom of her affectionate offspring."

~ Mercy Otis Warren

CHAPTER EIGHT

I.

As often happened when Guardians were in the pub, Valaria's announcement of last call was received as a suggestion rather than a mandate since the settlement's curfew didn't apply to them. Had anyone else still been around—other than the dissident sitting a few yards away at her dining table—she might have been more inclined to force the issue. But since their after-hours presence wasn't out of the ordinary, and because ordinary was a commodity in exceedingly short supply at the moment—and because there *was* a dissident sitting in her quarters!—she decided it probably was best not to rock the boat by insisting that they leave. As a result, it was almost two in the morning before the five men finally pulled themselves away from the vids, threw a few suggestive comments Valaria's way as she closed out accounts for the night, and headed up the entry steps laughing uproariously at the brilliance of their lewd suggestions.

Valaria gave the more-than-slightly inebriated quintet a few minutes head start before following them to the surface to make sure they weren't hanging around. She watched in relief as the dim taillights of their small transport vehicle disappeared down the main street, bidding them a grateful farewell with her classic one-finger salute. Yancy also seemed relieved to see them go, looking up at her for permission before trotting off into the dark to complete his own final transaction of the evening.

Valaria leaned against the curve of the dome, savoring the stillness for a moment before sliding down to a comfortable squat at its base, pulling out a cigarette and inhaling her own form of release as she waited for the dog to return.

When the duo entered Valaria's living quarters half an hour later, Quinn looked up from the dining table where he was still working. "Everything OK?"

"Yup, looks like everybody but us is all tucked in for the night."

Almost undone by fatigue, Valaria wondered if he had moved at all since she left to open the pub. When he stood and stretched everything from his neck to his fingers, putting a fist in the small of his back and cracking it loudly, she had her answer.

"Any progress?" she asked.

"Some, but I think I've reached the point of diminishing returns and should call it a day. I might tinker a bit more before bedding down, but in all honesty a fresh start in the morning sounds really good right now."

"So you're saying the table actually does hold more data?"

"Oh, no question about it," he said confidently, beginning to go through the steps to return his tech to dormancy. "There's definitely more to the puzzle here. I just can't quite get the pieces to fit together."

Valaria exhaled sharply and collapsed into one of the living room chairs. "Bloody hell, I feel like I grew up with a total stranger. Why didn't Otis ever tell me any of this crap?"

"I'm sure he intended to," Quinn replied. "Like I said before, I think he just waited too long. He was a strong, healthy guy; who'd ever dream he'd be killed by Freebooters? If that's who actually killed him."

"What the hell does that mean?" Valaria demanded.

"Well, think about it, Valaria. It's like I said before—Freebooters

Valaria wasn't at all convinced Otis had planned to tell her about his former life but was too tired to argue the point. And after spending the evening slogging her way through a churning morass of conflicting emotions caused by neighbors who showed all the backbone of an Omega wolf going belly-up in hopes of not being disemboweled by the Alpha, thinking about Otis's death was just one dagger too many in her heart that night.

Relieved when Gideon headed for the door, Valaria silently followed.

While he waited in the gloom at the bottom of the stairs, she went to the surface in order to be sure the area outside the dome was clear.

"I've been thinking," she began after gesturing Quinn to join her in the moonlight. "You might as well break camp in the morning and bring your stuff back here. There's no point going back and forth every day; somebody's bound to see you if it goes on much longer."

Quinn looked at her somewhat quizzically.

"I appreciate the offer, but are you sure?"

"Yeah, I'm sure. Like I said, the longer you go back and forth, the more likely somebody's gonna see you—and obviously you're not going to be leaving any time soon."

She gave him a frank stare.

"It's not as if I'm inviting you into my bed," she said pointedly.

He shot her a sleepy version of a fairly rakish grin.

"Down, boy; don't make me sorry already."

She pulled out a cigarette and lit up, squinting at him through the smoky exhaust.

"And wouldn't *that* be a match made in heaven," she continued sardonically. "Geez Quinn, I've probably got about ten years on you. You're what; all of twenty-five?"

"Twenty-eight."

"OK, twenty-eight—so you know about where that puts me. Granted, living in the Borders does shit for your sex life, but I'm not so desperate that I'm gonna hook up with somebody who's better cast as my little brother than my lover."

She took another long drag on the cigarette. "And, anyway, that's not what this is about. You need to finish your work, right?"

"Right."

"Well, the best way to accomplish that is to stay here and just do it ...*work*, that is."

A little surprised by her discomfort, he couldn't resist the temptation to add to it a bit. "I don't know, Valaria; you're kinda cute when you're flustered."

She shot him a fatal glare.

"I'm not flustered and I'm sure-as-hell not *cute*," she sputtered, spitting the adjective out in disgust.

"Regardless of the fact that if looks could kill you'd be a mass murderer," he informed her, "whether or not you admit it, you *are* cute. In fact, you're damn close to pretty—when you're not being a sarcastic bitch, that is."

More comfortable being described as a mass-murdering bitch than she ever would be with being called cute, Valaria let the comment pass with nothing more than a strong exhalation of cigarette smoke in his direction.

"But you're right, that's not what this is about," he continued, waving the smoke away, "and sex is a complication I frankly can do without right now. So—in spite of the fact that I think the difference in our ages is meaningless—I accept your invitation and promise to stay on the futon."

In response to her satisfied smirk, he launched a final incendiary as he turned to leave.

"Even if you come begging."

II.

Quinn returned to the pub the next morning just as the sun smeared the eastern sky with bold swaths of pink and lavender. Shouldering his rucksack, the predawn greeting he gave Valaria exuded a level of enthusiasm she only tolerated from Yancy because she could throw him outside to revel in the glories of morning without her.

Dog and man passed one another as Quinn entered the dome, leaving the enthusiasm quotient unchanged.

"Dial it down," Valaria insisted, just this side of comatose. "What've you got to be so excited about this early in the morning, anyway? All I can think about is going back to bed."

"No going back to bed today, my friend. We are going to celebrate!"

"Celebrate what?" she demanded morosely as she collapsed onto a dining chair, elbows on the table, hands clutching her head. "God, I feel like I've got the world's worst hangover and I didn't even do any drinking last night."

"Well then, I've got just what you need."

Enthusiasm undaunted, Quinn pulled several small packages out of his rucksack before tossing it onto the futon and heading for the kitchenette.

"The last of the coffee," he said, waggling one of the bags her way. "As well as a couple treats I've been saving."

Valaria was slowly beginning to emerge from the symptomatic grogginess typical of her chronic 'Loathing-of-Morning-Syndrome' but remained slumped at the table.

"Since we're celebrating, I take it you've got good news," she mumbled into the hands still clutching her head.

He placed a steaming cup of coffee in front of his skeptical host. "I do indeed."

Returning to the kitchen, Quinn activated internal heating elements in the slender plate-shaped metallic packets he had unearthed from his rucksack along with the coffee.

"I figured it out," he said with no small measure of satisfaction.

In a moment he resumed his now-customary spot at the table and handed Valaria a container that quickly began smelling suspiciously like buttermilk pancakes.

"This is your version of '*living rough*'?" she asked with no small measure of incredulity as she savored the aroma. "You've obviously never watched *Survivor*."

Ignoring what he assumed was another archaic cultural reference, Quinn launched into an explanation of the programming wizardry he had managed to perform but, more interested in the steaming plate of buttery maple goodness now sitting in front of her, Valaria immediately waved a fork in protest.

"Spare me the technical shit."

"Sorry," he replied. "Bottom line—Otis didn't just leave you basic plans for the Guardian Star, he left the elevator as well." He smiled slightly. "When I finally was able to manipulate the digitized table legs they combined to give me another pretty damn clear schematic. Beautiful," he added, patting the dining table in affectionate admiration. "Brilliant."

He glanced around the room with something close to wonder. "It was all right here. Right in plain sight where anybody could've seen it."

"Not just anybody," Valaria countered, her mouth full of pancakes. "I've been looking at it most of my life and never saw anything but my grandfather's carpentry." She swallowed and pointed her fork at him. "He'd be proud of you, Quinn. Proud to know you."

"Thanks," he said with grateful humility. "And on that very positive note, allow me to make an official presentation."

Reaching into a back pocket, Gideon extracted a small crumpled envelope and handed it to Valaria. He had used one of his shoelaces to add a festive—if rather frayed--bow.

"I'll need that back when you're done," he noted, directing her attention to the loose boot on his right foot.

She accepted the envelope gingerly, more than half expecting some crude male-bonding practical joke to come leaping out at her.

Inside was a narrow length of neatly hemmed polka dot fabric.

Recalling her polka-dotted-minion comment from the previous evening, a slow smile began to spread across Valaria's face.

"On behalf of the Sons of Liberty," Gideon intoned solemnly, "I hereby award you the rank of Official Minion."

"Where the hell did you find this?" she asked, wrapping it around her left wrist several times and using her free hand and front teeth to tie it off in a knot. "And where the hell did you learn to sew?"

"Just one of my many talents. You inspired me last night so I did a little foraging before going back to camp... You might not want to wear that around your friend Mavis—I tore it off one of those patchwork tent-things she left on her clothesline."

Valaria erupted into laughter, nearly choking on a bite of pancake. "She *wears* those 'tent-things' you moron!"

"Oops," he replied with mock consternation, smiling broadly.

They had shared other meals during the time Quinn had been working in stealth mode among the residents of Settlement #4 but this was the first one that could be called companionable. Valaria had come to a point where she no longer saw Quinn as a delusional troublemaker who was more likely to rain destruction down on their heads than accomplish any of his high-minded goals, sticking his nose prominently into her personal business along the way. In the short time they had known each other she had come to respect the man—status she didn't confer lightly. She also had grown increasingly interested in what he said about what the country *should* be compared to what it *was*. For his part, Gideon Quinn was more convinced than ever that his cause not only was just, it also now was more attainable than ever—and that people like Valaria Thorpe were crucial to its success.

When she left him midmorning for her shift at the farm, Valaria took with her a mind alive with challenging—disconcerting—possibilities, and left behind her a man pondering basically the same things.

In addition to being something of a magician when it came to brewing spirits, over the years Valaria also had become a reasonably expert horticulturalist. Assigned to one of the two domes devoted to crops, she was particularly successful caring for the squash, cucumbers, and tomatoes planted in rot-resistant nets suspended from poles several feet off the ground and the kale, spinach, and broccoli grown in vertical walls behind them. As time honed her skills, Valaria had discovered a strong sense of satisfaction in literally seeing the fruit of one's labor at harvest time and in making a contribution to the life of the settlement beyond enabling their inebriation. She also genuinely enjoyed working the soil—not to mention the fact that the smell of rich loam was much to be preferred over the cloying odor that seemed to permeate every pore of those assigned to the fish dome.

As was true of their homes, all three of the farm's environmentally controlled habitats were quickly passing from showing their age to shabby. Occasional incursions by Freebooters and the normal wear and tear associated with the passage of time had created a need for repairs that were increasingly beyond the exiles' abilities and resources. They managed to keep farm operations limping along, however, and thus far had always been able to meet their quota for the exchange of goods the government's Symbiosis program was supposed to facilitate—in their case, food in exchange for manufactured products. In spite of their success, however, they lived under a pervasive shadow, always afraid of failing to provide their mandated share. Symbiosis might lag on the government's end without comment or consequence but the system brooked no shortfall from the outcasts and any delay brought quick penalties—penalties that could be disastrous since the goods being exchanged definitely were *needs* rather than *wants*.

Because of that constant ominous shadow, Valaria grew increasingly apprehensive as she approached the farm for most of the work crew stood outside, clustered around the far end of one of the domes.

"What's going on," she called out.

One of the women shouted a response while waving Valaria toward them. "Freebooters broke in last night!"

Muttering a litany of expletives, Valaria trotted over to them, anticipating the worst.

Several of the dome's octagonal Plastipane panels just above the concrete foundation had been broken so to allow the thieves entrance. A few had sustained repairable damage—leaving thick milky-white pieces large enough to be glued back together—but others had been shattered.

These were the focus of the small knot of workers surveying the wreckage.

"I don't understand why they broke in," one of the men was saying from where he knelt, picking up jagged shards of Plastipane. "The next harvest is weeks away yet."

"You give them too much credit," another chimed in. "It's been a long time since they bothered us. They probably have no idea the next harvest won't be ready until October."

"Or maybe it's just plain vandalism," Valaria suggested.

"Vandalism?" asked the woman who had called her over. "Why vandalize us? They need the food as much as we do."

"Doesn't matter why they did it," the first man interjected. "We've gotta figure out a way to fix it."

They had almost finished cleaning up the debris and had formulated a rudimentary plan for replacing the panels that couldn't be fixed when someone noticed another small group approaching the dome.

Like deer turned to stone by an unfamiliar sound, the workers virtually froze where they stood as a squad of Guardians drew closer.

"What's going on here?" the lead officer demanded loudly.

Valaria threw her a look of contemptuous disdain. "What does it look like? We're working on this dome."

The officer directed an intense glare Valaria's way but didn't seem inclined to issue an official warning for her insolence.

"We can see that," she sneered. "What happened?"

"Someone broke in last night," one of the men offered, his eyes imploring Valaria to back down.

"Freebooters…" a mousy woman chimed in, edging away.

Valaria stared at the two. Was that the best they could manage? When it came to fight or flight, she wondered angrily, was it always going to be flight as far as their interactions with Guardians were concerned?

The lead officer backed away from the dome in order to better assess the extent of the damage.

"Freebooters," she repeated solemnly. "Well, if that's the case, you should find the notification we've been dispatched to bring you very reassuring."

She extended a gloved hand to the junior officer behind her who immediately removed a data tablet from the satchel he shouldered and gave it to his superior.

"You will share this information with your fellow residents," she began as she brought the tablet to life and started to read.

"By order of Colonel Seth Mertens, Commanding Officer, Guardian Star. Item #1: It is hereby ordered that a squad of Guardians of the Reorganized States of America be garrisoned among the residents of Settlement #4 forthwith. Item #2: One residential dome of said Settlement shall be vacated in order to facilitate the garrisoning of said squad. Item #3: Said residents of Settlement #4 shall provide all supplies necessary to facilitate the garrisoning of said squad. Item #4: Said quartering shall continue until such time as this Order is officially rescinded. Item #5: Non-

compliance with this Order shall result in arrest and detention of
any resident found to be in violation of its mandates."

When she had finished reading, the officer surveyed the group of workers with her chin slightly elevated and a *"Go ahead—I dare you"* look of superiority on her face.

"You've got to be kidding," one of the younger men blurted out.

"What have we done to deserve this?" another demanded.

"You would do well to receive this Order *graciously*," the lead Guardian cautioned, distinctly pronouncing each syllable of the last word and clearly savoring the absurdity of her suggestion. She looked around the small group as if evaluating an infestation of vermin, knowing full well the implication of her next words. "As you just told me, your community has been victimized by Freebooters—what better way to discourage such activity than by having Guardians present among you?"

Pinning each resident with a glare she continued, her voice dripping with false sincerity.

"And we Guardians will be here to protect you... as long as there's a threat of strangers endangering your community."

III.

The *Shoe and Gear* was filled almost to capacity as virtually every resident gathered to discuss the newest Guardian edict. Since personal electronics were nonexistent in the Borders, their overlords had transmitted the edict to the pub's entertainment screen and the conversation grew increasingly heated as more and more people familiarized themselves with the mandate's details.

"Quiet down everyone, please," Jasper Hahn called out, trying to make himself heard over the noise. He and the other members of the Settlement Council had been tasked with leading the impromptu town meeting but thus far had had little success in keeping things orderly. This time, someone at the back of the pub punctuated Jasper's request with an ear-piercing whistle which seemed to do the trick.

"Thank you," Jasper said, acknowledging both the whistler and the quieting crowd. "I know we're all upset about this latest action on the part of the Guardians, but we really need to discuss it calmly if we're going to make any progress."

"I don't see what there is to discuss," one of the men said loudly. "There's no appeal process so there's nothing we can do about it."

"Oh, there's something we can do," another countered boldly. "We can tell them to stay the hell out of town!"

Valaria was pleased to hear a murmur of agreement run through the crowd, finding comfort in the fact that at least some of her neighbors were more outraged than cowed.

"What good would that do?" a woman off to the side interjected. "We don't have any weapons so not only are we out-numbered, we're hopelessly out-gunned. How can you say no when you can't back it up with anything?"

"I'm afraid the Council agrees," Jasper said. "We recommend trying to figure out how best to fulfill the mandates of the Order while still preserving our way of life as much as possible. There doesn't seem much point in doing anything else."

"Well, before we roll over and give them one of our homes," a voice near the door called out. "I'd like to know why they're doing this. Obviously they're cracking down, but why an occupation? What have we done to deserve this?"

Mavis Pope stood and gestured that she wanted to speak.

"I think I can help there," she began. "Those of us who were taken into custody after the raid were questioned over and over again about whether any strangers have been around lately. I think they're looking for somebody."

Several residents who had been in the pub the night Gideon Quinn first arrived on the scene looked directly at Valaria and she felt her face reddening. Pete, who was sitting next to her, scooted his chair away a bit as if suddenly needing to distance himself from a contagion.

"They also asked about residents speaking out against the government," interjected Carlos Rivera. "So, they may be looking for somebody but they also just want to keep a lid on things in general."

Mary and Hector Johnson, who had spoken with Quinn that first night, made eye contact with Valaria, waiting for her to speak up.

When she didn't, Mary raised her hand.

"Well, there *was* a stranger in town," she informed the group. "He came into the pub a week or so ago looking for Otis Thorpe."

Valaria made eye contact with Mavis Pope who, recalling that Valaria had told her she had seen no strangers, shot an accusatory glare her way.

Valaria shrugged it off, thinking the other woman looked angrier than she had a right to be.

In a moment, the entire assembly was focused on Valaria.

"That was nothing," she assured them. "Just some guy looking for Otis. When he found out Otis had died, he left. End of story."

Hector, who had been particularly unnerved by Quinn, wasn't satisfied with Valaria's dismissive explanation.

"That's not exactly the end of the story," he said loudly. "The man said he was with the Sons of Liberty, for God's sake."

"The guy was a delusional asshole," Valaria said to the now silent room. "He also said the Thorpe he was looking for had a grand*son* and worked for the government. Does that sound remotely like the Otis Thorpe you all knew? Can't you just imagine an angry old carpenter in league with the Triumvirate?"

"Of course not," Jasper interrupted, coming to her rescue. "The whole thing was preposterous. And anyway, he's no threat to us; he's long gone."

There was a surge of conversation around the pub as those who hadn't known about Gideon Quinn digested this latest information.

"You should have reported him to the Guardians," Mavis called out angrily. "You could have spared us all a lot of grief if you had."

"Just what grief would it have spared us?" Valaria demanded. "You think the raid wouldn't have happened if they'd known someone from the Sons of Liberty had passed through the settlement? That would've brought them crashing down on us even harder than they did. You think knowing about him would have prevented this latest move? Hell, they'd've moved in the next day! Get a clue, we can't win one way or another with these bastards—they've got all the power."

"Which brings us right back where we started," Jasper interjected firmly, resuming control of the meeting. "We need to face facts. The Guardians are coming and we have to make a decision about how we're going to accommodate them."

IV.

"Delusional asshole, huh?"

Gideon Quinn was waiting for Valaria in her darkened living quarters, speaking from the shadows before the automated lighting could respond to her entrance and illuminate the scene.

"Thanks a lot."

"Well, what would you have had me tell them? That you've been here more than a week discovering all sorts of secrets about my grandfather? Yeah, that would've been really helpful."

"I guess I'm just struck by how far we've come," he observed. "There was a time when that's exactly how you saw me."

Valaria collapsed into the comfortable chair adjacent the futon Quinn and Yancy currently occupied.

"There was a time," she remarked sardonically, "when I was nanoseconds away from turning you into the Guardians just like Mavis insisted I should have done."

"Yeah, isn't she a pip?"

"She reflects the opinion of a lot of people. They've had it rough and don't want to rock the boat. Everybody bitches about the government but not very many are up to actually doing anything. Frankly, I'm impressed by the growing number of people who seem willing to even *consider* shaking things up a bit."

"They're the ones we're counting on."

"Well, there's also a lot of them you can count on to turn you in if they find out you're still here."

He leaned forward before responding. "That's exactly why I'm leaving."

"You're what?"

"I'm leaving—tonight. You think things are tense now? Once the Guardians move in, it's going to get worse; much worse. I've seen it before. A full-blown occupation messes with people's heads. Everybody gets so damn paranoid they stop thinking rationally and start looking out for themselves without any concern for their neighbors. And as fear ratchets up, one of two things happens—people either spend every waking hour just trying not to be noticed or they end up trying to ensure their own safety by turning their paranoia outward and looking for bogeymen among the people around them. Before you know it, everybody's rushing to denounce their neighbor before they have a chance to do it to them. It's ugly—and it's probably unavoidable when people live in fear 24/7. And it's exactly the way things are done in the Safe Zones. One wrong word, one wrong look and your life's not worth shit."

Valaria started to speak but he held up a hand to stop her.

"It's why I came here in the first place. It's what we're determined to change. I'm sorry things are going from bad to worse for your settlement; you're good people... And that's exactly why I'm leaving. I'm not going to put you or Jasper or anybody else in further jeopardy—and I sure as hell can't take the chance of getting caught, especially now that I've found your grandfather's schematics."

When Valaria had joined the duet lurking in her quarters, Yancy had deserted Quinn to come and curl contentedly at her feet. She reached down and began stroking his velvety fur as she replied. "You don't need to convince me; I totally agree. It's time for you to go."

Quinn nodded at her agreement—appreciating the fact that it was delivered without some kind of sarcastic punctuation.

"You found what you came for," she was saying. "And if things are ever going to change it's probably up to people like the Sons of Liberty to make it happen. So, bottom line, yeah, Marshall Dillon, it's time for you to get the hell out of Dodge."

Although he had no idea who 'Marshall Dillon' might be, Quinn caught the meaning behind her words and smiled. "You're right, I've got what I came for—thanks to Otis—and it's definitely time to go. You do realize he's a true hero, don't you? He's just as important to what lies ahead as any name on our Liberty Tree was to the first Revolution."

He glanced around the room before continuing. "God only knows what else he may have left behind for you to find, Valaria. Too bad I can't hang around to help you look."

"I won't be doing any more looking."

"Aren't you the least bit curious about what else may still be hidden?"

"Oh, I'm curious all right," she replied. "But I won't be doing any more looking because I'm not going to be here either. I'm coming with you."

Gideon stopped short. "Oh, no you're not."

"Oh, yes I am."

"No you're—" Quinn broke the childish cycle Valaria undoubtedly would have continued and gave her his best adult face. "Let's not play games," he said flatly. "You can't come with me. It's too dangerous."

"And you think staying here *isn't*? You should've seen the way everybody looked at me after what Mary and Hector said tonight in the pub. It was like I was a stranger. You say they're gonna start denouncing each other? Well, who do you think is gonna be at the top of their list?

143

Hell, if her fat ass could handle the trip, Mavis Pope would probably be half way to the Star by now!"

Quinn ran a hand through his shaggy hair as he considered her words.

"You know I'm right," she insisted. "And anyway, the data you've stored in your tat technically belongs to me and I'm feeling pretty damn proprietary about it right now."

He sat there silently appraising her while she continued her campaign. "Be honest. If you believe Otis decided to hide his data so it could be used against the Guardian Star, don't you think he also thought the day might come when I would need to leave the settlement? You're the one who said he's the only person who could've deactivated my tag. Looks like he's given me his blessing, huh?"

"You really think he would've wanted you to do this?"

"Like he always told me when I tried to shirk my chores... 'If not you, who? If not now, when?'"

"All right," Gideon replied without much enthusiasm, "I guess you can come along. Can't see how I can stop you."

Valaria arched an eyebrow and gave him a challenging smirk at the mere mention of trying to stop her. "Damn straight."

"But what about the pub? You just gonna walk away?"

"Jasper and Pete can move in and run things while I'm gone," she explained. "You heard the outcome of the meeting, didn't you? They volunteered to give their dome to the Guardians; felt it would be easiest for two old men to move and figured they might even be allowed to stay and keep house. This way, they don't have to do that; they've got somewhere to go."

He couldn't deny it was a fairly decent idea. "What're you going to tell them?"

"I'll tell Jasper a version of the truth. He can tell the rest that I've run off with my black market lover." She smiled at the prospect. "Shit, they'll eat that up!"

Still working through his reluctant acquiescence to the idea of taking her along, Quinn gave Valaria's suggestion of a black market lover a skeptical smile. He wouldn't be at all surprised if she had one.

In addition to the smile, he gave her an hour to pack.

The owner of *The Shoe and Gear* spent most of that time writing a terse letter to Jasper in which she cryptically explained her decision to leave, focusing on her desire not to endanger the settlement further and leaving out any reference to the plans Quinn had discovered. Once satisfied with the brief missive, Valaria directed her attention to packing. Heading out to the shed, she retrieved the small two-wheeled cart and oversized backpack Otis had used when he went out looking for wood. After giving the pack a quick cleaning she stuffed it with extra clothing, a few personal care items, a rain poncho, and a thick jacket. She slid her grandfather's chess set, now securely wrapped in a towel, along with her grandmother's Bible and the crucifix, into a large exterior pocket covered by a heavy protective flap. They used the deep rectangular cart to store blankets, food and water, a few tools, the tattered tarp that had shaded the front of the shed—and as much toilet paper as Valaria could stuff in.

When they were ready Quinn looked at her with a raised eyebrow and tightlipped half-smile.

"You sure about this?"

She raised her left hand slightly so the polka dot cloth wrapped around the wrist was visible; indicating her minion status with a smirk of her own.

"Let's go," she said simply.

Shouldering her backpack, Valaria preceded him up the stairs and into the expansive unknown that lay beyond the settlement, Yancy trotting devotedly alongside.

"...It does not require a majority in order to prevail, but rather an irate, tireless minority keen to set brush fires in people's minds..."

~ Sam Adams

CHAPTER NINE

I.

"Just where are we going?" Valaria finally asked, glancing back over her shoulder as her moonlit world disappeared behind them.

In spite of her fiercely independent spirit—and prickly bravado—as a child of the Borders, Valaria Thorpe had led a sheltered life in many ways. The exiles may have been second class citizens at best, living under the tyrannical thumb of an autocratic regime, but they were freer in some ways than their counterparts in the heavily monitored Safe Zones and, because they supplied an essential workforce, were far more secure than the scattered remnant scraping out an existence in the Wilds; especially Settlement #4 due to its proximity to the Guardian Star. It was this veneer of sheltered naiveté that had Quinn silently chiding himself for agreeing to bring her along. He was more than mildly concerned about the edge of excitement that made her question sound like they were embarking on a great adventure.

"Why?" he asked. "Having second thoughts now that you discover there's no yellow brick road to show us the way?"

She glanced over at him in surprise.

"Yeah," he smirked, "you're not the only one who can throw around archaic cultural references."

"So, if I'm Dorothy," she replied, "and Yancy's obviously Toto, who does that make you? Not the Wizard— the Scarecrow?"

As she spoke, the cart she pulled behind her snagged an unseen root in the darkness and she found herself momentarily unnerved by a sudden loss of balance.

"Just as long as you're not the Tin Man," she mused, regaining her footing and giving the cart a determined tug, "cuz I didn't pack an oil can."

After leaving Valaria's dome on the western edge of the settlement they had set out in silence to the south. The oblong domes of the three farming habitats shimmered in moonlit relief on their left and once past them they had cut sharply east, giving the settlement itself a wide berth.

It hadn't taken long to reach the farthest edge of Valaria's familiar territory. Despite the fact that they weren't detainees like those in the country's re-education centers, restricted freedom of movement was one of life's realities for Borders inhabitants—easily enforced by the surveillance drones that watched from above and the subdermal tags that could be used to track them down should the need arise. Although banished to the hinterland for some sort of social/political transgression, each decade following The Revanche had found most exiles growing less restive and increasingly docile. Whether from a measure of gratitude for the marginal autonomy their outcast status conferred or simple resignation to their fate, fewer and fewer of society's discards tried to use their exile as a bridge to the ungoverned lands lying beyond I-35 and life became progressively more routine. Likewise resigned or grateful, Otis Thorpe had never ventured beyond the official five mile limit and, since he hadn't told Valaria about the neutralized status of her tag, neither had his strong-willed granddaughter. As a result, the reality of just walking away from the confines of her previous existence—and away from everyone and everything she had ever known and trusted—brought an unexpected exhilaration Valaria was finding difficult to hold in check.

She was to receive what could only be called a rude awakening.

II.

"You never answered my question," Valaria said irritably. "Where are we headed?"

Silence had fallen between them after their *Wizard of Oz* exchange for the uneven terrain of the trail they blazed through the dark required serious concentration in order to stay upright. But as the sun began brightening the eastern sky walking grew less hazardous and Valaria was simultaneously growing testy.

"We're heading for the 55th," Quinn replied. "You know what that is, don't you?"

"Of course; it's the Borders's eastern border."

Gideon smiled. "Interesting way to put it. I'd have said it's the country's *western* border, but—as an exile—I can understand how you'd see it the other way around. We're lucky, actually. Even though your settlement's closer to the 35th it's at one of the narrowest parts of the Borders buffer so we've got less than two hundred miles to travel. If we keep a steady pace, we should be there in about a week."

The idea of walking for a week put just the hint of a damper on Valaria's exhilaration. "You guys don't have any transports?"

Quinn pulled up sharply and tapped himself on the chest. "Uh, hello, *subversive* here, remember me?"

Valaria gave him a snarky glare.

"Time for a reality check," he continued, shaking his head in mild disbelief. "I've got close to two hundred miles to cover, I've gotta do it in about a week, and no, there aren't any Sons of Liberty bus stops along the way. This isn't going to be easy, Valaria. We've got a long way to go and need to keep a seriously-low profile. Hopefully we won't run into any problems—I didn't see any Freebooters on the way out—but we have to be alert and we have to be careful."

He shrugged his rucksack off his shoulder, eased it to the ground and eased himself into a squat next to it. Pulling out a nutrition bar and a pouch of water, he continued. "I'm not saying this to scare you but you really have no idea what's out here." He broke the nutrition bar and handed her half. "Guardian drones keep an eye on things and ground troops take out Freebooters when they can but the government really doesn't give a shit about any of the pathetic scavengers wandering around so they're not going to come to our rescue if we get into trouble. Hell, they're part of the trouble we're trying to avoid. So face it, we're on our own, we're going to be living rough... and it's just possible we won't make it at all."

Convinced he was exaggerating for her benefit, Valaria glowered at him around the nutrition bar she chewed.

"It's the truth," he said simply. "That's why I said you shouldn't come. The Borders settlements are a helluva lot safer than the Borders itself, especially one as close to the Guardian Star as yours is."

He paused, hoping she was taking his words seriously. "You can still turn back if you want to. There's no shame in deciding this isn't for you."

"Who said anything about turning back? I just think I have the right to know where we're going. And I'm not as naïve as you apparently think I am. Freebooters murdered my grandfather in case you've forgotten, and they raid us on a fairly regular basis."

"True enough; if it actually was Freebooters who killed him."

Valaria balked at his words. "What the hell does that mean?"

"Ever since you told me how you grandfather died, it's bugged me. Just doesn't sound like Freebooters—killing somebody and not taking everything they had with them? Sounds more like a bush-league mistake made by some government lackey."

Valaria laughed. "You're saying the *government* killed Otis?"

"That's just as believable as blaming it on Freebooters; more believable if you ask me."

"OK, I will ask you—why would the government murder Otis? Geez, you really are nuts."

"Come on, Valaria, just think about everything we've learned about your grandfather. The government undoubtedly realized the potential threat he posed as a possible resource for the resistance—and they were right since contacting him is exactly what we tried to do. So why not be proactive and silence him for good? And he's not the only one who's dead. All the people at Telliman who worked on the Star have died; some from natural causes, some not."

When Valaria didn't immediately shoot him down—finally understanding his "last man standing" reference to Otis the night they met—Quinn continued.

"Hell, if they get wind of what we're doing, they'll be on our trail just as doggedly as any Freebooter who picks up our scent. It's like I said, you really need to go into this with your eyes open."

Still pondering his theory, Valaria recovered enough to give him a snarky, wide-eyed stare in response to his imperative. Quinn shook his head and they fell silent as their impromptu break came to an end; both hefting their packs back onto their shoulders to resume their eastward journey.

"So, why the 55th?" Valaria asked at length. "Are we gonna cross over into the States?"

"No," he replied simply. "We're going to St. Louis."

"OK, so what's in St. Louis?"

"One of our bases; not exactly a stronghold yet, but getting there."

"St. Louis is on the Mississippi, right?

Quinn nodded.

"Awesome. I've always wanted to see it."

"It's an amazing sight I'll grant you that. They called it '*The Mighty Mississippi.*' St. Louis was eventually abandoned after the plague, but it must've been pretty impressive, too. With the RSA just across the river it's a strategic location and since Freebooters and scavengers picked the city clean years ago we've been able to move in without any competition.

We've been quietly reinforcing our base there for a long time. The problem now isn't people as much as the feral dogs that roam the streets. There's been a lot of inbreeding with coyotes and they've become seriously aggressive."

He looked at Yancy with genuine affection. "We'll need to keep an eye on this guy."

Silence fell between them again and it wasn't long before they came upon the remains of an asphalt roadway Quinn had used on his original journey. Since only a few select arteries in the 'reorganized' portion of the country had been targeted for maintenance in the years since The Revanche, deterioration of the rest of the nation's roads was extreme. The thread they followed of what must at one time have been a major east/west highway disappeared sporadically into a tangled jumble of trees and underbrush thrusting impertinently skyward through increasingly compromising fissures in the cracked and decaying blacktop. In spite of gaps and unexpected obstacles, it nonetheless provided a much better surface for walking—and intermittent vestiges of roadside signage gave a clear indication that they were headed in the right direction. As a result, they were able to set a healthy pace of nearly three miles an hour.

The roadway fascinated Valaria as it appeared and disappeared tantalizingly before them. Dilapidated remnants of advertising billboards could be seen from time to time off to the side as they walked and, when their faded messages were discernible through the weeds that had shimmied upward over the years, she was captivated by the glimpse of history they provided; a car dealership promoted the newest in energy-efficient transportation, the best All-American burger was offered by a fast food chain, and something called a 'credit union' enticed patrons with promises of a secure future—perverse reminders of the world that had been decimated by plague and subsequently consumed by weeds and debris. They even came across the occasional rusted out skeleton of an old-fashioned car and these, in particular, held Valaria in thrall until Quinn almost physically pried her away. She had never seen anything like this new—*old*—world and it didn't matter that the relentless hand of nature was clearly winning the war against what previously had been a testament to humanity's progress; she stood in awe of both.

Valaria's sense of wonder did not, however, extend to the overwhelming 'aloneness' that surrounded them. Even though the settlement consisted of only the farm and a handful of domed dwellings, it provided a feeling of community that insulated residents from the stark isolation of their exile. Now that she and Quinn had left that tattered cocoon, the expansive emptiness of the Borders was downright foreboding and inspired an oddly claustrophobic reaction as it seemed to close in on her. Other than the constant sounds of nature it felt like they were as alone as Adam and Eve in the Garden. It was an apt analogy—except for the heat and humidity that was far removed from paradise, the distinctly un-Edenlike flying insects that began demanding an intimate acquaintance with them once the sun came up... and the fact that this Adam was far from pleased by the addition of this particular Eve.

They walked mostly in silence, Valaria's education entering a new phase when they came across their first abandoned town shortly before noon. A partially legible sign greeted them at the outskirts and, after she pulled away the weeds and wiped off as much of the accumulated grime as possible, it identified the once-thriving community as 'Concordia.'

What remained of the town itself, however, belied its harmonious name.

Like the roadway they had been following eastward, the streets of Concordia had long since been overtaken by weeds and saplings, many of the latter having already grown into mature trees. Some businesses and homes still retained their brick facades or vinyl siding but most buildings had been constructed primarily from wood which had quickly surrendered to an onslaught of moisture, insects and weeds once the town was deserted following the plague; what remained was a depressing tableau of little more than wet, crumbling ruins. Roofs also had resisted only temporarily before succumbing to nature's incursion and most no longer offered much protection from the elements. Throughout the small community, structures of every description were disappearing into tangled woodland that was happily reasserting itself now that man's dominance had ended.

"We need to be careful," Quinn said quietly as they began their trek through nature's carnage. "We'll pick up the highway on the other side of town but there's always the possibility of Freebooters hanging around a place like this—not to mention feral dogs and other animals—so we keep moving and keep conversation to a minimum, got it?"

"No problem," Valaria replied in hushed tones, spooked by the eerie emptiness that seemed to stalk them.

Picking up on the tension of his human companions, Yancy stayed close to Valaria's side but was frequently distracted by smells and sounds that nudged his instincts and urged him to come investigate. After increasing their tension exponentially by succumbing to temptation several times and impulsively dashing off into the underbrush or a dilapidated building, a possible solution occurred to Quinn.

They had just emerged from a particularly overgrown section of town onto a fairly intact expanse of asphalt framed at the far end by a large, single story L-shaped structure. The building had been divided into different sized segments, each fronted by large, plate glass windows and doors. Only dagger-sharp shards of glass still remained in most of the frames but it was clear to Valaria that she was looking at what the old broadcasts she watched referred to as a shopping center.

Before committing their trio to a trek across the open blacktop in front of them—what had been the parking lot—Quinn stopped in the shadows at its edge, one hand extended in front of Valaria as a signal to wait, the index finger of the other touching his lips, indicating the need to remain quiet.

"I've got an idea," he whispered.

After listening to the stillness and using Yancy's display of patience as a fairly accurate barometer, they began to cross the parking lot at a quickstep.

"I stopped here on my way to the settlement," Quinn continued, pointing to one of the few remaining signs visible over a doorway; it read 'Hanson's Hardware.'

"It was raining buckets," he explained, "and I came in here to wait out the storm."

They had entered the dim store and Quinn once again gestured for silence after their footfall had shattered the quiet as each step encountered broken glass and debris of every description. After a reassuring hush had once again fallen, they moved on. "I remember seeing something that might help us now."

They walked through a maze of collapsed shelving units that at one time had presented the shop's merchandise in orderly fashion. Whether the result of panicked townspeople stocking up on supplies at the time of the plague or Freebooters and scavengers in the years that followed, the store was in shambles and virtually devoid of goods. The chipped and broken tile flooring was filthy throughout and covered in spots by thick splotches of what must have been various forms of paint and stain, and the area designated for tools and hardware had long since been picked clean. In the aisles still indicated as the garden center, broken containers of all shapes and sizes had spewed forth fertilizer, potting soil, and sundry other plant-related products. Quinn ignored all these and walked with purpose toward the back of the store where a small sign labeled 'Pet Supplies' dangled from the ceiling on a broken clip.

An area set aside for dog and cat food was completely empty—long-absent pet owners having raided the shelves in order to provide for their four-legged companions—and various rodents had obviously feasted on the few packages of bird seed and rabbit pellets that had been left behind. But it wasn't food that brought Gideon there. With Valaria and Yancy following in his wake, he quickly made his way to a display that actually had a few products remaining.

"I know Yancy's always been able to come and go as he pleases," Quinn said, "but there are gonna be times when we need to keep him close."

He directed Valaria's attention to the display.

"Dog collars," she observed dubiously.

"Yeah," Quinn replied, scanning the area. "I don't see any leads left, but that rope you brought along should do the trick; tie it onto a collar and we'll be good to go."

"I'm not tying Yancy up," Valaria informed him. "That's a shitty way for a dog to live and he'd never get used to it."

"That's not what I'm suggesting. But if he's wearing a collar we can use the rope when we need to—protect him and us."

Quinn had already begun looking through the items remaining in the display and felt lucky to find one labeled for a dog of Yancy's size. He held it out for Valaria's inspection.

"*Pink*," she barked incredulously. "You expect Yancy to wear *pink?*"

"Who gives a damn what color it is," Quinn replied testily, pulling the collar off the warped card to which it was attached. "Says right here it's a deluxe model made of durable nylon with a rustproof D-ring—won't absorb water and is mildew resistant."

"Bloody hell," she sputtered grabbing it from him. "Stop advertising the damn thing and just give it here."

Pulling Yancy to her she fastened the collar around his neck, apologizing profusely and assuring him it was only temporary.

Reluctantly accepting Quinn's suggestion that they give Yancy some practice time on-lead while traversing what remained of the town, Valaria had pulled out the length of thin rope stored in the cart and tied it onto the D-ring attached to the bright pink collar now jauntily adorning the dog's neck. Unaccustomed to being restrained, however, Yancy immediately indicated his displeasure with seamlessly interwoven spells of lurching, low-belly skulking, and a reasonable facsimile of Irish folk dancing—throwing Valaria a mixture of imploring and accusatory looks between performances. She and Quinn had their own mixture of responses, ranging from barely contained laughter at his antics to moments of abject frustration where they found themselves yanking futility at the rope or reeling the dog in to try to placate him with offers of sympathy and reassurance.

It was the sympathy that slowly seemed to win the dog over—along with bits of nutrition bar offered in reward for any period of antic-free walking. By the time they reached Concordia's eastern edge and could once again see the ribbon of highway stretching into the distance, Yancy had come to the point of acquiescing to his fate and was growing increasingly willing to trot along at the end of a reasonably slack rope and only sporadically threatened to pull Valaria's arm out of its socket.

"I think it's about time to give Yance a break," Valaria suddenly informed her companion, breaking a long silence.

They had walked about a mile beyond Concordia, well past the point where the claustrophobic, eerie stillness of the town's overgrown ruins had given way to an open expanse of fairly uninterrupted roadway.

She stooped down in order to release the captive canine from his tether but a distant, all-too-familiar electric hum abruptly riveted her attention.

Her hands froze on the knotted rope.

Quinn turned toward the town, intently scanning the sky while shielding his eyes from the sun that was beginning its slow descent into the west.

"Is that what I think it is," he murmured.

"Oh yeah, there's no mistaking that sound," Valaria replied, beginning to evaluate the surrounding terrain. "What do we do?"

Gideon turned away from the hum, joining in her survey of their options.

"I really don't think they're looking for us," he began. "After all, nobody knew I was still around and your absence may not even have been discovered yet. But I still don't want to show up on their scans."

The hum was growing louder, the TOD now clearly discernible as it approached from the northwest.

Valaria looked back at Concordia. "Should we make a break for the town?"

"It's too far and we'd be running basically right at them."

Quinn grabbed the cart and headed off the pavement toward one of the patches of tall weeds and scraggly underbrush that was an omnipresent roadside companion.

"Come on," he ordered.

Reeling Yancy in on his makeshift lead—and inordinately thankful she hadn't told Quinn where he could put his whole collar idea as had been her first inclination—Valaria and the dog joined him as he flattened himself against the ground in the dappled shade of an accommodating patch of thick weeds.

They lay in the dirt with the dog wedged between them, fighting the urge to swat at the cloud of gnats they had disturbed, and waited for the drone to pass over.

III.

Due to its classification as a frontline military installation, both logistics and daily routine at the Guardian Star were strictly regimented. At ground level, a highly fortified security section presented an imposing face to the barren perimeter surrounding the tower and the thickly reforested area that lay beyond. Directly above security, huge sections of the daunting structure were used as storage and maintenance areas and one level above that areas almost as large were set aside for mechanical support. The five companies of Guardians stationed at the Star were divided into squads based on their role, with lower-level yobs being housed in spartan dormitory units above mech support and those reaching the status of officer being assigned, according to rank, only slightly-less austere single or double occupancy rooms on the floors just above that. Beginning at the next level, several floors were dedicated to physical training followed by three modestly-appointed cafeterias and two limited recreation facilities that served officers and enlisted personnel alike. Just above the tower's midpoint, hangars for the Tactical Observation Drones frowned down at their bleak surroundings from a large archway that slid open and closed for drones to pass through; the shallow flight deck from which they took off and landed fanning outward toward the barren expanse like a pouty lower lip. Access to the portion of the Star rising dramatically skyward from that point became increasingly restricted. As one gained altitude and the tower continued to narrow, slightly more posh accommodations for command officers were provided as well as levels used for administration and areas where Guardians possessing specific technical skills—controlling the drones and interpreting their data—served in twelve-hour shifts. Above them, the uppermost reaches of the mile high behemoth were an empty skeletal framework, the top of which sported the warning lights that turned the sharply tapering pinnacle into a manmade constellation and gave the tower its name.

Dawson Hayes was just coming off one of those marathon twelve-hour stints in the restricted portion of the Star. He paused outside the control room door, waiting for the distinctive electronic chirp that would indicate it had latched securely behind him. Dogged by troubling thoughts, he turned and walked toward the elevator. He was bone weary and after giving a half-hearted salute to the guard at the lift he put his right palm on the wall-mounted scanning unit that would grant him access to the only thing now standing between him and some well-deserved rack time.

Grateful to be out of anyone's line of sight who might require him to maintain a military posture, Hayes slumped against the wall as the elevator door slid closed behind him, folded his arms across his chest and closed his eyes. The lift flew downward with mind-numbing speed but its occupant was barely aware of any movement. In less than three minutes Dawson reached his residency floor but as the door opened his reverie was shattered by his exuberant—and well-rested—roommate, Roger Trineer, who was waiting for the secondary elevator across the hall.

"Hey Dawson," Trineer sang out. "Glad I caught you! Some of us are heading for the Settlement. Why not come along?"

Hayes shook his head. "I've just spent the last twelve hours peering through the eyes of a damn drone—my brain's fried. All I can think about right now is shutting down and getting some sack time. Go raise hell without me."

"Your loss," Trineer cautioned as the elevator door slid open. "Never know, this might be the night I get lucky."

He had stepped into the lift and treated Hayes to a crude sexual gesture in reference to the ongoing suggestive game he played with the sarcastically unresponsive proprietor of *The Shoe and Gear*.

Hayes gave him a solicitous smirk as the elevator door closed, muttering under his breath, "Not very damn likely."

Safely cloistered in his quarters a few minutes later, Dawson didn't even bother with a shower before collapsing onto his bed fully clothed. Still pretty wired after having a TOD in his head for twelve hours—the optical interface embedded in his right temple making him slightly blurry-eyed—he found sleep a frustratingly elusive commodity. Running a hand over his close-cropped hair, he shut his eyes and gave in to a review of the day's events.

Things had started out normally enough. After a quick breakfast, he and the other Guardians about to go on duty had reported to the briefing room for a routine update. Standing rigidly at attention with their arms behind them, right hand clasping left wrist, they had listened intently as the Duty Officer brought them up to speed.

"It has now been confirmed," he had informed them, "that agents of the Sons of Liberty have been sighted in the Borders—one as close as Settlement #4."

There was proof, he went on to say, that the Sons were actively seeking to enlist the aid of Pioneers in their campaign of insurrection against the Triumvirate. Again referring to Settlement #4, he alerted them to the fact that one of the exiles—Valaria Thorpe, proprietress of the local pub—had been reported missing and was presumed to be attempting to join the subversives.

"Although I am not at liberty to share many specifics with you," he had concluded officiously, "suffice it to say that your work has just become even more vital to the security of the Homeland."

Hayes had left the briefing and headed for his station in the TOD control room seriously distracted by what he had heard. Thorpe had always been a bit of an enigma to him and he wouldn't put it past her to suddenly discover a vein of latent patriotism but he found himself hoping she wasn't actually trying to cross the five-mile limit. It was more likely, he tried to convince himself, that she was off somewhere nearby shacked up with somebody in the black market.

Unfortunately, his worst fears had been confirmed when, after several hours spent seeing the world through the grid-like gaze of an observation drone, his scans had detected two people and what appeared to be a dog dashing into the underbrush adjacent old Highway 40. Random sightings of civilians were to be expected—Freebooters and scavengers being most common—but a second, lower pass had verified his suspicions for he would have recognized Yancy's distinctive black and white markings anywhere.

Well, at least it had been he who saw them.

His thoughts returning to the present, Dawson propped himself up on his pillow and folded an arm behind his head for extra support.

"Damn, Valaria," he whispered hoarsely into the darkened room, "what the Hell are you up to?"

IV.

"Do you think they saw us?" Valaria asked as she rose to a sitting position among the weeds and began brushing dirt from her clothes.

"Probably," Quinn replied. "That second pass was lower and slower than the first. They were taking a good look at something. Hopefully we just looked like a couple of scavs."

He rose to his knees and leaned back against his feet, absently picking at bits of dirt and weeds clinging to Yancy's fur.

"With my luck, it was that prick Roger Trineer," Valaria volunteered. "He's one persistent sonuvabitch—been harassing me for months with what he seems to think is enticing verbal foreplay. If he knows I've gone AWOL he'd undoubtedly love to be the one to track me down."

Quinn listened without comment as they gathered their belongings, waved off the swarming gnats, and once again headed east.

"I suppose it could've been Dawson Hayes," she continued. "Hell, what does it matter? One Guardian is as bad as another. They'd all turn us in if they got the chance."

"You've mentioned that Hayes guy before," Quinn interjected. "He's the one who came into the pub with Yancy when I was under the bar, right?

Valaria nodded.

"He didn't seem as toxic as most. Obviously likes your dog; seemed to like you, too. Think he might cut you a break if he was behind the drone?"

"I'll admit he seems OK—for a Guardian," Valaria replied, adding sarcastically, "but I wouldn't go as far as saying he *likes* me… Geez, what are we, twelve years old?"

Quinn smiled. "Hey, you said it yourself—the Borders puts a serious damper on a person's sex life. Right now, I wouldn't turn up my nose at a break from some Guardian who has the hots for you."

"*That* would be Trineer," Valaria scoffed. "And like I said, he'd be the first one to turn me in."

It was almost totally dark by the time they stopped for the night. They had been walking for close to seven hours and had covered nearly eighteen miles; not the twenty Quinn privately had targeted, but not bad for their first day out. When he caught sight of a thick stand of trees well off to the side of the roadway he thought it best not to risk ending up having to sleep out in the open and decided to call it a day.

Valaria was seriously relieved when Quinn announced it was time to make camp—although she wasn't going to subject herself to his smug "*I told you so*" by giving him the satisfaction of knowing it. She was in good physical condition and had found keeping up with Quinn's steady pace fairly easy. Her *feet*, however, were a different story. Even protected by a pair of secondhand work boots, their complaints were growing louder with every mile and she was sure even her blisters were going to have blisters before long.

As Quinn ignited the portable camp stove—a solar-powered unit that spent its days attached to the back of his rucksack where it could bask in the sunshine—Valaria painfully extracted her feet from torture chambers cleverly disguised as shoes.

"It might be a good idea to leave those on," Quinn commented, taking note of the care she was exhibiting in their removal. "You might not be able to get them back on again in the morning."

"I'll risk it," she snapped.

Quinn was announcing tomorrow's arrival hours before Valaria would normally be willing to concede its existence. Hobbling moodily off into the semi-dark with a roll of toilet paper firmly wedged under her arm in order to "see a man about a horse," she quickly discovered the painful reality behind his warning from the night before—her swollen, blistered feet were going to make the endless hours that lay ahead a real bitch! After finding an agreeably sheltered spot to squat, with Yancy alertly standing guard, she returned to camp, her sulky veneer masking genuine concern about the walk that awaited her.

Gideon acknowledged their return but wisely made no mention of Valaria's obvious discomfort. He had gotten food out in her absence and they refueled on thick slices of bread slathered with honey and even some fairly decent tea warmed over the diminishing heat of the solar stove.

When it was Quinn's turn to go inquire about that ubiquitous horse in the woods, Valaria took advantage of his absence to undertake the challenge of getting her feet back into her shoes. It was no easy task but she was determined not to be a detriment to their progress and through gritted teeth—and muted expletives—the deed was finally accomplished. By the time Gideon returned (she suspected he had dallied in order to facilitate her re-shodding ordeal—either that or last night's beans hadn't agreed with him!), Valaria had managed a few gingerly steps and was beginning to break camp.

"Here," Quinn said, unceremoniously handing her a tall, sturdy stick, "this should help you stay on your feet. I'll take charge of the cart today."

The walking stick did help. In spite of its support, however, Valaria lagged behind her guide for most of the day, receiving numerous backward glances but no criticism from her more seasoned companion. Although he said nothing, Quinn was clearly sympathetic to her plight for they were resting at more regular intervals than Valaria would have expected; something that brought her both chagrin and relief. Even the highway seemed to take pity on her as it stretched cooperatively before them with very few sections completely overtaken by nature's untamed hand.

Despite those regular breaks—and the highway's largesse—by mid afternoon Valaria's feet had slowed them to a snail's pace. They had managed only a little more than seven miles, not even half Quinn's daily goal. Her reliance on the improvised walking stick was becoming increasingly pronounced and it struck him that she was beginning to resemble a hunchbacked old woman as she leaned heavily on it.

It was clear they were going to have to stop.

"You better let me take a look at your feet," he said once they had set up camp and shared a light supper.

"I don't know, Quinn," she replied skeptically, "You think it's a good idea for me to take my shoes off? I really might not be able to get them back on this time."

She had stretched her legs out from where she sat on her bedroll next to the camp stove and it had given Gideon a clear look at her clunky boots for the first time.

"I think part of the problem," he observed, "is that your shoes are too big."

"Well, duh," she replied tartly. "It's not like exiles have much choice when it comes to things like clothes and shoes. We take what we can get."

"So all this walking in shoes that don't fit is what's killing your feet. Let's bandage the blisters, give your feet a breather overnight, and then you can add a pair of my socks to yours in order to take up some of that extra space in your shoes and cushion the sore spots."

Having reached a point where she was about ready to suggest amputation, Valaria was less than optimistic about what good Quinn's suggested ministrations might do. She was, however, totally willing to get the God-forsaken shoes off—and only slightly less willing to have him clean and examine her feet.

She slept that night with her ankles resting on an improvised pillow in order to allow the cool evening air full access to the freshly cleaned blisters. Upon waking, Quinn had finished playing doctor by adding antibiotic ointment and bandages to both feet and giving her two pairs of his thickest socks in an effort to add some extra padding to the sore spots. It was a prescription that proved fairly successful and over the next few days Valaria found herself thinking less and less about her feet and more about the increasing distances they were able to cover.

By the time they came to the outskirts of Columbia on the fifth day, they had almost regained their daily goal of twenty miles and Valaria was feeling pretty confident—if not actually a bit cocky—about life on the road as a renegade.

"Liberty must at all hazards be supported. We have a right to it, derived from our Maker. But if we had not, our fathers have earned and bought it for us at the expense of their ease, their estates, their pleasure, and their blood."

~ John Adams

CHAPTER TEN

I.

Despite the fact that The Revanche successfully vanquished the terrorists responsible for the plague, the months immediately following had seen the disease continue to spread with all the fury of a wildfire's inferno. Quickly gaining the status of pandemic, it had engulfed the globe.

For the generations rocked in the cradle of the twentieth century's Cold War between freedom and totalitarianism, the tenuous balance created by the sheer lunacy of mutual annihilation had somewhat mitigated the dark pall of a possible nuclear holocaust. But no such reductio ad absurdum existed in the lexicon of terrorism and in the myopic frenzy of their fanaticism, Islamic extremists failed to perceive the absurdity of an act of barbarism that ultimately would engulf *them* as well as the western world they despised. Within six months the plague inevitably spread to its place of origin; the architects of humanity's worst calamity bringing the disease as well as the wrath of a wounded world down upon their own heads.

It took more than three years for the infection finally to burn itself out—taking with it more than a third of the world's population in the process. In its wake, varying levels of collapse of both infrastructure and order had been inevitable.

As the plague gained momentum and it became obvious that the United States was going to be unable to adequately respond to the crisis, two panic-stricken migrations had ensued, the first *away* from population centers as people sought to escape the contagion, the second in the exact opposite direction as survivors began seeking asylum where they believed the only vestige of civilization was likely still to exist—*larger cities*. To its credit, the government attempted to facilitate this second migration, dispatching cobbled-together military units to gather those who remained and transport them to designated 'Safe Zones.' Over the months, those areas of refuge also began to be consolidated until, eventually, there were only five major population centers remaining—all sandwiched between the Mississippi River and the Appalachian Mountains; east of which the specter of radioactive contamination from the Eastern Seaboard's surfeit of decaying nuclear power plants was making the already plague-decimated Boston/Virginia Beach corridor as much a wasteland as The Wilds of the far west.

Expecting the government—what was left of it—to protect them, people in the five official Safe Zones had clung in exhausted desperation to an ambiguous 3-step plan outlined by the newly-formed Triumvirate and summarized in the first of myriad slogans to come, all designed to make martial law more palatable and draw attention away from the extreme cost of safety—

RESTORE stability
REBUILD the nation
RECLAIM The Wilds

They were a people grown complacent by decades of prosperity; relying more and more on what critics had referred to as the 'Nanny State.' And despite having witnessed barbaric acts of terrorism like New York in 2001 and its sibling attacks over the years in London, Paris, Tokyo, Dubai City and other centers of prosperity, such events were largely vicarious traumas that in no way prepared them for the worldwide cataclysm they faced as a result of the plague. As survivors in the U.S. licked their wounds and mourned their countless losses, they uttered barely a whisper of dissent when a dictatorial form of stability—accompanied by increasingly draconian laws—quietly began taking hold east of the Mississippi River.

In the thousands of square miles *west* of the Mississippi, however, recovery—if it could even be called that—took on a significantly *darker* tone.

As the disintegration of a civilized, albeit imperfect society spread, something decidedly *un*civilized began to rise from the figurative ashes in what the RSA now called The Wilds. For those who had been too isolated—or too independent—to participate in the government's evacuations, the vast western region of the former United States became a wilderness of Biblical proportions where they would eke out a marginal existence haunted by every imaginable form of deprivation and danger.

For those among them who had chosen not to leave for more *nefarious* reasons, The Wilds would become, essentially, their hunting ground.

Developing a fiercely territorial system loosely resembling a tribal confederation, this second group would come to be known as Freebooters—an archaic term for pirate one of the more learned among their early number had chosen due to the erudite veneer it added to their gang-like existence. Having crossed the Rubicon of whatever system of values might have held them in check prior to the plague, they were the antithesis of the rigid order being created in the cities and the mere mention of Freebooters became the boogeyman for every child in the RSA... for many *adults* as well.

It was a lifestyle with which Corsa was intimately familiar.

The lone survivor of a Freebooter raid on a small group of farmers when he was three, Corsa had become a full-fledged 'Booter' just a few months earlier. He bore the new scars from his teenaged rite of passage with honor; most proud of the broad gash that had left a discolored swath across his left check and jaw line. Haunted by nightmares in which everything familiar was being consumed by flames and a vaguely familiar woman's voice cried out to him from the heart of the inferno, Corsa embraced his Freebooter identity with a bravado born of anger and trauma; a reckless audacity that had brought him attention early on. He was smart, he was callous, and he now served a clan that was as adept at living off the land as they were at living off anyone unlucky enough to cross their path.

The ruins of what had been Columbia, Missouri were in the heart of their territory.

II.

"Having a little trouble keeping up," Valaria teased, taking lead for the first time.

Quinn had stopped to survey the remnants of the city that lay on both sides of the asphalt path they followed.

"Getting a little cocky, aren't you? Just remember those are my socks cushioning your feet—I can take 'em back you know."

"Sure you want them? It's not like they've been washed lately."

She returned to his side, pulled a water pouch from her backpack, and drank deeply.

"What gives?" she asked, handing it to him.

"When I came through here the first time I saw what looked like campfire smoke off to the south. It was still pretty light out so I left the

166

roadway just to be on the safe side and walked through the underbrush until I was well west of town."

He took a long drink. "We've got most of the width of the city to cross and I sure-as-hell don't want to meet up with any Freebooters along the way." He snapped the water pouch closed and handed it back to her. "I'm wondering if it's safer to stay on the highway or to cut through town."

"Cutting through town would take longer," Valaria observed, "but we'd be harder to spot. On the other hand, if there's a chance people live around here, it's probably best to go as fast as possible. They could be perfectly harmless but I agree, why take the chance?"

"Speed and visibility versus stealth and time," he mused.

"I vote for speed."

"I think I do, too. How about you, Yance?"

The dog's prancing impatience and wagging tail seemed to make it unanimous. He might have changed his vote, however, had he realized that in just a moment he would once again be tethered in order to guarantee his cooperation as they continued traversing the decayed ribbon of Highway 40 that ran across the city of Columbia.

They set off at a brisk pace, keeping a watchful eye out for any sign of activity on either side of the blacktop and making good time. The halfway point had almost been reached when they came upon an interchange where the artery they followed crossed over a street identified as North Providence Road. The years had been especially unkind to this particular section of highway. As it stretched away from them they could clearly see a huge gap near the middle where the portion intended to bridge the street below had collapsed onto the lower roadway in a formidable tangle of concrete and rebar that took on the appearance of poorly-executed modern art.

"We'll have to go around," Quinn said, indicating the remains of an exit ramp sloping off to their right. "We can go down here and then right back up the other side."

He took charge of the two-wheeled cart while Valaria reeled in Yancy's improvised leash and they slowly began to negotiate their way down the broken, weed-corrupted asphalt.

They had reached the bottom and were about to cross the street when a languid voice called out to them.

"Hey there…"

Turning toward the sound, they were greeted by the sight of two boys sliding down the embankment from the sheltered area underneath what remained of the overpass.

Instantly alert, Quinn stepped in front of Valaria and the dog.

"Relax," she chided. "It's just a couple kids."

He shot a murmured warning over his shoulder. "Scouts."

The boys were filthy, the older of the two about thirteen years old, the other no more than ten. Their ill-fitting clothes were tattered and grimy, their shaggy hair matted and snarled, and as they got closer it was obvious from the smell that neither had seen a bar of soap in a very long time.

"Hey guys," Quinn began lightly. "What're you doing way out here all by yourselves?"

"Aw, we're not by ourselves," the older one replied, dirty fingers toying idly with an old-fashioned referee's whistle suspended from a frayed cord around his neck. "We live here."

"With your folks?"

Both boys appraised Quinn and Valaria with totally blank expressions, although it was clear they were missing nothing.

The older boy picked up on Quinn's suggestion. "Yeah... with our folks."

He tilted his head at an odd angle and gave them a serene smile that was as eerie as it was placid—and there was something about the way he said *"our folks"* that sent a chill down Valaria's spine. The younger boy stood by, silently shifting his weight from one leg to the other in an odd and vacant rhythm as if enthralled by a tune only he could hear. His nose was running, creating a slick track in the grime between nostrils and upper lip that he repeatedly swiped at with his tongue.

They were ominously pathetic and it was difficult to look at them.

"What's your name?" Quinn asked.

"I'm Corsa, this is Milo... Who're you?"

"Name's John," he replied casually. His unwavering gaze stayed on the two boys as he identified his companions. "This is Susan and Buster."

Milo spoke up for the first time, his voice as flat and lifeless as his eyes. "I like your dog."

"Thanks," Valaria replied, pulling Yancy closer.

"Can I have him?"

More than a little off-put by the menacing edge to his quiet request, she gave him a look that clearly communicated the *"what the f—"* that ran through her head.

"Sorry, kid, he stays with me."

Quinn lightly touched Valaria's elbow and they began crossing the street.

The boys followed.

"Where ya goin', John?" Corsa asked benignly as they all started up the opposite ramp heading back to the highway. The whistle he had been absently toying with while they talked was now grasped purposefully between the thumb and index finger of his right hand.

"Gotta keep moving," Quinn glibly lied. "We're meeting some business associates."

Whatever the young 'booters might have in mind, he hoped the thinly-veiled reference to black market activity might give the duo second thoughts since those purveyors of illegal goods took no crap from Freebooters.

The boys stopped when they reached the top of the ramp.

Gideon began edging away. "Nice meeting you guys."

Before Quinn's brain had time to register movement, Corsa suddenly lunged forward, head-butting him in the gut. Taking his cue from the older boy, Milo shrieked incoherently and dove for Valaria's ankles.

Thrown off balance by the backpack she shouldered and the grimy child now wrapped around her feet, Valaria went down hard, the walking stick flying out of her hand and spinning heavenward like a propeller without a plane. Momentarily submerged in utter dismay at the insanity of fighting off a ten-year-old, Valaria wrenched a foot free from Milo's vice-like hold and kicked upward with all her might. It was awkward but effective. She connected with the boy's chin, flipping him unceremoniously onto his back, arms akimbo, head literally bouncing against the pavement.

In an instant he was back on his feet and Valaria thought she heard him growl.

The boy crouched slightly, like a wild animal about to pounce; lips upturned in a macabre snarl exposing a gap-toothed maw, hands extended before him, filthy fingers curled like claws.

It must have been the growl.

Yancy had begun barking frantically when Milo took Valaria down. Dashing back and forth, the dog initially stayed on the sidelines like a manager directing a fight from just behind the ropes. But when the young 'booter had lurched back to his feet after Valaria's kick threw him, growling at her in the split second before round two, Yancy had sprung into action. In a blur of black and white fury, the dog grabbed the boy's wrist with a bite that left no doubt as to his intentions. Bracing himself by leaning into his haunches, he had viciously wrenched Milo back down to the pavement. The young villain kicked out wildly at his canine opponent but Yancy was undeterred. Releasing Milo's wrist and snarling rabidly he grabbed an offending leg.

The child's heart-wrenching cry slashed the air.

For a moment Valaria was moved with compassion for the little boy now writhing on the asphalt clutching his blood-soaked leg, but only for a moment. Calling Yancy to her side, she adjusted the backpack that miraculously had stayed between her shoulders, ran to where her walking stick had landed by the side of the road, and turned toward Quinn.

What she saw amazed her.

Utilizing moves Valaria had only seen in old movies, Quinn was blocking, kicking, and throwing Corsa as if the two were sparring in some carefully choreographed fight video. Although outclassed, the teen obviously possessed rudimentary skills—or an excess of determination—and every time Gideon brought him down he was back on his feet almost immediately. The young 'booter's eyes were already beginning to swell and both opponents were bleeding from mouth and nose. Corsa's nose was visibly broken.

Stepping into a moment's advantage as Quinn regained his balance following a kick that hadn't connected, Corsa turned sideways and landed a solid right-footed strike against Gideon's rib cage.

Instantly winded, the older man went down.

Without pausing to think, Valaria grabbed the walking stick like an oversized baseball bat and jumped into the fray. Screeching like a banshee, she swung wildly in Corsa's direction. No contact was made but the teen stumbled to the pavement in startled amusement as he dodged the blow, giving Quinn time to stagger to his feet.

"*Run!*" Gideon commanded, grabbing his rucksack off the ground and jamming it into the cart.

Laughing almost hysterically as he rose, Corsa dragged Milo to his feet with one hand and thrust the whistle into his mouth with the other, bringing it shrilly to life. It took just a moment but they were precious seconds that gave Valaria and Quinn time to break into a reasonably effective sprint despite the damaged ribcage Gideon pressed tightly with his forearm.

Valaria threw a glance over her shoulder as they ran.

In response to Corsa's shrill alert, at least five older versions of the young Freebooters emerged seemingly from the ether, scrambling up both sides of the decaying highway like gangly-legged insects swarming their prey. Joining the chase, they were rapidly gaining ground.

An eerily-dissonant ululation filled the air, growing louder as unseen others picked up the cry.

"Don't look back," Quinn ordered. "Just run!"

Regardless of their head start, Valaria knew they were in very deep shit. Encumbered by rucksacks and the cart, there was no way they were going to be able to outrun the pack of wolves on their heels.

The urge to look back was overpowering.

The Freebooters had closed the distance between them to little more than 50 feet and Valaria was convinced she could smell their fury as the dissonant keening continued.

Distracted for a moment by a thundering rumble in the distance she almost tripped over Yancy as he zigzagged in front of her—were the Booters actually beating drums somewhere? The sound seemed to come from above, however, and pulled her gaze heavenward. Stumbling slightly in blind amazement, Valaria watched in awe as what looked like transparent waves warbled through the picture-perfect sky and engulfed the Freebooters, flattening them like ants beneath a shoe.

Although still some distance away, when the undulating waves hit their mark the force created a concussion that lifted Valaria and her companions off the ground and flung them like rag dolls a good twenty feet farther down the road.

"Bloody hell," Valaria cried out from where she lay sprawled on the ground, ears ringing loudly. "What was that?"

Bracing herself on her elbows, she looked skyward, raising a hand to shield her eyes from the glare of the sun. A sleek, aerodynamic drone— larger than any she had seen before—was circling away from them, apparently preparing for another pass.

Quinn helped her to her feet, wiping blood from his mouth and nose with the back of his free hand.

"That, my friend, is a Tactical Attack Drone—TOD's big, bad brother," he said breathlessly. "When I was in the city I heard they were taking some TADs out of mothballs but had no idea they'd already been deployed."

Although well out of range, they instinctively ducked as another low, thunder-like rumble erupted from the cloudless sky. In a heartbeat, a second warbling energy wave was momentarily visible as it distorted the air in the direction the remaining Freebooters were scattering.

"Helluva lucky break they're targeting the larger group," Quinn said. "Probably didn't even see us."

"Guardians versus Freebooters," Valaria observed stoically, "doesn't get any better than that."

III.

Determined to put as much distance as possible between them and Columbia before fatigue won out, Quinn and Valaria travelled fast and hard after encountering the Freebooters. Each was too focused on that goal—and on their respective aches and pains—to waste time on conversation. As a result the intervening hours were almost silent and it was well after dark before they surrendered to exhaustion and stopped to make camp for the night.

Blowing gently into the cup of hot tea she held with both hands to steady herself, Valaria stared into the black void beyond the reassuring light cast by the solar camp stove. She finally broke the silence with a question she was almost afraid to ask.

"Do you think they'll come after us?"

Quinn shook his head. "No; they've got bigger things to worry about right now."

They were seated on the ground on opposite sides of the solar stove with Yancy stretched comfortably between them. Gideon reached out and stroked the dog's flank before speaking again. "God, I can't believe how lucky we were that a drone came along right then. I don't even want to think about what could've happened."

Intercepting the glance he surreptitiously cast her way, Valaria knew it was for her he had been most concerned and a shiver raced down her spine at the thought of being at the mercy of Freebooters.

"Must've been a training flight," Quinn mused more to himself than to either of his companions. "Can't imagine they were actually tracking those 'booters. Sure hit the jackpot when a live target presented itself."

"I don't care what they were doing," Valaria interjected. "For the first time in my life I'm glad they're around."

"Well just don't forget—we could've been on the receiving end of that energy pulse if they'd seen us instead of those 'booters." Attempting to lighten the mood a bit, he changed the subject. "At least we didn't lose anything. I thought about dropping the cart—that might have satisfied them—but there's just too much important stuff in it."

"Yeah, like toilet paper!"

Quinn smiled.

"You could always use that," he jibed, indicating the polka dot cloth wrapped around his companion's left wrist.

"And lose my coveted status as minion? No way!"

He acknowledged her mock indignation with a salute that ended in a return to stroking Yancy's side as he slept between them.

"And what's up with those moves of yours?" Valaria demanded quietly. "That was pretty freakin' awesome. I never dreamed you could do anything like that."

Quinn tried to deflect the unexpected admiration. "Just one of many services I provide."

"Can all the Sons do that shit?"

"Not all of us," he replied. "But we've been training more seriously the past couple years."

"Well, that was as good as anything I've seen in the movies. Corsa never had a chance."

"I wouldn't say that," Quinn scoffed, gingerly touching his bruised ribcage.

Returning to the topic of Freebooters seemed to put a damper on the conversation and both lapsed into silence once again, each staring into a distance of their own measure.

"God, those poor kids," Valaria finally murmured over a contemplative sip of tea.

Quinn snorted. "Those 'poor kids' would've killed us if given half a chance!"

"I know... But can you imagine a more pathetic way to live? So scrawny and dirty—and obviously a little nuts! And did you see the scars on Corsa's face? What the hell's up with that; some stupid form of initiation, or just plain child abuse?"

"Both probably," Gideon observed, stifling a yawn.

Neither Quinn nor Valaria slept well that night. Turning the solar stove down to a barely visible glow—just enough light to hold at bay the menacing darkness edging in around them—they took turns on watch but both found it challenging to drift off once it was their turn to sleep. The only one who seemed able to take the day's events in stride was Yancy, resting peacefully between his two humans with legs jerking occasionally as he romped through an unseen meadow, lips chuffing comically in a silent bark, and tail wagging spasmodically in unconscious canine glee. Although mildly entertained by his antics, the dog's human counterparts spent most of the night envying his heavy slumber and even Quinn was somewhat less than enthusiastic when forced to deal with Yancy's zest the following morning.

Valaria was downright belligerent.

"Get away from me, you mangy prat," she snapped, pushing the dog off as he exuberantly embraced both the morning and his favorite person.

After fighting a kid who should have been playing baseball instead of marauder and spending a virtually sleepless night on the cold ground, Valaria was feeling every minute of her thirty-four years as well as willingly succumbing to her intense loathing of morning. She slumped down closer to the stove Quinn was reactivating and sullenly assessed the assortment of scratches and bruises with which Milo had gifted her.

Gideon wisely said nothing as he handed her a slice of bread and honey.

"I don't suppose we could take a day off," she grumbled morosely. As if to emphasize her moody displeasure, she picked an edge of blue mold off the bread's crust with a scowling flourish.

Quinn reached for the small kettle on the stove. The act clearly was painful and his free hand automatically pressed against his ribcage. "Sorry; too much ground to cover. And I think we'd feel even stiffer if we didn't keep moving."

She held the moldy bread crust out to Yancy who was skulking sheepishly in the background.

"Come here, bud," she coaxed. "It's OK now."

Not one to pass up bread and honey—moldy or otherwise—let alone a gesture of affection from his human, Yancy was at her side in a heartbeat, doing his best impression of a canine Sphinx as he quietly devoured the bread.

Much to the restless dog's delight—and his exhausted human's dismay—they were back on the road as soon as they could break camp.

It was another hot, humid day, the last vestiges of summer clinging to Missouri with the relentless tenacity of an addict in need of a fix—a comparison Valaria could relate to since she was down to her last five cigarettes and rattled by nicotine cravings as perverse as the daily torment of flies and mosquitoes. That seemingly omnipresent pestilence was beginning to dangerously fray their nerves if not their resolve; ragged edges unraveling even further due to injury, fatigue, and sudden jolts of alarm when any noise happened to stray from the ambient woodland backdrop of rustling leaves, chirping birds, trilling cicadas, and scrabbling critters. Acutely aware of the possibility of a Freebooter ambush, they would freeze in a hushed tableau at any unfamiliar sound—or at sound's abrupt cessation; Valaria dropping into a squat next to Yancy, hugging him to her and clamping his snout with her hand. By midday they had encountered nothing more menacing than rodents, deer and one very surprised, spindly-legged cow, but the lengthening trip was taking its toll.

They were as worn as the sparse coating of honey now left for their bread and spent most of each day in silence.

IV.

A little more than a week out—having lost time early on due to Valaria's ill-fitting boots—they came upon signage indicating a turnoff for the former city of O'Fallon. It was a point Quinn and been anxious to reach for it meant St. Louis was only about twenty-five miles away and gave them both a much-needed infusion of encouragement for there had been no reprieve from the heat, humidity, and bugs that continued to sap their strength and erode their morale.

As they forged ahead, still wary of every unfamiliar sound, they kept an eye on a militant cluster of thunderheads beginning to darken the eastern sky. A cooling rain would be more than welcome—refreshing their spirits as well as washing away some of travel's sweat and grime—but a serious storm would be another matter entirely and Quinn was racking his brain trying to recall any areas of shelter along the way.

They had been walking for almost an hour after taking a break for lunch, still eyeing the thickening wall of storm clouds forming an ominous dead end as the broken asphalt dissolved into the distance. The humidity was increasingly oppressive and the woodland progressively quiet as the breeze stilled and flora and fauna alike seemed to be hunkering down for nature's blitzkrieg.

Quinn had walked a bit ahead of his companions and stopped to allow them to catch up while studying the sky.

"This does not look good," Valaria said, stating the obvious as she joined him.

"I'd say it's still a few miles away," he replied. "Hard to be sure but I think it's tracking south."

A distant rumble of thunder followed by a jagged flash of lightning stirred the air a bit and a short-lived breeze swirled over them as they began walking again. Valaria closed her eyes for a moment, basking in the brief respite but Yancy was suddenly alert, ears at full attention and nostrils pulsating. In the moment it took for the breeze to be spent, he broke stride with his companions and dashed impulsively into the underbrush.

"*Yancy!*"

It was a cry shouted in stereo as Valaria and Quinn stared after the dog in dumbfounded dismay.

The only response was the sound of Yancy crashing through the thick woods to the right of the highway and an urgent bark calling for them to follow.

Without a moment's thought or hesitation, Valaria impetuously ran after her dog.

"*Wait*," Quinn shouted after her. "He'll come back!"

Ignoring the rational voice of the man behind her Valaria struggled on, tracking Yancy as best she could through the underbrush. She followed his insistent barking and fought her way through an uncooperative tangle of weeds and low-hanging branches that seemed to fling themselves about in a determined effort to thwart her.

Back on the roadway, Quinn uttered a vehement "*Shit!*" and started after his wayward companions, the deep, two-wheeled cart bouncing and tipping precariously as he angrily pulled and yanked it along behind him.

In the bushes ahead, Valaria made very little progress. Beginning to feel short of breath from the exertion of fighting the woods as well as the heat and humidity, she paused to get her bearings, straining to figure out which way Yancy's bark was leading. Drenched in sweat and wiping away a trail of blood trickling down her cheek from one of the new scratches adorning her face and arms, she leaned forward, hands on knees, allowing the backpack to slide to the ground as she did so and gulping in deep breaths of air.

"Are you out of your mind?" Quinn demanded as he came upon her a moment later. "This is exactly why I wanted him tethered. You've gotta let him go. He'll find his way back to us."

Valaria's indignant, expletive-peppered response was cut off in mid-sentence when Yancy abruptly stopped barking and the woods fell eerily silent.

"Oh my God," she cried out with a depth of emotion that rocked the man beside her.

She took a few steps forward. "*Yancy!*"

"Stop yelling, for God's sake," Quinn snapped, grabbing her arm. "You want the whole damn world to know we're out here?"

"I'm *not* leaving him," she snarled.

The look of desperation on her face gentled him.

"All right, but don't fly off half-cocked—and stop the goddamn yelling!"

Mopping his sweaty face with the back of his hand and surveying the area around them, he pointed to some nearby bushes that bore obvious signs of having recently been disturbed.

"Look," he said, "Yancy's a big dog; if we use our heads we should be able to follow him fairly easily."

They quickly discovered that the dog had, indeed, left a fairly clear path of destruction in his wake as he plowed helter-skelter through the underbrush. The duo forged ahead slowly, widening his route as best they could in order to keep injury and annoyance to a minimum. They hadn't gone far when an overpowering, putrid smell accosted them.

"Oh my God," Valaria whispered, wincing as if physically assaulted and putting her hand firmly over her nose. "What *is* that?"

"It's what Yancy must have picked up on," Quinn replied solemnly. "Something is seriously-dead out here."

"Well, this just keeps getting better and better. What do we do now?"

"We find Yance and get the hell out of here."

It became disturbingly easy to follow the dog from that point for the cloyingly rancid, fetid sweetness of decay increasingly permeated the air, souring their stomachs as they now followed their noses as much as the dog's path.

Convinced she must be turning a delightfully putrid shade of green—and finding it extremely difficult to contain the bile rising in her throat—Valaria was just about ready to admit defeat when Yancy suddenly came crashing back through the undergrowth.

Wagging all over in triumph, he bounded up to Valaria and dropped something at her feet.

It was the bloodied remains of a human ear.

"Oh shit," she sputtered in horror, staggering backward.

Without comment, Quinn tethered the dog and handed him off to her. Kicking the ear back into the bushes, he pushed through the underbrush from which Yancy had just emerged.

A long silence followed.

"You better stay where you are," Gideon cautioned soberly from the other side, his voice taut and thin.

Enticed by morbid curiosity and more than a touch of vainglory, Valaria reeled in Yancy's improvised leash and followed Quinn through the tangled barrier.

There was a sun-dappled clearing on the other side of the hedgerow, framed in brutal irony by the blue-black thunderheads rolling in from the east and the scene of carnage displayed in macabre tableau at its center. What obviously had been a long term campsite for a small group of scavengers had become a deathtrap when overpowered by either another group of scavs or, more likely, a gang of Freebooters. There appeared to have been five or six in the group—although it was difficult to be sure due to their state of decomposition and the fact that most had been savagely hacked to pieces. The metallic smell of blood merged with the stench of decay and thick, sticky pools coagulated darkly in the heat. Their meager homestead ransacked, the scavengers had been viciously slaughtered; stripped of what little they had and left to rot in the summer sun.

The sight was beyond horror and brutally scorched Valaria's mind.

The smell would linger even more vividly.

Instantly regretting her decision not to heed Quinn's warning, Valaria was overpowered by the stench and the sight of viscera glistening wetly in the midday glare. Falling to her knees she vomited until she was empty and reduced to nothing but painful, dry heaves.

"Come on," Quinn said with quiet reverence, helping her rise. "There's nothing we can do for these poor bastards. Let's go."

"Shouldn't we bury them," she managed to squeak out.

"Yeah, we should. But we don't have a shovel and—to be totally honest—this wasn't done all that long ago. I don't think it's a good idea to hang around too long."

Quinn's final observation was punctuated by a persuasive rumble of thunder as the storm finally overtook them; a gesture of absolution from on High affirming the need to move on.

"...To the persecution and tyranny of this cruel government we will not tamely submit — appealing to Heaven for the justice of our cause, we determine to be free or die."

~ Joseph Warren

CHAPTER ELEVEN

I.

It took a long time for the foul smell of human decay to even begin to release its ghoulish hold on them, every breath tainted by death's fetid olfactory fingerprint. Ill-equipped to bury the scavengers and finally overtaken by the storm, Valaria and Quinn had donned thin waterproof ponchos and moved on, but even the hard rain couldn't wash away the cloying stench that seemed to have permeated every piece of clothing, every strand of hair, every inch of exposed skin. Even the food they forced themselves to eat that night seemed to reek and taste of death.

Once sheltered from the rain beneath the tarp Valaria had wisely stuffed into the cart before beginning their quest, the quiet lengthened between them as each processed the day's grisly revelation in silence.

It was Quinn who finally edged his way reverently into Valaria's solitude. "I'm really sorry you had to see that but I tried to warn you off. Want to talk about it?"

"Nothing to say," she replied, her raspy voice almost lost to the rain spattering against the tarp.

She was sitting huddled up to Yancy and nestled into his soft fur. "I know things are bad out here. I know the country's basically a steaming pile of shit. But that doesn't make it any easier to accept—especially when it stares you in the face like it did today."

"But that's just it—we *shouldn't* accept it," Quinn observed with hushed ferocity. "Things should never have gotten as bad as they are. The government should never have abandoned so many people. It was inevitable they'd prey on one another."

"And you guys are gonna fix all that?"

"We're sure as hell going to try."

Valaria shook her head dubiously and stared into the rain. "You really believe things can change?"

Still troubled by bruised ribs from his encounter with Corsa, Quinn winced as he leaned forward and took one of her hands in his—more than a little surprised when she didn't pull it away.

"I believe law and order can be restored, yes. It won't be easy, it won't be pretty, and it won't happen overnight but I believe with every fiber of my being that we can make a real difference and make life better for people."

His look was intense and his words struck her more like an oath than an observation.

"God, I hope you're right, but after what we saw today I'm not so sure."

She withdrew her hand and began absently scratching Yancy's belly as he shifted position and lay down between them.

"I don't mean to minimize the tragedy represented by those dead bodies," Quinn continued, "but there's been a lot of death over the past decades and I'm afraid it's not over yet."

Space beneath the tarp was cramped and he shifted uncomfortably as rain dripped in from the drooping edge beside him.

"No one in his right mind takes the concept of collateral damage lightly," he said, "but the government and the Freebooters aren't going to just step aside. As awful as it is, 'booters have got a pretty good gig out here and the government's been safe and secure for a helluva long time now. So, yeah, there's gonna be more violence. And that's exactly what makes your grandfather's plans so damn important. If we can succeed in compromising the Guardian Star we should be able to get the attention of people who are quietly surviving out here as well as show the government that we mean business. It's got to happen, Valaria. Things have got to change."

Valaria nodded slightly, silently acknowledging that if the ranks of the Sons of Liberty were filled with men and women like Quinn they might just have a chance.

It was a prayer as much as a hope that they were.

II.

Rain was still falling when it was time to break camp in the morning and it would continue to fall off and on as they traveled the final miles now standing between them and St. Louis. They had reached the outer edge of the metropolitan area's fanlike expanse but a full day's trek still lay ahead before they would arrive at their final destination.

Although not yet completely out of the proverbial woods, Quinn visibly relaxed and his mood lightened as they entered territory patrolled by the Sons of Liberty. Neither he nor Valaria were much for small talk but he began to share things he had learned about the area's past and pointed out milestones as they continued walking.

About midmorning there was a lull in the rain and Valaria pushed back the hood of her oversized poncho, grateful for the reprieve and the trace of sunshine it brought with it. They were approaching a turnoff some ten miles west of the city center and Quinn paused when they reached it.

"Are we there?" Valaria asked hopefully.

"No, this is the exit leading to Chesterfield," he explained pointing toward the remains of an asphalt ramp shambling away from the highway.

"And?"

"And I'm considering a little detour."

She shot him an acidic *"you've got to be kidding me"* look.

"You've got to be kidding me."

"I know," he continued defensively, "we've been walking forever, but I really want to show you a little of this town."

"And just what's so special about this one? I've seen enough crumbling buildings and overgrown streets to last a lifetime."

"Not like this you haven't," he assured her. "Chesterfield's a real eye-opener."

She took some convincing but her curiosity was piqued and it wasn't long before they had snaked their way down the broken terrain of the exit ramp and set off exploring.

"It's not actually the town I want you to see," Quinn explained as they followed a reasonably intact street and stopped in front of twin stone walls that swept majestically away from both sides of an adjacent artery.

The name 'Sylvan Glen' was artfully carved into flat ovals of white granite embedded in the stacked stone of each curved wall and, although corrupted by time just as everything else they had seen during their nine-day odyssey, there was no mistaking the fact that this had marked the entrance to something special.

"This won't take long," Quinn promised as they turned in and began walking up the street.

He was right. In just a moment, Valaria stood gawking at the remnants of what must at one time have been an extremely upscale neighborhood. Like the rest of the yet-to-be-reclaimed portion of the country, it was slowly crumbling to ruins but enough remained of the oversized lots and huge brick and stone houses that had adorned them to serve as vivid testimony to the affluence of the former United States.

"Of course, not everybody in the country lived like this," Quinn said, stating the obvious, "but I thought it was worth a look."

He led the way up a long brick driveway curving gracefully toward one of the largest houses still visible through the previously coveted natural setting that was slowly devouring everything. Standing in derelict grandeur at the crest of a sloping lot, the two-story house boasted a steeply gabled four-car garage at the right hand end offset by an immense wing stretching to the left that had contained more than 5,500 square feet of living space. The architect had skillfully kept the house from appearing boxlike by adding two identical gabled sections extending from the front of the house toward the street, both of these further complimented by matching three-sided bay windows finished in contrasting smooth stucco and topped with copper roofs. Despite the fact that the house was slowly dying—almost none of the numerous windows retained any glass, the copper accents had long since turned green, and the roof had clearly given way in spots—it was absolutely stunning and Valaria couldn't take her eyes off it.

They made their way up the driveway and stopped in front of an oversized oak door. The wood was parched and pealing but it created an entryway still worthy of respect.

"Are we going inside?" Valaria asked in a hush one might expect to be reserved for entering a church.

"We won't chance going upstairs but, yeah, it's safe to go inside and take a look around. I stopped here on my way west."

Having lived most of her life in less than 800 square feet of space behind the pub, Valaria stood in open-mouthed wonder as she surveyed the interior of the opulent home that struggled valiantly against the relentless hand of nature that was intent on devouring it.

To the right of a large vestibule, a once-grand staircase ascended to the second floor looking as forlorn as an aging debutant still clinging to the last vestiges of youth. Its wide marble steps were cracked and broken, the missing spindles of its deteriorating banister displaying the debutante's pathetic gap-toothed smile, the walls streaked and blistered by her tears. Adjacent the staircase was a doorway into what must have been a combination study and library. Built-in bookshelves lined the walls and an expansive oak desk—now obviously home to a boisterous colony of chipmunks—still held pride of place at the far end of the spacious room. The mushy remains of a thick oriental rug squished soggily beneath their feet and the musty smell of moldering paper hung heavily around them, bringing Valaria close to tears at the loss represented by row upon row of wet, decaying books.

On the opposite side of the vestibule were the ruins of a formal dining room from which a pair of large, stubbornly resistant pocket doors led to an enormous kitchen and great room stretching in decaying splendor across the back of the house. Even this limited portion of the structure was many times larger than her living quarters in the dome and Valaria stared in amazement at the sprawling granite countertops that separated the huge open-concept kitchen from the rest of the space and the massive stacked stone fireplace covering the great room's far wall. Everything was filthy and falling apart but she walked reverently through the detritus, skimming her fingers across every surface, gently touching each piece of furniture and knick-knack that remained, opening every cupboard and door that still clung to a hinge... and trying to imagine the people who at one time had called this place home.

"There's a huge walk-out lower level beneath us," Quinn said, interrupting her reverie, "but the water and sewer lines have obviously ruptured so I don't recommend going down there."

"I can hardly believe this is real. Did *one* family really live here all by themselves?"

"Like I said, not everybody could afford to live like this but yeah, it's what they called a single family home."

"Ho-lee shit..."

"Yup," he agreed, looking around with a smile, "holy shit."

Once more girded against the persistent rain, the trio completed their brief detour through the splendor of suburbia and continued following what remained of Old 40 as it faithfully led them eastward.

Valaria listened politely—for the most part—as Quinn maintained a sporadic commentary on the area's background while they walked. She wasn't the most patient of audiences under the best of circumstances and was having trouble staying focused as she grew increasingly distracted and dumbfounded by the vestiges of extensive human habitation visible all around them through the tangled patchwork of weeds, trees, and ruins. Not only did the remnants of different forms of signage tell an abbreviated story of the metropolitan area, but from their often elevated vantage point along the asphalt path they followed, Quinn and Valaria could see a visual cacophony of what must have been a healthy collection of commerce and community stretching to the horizon on both sides of the highway.

"Hey Quinn," Valaria blurted rather suddenly, interrupting some insight he was sharing that she hadn't been bothering to follow. "I've got a question for you."

They had reached the point where Old 40 crossed a road identified as 'Big Bend' and she had abruptly stopped walking.

"OK..."

"I've seen signs for at least five colleges and universities today—Maryville University, Missouri Baptist, some Lutheran seminary, as well as Washington and St. Louis Universities; we've passed hospitals, golf courses, shopping malls—that Galleria thing was bigger than my entire settlement!—and look off across this area. There are more rooftops out there than I would've dreamed possible!"

"Yeah, well, it's like I've been telling you—millions of people lived in the greater St. Louis area before the plague."

"So, here's my question," she continued, resting her hands on a rusted length of metal guardrail and looking out across what must have been an extremely densely populated portion of the city. "Don't you think there are still some people out there?"

Quinn joined her at the rail, shrugging off his rucksack and stretching his neck and shoulders.

"Probably. No, make that *undoubtedly.*"

He sat on the edge of the guardrail, first testing its stability before trusting it with his full weight.

"It's more likely out in the hinterland where people could learn to live off the land again, but there are bound to be survivors scattered in cities and towns all across the country. It's what we're counting on."

"You really think they'll join your little revolution?"

"Yeah, I do. As the Sons get stronger and better organized we'll be able to start offering some of the things they've lost—security, healthcare, commerce; you sure as hell don't see the Triumvirate doing any of that."

Valaria digested his words in silence for a moment before indulging in another segue as she studied the overgrown vista before her. "God, why would anybody have wanted to live like that—so crowded and close together? Gives me claustrophobia just looking at it."

"Well, they brewed some of the best beer in the country here, played some of the best baseball—and apparently made *the* best frozen custard."

"Frozen custard?"

"Don't know just what it was, but you sure see enough signs around for it."

He stood and re-shouldered his rucksack.

"Come on, let's get going."

III.

Impressed as she had been by Chesterfield's unmistakable opulence, and as much as the densely populated outer ring of the city had been a bit overwhelming, nothing could have prepared Valaria for the awe-inspiring metal and glass canyons of the city's innermost rings.

At its zenith, St. Louis, Missouri had been one of the sparkling jewels of the Mississippi River basin. Having passed through Native American and French hands before becoming part of the United States in 1803, the Lewis and Clark landmark was trumpeted as the Gateway to the West; a title officially commemorated in 1965 by the iconic 630-foot-high stainless steel Gateway Arch. Not immune to the growing pains characteristic of metropolitan centers worldwide, the city had experienced both triumph and crisis as it matured. After riding the crest of prosperity in the decade following World War II, Missouri's riverside gem was burnished during the civil rights movement of the mid-twentieth century but was spared the violence that literally burned in cities like Detroit and Los Angeles during that era. Sparked by the thriving enterprise and pulsing nightlife at its sophisticated urban heart and enhanced by richly diverse neighborhoods like Clayton and Lafayette Square, the metropolitan area had quickly grown to embrace posh bedroom communities like Creve Coeur and Chesterfield in the spread of its outlying fan and became the proverbial poster child for the modern American city. Famous not only for its unmistakable 'croquet wicket' monument to Manifest Destiny, the city boasted world class education and health care, a plethora of public green space as well as museum, theater, and culinary opportunities rivaling those in much larger venues, with championship major league sports teams—and the best frozen custard in the country—rounding out the urban experience. As time passed, St. Louis had become a beacon of the American Dream, enjoying that status for almost a century by the time

Naomi Blanchard and the Neoteric Party took command of the national stage. It was an urban success story to be envied and emulated...

But like the rest of the world, one brought to its knees with devastating ease by the most insidious and invisible of villains—*bacteria*.

Due to the hiccup of geography that placed it almost at the center of America's portion of the continent, St. Louis was in many ways the nation's hub. Prior to the terrorist attack that unleashed a particularly virulent version of the pneumonic plague, the regional population had surpassed three million and Lambert Field, the city's burgeoning international airport, was serving more than 50 million travelers annually as tourists and entrepreneurs alike were drawn to the sparkling gemstone in almost equal measure. When the plague exploded—and the dominoes of infrastructure and order began to fall—it was like a puckish child sweeping away the playing pieces in a fit of temper; the entire St. Louis area staggered as the stench of death filled the streets of city and suburb alike and the loss of countless lives soon became the death throes of the thriving metropolis itself. Survivors of the plague eventually had been evacuated but the traumatized city continued to suffer, brutalized by the scavengers and elements to which it had been abandoned.

A stark microcosm of the results of the terrorist atrocity that had engulfed most of the developed world, the once proud beacon now stood as a tragic and lonely monument to everything the country had lost to the tsunami of fanatical extremism that had overwhelmed it.

Valaria and Quinn forged ahead through the detritus of that tsunami's wake, the more literal storm that had overtaken them west of the city having finally abated. Sporadic precipitation still dogged their heels, however, and although she had always loved the sound of falling rain, walking, eating, and sleeping in it for two days—accompanied by the persistent smell of wet dog—was beginning to eat away at Valaria's less-than-stellar reserve of patience. But after passing a vast natural area on the north side of the highway identified by Quinn as Forest Park, the personal thundercloud that had been making her mood as bleak as the weather began to lift as buildings of increasing height and various styles slowly started to command the emerging cityscape. In an amazing celebration of form and function, St. Louis seemed to reach heavenward with hundreds of distinctly different fingers and Valaria was once again dumbfounded.

"What's the matter?" Quinn asked as she slowed to a stop.

She peered at him from the recesses of her hooded poncho, gave him an incredulous smirk, and gestured toward the buildings clamoring for dominance in the near distance. "Gotta admit, the hick from the Borders is just plain gobsmacked by all this."

"Wow," he replied, eyebrow shooting up in mock disbelief. "Valaria Thorpe actually impressed by something—whodathunk it?"

"Well, who wouldn't be impressed by this?" she demanded. "Oh, but I forgot—you're such an accomplished world-traveler."

He ignored the sarcasm. "What's really impressive is the fact that St. Louis wasn't even all that big—would've fit in the hip pocket of mega-cities like Los Angeles and the New York/Philadelphia corridor!"

"New York," she murmured wistfully, still lost in the vista before her. "Can't even imagine it."

"Now *that's* a true wasteland. The whole eastern zone will still be deadly for another fifty years at least—a testament to the insanity of relying on a power source whose byproduct is as deadly as it is long-lived. The Triumvirate can *keep* it. We'll take what they've abandoned."

"Oh God, here we go again," she observed with dry disdain. "Shall I break out the fife and drums or will you be singing 'Yankee Doodle' unaccompanied?"

A bit of verbal parrying would have gone a long way toward shaking off the haunting debris of the last few days, but they were interrupted by the sudden appearance of a cadre of five men that materialized from the shadows and blocked their path.

"Hold up there," the apparent leader called out as they approached, extending his right palm toward them.

Not yet ready to surrender the sarcasm that was her stock in trade, Valaria leaned toward Quinn and referenced the men with a slight nod in their direction.

"Sons of Liberty or sons of guns?" she asked with a smirk. "Do you know the password or is there a secret handshake?"

It had finally stopped raining and both Quinn and Valaria pushed back the hoods of their ponchos and raked fingers through their unkempt hair. Taking his cue from his people, Yancy put an exclamation point on the drab autumn day by giving his drenched coat a thorough shaking.

Once the ponchos no longer hid their faces, the man in front called out to them again.

"Quinn, you bastard—is that you?"

"Dang," Valaria rasped. "Really wanted to see that secret handshake!"

Quinn walked away from her mordant humor, his right hand outstretched toward the man striding forward.

"Dodger!"

The two men met in the neutral zone between them, each grasping the other's right forearm while simultaneously clapping the other man on the right shoulder with their free left hand.

Valaria watched their reunion with cynical disappointment, glancing down at Yancy and cocking an eyebrow.

"Is that it?"

Quinn gestured them forward and, as introductions were made all around, Valaria warily evaluated her first group of dissidents.

They were a decidedly motley crew. Each wore blue jeans topped by a sweater or sweatshirt and were shielded from the elements by whatever raingear had been available—one obviously didn't receive a uniform when joining the Sons of Liberty. Two were well into middle age— brothers by the last name of Foster; strongly built but with plenty of grey in their hair and beards. The man Quinn had identified as Dodger— officially introduced as Levi Dodge—sported a close-cropped beard and clean-shaven head that perfectly accentuated his cocoa-brown skin and beautiful smile. The fourth, identified as Kevin Eldridge, clearly was still in his teens with just the whisper of a moustache above his upper lip and a rather serious breakout of acne peppering his solemn face. And one, Valaria was rather embarrassed to realize, was actually a woman. Field service obviously not being the place for a demonstration of femininity, she was dressed like her comrades, her hair pulled back in a gender-neutral ponytail, her name the gender-neutral Jordan; she looked like another adolescent boy and it was only when she spoke that a lilting, utterly feminine voice gave her away.

In spite of their general lack of uniformity, the one thing the patrol had in common was an impressive energy-pulse stunner holstered at their side—the standard issue Guardian weaponry referred to as StunStix.

Valaria wondered absently just what Dawson Hayes would have to say about that.

IV.

The last two miles of their journey were completed in the company of the patrol. Only half listening to the raucous—at times downright crude—conversation between Dodger and Quinn, Valaria walked along in silence as they finally said goodbye to Highway 40 and headed north on a major city street identified as Broadway. Still utterly beguiled by the glass and metal stalagmites reaching heavenward on all sides, she was more than mildly intimidated by a size and scope that the others all seemed to be taking in stride.

The exit itself had been a show-stopper for clearly visible immediately north from the crest of the highway were the remains of Busch Stadium, home of the legendary St. Louis Cardinals—and something akin to Mecca for a baseball fan like Valaria. Having followed the sport for as long as she could remember—no matter that the athletes for whom she cheered had all been dead for decades!—the decrepit bowl-like structure held a dispirited, mournful allure and she lagged behind trying to see as much of the stadium as possible while the others strode purposefully up the street.

"You a baseball fan?"

Kevin Eldridge, the pimply-faced adolescent, had slowed his pace so to join Valaria and Yancy. His voice was as dour as his expression and his gaze rarely left his mismatched shoes.

"You bet," she replied. "Never dreamed I'd have the chance to actually see a stadium in person; well, the remains of one at least."

Kevin squatted down so to be at eye level with Yancy and began scratching him under the chin, receiving a wagging tail and euphoric canine grin for his trouble. There was sad longing on his face as he interacted with the dog and Valaria felt surprisingly moved—silently chiding herself for the unexpected reaction; just what she didn't need was to pick up another stray!

"Here," she said, handing Yancy's rope to the boy. "Wanna take charge of him for a while?"

"Yeah... s-s-sure... thanks," he replied, stammering awkwardly and glancing up from his shoes just long enough to take the rope.

They walked along in silence for a bit, Valaria lost in her survey of the skyscrapers visible in every direction. A fascinating amalgam of various heights and designs, the buildings gaped at them through countless windows; dark, glassless frameworks that looked on with the vacant intensity of a blind man's stare. Every structure showed signs of significant exterior decay, an entire section off to the west bearing livid scorch marks from the tongues of an angry inferno whose insatiable hunger had obviously licked many an upper floor before finally burning itself out. Just as on the roadway, weeds of every description had infiltrated virtually every crack and crevice of the downtown area, and trees unexpectedly grew from even the loftiest of upper floors and rooftops. Wherever the hand of man had been removed, the hand of nature had gleefully reasserted itself.

As they continued walking a cold chill ran down Valaria's spine; was that movement she had she seen at an adjacent upper window? The overwhelming feeling of being watched filled her with sudden dread as she remembered their encounter with the Freebooters.

"You sure there aren't any people around here?" she asked Kevin, adjusting her backpack while scanning the panoply of windows on both sides of the street.

"Oh, I suppose scavengers still come through once in a while—and there are more of us Sons all the time—but the city's been deserted for years."

"Maybe it's just rats," Valaria mused.

"Not rats," he corrected quietly. "They're the first things to disappear after people leave. No people, no garbage; no garbage, no rats. No cockroaches either. In some ways the city's probably cleaner now than it's ever been."

Valaria pondered the young man's insights for a moment, noting as she did so that Kevin's demeanor was undergoing a subtle transformation as he spent time with her and Yancy—the dog probably deserving most of the credit. He no longer stared at his shoes—undoubtedly a serious impediment to being effective while on patrol—and his dour voice and expression were slowly warming.

She liked this kid.

She also liked what she was suddenly looking at.

"Bloody hell," she sputtered, "what is *that?*"

They had reached a break in the manmade canyon through which they passed. There was a large area of overgrown green space on the west hand side of the street that had obviously been intended to accent the historic building preserved at its eastern end. But it wasn't the open space or the tribute to history that had riveted Valaria's attention. Farther east, towering above the building Kevin identified for her as the Old Courthouse, was an enormous metal arch at the river's edge, glinting majestically in the setting sun.

"That's the Gateway Arch," Kevin informed her, smiling for the first time. "Haven't you ever heard of the Gateway Arch?"

Without replying, Valaria set off across the street and headed past the Courthouse at a determined trot. Kevin and Yancy caught up when she stopped on the other side.

"It's an old monument," he explained. "St. Louis was called the 'Gateway to the West'—you know, Lewis and Clark... Manifest Destiny... all that shit."

"This is *amazing*," she said, staring up at the arch and surveying the warren of walkways and overpasses designed to facilitate the flow of transports and pedestrians that must have flocked to the site when the city was alive.

She was heading for one of the walkways with Kevin and Yancy at her heels when they suddenly heard Quinn and the others calling to them.

"There you are!"

Dodger's voice scalded them as the patrol drew near

"Just what the hell do you think you're doing, Eldridge? You know better than to wander off."

"And if you're done *sight-seeing*," Quinn said to Valaria with a heaping spoonful of disapproval, "we need to move on."

In a retort peppered with an array of favored expletives, Valaria informed the group of her intention to go exploring, only to have Levi Dodge inform her in barely civil terms that the Arch was unequivocally off limits.

Snatching Yancy's rope away from Kevin—who had taken his superior's reprimand thoroughly to heart and returned to dour, shoe-staring silence—Valaria fell into sullen step next to Quinn, moody storm clouds once again gathering at her shoulder as the group resumed its trek up Broadway.

The detour to the Arch had taken place under the bemused eye of the setting sun. Playing its daily game of hide-and-seek with the city's skyscrapers, it began casting distorted shadows everywhere—constantly shifting, darkly ominous companions that rounded the edges of Valaria's petulance and made her begrudgingly glad to be in the company of a well-armed patrol.

As a result of their late-day arrival—and Valaria's impetuous excursion to the river—the game was over and it was dark when the patrol finally delivered them to their ultimate destination.

V.

Valaria slept late the next morning, luxuriating in a newfound appreciation for a real bed and stretching languidly beneath blissfully clean sheets upon waking. It was almost cold in the room, the rain that had chased them the last few days being the vanguard of a front that had brought the first chill of autumn. Still huddled under a thin blanket, she reached down to absently scratch Yancy's upturned belly where he lay sprawled on the floor beside her. Staring broodingly at the exposed springs supporting the mattress of the empty bunk above her head, she replayed the 'scolding' received from Dodger and Quinn the night before.

After a terse and grumpy goodnight to the two disciplinarians, Jordan Keller—the female member of the Sons' patrol—had escorted Valaria and Yancy through a confusing maze of corridors leading to the women's dormitory. Although clearly improvised, the dorm was surprisingly well-appointed with neat rows of metal bunk beds arranged at regular intervals around the periphery of the narrow room. The woman in charge, a large Amazon with a brusque, no-nonsense manner, had balked at first when Valaria appeared on the scene accompanied by a dog. Not entirely certain which of them the woman objected to more and although bone-weary, Valaria had stood her ground when the matron insisted the dog be housed elsewhere. Seeming to sense the precarious nature of his status, Yancy had wisely displayed his most civilized behavior while Valaria argued his case, staying seated docilely at her side, looking up at them with pathetically-pleading big brown eyes, tongue-lolling in a canine grin. A few tense minutes of heated debate between equally stubborn contestants had followed but the two women finally reached an almost respectful impasse and Yancy had been allowed to stay—for the time being. Flush with victory and momentarily energized, Valaria had followed Private Keller who helped her put linens on the bunk to which she had been assigned, accompanied her to the women's bathroom, and had gone through her own nightly ablutions while Valaria indulged in a long, steaming shower.

Now, as she slowly surfaced from sleep—thoroughly clean and rested for the first time in more than a week—Valaria found herself intensely curious about the monolithic facility she had barely glimpsed the night before.

As she would discover, it truly was a colossus.

After beginning its life as the *Dome at America's Center,* the site chosen by the Sons of Liberty for their official 'hideout' had passed through numerous incarnations before finally being christened *The Hubbard Dome and Convention Complex* in honor of William Hubbard, one of Missouri's own who had served as Vice President a decade before the plague. Nicknamed 'The Hub,' it had been a regional hotspot for conventions and concerts alike and home to another St. Louis sports franchise, a professional football team called the Clydesdales. Through some mixture of miracle and chance, the dome had withstood everything fate had thrown at it in the years following the plague and, although beaten and bruised, stood largely intact—the multi-sectioned cover that still managed to protectively hug the huge expanse being its most appealing feature for renegades trying to avoid detection.

Rising to a height of 210 feet, the domed portion of The Hub had been expanded over the years to cover slightly more than twenty acres and everything had been state-of-the-art when the world had abruptly been brought to its knees. In the dome itself, the lowest levels of permanent seating retracted so to maximize available space during non-sporting events and the artificial playing turf could be stored automatically beneath a beautiful hardwood floor that seamlessly glided into place in invisibly jointed sections. From mammoth ultra high-definition viewing screens and fascia boards around the dome's bowl to extensive concession and public access areas, the arena had hosted its 75,000 potential guests with grace and ease. Although most of its sophisticated automation no longer functioned, the dome and convention center offered more than three million square feet of space; more than enough to house, train—and hide—a small army.

For all it had to offer there was one more box The Hub ticked off on the Sons' list of priorities when choosing a hideout—only the Mississippi River and about 5 miles stood between it and one of the RSA's few transportation centers at the convergence of Interstates 70, 55, and 64 in the ghost town of East St. Louis, Illinois. From that serendipitous intersection, the highways were restored and maintained as they fanned out to connect the five Safe Zones created after the plague—access to which would become vitally important in the months ahead.

It was Yancy who eventually persuaded Valaria that it was time to get up and go exploring. Beginning to go through one of his most entertaining canine routines—a series of low bows, tight spins, and throaty chuffs she referred to as the 'piddle-prance'—he conveyed in no uncertain terms that his need for an excursion to the great outdoors was approaching critical mass. It was still comfortably dim in the room—all the windows being securely covered with blackout material—and Valaria would have loved to stay in bed but knew from experience that ignoring the dog for too long would result in an unwelcome urinary monsoon. Not wanting to give the dorm's matron any excuse to banish him, she reluctantly emerged from her comfortable cocoon and dragged her backpack from under the bed to extract the last clean clothes. Pulling on a pair of jeans and a turtleneck sweater, she set out to find an exit.

What she found was an armed young woman sitting on a chair in the hallway opposite the dormitory entrance, eyes riveted on the door.

"Whoa—hi there," Valaria said, pulling up short and reigning in Yancy's rope lead. "Didn't expect to find anybody out here."

"Good morning Ms. Thorpe," the young woman replied, rising. "My name is Ella Lansing and I've been assigned to assist you today."

"Assist me?"

"With whatever you need."

"OK, that's cool," Valaria said, instantly realizing that—of course—the Sons wouldn't automatically allow her free run of the place.

She gave the young woman what she hoped was a reasonably friendly, diplomatic smile.

"Well, right now we need a place for my dog to take a leak and then we could both use some food."

Ella led them to a side door that opened onto what had been part of an extensive paved area. Since every yard, walkway, street, and parking lot in the country had long since literally gone to the dogs, it was easy enough to find an appropriate place for Yancy to hike his leg.

Their young escort waited in the doorway for Valaria and the dog to return. Once back inside she took them through a warren of passageways—some of which Valaria thought she recognized from the night before—until finally entering a large, open area set up as a cafeteria. It was late morning and Valaria could hear people in an adjacent kitchen, probably working on preparations for the noon meal.

"This is where we eat," Ella explained as they sat down at one of the many tables. "Can I get you a cup of coffee?"

"Yes, thanks."

The young woman kept an eye on Valaria as she went to get coffee from a huge urn on a table near the kitchen door and grab a couple apples from a large bowl next to it. Valaria chuckled softly at Ella's wary surveillance wondering if they expected her to suddenly bolt and run helter-skelter through the facility somehow garnering intelligence to pass along to the Triumvirate.

She put her hand on Yancy's head and waggled his ears. "Got that hidden camera running, Bud?"

Ella's brief absence gave her a chance to take a look around. Here, as in the dormitory, all the windows at ground level were securely covered, the only natural light coming from a secondary bank of glass panels high up under the eaves. Everything was extremely utilitarian but, as in the dorm, surprisingly well-appointed. She said as much to her escort as the young woman placed the coffee and apples in front of her.

"This was a regional evacuation center after the plague," Ella explained, sitting down across the table. "Hundreds of people stayed here before they were sent on to the Safe Zones. When they were done I guess they basically just walked away and left everything."

"And you guys eventually walked in and started using it again."

"Pretty much. From what I'm told it was a total mess. Scavengers had thoroughly picked through things but they left the tables and chairs, beds, stuff like that. We're still working on cleaning things up and putting it all back together again."

"Just how many Sons are posted here?" Valaria asked, offering Yancy a chunk of apple.

"Sorry, ma'am, I'm not at liberty to share that kind of information."

"I'm not the enemy, you know—I came here with Gideon Quinn."

"Good to know, ma'am," she replied but offered nothing further.

Valaria considered drawing Ella's attention to the freshly-washed polka dot fabric adorning her left wrist and telling the other woman about her hard-earned status as minion but thought better of it—chances were the well-trained dissident would fail to appreciate the humor or grant any privileges on the basis of their shared status as Sons of Liberty flunkies.

They were just finishing their second cup of coffee—Valaria finally having succeeded in convincing Ella to join her—when Gideon Quinn came on the scene. He, too, had taken advantage of an opportunity to shower and looked much as he had the first time they met—wearing blue jeans and a black turtleneck sweater topped by his prized calf-length suede duster that had spent the last week carefully rolled up in his rucksack. Shaggy hair brushing against the collar, neatly trimmed stubble shadowing his face, he looked almost good enough to eat. As always, his signature half-gloves covered his hands.

"Here you are," he said, responding to Yancy's enthusiastic greeting and pulling up another chair. "So, what've you two been up to this morning?"

"Just pumping Ms. Lansing for all the dope on the Sons so I can pass it on to the government."

Ella looked more than mildly horrified and almost choked on her coffee.

"A joke, Ella—just joking," Valaria assured her.

The younger woman smiled meekly, the color slowly returning to her face, but looked like she was trying to recall exactly what 'dope' she might have inadvertently disclosed.

"Well, putting your espionage mission on hold for the time being, you ready for the grand tour?"

True to his word, over the next hour Quinn showed Valaria around the enormous convention center, pointing out areas that had been fully reclaimed and explaining projects yet to be accomplished. Along the way they encountered more people than Valaria had expected—she stopped counting after losing track and having to start over several times. For a girl from the Borders—someone who had encountered crowds only when gazing at the multitude of stars peppering the vast night sky—it was all more than a bit overwhelming. And in addition to their unanticipated numbers, everyone they met referenced Quinn with a significant degree of deference, causing Valaria once again to wonder about his status in the organization.

When they finally reached the dome itself, Gideon led her to the front row of an upper level section of seats where they could watch several squads working through various physical fitness and martial arts training drills out on the field.

"So, what do you think?" he asked with more than just a trace of pride in his voice.

"I think this is amazing," she replied in genuine awe, surveying the thousands of seats circling the arena. "Apart from the fact that I can't believe the number of people it would've taken to fill this place, I had no idea you Sons of Liberty were so well organized. You'd never dream all this was going on in here—the outside looks as bad as the rest of the city. Why didn't you tell me about all this?"

"Now that would've made a lot of sense, wouldn't it," he chided. "When you're the underdog you don't go around laying all your cards on the table just to get people to take you more seriously—not if you want to *keep* those cards."

She conceded he had a good point.

"Anyway," he continued, "once you announced you were coming with me I figured you'd see it all firsthand soon enough. And be honest, would you have believed me if I'd tried to describe this to you back at the settlement?"

Valaria indulged in a sardonic chuckle.

"No," she admitted, "I probably would have called you—"

"—a delusional asshole," he interjected without missing a beat, remembering her characterization of him at the town meeting.

"Well, yeah."

"I understand," he assured her. "We've kept an intentionally low profile even as our numbers have grown. The government isn't as all-powerful as they make out but they're still a helluva lot stronger than we are. I'm actually glad a description of this place would have struck you as delusional."

"Just how many of you are there?"

"There are about four hundred at this facility and we've got other, smaller, outposts scattered north into Iowa and as far south as Arkansas. We've even got a patrol out in The Wilds right now—our own Lewis and Clark Expedition if you will—trying to make contact with the people out there."

Valaria leaned forward, crossing her forearms and resting them on the railing as she continued to look around in wonder.

"Got a question for you," she said at length. "How do you keep the government from finding out where you are just by using people's tags?"

"That *is* a good question. Tags are definitely an effective means of identifying and tracking people but not everybody here is tagged and they're not hardwired into the nervous system or anything like that—a direct hit from a StunStik and they go dark without any lasting damage to the host."

Valaria winced inwardly at the thought of being hit by a stunner. Even at the lowest setting they still packed a serious punch.

Quinn had switched into lecture mode once again but this time his audience wasn't distracted.

"St. Louis is a nearly perfect spot for all this," he was saying. "Not only is it centrally located, it's close—but not too close—to one of the RSA's transport hubs about five miles the other side of the river. On top of that, this place offered an amazing amount of space and by some miracle it's still in decent shape. The fact that this dome still exists was *huge*—gives us a shielded area where we can train."

He gestured toward the people out on the field before continuing to tick off additional advantages. "There's tons of storage space, we've been able to repair a lot of the solar panels so we've got electricity most of the time, and we're even connected to the MetroLink."

"The 'MetroLink'?"

"The city's mass transit system. It ran mostly underground and had just been expanded and converted to magnarail around the time of the plague. Getting it up and running is one of our top priorities."

He glanced at one of the stadium's computer displays to check the time. "And you get to see it firsthand 'cuz we're gonna be using the only run that's been repaired—we've got an appointment at headquarters this afternoon."

"I thought *this* was headquarters."

"This is the bulk of the iceberg. You have yet to visit the proverbial tip."

They returned to the cafeteria where they ran across Levi Dodge and his squad as they arrived for the first lunch shift. During a quick meal with Dodger's team it was decided that Kevin Eldridge would take on dog-duty while Quinn took Valaria to headquarters for the mysterious meeting he kept dangling tantalizingly before her but about which he refused to give any details. Both Kevin and Yancy seemed happy with the arrangement—the human portion of the equation nearly falling over a chair in his eagerness to take the dog's lead.

The Hub's MetroLink station was in an underground section of the complex where the convention center and dome conjoined. Two miles of the station's eastbound tunnel, and the southern leg of the U-shaped spur they would need, had been cleared of debris but a lot of work remained to be done. As a result, the tram they boarded rocked and creaked like a ship adrift on sullen seas as it traversed the magnarail track and lights flickered sporadically overhead giving credence to Quinn's earlier observation that they had electricity "most of the time." Between the two, a feeling of disorientation kept Valaria from being sure of what direction they were traveling.

It took more than thirty frustrating minutes to get to headquarters—including several delays when the tram temporarily stopped altogether—but they finally pulled up to a sprawling underground siding that easily could have accommodated a hundred people at a time. Only a portion of the platform had been rescued from the debris and fallen ceiling tiles that littered most of its surface, marking an unmistakable path for disembarking passengers to follow.

They crossed the siding toward large, plate glass double doors flanked by two unsmiling guards armed with pulse rifles and StunStix. Acknowledging Quinn with a silent salute, one of the guards unlocked the door and the duo entered a huge, dimly lit expanse. Myriad objects were scattered throughout the vast, poorly lighted space, barely discernible in the muted light. There might have been some sense to the arrangement but the room's shadowy condition presented neither rhyme nor reason to the casual observer.

"Where are we?" Valaria asked in a hush. "What *was* this place?"

"This was the Museum of Westward Expansion and we are directly beneath the Gateway Arch."

Valaria's head swiveled upward almost as if expecting to see the mammoth structure that arched 630 feet into the sky from ground level somewhere above them.

She peered into the shadows shrouding the room. "This is headquarters?"

Quinn nodded. "And that's why the Arch most definitely is no longer on the city's walking tour."

"Why didn't you guys just tell me that last night? Why all the cloak and dagger?"

"Need-to-know, Valaria, need-to-know."

"What the hell does that mean? You're telling me now."

"Yeah, but the rank and file only know there's a command center *somewhere*, not that it's so close by. So the grunts on Dodger's patrol are in the dark about this place. All they know is the river's off limits because it's so open to observation…"

"And we'd like to keep it that way," a commanding male voice interjected from the shadows.

As they turned toward the sound, three forms emerged from the darkness, the man in the center—apparently the owner of the voice—striding energetically forward with an outstretched hand.

"General Quinn—Gideon—good to see you again!"

"*General* Quinn?" Valaria asked in a sardonic hush as the trio grew closer.

Her companion ignored both the question and the tone in which it came gift wrapped.

With eye contact as firm as his grasp, the man who had spoken took Quinn's hand in both of his, greeting him with genuine warmth before directing his attention to Valaria. "And this must be Ms. Thorpe."

The two appraised one another somewhat warily but Valaria liked what she saw.

He was elderly. Short and stocky, his heavily lined face was accented by bushy white eyebrows and an equally bushy white fringe encircled his shiny bald pate. At first glance he appeared to be the type of unobtrusive old person society easily ignored but he was clearly in charge and possessed a confidence and magnetism that were unmistakable.

Valaria's instincts told her this was one old man who should not be dismissed lightly.

After a moment's silence, he continued.

"Although," he observed with a thoughtful smile, "we thought you were a grand*son* and, quite frankly, I never expected to have the privilege of actually meeting you."

She bristled slightly. "Sorry if either of those are problems."

"Not at all," he assured her. "Not at all."

"Valaria," Quinn interjected, "this gentleman is James McFarland—Congressional Speaker of the House at the time of The Revanche."

"*Until* The Revanche," Mr. McFarland corrected, nodding somewhat sadly. "I made the mistake of resigning the next day and inadvertently allowed President Blanchard to create the Triumvirate in her own image as a result. But come; let's continue this conversation in my office."

Accompanied by the two men who had emerged from the shadows with him but had thus far remained silent—Assistants? Bodyguards?—Speaker McFarland led the way through the gloomy maze to a secured area deep in the bowels of the museum's basement.

"I'm from St. Louis originally," he told Valaria as they walked. "Always loved this place as a child and find delicious satisfaction in the fact that our modern incarnation of the Sons of Liberty is housed in one of the Old Nation's crowning tributes to the republic." He smiled almost mischievously. "I'd love to see Naomi Blanchard's face the day we finally make our presence known!"

They walked on, passing through a heavily guarded checkpoint before entering a secluded area where half a dozen technicians were working at virtual computer screens projected above makeshift work stations. McFarland led the way into an adjacent office, leaving his two silent shadows outside the door.

"Well, Gideon," he began, settling in behind a massive mahogany desk and indicating two chairs in front of it. "I know, of course, of your mission's success and the plans you've brought back for us but tell me more about your time in the Borders."

Quinn proceeded to provide a quick rundown on his experiences in the settlement, focusing on their discovery of the tech hidden in Otis Thorpe's chessboard and the schematics Valaria's grandfather had skillfully embedded in his designs on the legs of the dining room table.

"Amazing," the former Speaker of the House chortled. He directed his attention to Valaria. "Your grandfather truly was one of the great minds of my generation. And, as we now know, also a great patriot."

"Guess I'm still coming to terms with all that," she replied impassively.

Mr. McFarland considered her words silently for a moment; Valaria wondered if he was waiting to see if she would begin to squirm under his scrutiny. She sat ramrod straight, meeting his unwavering gaze with her own steely stare.

"So tell me," he said at last, "just how did you end up accompanying Gideon on his return trip?" His sharp eyes pinned her in place and his voice carried an edge of skepticism. "What is your purpose here?"

It was beginning to sound slightly more like an interrogation than a conversation and Valaria took a slow, deep breath before replying, wisely realizing that—as a stranger—it would be foolhardy on their part not to be at least mildly suspicious of her. Making a conscious decision to accept the ramifications of her status as outsider, she explained the circumstances surrounding Quinn's rather sudden departure—the Guardian occupation of the settlement and the contentious town meeting that had left her feeling unmoored and vulnerable. She finished her account with an admission that the stark drama of the trip had been a real eye-opener.

When she fell silent, the former Congressional leader nodded slowly and held a hand up toward Quinn who looked ready to speak.

"I'm not saying you're unwelcome," McFarland said. "To tell the truth, it's something of a coup to have Otis Thorpe's heir join us. We do, however, tread very carefully where newcomers are concerned. This is no Hollywood confection that portrays Armageddon as crazed zombies climbing over the walls or casts teenagers as the heroes of some ludicrous dystopian scenario. That being said, something sinister is going on across the river and we need to find out what it is and—ultimately—convince the regime that it's in their own best interests to let us go."

He looked pointedly at Valaria.

"So I ask you again, Ms. Thorpe—what are your intentions here?

"The eyes of our countrymen are now upon us, and we shall have their blessings and praise if we are the instruments of saving them from the tyranny mediated against them. Let us therefore animate and encourage each other, and show the whole world that a free man contending for Liberty on his own ground is superior to any slavish mercenary on earth."

~ George Washington

CHAPTER TWELVE

I.

Five months had passed since Valaria and Quinn's arrival in St. Louis. Five months that had seen summer take its final bow, autumn dash through like an Olympic sprinter and winter settle in with all the tenacity of a predator guarding its kill. The heat and humidity of a Missouri summer had always been an enervating precursor to the surprisingly frigid counterpoint that was St. Louis in winter and its current bluster was to be no exception. By February the streets were buried beneath more than two feet of accumulated snow and temperatures struggled to climb above freezing. Since most of the Sons of Liberty lacked appropriate winter outerwear and moving around much in the snow—or worse yet, clearing it away—would have made their presence in the city far too obvious anyway, the Sons of Liberty stationed at The Hub dug in for the duration, focusing on repairs, planning, and—most importantly—training.

Valaria was proving to be something of an anomaly among the recruits with whom she worked and trained. Although nothing had ever been said to the rank-and-file, it was clearly understood that she was directly connected to whatever Gideon Quinn had brought back from his time in the Borders and that she enjoyed somewhat enhanced status as a result. After all, no ordinary yob was allowed to keep a dog with them or assigned private quarters in order to do so—no matter that the room was a former storage room and actually still smelled faintly of bleach. No one overtly resented what could have been perceived as special treatment but they certainly were curious—curiosity routinely deflected by Valaria's abrupt, porcupinesque personality. She wasn't exactly unfriendly just predisposed to holding people at bay and imbued with a more than slightly abrasive temperament that kept her prickly quills well-sharpened.

Although not officially assigned to a specific squad (Quinn had laughed out loud when the topic had been broached), Valaria spent her days working and training alongside everyone else but took most of her meals with Gideon and—although not privy to actual strategy sessions—accompanied him to headquarters on a fairly regular basis; James

McFarland had apparently taken a liking to the brusque newcomer and enjoyed picking her brain about life in the Borders as well as meandering through her memories of her grandfather.

McFarland's final question during their initial conversation had burrowed its way into Valaria's brain like a fragment of song lyric that nags interminably. When asked about her purpose in accompanying Quinn to St. Louis a response had come easily enough—she intended to see to it that her grandfather's plans were used in a way she believed he would have wanted. She had made it clear, however, that although definitely not aligned with the government it was *not* her intention to join the Sons of Liberty in the literal sense. It was that last observation—stated perhaps a bit too boldly in light of her rather ambiguous circumstances—that had led her to the realization of what her ultimate goal actually was.

Valaria Thorpe intended to develop a skill set that would enable her to participate when it came time to use her grandfather's plans in an assault against the Guardian Star.

II.

"Come on, Thorpe, move your scrawny ass!"

The high-pitched, mocking voice sliced through both the momentary lull and Valaria's tenuous veneer of compliance. She shot a withering glare toward the drill instructor shouting at her from midfield but did as she was told and ramped up her pace as she and her training team completed their last lap around the track that encircled The Hub's expansive playing field.

Sheltered by the dome, both track and turf were in remarkably good shape considering the fact that neither had received proper care for decades and clearing away debris and cleaning the surfaces had been fairly straightforward tasks. The field's artificial grass—a synthetic polymer emulating the look and feel of natural sod—had been installed just a year before the plague and was almost as lush as when the St. Louis Clydesdales had faced their NFL opponents across the gridiron. Valaria routinely shed her ill-fitting shoes and ran barefoot on the pliable greenery that abutted the six-lane track. The equally ill-shod recruits with whom she trained often followed suit, running on the track or in the turf along its edge without the impediment of the blister-inducing, make-do footwear that seemed to be a universal post-plague reality.

Their run completed, Valaria and her team trotted midfield to join the drill instructor. As they gathered, Sergeant Edwards took a few purposeful steps away from them in order to focus on a message that had just come up on the data pad she carried. The momentary distraction presented an unexpected reprieve that found most of the trainees leaning forward with hands on their knees, gulping refreshing draughts of air while their heart rates slowed and they waited for the sergeant to return.

Walking the group's perimeter with her hands on her hips, Valaria inhaled deeply with each stride, savoring the exhilaration of her rapidly beating heart. As was true of all the men and women with whom she trained, Valaria's stamina had improved exponentially over the five months she had been at The Hub and she no longer dreaded the daily laps around the arena—although running the stadium stairs would probably always be a killer.

"Count off," Edwards barked as she rejoined the group and they scuttled into formation.

She waited as each in turn shouted out their number in quick succession.

"There's been a change in our schedule," she continued, her voice edged with frustration at the intrusion into her carefully choreographed routine. "One through nine, you're needed in the MetroLink tunnel— apparently there's been another collapse and they could use more hands. The rest of you report as planned for MMA."

After a silent beat, Edwards glowered at the twenty grunts gathered before her.

"What say you?"

The team snapped to attention where they stood.

"*Yes sir; yes sir,*" they shouted in unison, their voices echoing shallowly in the cavernous space.

Valaria swallowed the smirk that automatically creased her lips as she half-heartedly joined the ubiquitous display of military discipline, fighting the urge to give Edwards a lopsided, derisive salute.

As half the squad jogged off toward an officer waiting to take them to the tunnels, the rest headed for the opposite end of the field and the MMA training for which they were scheduled.

Counted among the second half of the team, Valaria fell into step slightly behind them.

Once out of sight and earshot of Sergeant Edwards who accompanied the squaddies headed for the tunnel, all vestige of discipline quickly evaporated and several younger recruits began exaggerated horseplay in anticipation of the martial arts session to come.

Valaria watched them with a reproachfully snarky smirk—the intricacies of MMA training were lost on some of the grunts; just throw a StunStik in their hands and call it good.

Tom Braddock, a slightly older recruit who had both feet stoically planted in reality watched their antics with mild disdain and also lagged behind.

"Nice to get out of an extra work detail, huh?"

"I can take it or leave it," she replied. "Not much different from putting in time at the settlement farm."

"So you're from an agricultural settlement?"

Not one to make reassuring noises to statements of the obvious, Valaria walked on.

"I'm from a settlement, too," he remarked, his conversational confidence beginning to waver. "I suppose quite a few of us come from the Borders."

She gave him a noncommittal nod and continued walking.

"Being here's been a real education," he persisted. "Not just the training, but the chance to meet so many different people. There were only about thirty left in my settlement—barely enough to keep up with our work quota. There had been a few off-grid births, but no exiles in years. Thought our numbers must really be dwindling until I got here; felt guilty about leaving but the time had come. How about you?"

His words took her back to the contentious town meeting that had inspired her departure and Valaria gave her companion another neutral nod.

"Yeah, I guess you could say the time had come."

They had reached the far end of the field where an improvised martial arts training area had been set up.

Initial exploration of the abandoned NFL facility had yielded a variety of tattered and decaying accoutrements of professional athletics. Most were of no use to them but among the sundry items was the happy discovery of two dozen large wrestling mats, fifteen of which had been patched and returned to reasonably serviceable condition. Those mats— along with makeshift practice dummies and hand drawn diagrams illustrating key impact points on the human body—created the ad hoc dojo where Valaria and her fellow trainees silently began working through a series of stretches while waiting for the session to begin.

Their instructor, a rather diminutive African-American man just beginning to grey at the temples, didn't keep them waiting long. Striding purposefully across the field and pausing at the edge of the mats, he watched for a moment with composed detachment before silently signaling them to the center.

Marcus Griffin, sporting the rank of lieutenant, was purported to be a Guardian defector but looked more like an accountant than a government enforcer specializing in martial arts—a fact he capitalized on since being the personification of the old adage 'looks can be deceiving' often worked to his advantage in a fight. Griffin taught a blend of martial arts he referred to as 'Situation-Specific Skillsets,'—a use of alliteration Valaria had scoffed at until she got to know the man better and began paying him the respect she discovered him due. Beginning with basics similar to what anyone might study—how to punch, kick, and utilize various takedown moves—martial arts training under Marcus Griffin then focused on learning to dominate an opponent through superior body positioning, controlling someone during clinch fighting, and utilizing a variety of different chokeholds. Once these primary skills had been covered they became part of the Sons' daily drill so that, eventually, muscle-memory began to kick in and the moves slowly became instinctive to most trainees.

This was the point Valaria's team had reached. The group had already been working together for several weeks before she came on the scene and she initially experienced some unexpected odd-man-out trepidation as a result. It hadn't taken her long to catch up, however, for she was intensely motivated and Lieutenant Griffin was equally determined that all his students succeed.

Having reached the reinforcement phase of basic martial arts training, over the last week Griffin had begun introducing Valaria's team to his specialty, what he rather ominously called 'Kinetic-Kills'—alliteration she now found more chilling than laughable. This next level of training ultimately was for a select few to be singled out during the introductory phase. More intense and challenging, it included no defensive actions— something most trainees found extremely difficult to master—all counter moves taking the form of strikes to specific, vulnerable points on the body.

One of the Masters under whom Griffin had trained taught that every human body reacts identically to certain injuries and, as a result, if you know how the body will respond the instant it's struck you can incapacitate any opponent through focused strikes to specific nerves, joints, and organs. For a man of diminutive stature like Griffin—and for women serving alongside their larger, more heavily-muscled male counterparts—this was a leveling of the playing field that literally could mean the difference between life and death in a fight.

The concept of Kinetic-Kills held Valaria in thrall and she was determined to be among the elect selected for further training.

Automatically pairing up with her chatty companion for some skill-review sparring as the session began, Valaria stretched extensively and loosely shook her arms as she anticipated moving through the basics. Taking up a position opposite her, Braddock did likewise. As they referenced one another in prelude to the drill, Griffin's voice interrupted their concentration.

"Thorpe," he shouted, "front and center."

"Oh *shit*," she muttered under her breath.

Because there usually was an even eighteen in their group, Griffin rarely participated in the preliminaries and more than a month had passed since Valaria had been singled out to assist in a demonstration. With half their team sent to help clear the MetroLink tunnel—leaving them at an uneven nine—it was logical that the lieutenant would become the extra man needed for paired sparring but she had assumed—*hoped*—he would partner with one of the men.

Her mouth was suddenly dry and her heart began to pound; she didn't just want to show progress, she hoped to come away from the encounter with no broken bones!

The first strike came before Valaria had time to gather her wits about her, leaving her flattened on the mat and glowering up at the lieutenant with barely suppressed fury. Instantly frozen in their tracks the other trainees stood silent at the periphery, the youngest of the group—Chad Brooks—looking like he was about to wet himself.

"What'd you expect, Thorpe," Griffin scoffed with a hissing chortle. "Think your opponent's always going to bow politely before an attack?"

He stretched out a hand to help her rise.

She considered the gesture suspiciously and, with a narrow-eyed sneer, locked her hand around the wrist of his outstretched arm. In the heartbeat before Griffin again exploited her vulnerability Valaria used his counterweight to her advantage, lurching forward and wrenching the lieutenant's arm in a circular motion that threw him off balance and brought him down to his knees.

In the blink of an eye, Griffin rocked backward slightly and sprang to his feet with the grace and agility of a gold medal gymnast.

With markedly less elegance, Valaria also rose.

"Nicely played," Griffin observed with just a trace of genuine admiration in his voice.

It was the first time Valaria had heard the lieutenant say anything remotely positive and it was all she could do to keep from falling at his feet in a puddle of sycophantic drool.

III.

Kevin Eldridge, Yancy's pimply-faced, ad hoc au pair, was waiting for Valaria when she returned to the convention center. He and the dog greeted her with similar, unrestrained enthusiasm and she found herself thinking that, if he had a tail, Kevin undoubtedly would be wagging just as much as her other perpetual shadow.

"You're limping," he observed with hushed concern when she reached him.

"No kidding? I hadn't noticed."

"You all right?"

She heaved a sigh that, under ordinary circumstances, would have dripped with annoyance and triggered the launch of a sarcastic incendiary but, directed at Kevin, was laced mostly with resignation. "Yeah, I'm fine—just got a little more than my share of attention from Lieutenant Griffin today, that's all."

Kevin literally shuddered.

"That guy scares the crap out of me," he admitted. "Nearly pee my pants every time he looks my way."

"He's no 'Mr. Rogers,' I'll grant you that."

"Who's 'Mr. Rogers'?"

"He was on an old-time kids' show. My God, where'd you grow up? Didn't you ever watch any old vids when you were little?"

Kevin shrugged diffidently and fell silent. They had reached the cafeteria and he stopped short, holding out Yancy's lead before heading toward an exit without comment or eye-contact with the dog's owner.

Valaria scowled at his back. "Where're you going? Thought you wanted another chess lesson after supper."

The teen had thrust his hands into the pockets of his well-worn hoodie and walked away in a bruised and brooding silence.

"Was it something I said?" she asked Yancy as they watched him go.

The dog gave her a mildly reproachful look.

"*What?*" she insisted. "Shit, it was only 'Mr. Rogers.' What's wrong with that?"

"What's wrong with what?" a voice from behind asked.

She whirled around to find Quinn standing at her shoulder.

"Geez, don't sneak up on me like that," she snapped, dropping Yancy's lead and taking an exaggerated defensive stance, hands raised in mock-karate fashion. "With these finely-tuned reflexes I could do some real damage!"

"Yeah, right," he scoffed, reaching down to pet Yancy's head. "Was that Kevin I saw leaving? What'd you do to chase him off this time?"

"Nothing," she replied innocently. "Just asked if he ever watched any old kid's shows when he was growing up. What's wrong with that?"

"Probably salted some old wounds; I think the kid's background's pretty brutal."

Valaria fell silent for a beat, pushing her hair away from her face by running her fingers through the shoulder-length waves.

"Shit," she muttered, succumbing to a moment's self-flagellation. "Well, how the hell am I supposed to know that? I'm not used to having to treat people with kid gloves."

"I don't think you even *own* a pair, do you," Gideon chuffed.

Valaria shot a narrow-eyed glare his way before looping Yancy's lead loosely around the back of an adjacent chair and heading for the cafeteria's serving window. "I can be diplomatic when the situation warrants," she observed. "Hell, I was the picture of restraint when you bullied your way into my life."

Quinn choked back a laugh. "*Restraint?* I don't know if that's quite the word I'd have chosen."

Having reached the line of recruits worming its way past the servers doling out a rather pasty stew concoction accompanied by thick slices of bread, they each picked up a tray and waited their turn.

"Did I rat on you?" she demanded. "Did I throw you out on your ass?"

"No," he admitted with a smile.

"Well, I'd call that some pretty serious restraint on my part."

Quinn conceded the point without further comment as they retrieved Yancy and headed for a table well off to the side, conversation dwindling as the duo tucked into their meal.

"You got time for a game of chess?" Valaria asked as she wiped her plate with the last of the bread and offered it to Yancy. "Kevin and I were gonna play but apparently I'm persona non grata tonight."

"Sure," Quinn replied. "As a matter of fact, I want to talk to you about something."

"What've I done now?"

Quinn cocked an eyebrow and couldn't resist throwing a rather taunting '*I-know-something-you-don't-know*' grin her way.

Intrigued, Valaria waited impatiently for Gideon to finish eating and hurried to bus the table before they could be joined by some officers who had just come on the scene and were acknowledging Quinn from the serving line. Once back in her tiny room, Gideon took the only chair while Valaria perched on the edge of the narrow bed, Yancy curling contentedly on the blanket draped across its foot.

"How's the power holding out?" Quinn asked as Valaria put the chess set on an upended foot locker she had placed between them.

In order to demonstrate some of Otis Thorpe's genius for Speaker McFarland, Quinn had worked tirelessly to recharge the power cell incorporated into the chess board's surface. McFarland had been enthralled by Thorpe's skills and touched by his whimsy. Smiling in admiration when Quinn described the 'treasure box' that only Valaria's fingertips could open, the old man had then touched her arm in warm acknowledgement when told about the sentimental chess game that triggered the chessboard's display of the Guardian Star schematic.

"So far, so good," she said in reply to his question.

Sharing Otis's work with Mr. McFarland had been gratifying but having access to her grandfather's plans was particularly fortuitous; ever since the demonstration Valaria had been studying the diagrams as part of her goal to become a member of any team assigned to use them in an assault on the Guardian Star. In the process, she had discovered she had at least a smattering of the elder Thorpe's aptitude and, at this point, felt she probably knew the Star as well as anyone else at The Hub; or at least she liked to think so.

They executed a few moves in silence before Valaria reached the extent of her meager reserve of patience and could wait for Quinn no longer. "OK, so what did you want to talk to me about?"

Gideon focused on his next move with a satisfied tight-lipped smile. "I was wondering if you felt ready to go on a mission with me."

"A mission? Are you serious?"

Quinn leaned away from the chess board and folded his arms across his chest, the memory of his first encounter with Valaria—when she had ridiculed his use of the word—bringing the trace of a smile to his face as he considered the woman before him. "Yeah, I'm dead serious. And if you want to go I have to know right away 'cuz we're leaving at first light."

"Of course I want to go... Where're we going?"

Gideon shifted position, leaning in and resting his forearms on his thighs. Even though they were alone, he lowered his voice.

"We've got an outpost about a two-day walk south from here," he began. "It's a small storage facility where we've been stockpiling supplies—mostly armaments. We've received word that the government knows about it and plans to take it out. Problem is, it's snowing down there and the storm's keeping us from being able to hijack the government's telecom array; that's how we communicate since we have no array of our own. It's hard enough to stow away under GovNet's signals in the best of circumstances but we're down now because of the storm so there's no way to warn the depot without actually sending someone. Bottom line, we've gotta get there before the Guardians do and move those supplies."

Quinn fell silent but looked like he had more to say.

"And..." Valaria prodded.

"And," he continued with mild reluctance, "there's some*one* we need to get out of there even more than the supplies. 'Sam Adams' was overseeing the latest delivery of weapons and as far as we know, he's still there. If the government gets its hands on him it could be game over for us. And there's no way in hell we're gonna let that happen!"

IV.

They left just before dawn the next morning.

Valaria's inclusion on the ten-man patrol was a tribute to Quinn's status; she wasn't anyone's first choice since her training was incomplete and she wasn't even officially a member of the Sons. The fact that she came equipped with a dog made her even less appealing to some but Gideon was in charge of the mission and his faith in the black and white mutt convinced many that a dog might actually prove useful. And if the dog was coming along his 'handler' had to come as well.

Other than Valaria's somewhat questionable inclusion, selecting personnel for the mission had been the easy part. Quinn knew his fellow dissidents well and created a skillfully forged chain, among whom were his friend Levi Dodge and Dodger's right-hand man, a tall, gangly Texan named Farley Donovan. Donovan's shoulder length ginger-colored pony tail and dusting of freckles was a striking counterpoint to Levi's shaved head and café au lait complexion and Quinn always had to smile when he saw the two of them together. And with his southwestern drawl there was no mistaking that Farley was an import from the Lone Star Republic, something Valaria found intriguing since she had never met a foreigner before.

Once the 'who' had been decided, the problem of 'how' needed to be addressed and it had taken true teamwork to outfit the group for a walk through the remorseless Missouri winter. Insulated coats and boots were a standard of days long gone and anyone scrounging for survival in the hinterland basically hunkered down and hibernated during the colder months. As a result, the patrol ended up looking more like a band of scavengers than a military squad, dressed in multiple layers of socks, sweaters, and jackets donated by their peers and wearing the stoutest pair of shoes or boots they could beg, borrow, or commandeer.

Fortified against the elements—and armed with captured StunStix and pulse rifles—the patrol left The Hub by dwindling starlight.

Their destination was a town by the enticing name of Eureka. Although less than thirty miles away it would take two full days to get there—more if the weather turned against them. Before the plague Eureka had been a quick twenty-five minute drive down Highway 44. Even now, under better circumstances, following the degraded roadway would have made the trip reasonably straightforward. But with the addition of snow all bets were off and the patrol would need to follow a compass—and their noses—more than patchy remains of asphalt in order to successfully reach the outpost.

They set out at a determined pace, trudging through the snow and weaving their way out of town by way of side streets that were less likely targets for surveillance should government drones sent to attack the storage facility already be aloft and the scope of their sweep broad enough to include the outer edges of the expansive St. Louis area.

There was little conversation as the patrol wormed its way down streets choked with snow. Valaria had been fortunate enough to find an actual pair of boots to borrow for the trip and was supremely grateful for dry, reasonably warm feet as she contemplated two days of winter walking. Yancy's fraying rope leash had been replaced by a length of chain with a clip at the end dug up by Kevin and—whether it was the allure of a new lead or the urgency he sensed from his human companions—the free-spirited dog was responding reasonably well to his role as a charter member of the Sons of Liberty Canine Corps. With her dog by her side, weeks of MMA training under her belt, and the improvised walking stick Quinn had given her months before firmly in her grasp—not to mention her minion polka dots securely wrapped around her left wrist—Valaria felt optimistic about whatever lay ahead. And trudging through the snow with her Sons of Liberty compatriots, she found herself reluctantly acknowledging a sense of purpose unlike anything she had ever experienced.

Something that might actually be worth fighting for.

"Do you think they'll send drones or Guardians?" she asked Quinn as they slogged along.

"Hard to say," he replied. "President Blanchard got her taste for drones during The Revanche and the government's been improving them ever since—you saw for yourself what the latest TAD is capable of when it flattened those Freebooters that chased us. Assault drones have always been a force to be reckoned with and we don't have much that can stand up to them. Still, there's nothing like boots on the ground so we'll have to be on the lookout for either—or both, I suppose."

They had traveled a little more than half way when Quinn gave the order to stop for the night. The wind was picking up, temperatures were dropping, and the slow-moving storm front that had knocked out communications was definitely closing in on them. Coming across the shell of an abandoned house shortly after dark, Gideon decided that something offering a modicum more protection than their two tents could provide shouldn't be taken lightly and ordered the patrol to make camp. The integrity of the structure had long since been compromised by weeds, trees, and wet moldy drywall but a corner of the house stood in proud defiance of its present circumstances, leaning heavily against an expansive brick fireplace and sporting a crumbling roofline balanced precariously at a rather jaunty angle that made the remaining windows look as if they were winking at you.

Sentries were posted, a cold supper was shared, and the patrol settled in for a restless night's sleep huddled around two small heating units.

By 3 a.m. the storm had blown itself out leaving nothing behind but a brittle night sky peppered with stars—and three additional inches of snow. Coming off his stint on guard duty, Quinn settled in next to Yancy and Valaria. Wrapped in the coarse blanket forming his makeshift cocoon and using his rucksack as an improvised pillow he was just beginning to drift off when crackling static emitted from the communicator attached to his belt jarred him back to wakefulness.

"What is it?" Valaria asked groggily, surfacing from sleep on the other side of the dog.

"Quiet!"

The static continued and soon the entire patrol was awake and alert, leaning in and straining to decipher what was being said through the interference.

"...*George this is Mar—a... Geor— this is 'Martha, are – out there?*"

Quinn shot a relieved glance toward Dodger and responded eagerly.

"Hello Martha, this is George. Martha, this is George. We hear you..."

"*You're breaking up, George...*"

"Martha, this is George. We're on our way to you. You're about to have some unexpected company so you'll want to *make room for them*. Do you read me? You need to make room for the guests."

"*Got most of that, George... could use some –elp with the preparations. Did you –ay you're com— here?*"

"Damn," Quinn muttered, rising to his feet and moving into unobstructed starlight before activating the communicator again. "Yes, Martha, we're on our way... Do you read me? We're on our way..."

Empty static was the only response.

"Martha? Martha, this is George, do you read me? ...Martha?"

Everyone stared at the communicator in hushed anticipation, willing it to speak.

"Martha?"

Quinn raised a level gaze to the patrol clustered around him. "Break camp; we move out in five."

It wasn't a good night's sleep that energized the squad as they silently followed Quinn's order; brothers-in-arms lay in harm's way and they were the only ones who could do anything about it. Disillusionment and dissatisfaction with the government in Columbus had been festering for decades and those who finally were standing up—those aligned with the Sons of Liberty—might be facing improbable odds but they had discovered something within themselves common to every generation of soldier before them—a sense of duty and brotherhood that was as intense as it was unfathomable to the uninitiated.

Even Valaria Thorpe—the skeptical outsider—sensed something special in men like Gideon Quinn and Levi Dodge. And despite still accusing Quinn of speaking in platitudes and basking in the banal she also found him inspiring—although she was loath to admit it—and was finding in herself a sense of resolve she normally reserved for nothing more significant than procuring a regular supply of smokes.

"Think they understood your message?" she asked once they were underway, pulling a battered cigarette from the ever-present pouch tucked in the pocket of her jeans. She passed Yancy's lead to Quinn in order to free both hands for the all-important task of lighting up.

Gideon took the dog and fed out some slack in the chain before responding. "I'm sure they did—if they heard it properly. 'Visitors' or 'guests' is how we refer to government movement. Kinda lame as far as codes go but we need to be short and to the point since we communicate by riding piggyback on the regime's GovNet signals."

Valaria nodded, exhaling a cloud of pungent smoke that wafted into Quinn's face.

"Geez, woman—when are you going to break that disgusting habit?"

He was about to launch into his well-worn tirade about the vile and self-destructive nature of smoking but Valaria had an agenda of her own.

"So, guess I finally know where you perch on the 'ol Liberty Tree, huh," she said in reference to his thinly veiled conversation with Eureka.

Gideon walked on in silence.

"They called you 'George'—as in George Washington, I assume. That's pretty impressive."

Quinn glanced over his shoulder toward the rest of the patrol before responding.

"Oh, I don't know about that," he murmured with a diffident shrug.

"Drop the humility, *General*," Valaria chided. "I've always known you were higher on the tree than you implied—your rank and the way people defer to you make it pretty damn obvious."

Both the tone and temperature of Quinn's response were markedly cool. "What's wrong with a little humility? And if it's that obvious to you maybe it should also be obvious that it's a role I'm not entirely comfortable with."

He would have continued but Farley Donovan, currently walking point, had stopped short at the crest of a steep knoll and held up a hand to stop and silence the patrol.

As one, the squad dropped into a silent, alert crouch.

After a moment, Quinn moved forward to join Donovan who was squatting next to a tree on the ridgeline. A half-frozen pond lay at the bottom of the slope on the opposite side. As Gideon reached the top, several dozen Canadian geese took to the air in a frenzy of flapping wings and mournful honking that ruptured the frigid stillness around them. For a moment, Quinn thought Donovan's signal must have been just a precaution as their approach disturbed the wary flock but as he drew up next to him Farley again indicated the need for silence and pointed toward the woods encroaching upon the pond's western shoreline below them.

Quinn's heart skipped a beat.

Moving stealthily through the trees and undergrowth was a group of at least twenty Freebooters!

V.

The patrol looked on in silent anticipation from its uniform crouch at the bottom of the knoll. Valaria loved the haunting call of wild geese and relaxed a bit as they ascended, wings beating in rhythm, slowly moving into their instinctive V formation as the tumult of their exodus abated and they headed east. Knowing that Yancy's love for the Canadians extended beyond mere esthetic appreciation, she drew the dog close and clamped her hand around his muzzle; if he decided it was time to hunt the last thing they needed was him bellowing out his intentions. She shushed him quietly, eyes riveted on Quinn's back, as a throaty growl rumbled through the dog.

After watching the Freebooters slither out of sight into the woods extending beyond the pond, Quinn and Donovan slid down their side of the slope and rejoined the patrol.

"Freebooters," Quinn explained tersely to the unwavering eyes waiting for them at the bottom.

"Well that's some shit-ass bad luck," Dodger hissed.

Gideon considered his words in silence for a beat, beginning to scowl.

"I'd say it's more than just bad luck," he replied with a skeptical huff. "It's one helluva coincidence, don't you think? I mean, what are the odds that a gang of 'booters would just *happen* to cross our path out here in the middle of nowhere in the middle of winter?"

"What are you saying?" Dodger asked. "You think they knew we were coming? How could they possibly know?"

"That's a really good question."

"Maybe the government told them," Donovan suggested.

The patrol looked at him, dumbstruck by the suggestion.

"Holy shit," Dodger said. "I don't even want to *think* about what that would mean."

"But that doesn't make any sense," Valaria interjected. "Why would the government send them? They hate 'booters. Guardians hunt them all the time."

"Just think about it," Farley drawled, warming to the idea. "Down in Texas we don't have trouble with Guardians but Freebooters are a constant pain in the ass. If the government and the 'booters ever joined forces that could be one helluva game changer for y'all."

"You gotta admit, Freebooters are damn good at what they do," another man observed. "I could see the government teaming up with them. What's that old saying… '*The enemy of my enemy is my friend*'?"

"Talk about a match made in Hell," Dodger muttered.

"I think we at least have to consider the possibility," Quinn said, pulling a map and compass out of his rucksack. "I think we're about here," he continued, pointing to the map. "Eureka's still three or four miles away. Let's come around on the 'booters flank and follow them for a while. If they continue on, all well and good, but if they're heading for Eureka we're gonna have to stop them—or at least slow them down."

Dodger nodded. "I hope you're wrong but I agree; we've gotta know for sure."

Without wasting any time, the patrol set out in the opposite direction the Freebooters had taken. They trudged through the snow at a quick step for about a quarter of a mile before turning sharply toward Eureka once again. If the 'booters were part of the government's plan of attack they'd also be heading south and, with any luck, the patrol would come in from the side and catch sight of them before being discovered themselves.

They moved as quickly and stealthily as possible through a tangle of underbrush now further congested by snow. Quinn took lead and had just about decided the Freebooters must have moved off in a different direction when Yancy stopped short behind him and almost literally went on point.

"Gideon," Valaria hissed with quiet urgency, indicating the dog.

Quinn glanced back and held up a hand to halt the patrol.

Without comment he and Dodger moved forward until they heard voices in the near distance and dropped into a squat at the edge of a small clearing.

Quinn smiled faintly in tribute to a mongrel's sharp instincts.

Apparently having stopped to get their bearings, the group of Freebooters they had been tracking was milling about the clearing trying to stay warm. A small clutch of men was almost on top of Dodger and Quinn arguing over a rabbit they had killed and debating the merits of eating it raw. Moving away from his companions, one of the men edged even closer to the tree line behind which Quinn and Dodger hid, unzipping his jeans and relieving himself in the snow.

As steam from the hissing snow rose just inches from in his face and the foul smell of urine filled his nose, Quinn found himself fleetingly longing for the smoky exhaust from Valaria's cigarette. He glanced at Dodger who gave him a *"This just keeps getting better"* look before slowly retreating into the woods.

Quinn silently followed.

Once back with the patrol, it was Farley Donovan who spoke for the group.

"So?"

"Well, they're definitely out there," Quinn replied.

Farley reached down and waggled Yancy's ears with one hand while clasping Valaria's shoulder with the other.

"Good job, boy," he said to the dog before turning to smile at its owner.

Realizing that a group of Freebooters at rest was a much easier target than when they were once again alert and on the move, Quinn instructed the patrol to get ready to go on the offensive—and ordered Farley and Valaria to continue on to Eureka to warn the outpost. It was a mandate accepted with smoldering frustration on Thorpe's part but Donovan again put an encouraging hand on her shoulder and they silently moved on while the rest of the patrol headed back to the clearing.

VI.

It was never to be more than a delaying maneuver. Although well trained and highly motivated, a patrol consisting of only eight Sons of Liberty was hardly a match for twenty mercenaries, for that was what the Freebooters essentially had become. Now loosely affiliated with the Triumvirate's oppressive regime the 'booters had even more incentive to harass those in the hinterland...

Apart from the sheer joy they derived from terrorizing civilization's tattered remnant, they now were being quite handsomely rewarded for doing so!

Quinn and his squad approached the clearing to the sounds of a loud argument emanating from the gang of heavily armed 'booters tensely knotted in its center. Taking advantage of their quarry's coarse discussion about just where the town of Eureka actually was, the Sons silently moved into position behind whatever form of protection they could find, Quinn gesturing three into large evergreens bordering the clearing's southern end.

Focused on Gideon and hardly daring to breathe, the squaddies waited for the signal to strike.

As they watched—tightly wound and ready to spring—a particularly burly Freebooter strong-armed his way to the center of the roiling gang and shoved the combatants apart.

"Knock it off, you stupid bastards," he growled fiercely, spittle flying as he snarled at his companions. "We've got a job to do and you're wasting valuable time."

He looked up at the clearing sky and the position of the morning sun before pointing almost directly at the Sons' patrol and continuing with both confidence and authority. "Check out the sun you brainless prats. It rises in the east, doesn't it? That means the town's this way."

Before the other 'booters had a chance to act on the man's insight, Quinn gave a shrill whistle and the Sons opened fire.

With the advantage momentarily in their favor, eight Freebooters went down in sprays of red.

Shouts of enraged surprise radiated from the remaining mercenaries as they sprang into action and rushed the clearing's perimeter. Known for working well as a unit—and for being extremely adept at self-preservation—they began returning fire in a heartbeat.

Quinn knelt beside a patch of lanky saplings and fired into the scattering gang but as he shifted position in order to take out a 'booter zeroing in on one of his snipers, the searing heat of a pulse burst skimmed the surface of his upper arm. It was a ragged jolt that surged downward into his fingertips wrenching the rifle from his grasp and spinning him sharply to the ground. Wincing in pain and slightly disoriented by the force of the blast, he looked up just in time to see the dissipating energy wave—still potent and deadly—obliterate the face of the squaddie charging forward to help him, the force of the blast lifting the man off his feet and flinging him backward into the trunk of an adjacent tree. He flopped forward like a rag doll, smoke rising from his ghoulish wounds. Quinn retrieved his pulse rifle with his uninjured left hand, swung it upward and with a furious cry shot the offending Freebooter before he had time to fire again. The 'booter dropped his rifle and clutched futilely at his gaping belly, looking at Gideon with a mixture of rage and startled anguish as he sagged to his knees. The snow beneath him was now a slippery red slush and the man's knees splayed outward in opposite directions, bringing him down face first into the blood pooling beneath him as it gushed from between his fingers.

Gideon staggered a bit as he struggled to stand in the slick snow, the shooting—and the ululating howls of the Freebooters—filling the clearing with an unearthly dissonance. Determined to check for signs of life in the man who had fallen in his defense, he knelt next to his comrade, knowing full well no one could survive such injury. The bloody pulp that had once been the face of Taylor Ramsey, the squad's jokester, smelled slightly of cooked meat where the edges of his gruesome wounds had been cauterized by the energy pulse.

Bile burned the back of Quinn's throat but the melee around him brought him fully back into the moment.

He glanced at his watch. Their encounter with the Freebooters had been going on for a mere ten minutes—not nearly long enough to give Donovan and Thorpe an adequate head start. If they could hold the 'booters for another fifteen or twenty minutes the pair would have a real chance of getting to Eureka in time to warn the outpost and help clear out whatever evidence of their presence remained.

His right arm hanging uselessly at his side, Quinn continued firing the pulse rifle with his weaker left hand—evading more shots than he was able to get off. Ducking behind an obliging tree, he paused to take stock. In addition to Ramsey and a healthy quota of fallen 'booters, he could see the corpses of two men who shortly before had been vibrant members of his team—one of whom dangled unceremoniously from a nearby tree, a look of utter surprise etched into his dead face, a shocking red tangle of viscera lying draped down his chest and resting in the cradle of his sagging neck and chin.

Turning away from the impact of the gore, Gideon looked for Levi Dodge and finally caught sight of his friend facing off with a 'booter almost twice his size.

Both had somehow lost their rifles and they were fighting hand-to-hand, grappling in a macabre ballet to the accompaniment of the Freebooters' ululating cries and the pulsating bursts of energy weapons. Dodger was bleeding profusely from his nose and his opponent appraised him with an open-mouthed sneer that exposed a bloody maw where his front teeth should have been. Every time Levi was able to bring the 'booter down, using throws and body positioning that would have made Lieutenant Griffin proud, the ponderous Baryshnikov with whom he danced rose and hurled himself forward again.

Winded and bloodied, Levi Dodge stood his ground.

Gideon headed toward him, determined not to lose another man. He watched as his friend darted agilely away from the 'booter before doing a half-spin and planting an impressive sideways kick squarely into the man's chest.

"Dodger," Quinn shouted as the Freebooter went down. *"Dodger..."*

Levi gave him a lopsided salute while wiping his bloody nose and giving his face a swath of crimson in the process.

His equally determined—decidedly less flamboyant—opponent had risen once again, managing to pull a knife from somewhere within the folds of his torn and bloodied coat.

Literally snarling at Dodger, he stumbled forward.

In an act of reckless desperation, Quinn whistled shrilly and hurled his pulse rifle toward his friend. It flew awkwardly end over end in a high arc and Gideon cursed his injured right arm for forcing him to throw from his left. But miraculously Dodger was somehow able to snatch the rifle in midair, grabbing it by the muzzle end. Planting his feet, he gave it the most enthusiastic wind-up his exhaustion could muster and—in a masterful merger of baseball and golf—swung straight into the gut of the oncoming 'booter, then pulled back to swing forcefully upward under the man's chin sending him sprawling backward into the bloody slush.

This time the 'booter didn't rise.

VII.

Donovan and Thorpe were still well within earshot when the shooting began.

A frisson of fear coursed through Valaria. She pulled Yancy's lead up short and turned back toward the sound, surprised to realize how much these people—how much Quinn—had come to mean to her.

Farley also paused, his hand once again on her shoulder.

"Come on, Thorpe," he said quietly. "They've got their job to do and we've got ours."

"Do you even know where we're going?"

He smiled through her dubious sarcasm.

"Of course I do—and it's not much farther but we've gotta keep moving."

They soon reached an area where markedly less snow had fallen and were finally able to find and take advantage of the degraded asphalt ribbon that had once been Interstate 44. Within minutes remnants of signage indicated that the town of Eureka was all around them.

Eureka had been established in 1858 along the route of the Missouri Pacific Railroad, an early attempt to connect the Midwest to California. The story was told that when railroad workers clearing land ran across a flat area with little to impede their progress they cried out, "Eureka!"—and the name stuck. Once the community was entrenched along the tracks it grew quickly, becoming known for being home to the St. Louis Children's Farm, an outreach program giving kids from the city's tenements temporary escape to the country.

Almost a hundred years later it had become home to escapism of a decidedly modern nature.

"What in God's name is *that?*"

They had walked past most of the long abandoned town and Valaria was just about ready to question Farley's claim that he knew where they were going when the acerbic challenge was totally derailed by an other-worldly assortment of huge, oddly shaped structures suddenly visible in the near distance above the trees.

Farley's easy smile returned. "That, my friend, is our destination. It was what they called an amusement park."

"A what?" Valaria asked, thoroughly *un*amused by the ungainly tangle of ominous shapes that loomed ahead of them.

"An amusement park," he repeated. "It was called 'Six Flags.' There apparently was a whole bunch of 'em around the country all by the same name. We've got one in Texas; I've seen it."

Shifting the strap of his pulse rifle where it strained against his shoulder, Farley started to move on but turned back when Valaria hesitated. Yancy paused between them, his chain pulled taut in her hand as he encouraged his reluctant human forward. Something about the unearthly tableau unfolding before them had reached in and seriously rattled her calm and Valaria stood momentarily rooted to the spot. Feeling rather foolish for her reaction to the haunting eeriness that lay ahead, she nonetheless shuddered involuntarily.

"Come on, Thorpe," Farley drawled, "we need to hurry."

Turning off the main road, Donovan led the way down a broad avenue which, in its day, had provided an impressive approach to the park but now—like every other road in the country—was dry, cracked, and mercilessly compromised by weeds. Wide enough to accommodate more vehicles than Valaria could even imagine, it passed beneath an enormous weathered sign proudly identifying the park and welcoming visitors. The sign had come loose from one side of its imposing brick moorings and now lay restlessly askew across the roadway, squeaking mournfully in the winter wind as it rubbed against the rusted cable that had once secured it and adding to the desolate loneliness the abandoned park exuded.

Valaria glanced around, almost expecting to see the specters of long-dead patrons basking in the fun of carefree days.

She quickened her pace in order to catch up with Donovan.

Once past the huge sign the broad avenue was easy to follow and the trio broke into a determined jog through wisps of aggrieved snow that swirled around their feet in the brisk winter wind.

Ahead of them lay a vast parking area, faint yellow grid lines still visible in places. Here too vegetation of every description had long since forced its way through the sprawling asphalt; plants that now stood sadly bereft and brittle in the snow that blew and drifted aimlessly about them like wisps of low-lying fog.

The park's main entrance was marked by a large oval fountain. Choked with debris, a thin layer of ice formed a murky crust over the putrid water resting at the bottom of its wide, shallow bowl. The far curve of the derelict waterworks was rimmed by six tall flag poles, only one of which still sported a recognizable flag.

It was the stars and stripes of the old United States.

Valaria had never seen a U.S. flag in person—the RSA having reduced the stripes from thirteen to five (one for each Safe Zone) with only three stars in the upper left field of blue to represent their venerated Triumvirate. Even though it hung in filthy tatters, flapping despondently in the frigid wind, she was moved by the archaic banner and paused for a moment, thinking of Otis.

Donovan reached out and gently took Valaria by the wrist, glancing around cautiously and heading for a series of interconnected booths designed to funnel patrons into the park. He led the way through turnstiles where darkened display screens waited patiently for a public that no longer existed and they entered a section of the park that looked like something straight off a history disc. Although dilapidated, decayed and littered with debris, the once-charming storefronts lining both sides of the cobblestone street were designed in the Victorian style popular at the end of the nineteenth century. Valaria hardly noticed, however, for her eyes had been drawn to a gigantic wheel rising majestically above the snow covered tangle of trees, vines, and underbrush seeking to overwhelm it and—even more astonishing—to a towering web of intricate scaffolding far beyond that appeared to support some type of railway. Rising to a staggering height that must have been at least four hundred feet, the system of track was apparently designed to intentionally take the most harrowing path imaginable. After plummeting downward from its zenith, Valaria could see multiple loops of varying sizes and—although now thoroughly impeded by vegetation—the track even appeared to form a tight corkscrew along the side closest to them.

She scowled in utter amazement, mouth slightly agape. "What am I looking at?"

Farley gestured to the colossal wheel.

"That's called a Ferris Wheel," he explained. "People would sit in those attached gondolas and then the whole thing would turn; on one that big you could see forever!"

"And *that?*" she asked, pointing at the huge, ramshackle track beyond.

"That's a rollercoaster. I've been on one in Texas that still works—although it's nowhere near that big."

"People would actually *ride* that thing?"

"You bet; why not? Before the plague places like this were wildly popular—and mostly for the thrill rides. I remember my dad saying that parks had moved to computer-generated *virtual* rides in his day—they saved space and could create unbelievable thrills—but that lots of people still wanted the outdoor, visceral experience of the real thing." He pointed toward the track. "And that's what you got as a result."

"Holy crap, you couldn't pay me to get on that thing!"

"Aw, come on—where's your sense of adventure?"

She gave him a cynical smirk. "Sense of adventure? Death wish is more like it."

Fighting the urge to take a detour across the park to investigate the coaster up close and personal, Valaria followed as Donovan headed toward an adjacent section of the midway.

They entered a portion of the park added during Six Flags' final expansion prior to the plague, the wide archway leading to it identifying the area as 'Virtual Valhalla.' This modern version of mythology's paradise consisted of a long circular avenue lined with buildings of differing shapes and sizes, the exteriors of which were festooned with thematic facades designed to entice passersby to come in and experience the mechanized mayhem within. Through virtual reality, everything from personally programmable roller coasters to a mission to an embattled alien planet had awaited those eager to indulge their lust for the next big thrill.

As they walked they came upon a building whose exterior emulated a typical pre-Revanche cityscape. The sign—partially destroyed by design—touted the experience within as a 'Terrorist Take-Down.'

"That's a shit-load of irony, isn't it?" Farley observed dryly as they passed. "If we'd been *able* to take them down, this park—hell, the whole damn world—wouldn't be the wasteland it is now."

Valaria acknowledged his insight with a glum nod, looking around in wonder at yet another example of what the world had been like before religious extremism became gangrenous fanaticism that ended in a totally pyrrhic victory over the despised infidel.

A cold chill of apprehension ran through her and she grasped her walking stick more tightly and reeled in Yancy's lead.

From the moment they entered the park Valaria had had the sensation of being watched. Trying to dismiss it as a byproduct of her intense reaction to the eeriness of the place—and taking her cue from Yancy who was fairly reliable at alerting to the presence of others—she nonetheless kept glancing over her shoulder.

"Would you relax," Farley chided.

"I can't help feeling like we're being watched."

"Of course we're being watched. Do you think we'd make this an outpost and then not protect it?"

"So why don't they make contact?"

"They have," he informed her. "We've been following their signals ever since entering the park. If I hadn't known how to read them I can guarantee you they'd have made *physical* contact long before now."

"What are you talking about? What signals? Why haven't you said anything?"

"Sorry, guess I didn't think it was important."

Valaria heard Quinn's 'need-to-know' echoed in Donovan's words.

"Oh my God," she moaned, "not you too."

Farley was about to ask what she meant when a low whistle drew their attention back to an attraction offering the beguiling opportunity to take on hordes of grossly disfigured mutants. A petite Asian-American woman wearing shabby clothing, her face smudged with dirt, silently gestured them toward her. Valaria realized the woman had been part of the grisly tableau of mutant and human automatons forming the approach to the building and that they had walked right by without noticing one of the inoperative machines was real.

"Nothing like hiding in plain sight," she murmured to Farley as they followed the woman inside. "And what the hell good are you," she added to the dog trotting along at her side.

The woman continued on in silence, escorting them down a long serpentine hallway intended to lead patrons slowly into the bowels of the building while waiting their turn in line.

Donovan gestured toward opaque panels lining the walls. "Bet those were used to startle and scare people waiting in line with projections of the 'Mutant Mayhem' awaiting them. Wonder if they were in 4-D..."

He sounded wistful and Valaria imagined him anxiously standing in the queue, reacting to the shocking images being projected at unexpected intervals and filled with anticipation for the vicarious horror that lay ahead.

The hall finally opened into a dark apocalyptic landscape where a scattering of enclosed booths designed to look like makeshift shelters stood ready to insert visitors into five minutes of virtual mutant vs. human carnage. Their silent escort led them around the perimeter of the booths to a door at the back that was barely discernible from the black wall in which it nestled. The woman keyed in a pass code, gesturing them through but not following when the door burped opened.

Another dark corridor stood before them but this one was quite short and an inviting pool of light at the end beckoned them forward.

As they paused to let their eyes adjust, two men appeared in the light.

"Welcome to Valhalla," one of them called out. "Welcome to paradise." Just this side of elderly he stood tall and lean, his face creased with the lines of a life well-lived as he smiled warmly.

"*Paradise*," the other, far younger, man chided with a scoffing chuff.

"Well, it sure was when I came here as a kid," his companion assured them.

The newcomers were ushered into what must have served as the control room. Like The Hub, the room's long-neglected surfaces had been cleaned and repaired as part of its transformation into a Sons of Liberty outpost.

Looking around for traces of weapons, Farley wasted no time in completing their mission.

"We're part of the patrol that's coming to help you. We've been sent ahead to let you know there's a gang of Freebooters headed this way."

"Slow down, son," the older man replied. "'Booters pass through from time to time but they never come close to finding us. They don't even know we're here."

"This time is different," Farley insisted. "They're definitely heading this way—we think they were sent by the government."

The two men were obviously surprised by Donovan's suggestion, the younger man looking as if he found him intellectually lacking.

"That seems pretty far-fetched," he scoffed. "What would the government want with Freebooters?"

"That's what we thought, too," Farley agreed. "But it seems like one helluva coincidence that they're heading this way at the exact time the government's planning a raid. And think about it, if those two are scratching each other's back it could be a real game changer. That's not something our patrol leader's willing to gamble on; he sent us ahead while the rest of the squad tries to slow them down."

"We've been expecting *drones*," the younger man said, more to his companion than to Donovan and Thorpe. "Sam didn't say anything about the government sending troops—let alone '*booters*."

"Is he still here?" Farley asked. "That's another reason we were sent ahead. If Adams is still around you've gotta get him out of here."

"He left once we saw you enter the park," the older man assured him.

"He'd be safer than the rest of us anyway," his companion added under his breath.

The older man shot him a meaningful glare, intentionally deflecting the younger man's offhand comment by apologizing for their lack of manners and taking time out for introductions to be made. He identified himself as Roscoe and the younger man as Paul.

Farley and Valaria exchanged glances while introducing themselves but neither pursued what Paul had said.

"Have all the weapons been moved?" Valaria asked instead.

"Almost everything; the rest of the garrison moved out about twenty minutes ago. We held a few things back in case we need them."

"And this is a new fall-back location," Paul added pointedly, "so if government drones do attack they won't hit us unless they take out the entire park. And with the whole place at our disposal your 'booters would be looking for a needle in a haystack if they come for us."

He paused, making cool eye-contact with Farley before continuing.

"Bottom line, there's really no reason for the two of you to hang around."

Roscoe placed his hand on the younger man's shoulder in an attempt to soften the blow of his bluntness. "Sorry if Paul comes on a bit strong.

But if what you've suggested about Freebooters heading this way is true, it might be best if you moved on—the risk of being discovered increases exponentially the longer you're in the park."

Farley smiled faintly at the older man's conciliatory words and looked at Paul with a level, confident gaze. "If you don't need our help, I agree there's no reason for us to stay— and we're eager to get back to our patrol."

Suddenly alert, Yancy turned toward the door where, responding to some unseen signal, the grimy woman had silently joined them. Without comment, she took the trio back the way they had come.

"Stay safe," she said quietly as they walked away and she resumed her post in the macabre tableau outside the building.

"Did you catch Paul's comment about Sam Adams being safer than the rest of us?" Valaria asked once they were out of earshot. "What do you think he meant?"

"Bet he's infiltrated the Freebooters—hiding in plain sight like our guide back there."

VIII.

Before sending them ahead, Quinn had pulled Donovan aside to look at the map and choose a rendezvous point well away from the park in case the Freebooters tracked them. They had selected an area just off the highway a mile north of the exit leading to Six Flags, a siding identified on the map as a 'Rest Area.'

By the time Farley and Valaria arrived, the lowering afternoon sun had begun casting elongated shadows across the short road leading from the highway to a small building where travelers had been able to stretch their legs and use public restrooms. Pausing along the edge of the road, they quietly watched for anything that might betray the presence of 'booters. After a long, reassuring silence, Farley moved on to scout the periphery, leaving Valaria and Yancy hidden among the trees.

Valaria crouched next to the dog, hugging him close.

"C'mon, c'mon..." she murmured into the frigid air, willing Donovan back into sight.

He emerged from the shadows at the far side of the parking lot a few minutes later and gestured her forward.

"Nobody's here," he said when she reached him. "We might as well get out of the wind and wait inside."

Almost completely covered by layers of thick deciduous vines that had slowly devoured it over the years the squat structure looked more like a basket than a building, the twining network of creepers now brittle and leafless in the cold winter wind.

It did not look particularly welcoming or restful.

"Think the toilets still work?" Valaria asked, recognizing the symbol for restroom on a broken sign.

"Hardly, but what harm's a little more pee gonna do?"

Moving inside out of the wind, they cleared away some of the accumulated debris next to a corner window. While Valaria went to check out the toilets, Donovan settled in to wait for the rest of the patrol.

The restroom proved to be just as disgusting as expected and after returning from her enlightening excursion to the world's filthiest toilets, Valaria managed only a few minutes of silence after sitting down on the grimy floor. "Shouldn't they be here by now?" she asked restlessly.

"Frankly, yes," Farley admitted. "We'll give them 'til morning and then head back on our own."

Valaria stood and looked out the window, staring anxiously into the semi-dark before once again huddling on the floor with Farley and Yancy.

Pulling her knees up to her chest and wrapping her arms around them for a little added warmth, she considered the foreigner next to her. "Can I ask you something?"

"Sure."

"I've been wondering just what you're doing here. You're from Texas, right? So why'd you join the Sons? This really isn't your fight."

"It's true that the Triumvirate poses no direct threat to us down in Texas," he replied in his smooth, southwestern drawl, "but a lot of people look at what the Sons are doing and see a real chance to finally restore stability across the country. Mexico's already claimed parts of what used to be California, Arizona and New Mexico; guess we'd like to see them stopped before they take even more of the old United States."

"But why does any of that matter now? Who gives a shit about The Wilds—it's all just a wasteland. And anyway, the southwest used to belong to Mexico, didn't it?"

Farley bridled at her words. "More than two hundred years ago. Listen, you can debate the whole Alamo/Mexican War thing 'til the cows come home—justified, unjustified—but the bottom line is that after winning the war the U.S. *paid* Mexico for the land—to the tune of about twenty-five million bucks! How often in history has *that* happened? How often does the winner *pay* the loser instead of just taking the land they fought over and subjugating or annihilating the people? Granted, that's not to say things were hunky-dory once the dust settled but, no, quite frankly I don't think Mexico has any particular claim left on the southwest."

Valaria conceded that the patriotic Texan had a decent point and the duo fell silent as a cold winter night wrapped its frigid arms around them. Neither felt inclined to discuss their concerns for the long overdue patrol, the stillness around them growing heavy with what wasn't being said as the hours lengthened and the pair dozed fitfully.

Dawn was just beginning to paint the eastern horizon an optimistic rosy pink when Valaria awoke with a start as Yancy shifted into an alert position. Realizing she had fallen asleep gracelessly draped across the dog with her head resting against Donavan's chest, she jerked herself away.

Farley held up a cautioning hand.

"Something's out there," he said in a hush, indicating Yancy.

With a throaty growl the dog tried to move forward but Valaria reeled him in and put her hand around his muzzle.

"What is it," she whispered.

"Probably just an animal. I don't hear anything but he sure does."

Now fully awake, the pair strained to hear what had alerted the dog. In a few moments the stealthy crunching of leaves was barely discernible outside the broken windows on the opposite side of the room.

Donovan slowly stood, lifting his pulse rifle to his shoulder and indicating that Valaria should move behind the remains of an adjacent display cabinet. She slid into position as quietly as possible, keeping Yancy at her side. With one hand around the dog's snout and the other firmly grasping her walking stick, she peered around the cabinet's edge.

The distorted shadow of a man fell across the threshold as he pressed himself against the wall by the gaping doorway.

Valaria held her breath as Donovan took aim.

"Farley," a raspy voice called out quietly. "Farley—you in there?"

A surge of relief coursed through Valaria and she sagged back against the cabinet, releasing her hold on Yancy.

The dog responded before Donovan could, barking loudly at the familiar form of Levi Dodge that now filled the doorway.

Farley lowered his rifle and smiled at his friend. "Geez Dodger, I almost shot you!"

"Well that would have been inconvenient."

The two friends met in the middle of the room and shook hands.

"Where's the rest of the patrol?" Donovan asked.

"Out in the woods. We've been playing hide-and-seek with 'booters all night."

Before the question could be asked, Dodger continued. "Ramsey, Tate, and Martinez are down." He stepped to the door and gave a short, sharp whistle. Turning back, he appraised the duo in front of him. "How about you two; you OK?"

In response to Dodger's signal, the remaining four members of the patrol did a quick jog to the building and entered as Donovan replied. "Yeah, we're fine."

"But *you're* not..." Valaria interjected as Quinn stepped forward, right arm tightly secured across his chest in a makeshift sling, with an equally makeshift bandage wrapped around his upper arm.

"Nothing to worry about," he assured her. "It's just a flesh wound."

"Oh my God, leave it to you to go all 'John Wayne' on us," she retorted tartly.

Dodger observed their exchange with a quizzical look. "John *Who?*"

"Undoubtedly some old movie reference," Quinn replied with a smirk. "Don't encourage her." He directed his attention to Donovan. "What about the park? Everything all right there?"

"Mission accomplished," Farley informed him. "Supplies were moved and they'd even relocated to a new fall-back position by the time we met up."

"How about Adams?"

"Safely dispatched just before we got there."

"Good," Quinn said, wincing as he inadvertently moved his injured arm. "Well done."

More than an hour remained before the sun fully rose and since everyone was cold, tired, and hungry Gideon ordered a brief bivouac. Almost before the small heaters were ignited and food was passed around most of the patrol was sound asleep.

Quinn assumed his customary position on one side of the dog while Valaria settled in on the other.

"Are you really OK?" she asked, offering him a hand as he lowered himself awkwardly to the floor. "You need any help?"

"I'm fine," he insisted in a strained hush. "What about you and Donovan? How'd you two do out here on your own?"

"It went well," she replied, absently stroking Yancy's side as he twitched in his sleep. "He's easy to work with. And that park was amazing; weird and creepy, but amazing."

"Thought you'd like it."

Valaria continued petting Yancy, keenly attuned to the intense knot of pain the man next to her was struggling to ignore.

"We had an interesting talk about Texas," she said at last.

Gideon leaned his head back against the wall and closed his eyes. "Learn anything worth sharing?"

"Donovan said lots of Texans are paying close attention to what the Sons of Liberty are doing."

Quinn nodded with genuine satisfaction. "That's good to hear. I've always believed Texas is the key."

"Texas? Why're they important?"

He shifted slightly to look at her. "Think about it Thorpe. Even as organized as we've become, the Sons really haven't *done* anything yet and the government pretty much thinks we're an anomaly—about as threatening as a mosquito. But if Texas is watching—and if we succeed in taking down the Guardian Star—then they'll see we're not just a bunch of rabble and might decide to support us. And if Texas comes in on our side the Triumvirate will have to take us seriously."

"So tenacious are we of the fair possession of freedom, which no power on earth has a right to curtail, that we shall never give up our invaluable claim."

~ Mercy Otis Warren

CHAPTER THIRTEEN

I.

It took a full month for Quinn's injured right arm to heal. As he claimed, the wound itself had been superficial, leaving nothing but a jagged scar across his right bicep that he wore as a badge of honor. Muscular damage from the pulse rifle's voltage, however, was extensive and the arm required time and physical strengthening before full use could be restored; time that—in his mind—was better spent on more productive pursuits and found him chomping at the bit while failing miserably to demonstrate any of the characteristics being a 'patient' implied.

"God in heaven, why do you have to be such a prat," Valaria chided one afternoon in early March as she watched Quinn slip his right arm from the sling that supported it in order to join some workers who were unloading boxes of supplies. "You're supposed to be *supervising*," she reminded him.

It had become a familiar theme and Gideon's response was equally predictable.

"I'm fine," he insisted. "If I don't start using the arm it'll never get back to full strength."

"If you keep overdoing it and don't start listening to what the doc advises it may *never* get back to normal, you moron!"

Quinn grabbed Valaria's left wrist with his good hand and indicated the polka-dot cloth it sported. "Watch it, grunt," he said in reply to her cheekiness. "That's *General* Moron to you."

With a rueful shake of his head he went back to work and Valaria noticed that the boxes he and his crew were shelving bore the Triumvirate's official seal. "Bloody Hell, Quinn, what've you guys been up to now? Don't tell me you've started stealing from the government."

"It's time the mosquitoes began biting," Gideon explained, leaning against one of the larger crates and crossing his arms in satisfaction. "Time we began making our presence felt a bit more directly in the good ol' RSA."

"So you're hijacking supply transports? Brilliant move, Quinn; yeah, that's a real stroke of genius. The only ones likely to get *bitten* by that mosquito are the people of the Borders."

"They're already being bitten. Who's more likely to be sure Pioneers actually get what they need, the government or us? Their claim that Symbiosis takes care of everybody is a load of crap."

"So making sure exiles get supplies makes you the good guys, right?"

"Something like that."

Surveying the growing mountain of crates, Valaria hoisted herself nimbly atop an adjacent stack. The canned goods and miscellaneous products they represented were routinely promised but rarely delivered.

"I suppose that actually is kind of smart," she conceded. "But it also makes the government even more pissed—ever stop to think about that?"

"The cost of doing business."

As the team continued to work Valaria noticed that Quinn was trying to nonchalantly slip his right hand back through the sling. It was trembling slightly.

"Why'd you send for me anyway?" she asked, resisting comment on his obvious over-exertion.

"Speaker McFarland asked to see us. I thought we could head for the MetroLink from here."

"Know what he wants?"

"Nope."

Quinn smiled, offering up his good hand to help Valaria down from her perch atop a gross of toilet paper. "But he's The Man so I don't ask questions when he calls, I just go."

Valaria ignored the proffered hand and Gideon was struck by the grace and physical confidence displayed as she sprang agilely off the crates. This was not the same woman who had struggled with a day's worth of walking the previous autumn. Training and determination had almost completely transformed her into her own personal version of what she called the 'Warrior Princess'—another archaic cultural reference the meaning of which he only marginally understood as she laughingly referred to herself as 'Xena.'

Leaving a few terse orders in his wake, the duo left the work crew to their task and headed for the tram.

Significant progress had been made on the MetroLink system over the winter. Restoration was complete on the run connecting The Hub to

McFarland's headquarters beneath the Gateway Arch and work was proceeding apace on other routes deemed essential to using St. Louis as the Sons' base of operations. As they boarded the underground transport Valaria recalled the first time she had made the trip. It had taken more than half an hour to travel the short distance, the tram rocking and jerking spasmodically through a poorly-lit tunnel still littered with debris. Each subsequent excursion had been marked by substantial improvement and they now moved at a smooth and steady clip along the restored southbound portion of the U-shaped spur that had transported tourists from the main line that served a busy area called Laclede's Landing over to the Gateway Arch and back again.

After emerging from the tram at the now-familiar siding beneath the monument, a matching set of unsmiling guards once again materialized from the shadows and escorted the pair across the wide platform originally intended to accommodate an onslaught of visitors. They opened the doors without fanfare, the dimly-lit Museum of Westward Expansion yawning silently before its two lone guests.

The former Speaker of the House had taken a liking to Valaria and she often was included when Quinn's presence was requested. The subject was always politics but the trio usually ended up talking about her grandfather before Valaria would be ousted from the confidential portion of the meetings. As a result of being left on her own, she had had ample opportunity to wander the myriad objects standing shrouded by shadows in the muted light of the museum. At first it had seemed that the vast space retained no coherent pattern and merely held the scattered remnants of a once proud national treasure. But the more she explored, the more Valaria was able to suss out the thematic order of the displays and wished she could have visited when they would have been enhanced and linked by the series of virtual reality experiences she had discovered evidence of.

Once Valaria and Quinn were inside, the two men accompanying them secured the entrance and returned to their posts. Snaking through the museum's gloomy maze, Gideon led the way toward another security checkpoint at the far end. Once final clearance was achieved three flights of stairs brought them to a heavily guarded office area in the building's lowest level.

A young woman rose from one of the workstations to greet them. She was pert, short and extremely curvaceous.

Not immune to her obvious attributes, Gideon's smile was instinctively disarming. "Afternoon, Kelsey."

"Down boy," Valaria murmured, rolling her eyes in mild derision.

Kelsey bobbed her head deferentially. "General Quinn. Speaker McFarland is expecting you."

"Don't think I'll ever get used to that," Valaria whispered as Kelsey led the way toward a door at the back of the room.

"It's nothing," Gideon replied dismissively. "They're trying to build an army, gotta have a few officers of rank."

She threw him a sarcastic smirk. "Your *explanation* is 'rank,' I'll grant you that. Geez, why can't you just accept the recognition you deserve?"

Quinn looked relieved that Kelsey had already opened the Speaker's door thus eliminating—or at least postponing—the need for a response.

"General Quinn and Ms. Thorpe are here, sir."

The portly old man across the room rose from his desk, his face animated by deep smile lines as he gestured the duo forward.

Kelsey silently closed the door behind them and returned to her workstation.

"Thank you for coming," McFarland said, reaching out to shake hands.

"Of course, sir," Gideon replied. "It's always a privilege."

The former Speaker of the House wheezed a bit as he chuckled softly. "Well, I don't know about that, but I hope I at least make it interesting."

"Always, sir," Quinn assured him. "What can we do for you?"

"I want to bounce an idea off the two of you. Let's go into my quarters where we can be more comfortable."

McFarland led the way through an adjacent door into a suite of rooms that had been converted into living space for him. Indicating two overstuffed chairs on either side of a small table, he sat across from them in a rocking chair, the cushions of which were rather threadbare but obviously a favorite. Almost immediately, a sleek calico cat darted out of the bedroom and leapt onto the old man's ample lap.

"Ah, Winston, always ready to welcome me home."

Gideon and Valaria waited in respectful silence for the Speaker to gather his thoughts as he scratched the cat under its chin; its deep, droning purr filling the room.

"Miss Thorpe," McFarland began, "I've been following your progress. If we had a newspaper you'd be front page news."

"Sir?"

"As I've mentioned, having the granddaughter of Otis Thorpe join our team is quite the coup."

"I'm afraid I've never quite understood that. Otis may have been more than I ever realized but he certainly couldn't have been famous."

"Not famous exactly. Your grandfather worked for a man named Carson Telliman. He was a member of the 'Telliman Think-Tank,' a select group brought together to brainstorm solutions to security issues of the day. It was called the 'Triple-T' for short and, as a contributor, your grandfather actually did garner a certain level of celebrity among those paying attention—especially as the Guardian Star began reaching toward heaven..."

He appraised her for a beat with benign intensity.

"...So you see, it truly is no small thing to have you on our side and highly gratifying to be informed that you've become one of Lieutenant Griffin's star pupils."

She met the old man's level gaze with one of equal measure but chose to focus on the reference to her training rather than McFarland's suggestion of a vicarious claim to her grandfather's status. "Lieutenant Griffin is an excellent teacher."

"And you, I am told, are a most apt student."

Her response was carefully weighed. "I want to make myself useful."

Benign gaze intact, McFarland considered her words for a moment before reaching for a data pad lying on the ottoman next to his chair.

"Yes," he mused. "Useful."

A thought seemed to strike him and he smiled sardonically as he followed its divergent thread. "With their compulsive social meddling, Naomi Blanchard and her Neoterics give unique meaning to that word." He shook his head mournfully and his voice dropped away. "They were a threat to liberty from the moment she was elected, we just didn't see it."

The elderly gentleman fell silent while accessing information on the pad.

"But after the plague," he resumed with renewed intensity, "and now after almost forty years in power, there's no denying that Naomi's imperious governing has caused the country to devolve into nothing short of a totalitarian state. Gideon, you've infiltrated the RSA on several occasions and have seen firsthand what life is like under the current regime; you and I have spoken of this at length."

"Yes sir."

"Martial Law may have been unavoidable in the wake of a catastrophic terrorist attack like the plague, but the Triumvirate's refusal to reinstate the Constitution and their subsequent draconian measures—what they've euphemistically christened 'The Patriot Protocols'—have undermined everything the United States stood for. The Eugenics laws, suspension of the Bill of Rights, the Borders... these and countless other actions—including creating the Guardians in order to enforce everything—nullify the most basic freedoms of the very people Blanchard claims to be protecting."

The top of his bald head had grown ruddy from the heat of his conviction and he ran a hand vacantly across it as if expecting hair in need of straightening. "She may call them her 'Precious Remnant' but they are nothing more than meaningless pawns she and her Neoterics manipulate in their quest to create Utopia. I curse myself every day for the tragic error in judgment that led me to resign when Naomi wouldn't be dissuaded from initiating The Revanche."

Quinn was quick to protest. "You were standing up for what you believed in. There was no way of knowing what President Blanchard would do once she consolidated power—*she* most likely didn't know. If you had stayed on and joined the Triumvirate she very likely would have had you eliminated as the regime became more ruthless since you never would have gone along with what they ended up doing. Frankly sir, I believe your decision to walk away was one of the best things that could have happened."

McFarland once again straightened hair that wasn't there, his head glistening under his touch like a well-polished billiard ball.

When he spoke his voice had softened. "Kind words, Gideon, but I can't help thinking about what might be different had I stayed in Washington. At the very least I could have objected to distilling the national government down to the President, Speaker, and Chief Justice—their vaunted Triumvirate. That alone was a total perversion of what the Founding Fathers intended when they established the three branches... what has come since is nothing short of an abomination."

The elderly Speaker glanced again at the data pad he still held before clearing his throat and continuing. "But I should get to the point lest you think me guilty of aimless rambling."

Undeterred by the fact that her comment smacked of impertinence, Valaria couldn't resist the opening he provided. "Your ramblings are never aimless, sir."

McFarland responded with his characteristic wheezy chuckle. Thorpe's Granddaughter—capitalized in his mind in the manner he often thought of her—was gratifying proof that there were plenty of people out there who had the chutzpah to stand up and take back what had been relentlessly usurped over the years.

As his chuckle subsided, he handed the data pad to Quinn. "Take a look at these figures. If our sources are correct—and we have no reason to doubt them—over the past three years there has been a steady decline in the number of exiles sent to the Borders; in the last 18 months the drop has become precipitous."

"Yes sir," Gideon replied. "I brought some of that information back myself."

"The Continental Congress—of which I am a member—" he added as an aside to Valaria, "is growing increasingly concerned about those numbers."

Quinn looked up from the data he studied. "Does the Congress have any theories?"

"Seems like a decline would be inevitable," Valaria ventured. "After all, the Revanche generation is almost gone—no offense, sir."

"None taken," McFarland replied with a smile. "I know I'm as old as dirt. Finish your thought, please."

"It's just that I'm remembering what Mavis Pope told me—she was the most recent exile sent to my settlement. She said people in the cities had pretty much come to terms with life as it is. As your generation passes, fewer and fewer people remember what life used to be like so there are probably just fewer people rocking the boat. And if that's the case, wouldn't a drop in exiles be expected?"

Quinn was quick to interject. "I'll acknowledge that possibility, but I wouldn't trust Mavis Pope any farther than I could throw her— and considering her size, that's not very far!"

"She ended up in the Borders basically because she's obese," Valaria explained to the rather perplexed-looking gentleman across from her.

McFarland sighed, shaking his head. "Ah yes, appearance is as important as compliance when Utopia is at stake."

"Congress undoubtedly has considered the impact of a generational decline," Quinn continued, "but the graying of the nation can't be the only reason for the numbers we're seeing. After all, citizens routinely denounce each another just to deflect attention from themselves or to get extra rations so there should still be at least a trickle of exiles. I'm assuming there are other—more troublesome—theories being kicked around. Am I right, sir?"

Speaker McFarland nodded.

"Am I also correct in assuming that's why we're here?"

"Yes," the old man said simply.

II.

The idea Speaker McFarland had outlined was as straightforward as it was daunting: infiltrate the RSA and find the cause for the drop in exiles. Gideon and Valaria agreed to go partly out of respect for James McFarland and partly because—if they had admitted it—they were flattered he thought them able.

Quinn had undertaken such missions before, using his technological expertise to pass among the RSA's five Safe Zones far more freely than any of its citizens. His exploits had always been solitary, however, and there was no denying he would have preferred to go alone and felt more than a dash of reluctance about taking Valaria with him. There was no disputing her bravery and she was smarter than most people he knew— and it certainly wasn't that he doubted her skills, quite the opposite; after being selected for specialized training by Lieutenant Griffin, Valaria had reached the point where she decked Gideon with unnerving regularity when they sparred. Nevertheless, he couldn't help still feeling somewhat responsible for her—and also feeling a certain amount of accountability to Otis Thorpe to keep her safe. Theirs was an undeniably complicated relationship—sometimes an extremely rocky one—and Quinn simply had misgivings about placing Valaria in harm's way.

Misgivings he wisely kept to himself.

Despite his qualms, when Gideon considered McFarland's reasons for sending a pair of agents this time instead of just one, he had to admit they were sound enough—he also acknowledged he had no authority to question them. The Speaker simply believed a two-person team was more likely to succeed. Characterizing the nature of the mission as exceptionally risky, he had told Quinn he felt it essential that someone would—as he put it—"have your back." He also believed that a man and woman would more easily blend in and, finally, that Thorpe and Quinn were uniquely qualified to fill that role.

"There's such an obvious spark of kinship between the two of you, your partnership is a natural," the old man had observed, "and," he added bluntly, "there's also obviously no romance lurking beneath the surface to complicate things and impede your ability to work together."

McFarland's comment about their bond of kinship had provided ample fodder for sarcastic debate between the two but it was his second observation on which Quinn and Valaria fixated—a remark they found almost laughable since the majority of their comrades totally lacked the old man's insight and assumed they were sleeping together.

"Damn, Quinn," Valaria had quipped once back on the tram, "if McFarland would post his opinion to the Liberty Tree maybe we'd finally be able to convince everybody that we don't f-around in the literal sense." She threw him a snarky smirk before adding, "I'm tired of people thinking I get preferential treatment 'cuz I'm sleeping with the *general*."

"I know at least one person who would appreciate that," Quinn replied, deflecting her reference to his rank onto the fact that Farley Donovan had become a fairly regular source of diversion for Valaria since their return from Six Flags.

As a result of the bonds forged during that first mission, it was Farley Donovan and his squad leader Levi Dodge the duo entrusted with news of McFarland's request and to whom they turned for assistance during the planning stage. Under the guise of playing poker, the four began meeting for strategy sessions in Quinn's quarters each evening, Valaria listening intently as the three experienced 'spies' discussed priorities such as falsifying the various documentation proofs they would be required to provide as they moved around the Zones. Eager to understand the dynamics involved in what they were attempting to do, she made quick work of studying the protocols, maps, and diagrams Quinn had downloaded to the data pad he gave her and soon was able to begin making what she hoped were reasonably intelligent contributions to their nightly conversations.

"You've been focusing on forged proofs but what are we going to do if some Guardian along the way simply wants to scan our *tags?*" she asked one evening during a lull.

"We've both got them," Quinn replied. "Yours is real but deactivated, mine's a reasonable facsimile. We're going to insert temporary dermal chips that'll hopefully fool the low grade scanners carried by most Guardians out in the field."

"That *'hopefully'* qualifier is a real comfort," Valaria scoffed, throwing Quinn the first derisive glare she had sent his way in quite some time.

"Well," Dodger interjected, "*hopefully* you won't get scanned."

"And if you do," Farley added, "*hopefully* you'll be able to outwit the bastard if the scanner isn't fooled."

Valaria glowered at all three men before playing what she believed to be the Ace up her sleeve.

"OK, here's another one for you—what about your tech-tat?" she asked Quinn. "How are you gonna keep that thing from triggering every damn alarm in the country once we cross over? Hell, are people in the States even allowed to *have* tattoos?"

Gideon glanced at the elaborate pattern inked across the back of his left hand.

"That's actually an easy one. When it's out of juice it really is nothing more than a tat so once it's dormant it poses no danger at all."

"And *do* Americans have tattoos," Valaria persisted.

"Some," Dodger said. "Personal expression among the rank-and-file is limited to say the least but the upper echelon has a lot more latitude so you'll see tats among the 'more equal' residents of the Zones."

"See? No problem," Quinn assured her. "We'll be 'middies' for most of our time in the Zone so the tat shouldn't raise any eyebrows. And we're going to be keeping a very low profile—get in, look around, get out—so we should be able to avoid drawing unwanted attention and backing ourselves into a corner."

Valaria admired his confidence—and shared it to a certain extent. They had studied and discussed so many aspects of the RSA and so many possible scenarios she almost felt like she lived there. But, being a self-proclaimed pragmatist (Quinn called her a cynic!), she also felt encounters with Guardians were inevitable—especially in light of heightened security since the Sons of Liberty had become more active. Increased drone activity, random identity checks and even home incursions were facts of life for citizens of the RSA; all portrayed as necessary precautions against what the government labeled acts of terrorism by those they called the 'Sons of Chaos.' As a result, Valaria thought it naïve to think they could avoid being subjected to similar scrutiny—and since Quinn was anything but naïve as well as being a man with few 'tells,' she also trusted that his comment about not "backing ourselves into a corner" meant he had a few tricks up his sleeve that his poker face wasn't giving away.

If not, their jaunt into the Zones was likely to be anything *but* safe.

III.

The so-called Safe Zones—five metropolitan areas into which evacuations following the plague had slowly been consolidated—were all located west of the extensive Boston/Virginia Beach corridor as contamination from the region's forty-nine abandoned and decaying nuclear power plants relentlessly transformed the area into a radioactive deathtrap. Unlike the historic nuclear meltdowns of Three Mile Island in the U.S., Chernobyl in Ukraine, Fukushima in Japan and Lufeng in China where containment and clean-up became immediate national priorities, post-plague nuclear contamination worldwide was ongoing due to the collapse of global infrastructures. In the U.S., where nuclear facilities were scattered across the fifty states, occasional low-grade explosions continued to expel irradiated particulates into the air but the concentration of nuclear plants along the eastern seaboard made that region particularly dangerous. Up and down the east coast, dozens of fractured cooling chambers gradually leaked billions of gallons of radioactive water into the environment. Vast areas from New York State to Florida had been rendered virtually uninhabitable and, as a result, the five Safe Zones were established between the natural barriers of the Appalachian Mountains and the Mississippi River.

Out of those five Zones—Indianapolis, Columbus, Louisville, Nashville, and Atlanta—Columbus (coincidentally located in Naomi Blanchard's home state of Ohio) had emerged as the RSA's new capital. Pristine and fully restored, Columbus now stood as the RSA's model of modernity.

As such, it was *not* Quinn's choice for the city to be breached.

"Not only is it the capital," he explained early on, "and they double-down on security as a result, but other than Atlanta it's also farthest away; Indianapolis or Louisville make much more sense."

"Both are about the same distance from here," Dodger observed. "And since all the Zones are linked by GovNet, you breach one you've essentially breached them all."

In principle Quinn agreed with his friend's glib comment but as a 'technoid' he knew that breaching the government's heavily encrypted communications network was going to be more like *building* a mile-high Guardian Star than *designing* one; challenging in theory, nearly impossible in reality.

After the plague, creation of the GovNet system had been deemed every bit as essential to recovery as shoring up the nation's porous borders by means of the so-called "NAB'D" project—the North American Border Defense initiative on which Valaria's parents had worked. Designed to establish real-time communication between the Triumvirate and the sprawling system of bureaucratic minions that did its bidding, GovNet inexorably shut down its Internet predecessor and successfully smothered the cyberspace free-for-all that had connected the average American not only to countless incarnations of vacuous social media but to the broader world as well. Relying on the government to protect them, plague survivors had clung in terrified desperation to the Triumvirate's promise of restored stability and were so consumed by fear and grief they uttered barely a whimper of dissent when a dictatorial form of stability quickly began to rise from the ashes and close the door on the rest of the world as well as on personal freedom. When President Blanchard's 'Precious Remnant' finally surfaced from its catatonic stupor it was a tightly confined, strictly controlled existence that awaited them—one completely devoid of personal tech and relentlessly monitored by electronic as well as human eyes and ears.

This was the system James McFarland had charged Gideon Quinn with breaching.

IV.

Quinn and Thorpe set out for the Indianapolis Safe Zone on April 1st; the date's significance not lost on the more cynical—more *pragmatic*—of the two.

Kevin Eldridge was also aware of the date and assumed himself the target of a none-too-creative April Fools prank when Valaria brought Yancy to him shortly after midnight and asked him to care for the dog during her absence. It wasn't until she pressed her grandfather's chessboard into his hands and made him promise to make sure Levi Dodge got it to Speaker McFarland if she didn't return that he realized she wasn't having him on and discovered a growing knot of dread beginning to roil in his belly. Succumbing to a momentary surge of unexpected emotion, Valaria had actually hugged Kevin before turning on her heels and leaving him dumbfounded in her wake—and instantly dooming the teen to endless nights of insomnia as he waited for her to return.

After leaving Yancy in Kevin's care, Valaria also found sleep elusive that last night at the Hub. She tossed and turned fitfully, her dreams haunted by enormous all-seeing eyes that followed her every move and Guardians she couldn't outpace as she struggled to reach her imperiled grandfather across a barren expanse that absorbed every footfall like gooey quicksand. Each time she woke, she would lie very still and concentrate on breathing as she willed herself back to sleep. Her efforts met only marginal success but—despite appearing somewhat bleary-eyed (which wasn't at all uncommon for someone who thought morning should begin around noon!)—by the time she joined Quinn, Farley, and Dodger for a pre-dawn breakfast the demons had been purged and she exuded nothing but quiet confidence as the four began their final briefing.

"It should be easy going at least until we reach Terre Haute," Quinn reiterated while the quartet savored fresh scrambled eggs and orange juice supplied by Speaker McFarland. "There are only two checkpoints before that and I don't expect any trouble since they're not heavily manned and drone flyovers are fairly predictable. Since we'll be using one of the government's own transports, no one should suspect we're anything other than what we appear to be."

"Just be careful not to miss the turnoff north of Highway 231," Dodger interposed. "It's only a mile from the Amtrak spur so patrols pick up at that point. You won't have much time to ditch the transport, change clothes, and melt into the workers waiting for the Bullet back to Indy."

"And there'd be no reason for a worker to miss that train so if you do you'll stand out like a whore at a church picnic," Farley cautioned, glancing Valaria's way with no small measure of concern.

"Hey, don't look at me," she assured him. "I don't go to church picnics."

The detritus of breakfast lay strewn across the table, the briefing was essentially complete and there really was nothing left to say. The four friends sat in silence for a few moments before Gideon tactfully suggested that Dodger help him with one final supply check. When the two men had left the room Donovan's eyes sought Valaria's across the table.

"I know I don't need to tell you to be careful," he began in his easy Texas drawl.

"No."

"Be careful."

She smiled and stood. "And you keep an eye on Kevin and Yancy for me."

"You know I will," he said earnestly. He came around the table and gently touched her face with the back of his hand. "Be sure to come back."

"You know I will," she said with a wry smirk. "In the meantime, hang onto this for me, OK?" She held out her polka dot minion bandana and wrapped it around the wrist he offered. "Don't think I should wear that while trying to pass as a citizen of the RSA."

"Probably not," he agreed.

Something of an awkward silence washed over them until Donovan stemmed the tide by lifting Valaria's chin and kissing her.

An unspoken longing passed between them; a longing that gave new purpose to one and gentled the other.

V.

Directly across the Mississippi River from its mega-city counterpart, East St. Louis, Illinois had begun life as a prosperous community in its own right. At one time the fourth largest city in the state, it had shown all the signs of continuing to benefit from a robust industrial core as well as its proximity to the 'other' St. Louis across the river until the demise of the nation's industrial 'Rust Belt' brought about a ruinous decline. By the time the terrorists' plague decimated the world's population, East St. Louis was already essentially a ghost town with fewer than 10,000 residents but the highest per capita crime rate in the country—the fruit of poverty's trifecta of hopelessness, resentment and disenfranchisement. A sad and desolate place before the plague—and the unintentional prototype for every post-plague community across the country—the city became a frightening wasteland in the years that followed.

But in spite of its vast misfortune and dark reputation, East St. Louis did have one thing in its favor—on the northwest edge of town stood the confluence of three major interstate highways; three highways that just happened to ultimately connect the Borders in the west to all five of the RSA Safe Zones in the east. As a result, a government that had no use for a city that was the quintessential apocalyptic nightmare (lacking only Hollywood's shambling hordes of blood-thirsty zombies!) found itself in dire need of the seamless transportation system languishing on its northern periphery. Within months of finalizing the Safe Zone system, an RSA outpost had been established at what came to be called 'The Convergence' and precious resources were allocated to upgrade and maintain the three Interstates radiating east and south from that point.

It was one of those roadways Quinn and Valaria would be traveling into the proverbial belly of the beast but the initial leg of their trip would once again be on foot as they took advantage of the MetroLink system that connected the two St. Louises. In spite of the fact that tracks had degraded over the years and underground spans were littered or even blocked with debris, the Metro provided not only an efficient way to cross the Mississippi but, once across, supplied a shielded route that would bring them within a mile of Convergence and the abandoned house where a stolen government transport vehicle would facilitate the next stage of their journey.

"We seem destined to take long walks together," Valaria observed, referencing the U-shaped spur's deserted northbound tunnel on her left.

The tram once again had deposited them at the Gateway Arch siding and she turned from the abandoned tunnel—twin to the one they had just traveled—to shrug into the heavy backpack she would be carrying during the first leg of the trip. Quinn had already shouldered his load and helped her balance the pack more comfortably before replying.

"All we need is an impulsive dog, a vicious thunderstorm, and some crazed Freebooters and it would be just like old times," he mused.

Jumping down from the raised platform onto the tracks below, they began heading toward the unrestored leg of the Arch's U-shaped MetroLink spur, pausing at the mouth of the derelict expanse of tunnel and taking stock of the darkness ahead. To help dispel the gloom, they switched on trail lights attached to the front straps of their packs. The lights flickered to life just as a shrill whistle drew their attention back to the siding.

Speaker McFarland stood on the platform flanked by the two omnipresent guards. As Quinn and Valaria turned back, the trio snapped to attention and offered up a farewell salute.

"Wow," Valaria murmured, raising her hand in recognition while Quinn returned the salute with solemn respect.

The Speaker watched them go, the dual halos of soft light that surrounded them slowly bobbing out of his line of sight as they moved deeper into shadow. Grateful that he hadn't missed their departure he turned and, with the measured steps of age, returned to his office once Gideon and Valaria had disappeared into the gloom.

They followed the abandoned track as it banked gradually and began a slow rise toward the point where it surfaced well north of the famed Arch. Once above ground, the abandoned portion of the Gateway Spur would curve east, exposed for only a short distance before rejoining the Laclede's Landing run and heading east across the Mississippi River sheltered from view as it ran beneath the roadway of the Eads Bridge. The usefulness of this northbound tunnel was a subject of debate and Quinn was well aware that plans were moving forward to destroy that section of the U due to its potential as a point of ingress to their base of operations under the Arch. As a result of its possible demolition, the northbound leg of the Gateway Spur hadn't even been explored and Quinn fully expected its condition to be like the tunnels they had cleared—congested with all manner of dirt and debris as well as fallen ceiling tiles, collapsed walls, and exposed wires.

His expectation proved to be spot-on but despite the tunnel's challenging condition the duo made good time until they came upon a derailed three-section tram. It was lodged in a portion of the tunnel that had almost completely collapsed—undoubtedly the cause of its capsizing. Lying on its side and wedged into the void by chunks of concrete and miscellaneous rubble, the tram effectively barred their way leaving nothing but a small opening barely the height of a man between it and the top of the tunnel's curved walls.

"OK," Valaria said, surveying the blockage and clasping the front straps of her backpack as if they were suspenders, "what do you suggest? Do we climb over or try to go through?"

"I'm thinking over," Quinn replied while doing his own assessment of the rather daunting obstruction. "All the seats and broken glass inside could make 'through' a pretty dicey proposition."

Valaria agreed and the two lost no time checking the tram's stability and stepping up onto the now-horizontal handrails that flanked the rear entrance. Balancing rather precariously on the narrow metal bars, they placed their palms on what had been the side of the tram but was now its top and hoisted themselves onto the windowed surface that would serve as their walkway.

"Watch your step," Gideon advised as Valaria moved out ahead of him across the first car. "Almost all the window glass is gone; don't want to end up falling in and breaking something."

"By 'something' I assume you mean a bone since everything inside is already—" Valaria broke off mid-sentence as she glanced into the passenger area illuminated by the trail lights she directed toward her feet. "Oh *shit*..."

"What is it," Quinn called out from several yards behind her. "Did you hurt yourself?"

"No, I'm all right," she shot back over her shoulder. "But there are people in here!"

"What do you mean there are people?" Gideon asked, darting agilely across the window frames that separated them.

Valaria stood at the end of the first car and when he reached her she pointed down into the open area between the last row of seats and the next doorway.

The skeletal remains of three people were clearly visible.

The scene was as surreal as it was macabre since the orientation of the tram was askew due to lying on its side. The trio below them appeared to be huddled around a makeshift campsite. They could see the remnant of a blanket that had been spread beneath them and what looked like a portable camp stove as well as related camping detritus still sitting virtually undisturbed. Everything was filthy and nothing but tattered remains of nondescript clothing clung to the bones. One skeleton lay off to the side curled into a fetal position and partially covered by another ragged blanket but the other two were together, the larger leaning at an odd angle against what should have been the floor of the tram, its arm across what could only be a child lying with its head in the adult's lap.

"Oh my God," Valaria breathed, dropping into a squat to get a better view. "What happened here?"

"Hard to say," Gideon replied quietly as he surveyed the mournful tableau. "By the look of things they've been here one helluva long time."

"Did Freebooters do this?"

"I don't think so. It's not messy enough and they don't look like they've been attacked; maybe a family trying to escape the plague—only to fall sick and end up dying here all by themselves."

"Poor bastards," Valaria observed. "Try to outwit the plague and end up dying in the dark."

Quinn nodded in solemn agreement, the irony of her suggested scenario registering somewhere between tragic and pathetic.

"What should we do?" she asked.

"Nothing. This is already their tomb. If the tunnel's destroyed at some point that'll just make it official, if it's eventually cleared then the Sons will bury them."

He touched her shoulder lightly before moving ahead and jumping across the narrow gap between cars.

When Valaria didn't immediately follow, Quinn glanced back. She had paused with her head slightly bowed as she made the sign of the cross in reverent recognition of the loss of life below her. Gideon smiled faintly and shook his head; the woman's quiet spirituality was such a stark counterpoint to the cynical, sarcastic front she presented to the world. Turning away out of respect he basked in its wonder for a moment, appreciating anew the complexity of his partner.

Valaria was at his shoulder almost before his thoughts had crystallized.

"What the hell are you waiting for, the next train?" she asked with a mordant smirk.

He laughed out loud at the fleeting nature of sentiment.

"What?"

Quinn just shook his head and set out across the second car.

They reached the end of the over-turned tram without further incident, climbed down and made their way through the debris standing between them and the mouth of the tunnel. Blinking into the bright sunlight that was enthusiastically caressing the distant horizon, the pair ventured into the open air and sprinted up the inclined tracks to where they once again merged with the Laclede's Landing run as it headed east.

The magnificent Eads Bridge and the Mighty Mississippi waited.

When the decision had been made to extend the MetroLink system across the river into Illinois it also was decided that the most efficient way to accomplish that goal was to utilize the rail line that already existed as part of the historic span designed two centuries earlier by James Eads. That iconic structure—the world's first steel bridge and the first to cross the Mississippi—had originally been dedicated on July 4, 1874. Designed with an upper deck that in the modern era carried vehicular and pedestrian traffic, the bridge also included a lower deck for railroad tracks which the MetroLink had adapted for its light rail service in 1993.

"Holy crap, this is pretty intimidating," Valaria commented once they began walking the tracks.

They had exited the landward portion of the bridge where shelter was provided by wide stone archways stretching across a long platform for boarding and exiting the trams. Now on the rail bed with only an intricate web of tubular steel supports standing between them and the Mississippi River a hundred feet below, Valaria was feeling more than slightly overwhelmed.

"Don't tell me you're afraid of heights," Quinn chided. "Better get over it 'cuz we're gonna be up here a while."

"Not afraid," she assured him. "This is just a little daunting."

She looked out across the muddy expanse churning below them on its relentless journey south. "Otis used vids to teach me geography but they sure didn't do the Mississippi justice—this thing's huge!"

"One of the world's perfect natural boundaries. And if full scale war comes, controlling the Mississippi will be crucial—keep RSA troops on the other side, shoot down drones and incoming missiles and you've got yourself a victory."

"You really think that's possible?"

"Hell," he admitted with a smirk, "you know me—I think victory's a sure thing."

The words were barely out of his mouth when an all-too-familiar resonant hum was suddenly audible above the sound of the river.

"*Down*," Quinn ordered sharply, grabbing the strap of Valaria's backpack and wrenching her to the rail bed.

Just a few hundred yards north of the bridge a sleek and deadly RSA attack drone glistened in the reflected light of the early morning sun as it flew slowly west across the river.

"Think it saw us?" Valaria asked.

"No; although they're damn good at detecting movement."

He remained in a motionless crouch for a moment before scowling fiercely and muttering an angry "*Shit!*" under his breath.

"What? You just said it didn't see us."

"Drones don't fly *west* from the states to patrol the Borders. They fly *east* from the Guardian Star and never cross the river. Makes me think we may have been blown."

"You're over-reacting," Valaria scoffed. "They've probably just added additional patrols since the Sons have become more active."

Gideon scowled and shook his head. "I'd like to think so but it's just as possible one of our contacts has ratted us out."

Valaria slowly shifted to her knees and peered through the metal supports at the drone disappearing into the west. "Do we go on?"

"Absolutely," Quinn chuffed. "Even if they know a mission's in play—know about the stolen transport—they don't know who's coming, where we're coming from, or where we're going; each contact only knows what's needed for them to play their part. And the government definitely can't know what our goal is—none of our contacts know that."

"Good, so let's keep moving."

Her easy determination made him smile.

VI.

Once on the Illinois side of the Mississippi, the MetroLink passed under stone and brick arches identical to those framing the western portion of the bridge and then descended through a few hundred feet of discolored acrylic shielding before the tracks emerged into the open at ground level.

Quinn and Valaria emerged with the rails, now less than a mile from the Convergence transportation hub.

They moved forward in full stealth mode, two sets of wary ears listening for the familiar hum of an approaching TAD while simultaneously alert to any potential threat in the immediate vicinity.

Although choked by weeds and thwarted by the intrusion of an occasional tree growing triumphantly between the tracks, the MetroLink was much easier to follow than any road they had used in the past, steel rails being much less vulnerable to decay than asphalt. Unfortunately, the rail line eventually veered sharply away from the RSA's prized convergence of crisscrossing highways forcing Quinn and Valaria to leave the well-defined route and head off on their own.

Their goal was a long-abandoned house on the southeastern side of the blacktop labyrinth that formed The Convergence; their prize, a stolen government transport vehicle stashed away in the dilapidated garage.

As expected, the street and environs were hushed and deserted as the pair approached.

"Hold up," Quinn whispered suddenly.

Valaria had started moving through the underbrush toward the broken pavement of the residential street when Gideon put a cautioning hand on her arm. "Don't you think it's a little too quiet?"

"*Too quiet*," she repeated skeptically. "How can it be too quiet? It's an abandoned town."

"Listen," he said, lowering into a crouch behind some bushes and drawing her down beside him. "It's not just the absence of human noise—you'd expect that—but there's nothing else going on... no birds, no bugs, *nothing*."

Valaria's head tilted instinctively as she leaned into the silence.

Quinn was right, the stillness was virtually absolute. And if she had learned anything from their previous walkabout it was that nature was one helluva a noisy place unless there was good reason for it to fall silent.

"So what are you thinking?" she asked.

"I'm thinking we're not alone."

She had to agree with him. And in light of his concern about the unusual drone flyover she began to wonder if this portion of their mission really had been blown and that the silence might be warning them of a serious threat.

"Couldn't it just be a routine patrol," she suggested hopefully. "We're so close to Convergence they're bound to make the rounds on a fairly regular basis. It doesn't necessarily mean they're looking for us."

"So, let's just wait and see what happens," he replied quietly. "If it's a patrol then they won't be hiding and we should see and hear them. If we don't, then something else is on their agenda and we'd be stupid not to assume it's us since this is where the transport is supposed to be stashed."

They stayed where they were, crouching uncomfortably in a thicket of weeds until a flash of light in an adjacent coppice of trees rescued their stiffening muscles—something metallic had been shifted, reflecting the sharp rays of the morning sun for just an instant.

"Point, set, and match," Quinn murmured, his words devoid of the satisfaction they implied. "We're not alone and they're not just passing through—they're watching that house. Let's go."

Giving the entire area a wide berth, they walked for close to half an hour before curving northward and crossing Interstate 64 as it headed southeast away from Convergence on its way to Nashville. Their target was the other leg of prized asphalt—I-70—which would take them northeast toward Indianapolis. Now well beyond view of Convergence they came around the transport hub's far eastern flank until finally catching sight of their goal.

Gideon still felt confident. Although convinced that something had gone wrong regarding commandeering a government vehicle he was equally sure that the odds were still in their favor since none of their contacts knew anything beyond the portion of the plan in which they played a part. Unfortunately, losing their means of transportation meant that a three hour drive to the rendezvous with the Amtrak Bullet had just become a three *day* walk. It was a trek that once again required crossing uneven, overgrown terrain since walking the pristine highway would be tantamount to conceding defeat—*transports* were routine but *pedestrians* definitely were not.

Valaria threw Quinn an *"I told you so"* smirk as they began another long walk apparently placed before them by Destiny.

By the end of that first day they had covered more than twenty miles and successfully avoided discovery by three transports and five drone flyovers—not an easy task in light of the fact that spring foliage was nothing more than embryonic buds at that time of year and offered scant camouflage.

Although traveling by foot was unexpected they weren't unprepared—at least in terms of ability; both were now in peak condition and more than up to the challenge of maintaining a brisk pace over uneven ground. In terms of supplies, however, they came up short. The backpacks they shouldered contained emergency rations but not much more—a dozen nutrition bars as well as four slender, self-heating meal packets. Valaria had marveled at the ingenious containers months before when Quinn had contributed pancakes for breakfast after his final over-nighter on her futon; now she only wished they'd had the foresight to stuff a few more into their packs. But apart from that emergency supply most of the space in their backpacks had been reserved for the clothing and accoutrements needed to transition from government transport drivers to workers heading for the Indianapolis Zone. As a result, they were on their own in terms of shelter and literally out in the cold as the sun went down and temperatures dropped precipitously.

When Quinn's voice nudged her back into the world the next morning, Valaria found herself dappled in dew, chilled to the bone and instantly longing for the additional body heat Yancy had provided on more than one occasion. Reluctantly relinquishing the negligible heat of the stiff

'WarmWrap' that came with the backpack, she yawned widely and tried not to blame Quinn for the rotation of the earth.

Dawn was just beginning to grace the horizon with promises of a brilliant sunrise yet to come. Unfortunately, neither member of the audience took much notice; one being occupied with the business of departure, the other preoccupied with shaking the dew from her hair while silently reciting a litany of loathing for the inevitability of morning.

"This just doesn't get any easier for you, does it?" Gideon asked as he finished repacking his rucksack.

If looks could kill, the potent glower she directed his way would have been worthy of a Freebooter initiation.

"Here," he said, tossing Valaria a packet of compressed toilet paper. "Go find yourself an accommodating tree while I pack up your stuff."

She returned a few minutes later, less bleary-eyed but only slightly less hostile.

Quinn wisely curtailed further comment and after a quick breakfast they moved out, once again travelling overland while consciously resisting the urge to use the intoxicatingly-smooth—but totally exposed—ribbon of Interstate 70.

Just past noon on the third day the turnoff for Highway 231 finally came into view. The original plan would have had them ditching the stolen transport at this point and changing into workers' garb before heading for the Amtrak spur. But since securing a vehicle had passed from risky to reckless in light of their suspected betrayal they were spared the necessity of getting rid of it and continued past the turnoff deciding to wait until the Amtrak spur was in sight before morphing into laborers.

A few miles farther on a sprawling industrial complex spread across the horizon. Most of the buildings were deserted but a section had been restored and now served to convert reclaimed metal from across the region into building materials unavailable in raw form since The Revanche. It was a visually depressing vista and an equally bleak place to work—noisy, filthy, and physically demanding—but about a hundred low-ranking residents of the Indianapolis Zone were assigned here and made the daily commute with little more than detached resignation etched into their compliant faces.

The Amtrak spur had been constructed on the eastern edge of the complex and as Quinn and Thorpe headed toward it the ominous hum of a drone pierced the cacophony emanating from the factories around them.

Thinking as one, they headed for the nearest building and plastered themselves against a side wall.

"I know it's irrational but I always feel like they're looking for us," Valaria commented from where the two watched the TOD pass from menacing to innocuous as it slowly disappeared into the distance.

"They may not be looking specifically for us," Quinn replied, "but they're always looking for someone so your paranoia is actually a pretty healthy defense mechanism."

He peered around the corner of the wall that shielded them. The restored portion of the complex was only a few buildings away. "This is probably as good a place as any to change clothes."

Without waiting for a response, he moved toward a gaping entryway.

The interior of the building was even less appealing than its decaying façade. What apparently had been some type of assembly line now stretched away from them in three collapsed parallel runs. Shattered windows long ago had stopped offering any protection from the elements and the abandoned machinery was terminally rusty and covered with debris. Augmented by the filth of untold numbers of animals and birds— and a smell registering somewhere between disgusting and nauseating—it ranked high on Valaria's growing list of depressing tableaus.

"You sure know how to show a girl a good time," she observed as she pulled worker coveralls out of her pack and shook life back into the purportedly wrinkle-proof fabric.

Quinn threw a smile over his shoulder, shedding the transport driver's uniform they had ended up not needing and pulling on his own set of coveralls.

Once dressed, Gideon laid his backpack on an adjacent conveyor belt and began a methodical inventory of the miniaturized data components they would need at points yet to come. After carefully stowing each in the hiding places skillfully integrated into his new set of clothing, he stuffed the backpack into the recesses of a rusty bin and headed for a side door in order to stand watch while waiting for Valaria who had taken a detour in order to empty her bladder.

As Quinn approached the doorway, a small flock of startled pigeons suddenly took flight in front of him; a flurry of beating wings that stirred up a whirlwind of debris as he inadvertently disturbed their roost. It was only a moment's distraction but it was enough to keep him from noticing the black-clad Guardian rounding the corner of the next building.

"What the hell are you doing in there," the man barked officiously.

Approaching Quinn with a crackling StunStik held out in front of him, he glanced inside the shadowy interior just in time to catch sight of Valaria zipping up her coveralls.

A lascivious sneer smeared the Guardian's face as he drew a distinctly carnal conclusion.

"This is one helluva stupid spot for a hook-up," he said.

The man's eyes raked over Valaria. He started to laugh but it wasn't mirth that ignited his pleasure.

"But then again," he added as he took note of the drooping conveyor belt behind her, "maybe this isn't such a bad place for a shag."

He moved forward, StunStik now crackling in Valaria's direction. "Just what's it worth the two of you for me not to turn you in?"

Quinn started forward but the Guardian whirled in his direction.

"Stay where you are, Romeo."

Quinn raised his hands in feigned acquiescence and the man continued toward Valaria. His hair was dirty and his breath was foul; he would never be chosen for a Guardian recruitment poster but then, a decaying factory was hardly a posting for first-rate officers.

Valaria stood her ground, her face unreadable.

Referencing the StunStik, she finally spoke. "That's not the most appealing thing to offer a woman, you know."

The comment was unexpected and his eyes involuntarily darted to the weapon.

It was just the lapse she had hoped for and she spun into a kick that landed powerfully on the Guardian's left kneecap.

Still brandishing the StunStik, the man stumbled away from her bellowing in pain and waving the crackling stunner toward Quinn as he darted forward. The weapon was easily evaded as the hobbled Guardian lurched in Gideon's direction and Quinn landed a convincing kick of his own that sent the man reeling back toward Valaria, muttering obscenities.

He threw the stunner aside and pulled a pulse gun from the holster strapped to his leg.

Quinn skidded to stop about a yard short of his quarry.

"What you gonna do now," the man snarled, pointing the gun at Gideon's head.

It was Valaria who answered.

Moving in from behind, she felled the Guardian with a kick to the back of his injured knee, locked him in a chokehold as he crumbled backward, and wrenched his neck sharply as she heaved him to the floor.

The silence that followed was deafening.

"Well shit," Quinn said at last. "Now we've got a dead Guardian on our hands."

"Better him than you," Valaria replied.

Struggling for emotional purchase, she leaned heavily against the rusting hulk of the nearest machine.

"And anyway, he'd have to be a helluva lot better looking before I'd be willing to make that particular sacrifice for The Cause," she added with dry sarcasm.

Quinn appraised her coolly as he grabbed the Guardian's ankles and began dragging him toward the back of the building. "Bloody Hell, when did you become Griffin's doppelganger?"

She took his words as a compliment.

VII.

Boarding the Indianapolis Bullet was surprisingly easy. They had blended into the waiting group of freshly-showered workers without inspiring more than one or two curious glances. The crowd moved passively toward the checkpoint standing between them and the waiting train, reminding Valaria of the clueless salmon back at the settlement fish farm that swam unwittingly into bins collecting them for harvest. Moving with the flow she experienced a momentary rush of adrenaline when it came time to be scanned by the Guardians manning the depot but the tiny dermal chips inserted into the tags on the back of their necks worked perfectly and they were passed on without incident.

Entering the train with the others, Quinn gestured Valaria to the second of the four seats in each row while he sat next to her on the aisle.

No one was talking—whether from fatigue or the presence of government watchdogs was hard to tell. The only sound was the rhythmic thrum of the magnarail as the sleek, aerodynamic train effortlessly gained momentum and flew forward at amazing speeds, glistening like quicksilver in the spring sunshine. Under ordinary circumstances Valaria would have been intoxicated by the new experience but instead of drinking it in she kept finding herself back in the debris and grime of the derelict factory clutching the corpse of a foul-smelling Guardian.

Lieutenant Griffin would have given her high marks. She had faced the enemy and her response had been instinctive and effective; she had saved her partner's life.

But in doing so she had taken another's.

The reality was heavy and cloying; a darkly fetid albatross she knew she would shoulder for a long, long time.

Dragging herself back into the present, Valaria held her emotions in check by drawing the right side of her lower lip between her teeth and biting down. With slow, steady breaths she tried to distract herself by surveying the impassive faces of the other passengers. Most were comfortably slouched in their seats quietly dozing. Some, however, looked more dazed than tired; their expressions dull, their eyes disturbingly vacant. She couldn't help smirking; they looked kind of stoned. She found their obvious acquiescence seriously disheartening but was struck by the thought that at least the poor sods got to go back to the Zone each evening and didn't have to live where they worked. That would have been a fate worse than exile and undoubtedly was the carrot that accompanied the stick.

Isolated and adrift in her grim reverie, Valaria hadn't noticed that Quinn was caught up in observations of his own. He sat slumped beside her, arms casually folded across his chest, eyelids drooping as he assumed the posture of just another tired worker. Dozing was a well-practiced ruse, however, and in reality he was totally alert. Occasionally shifting position, his veiled eyes scrutinized passengers and Guardians alike for signs of danger.

One worker in particular had garnered his attention.

The man sat next to the window across the aisle and three rows ahead. Although appearing just as tired as everyone else, he sat at an angle in his seat and was watching his fellows with deceptively keen eyes and sly glances—glances that seemed particularly interested in Valaria and Quinn.

About fifteen minutes into the trip the man appeared to have made a decision. He rose from his seat and wormed his way past the three other people in his row toward the center aisle. With a final surreptitious glance toward the dozing Quinn, he headed for the Guardian stationed about ten rows ahead at the front of the car.

Gideon was immediately on his feet and heading down the aisle in the opposite direction, Valaria looking on with confused concern.

"Excuse me, sir," he said to a Guardian approaching from the rear. "May I speak to you, please?"

The officer glared at Quinn and for a moment Valaria fully expected him to respond by simply stunning Gideon back into his seat. Instead, he grabbed Quinn by the sleeve and shoved him toward the back of the car.

Realizing something must be seriously wrong, Valaria quickly took stock of their surroundings. One of their fellow passengers had moved to the front where he apparently was waiting to speak with a Guardian who was preoccupied on his communicator. Other than that, nothing had changed; people dozed, stared out the windows, stared vacantly into space.

In just a few minutes, Quinn had been deposited roughly back into his seat and two Guardians strode purposefully up the aisle.

"What's happening," Valaria whispered.

Quinn nodded toward the man still waiting for the Guardian at the front of the car. "I told them I'd heard that guy bad-mouthing the regime while we waited for the train."

"Why'd you do that?"

"Because he was about to denounce us."

Three black-clad officers had converged upon the worker who was loudly denying the accusations they leveled against him.

The entire crowd of workers seemed to wince as one as the man was repeatedly stunned before being dragged from the car in a semi-conscious stupor.

It had been silent before, now it was deathly still.

Valaria leaned into Quinn's shoulder.

"How can you be so sure he was going to denounce us?" she asked in a barely audible whisper.

Quinn slouched a bit more and closed his eyes.

"He obviously wanted to talk to them about something," he said in a hush, "and he'd been watching us since the depot. He's either a plant or a snitch; either way, we needed a distraction and he provided it."

"What'll happen to him?"

"Don't know," Quinn replied stoically. "But it's like you said about the Guardian— better him than us."

"When government violates the people's freedoms, insurrection is the most sacred of rights and the most indispensible of duties."

~ Marquis De Lafayette

CHAPTER FOURTEEN

I.

Regina Agnew swiveled her chair away from her desk to gaze across the panoramic vista of the city far below the wall of glass at her back. The people scurrying around the open expanse at ground level were little more than insects from this vantage point and she smiled at the deliciously apropos metaphor for she experienced an almost morbid satisfaction in squashing them underfoot. Like the squirming, crawling, and flitting creatures of which they reminded her, the residents below were an interesting study and, yes, even necessary in the broader scheme of things. But just as with those other pests, there were times when she would have taken great delight in holding a magnifying glass over them and watching the sun's intensified rays reduce the hoi polloi to nothing more than smoldering husks.

Regina Agnew was not a nice person.

But she was powerful and, like many in whose footsteps she followed, she was addicted to power's exhilarating rush.

A skillful manipulator, over the years Agnew had honed her talents and played the game of power masterfully, allowing nothing and no one to stand in her way. Before the age of thirty she already was an integral member of the Telliman Institute, an influential think-tank that rose to prominence in the years before the plague. Ingratiating herself into the director's life until he couldn't even sneeze without her holding the tissue, Regina Agnew had polished her self-serving dexterity to razor sharp perfection on the whetstone of her ambition. Ruthlessly determined to be the architect of her own destiny not even something as bothersome as a pandemic could thwart the young tyro's insatiable desire for power, and the nation's subsequent collapse had simply provided countless opportunities to fill whatever niche best suited her purpose at the moment. And so, resolved not merely to survive but to thrive after The Revanche, Regina Agnew had joined the Neoteric Party and embraced its values and dogma with an enthusiasm rivaling St. Paul's conversion on the road to Damascus.

So far, it had served her well.

"...Excuse me. Overseer?"

From the other side of the room, the obsequious voice of her assistant interrupted her reverie.

Agnew's voice in return dripped with annoyance. "What is it?"

"There's a problem with the distribution of Radiance. Shall I look into it?"

"No," the woman's boss replied curtly, swiveling her chair back toward her desk. "I'll handle it."

Her ruminating interrupted, Agnew watched the younger woman move gracefully to the office door before activating her computer. Its translucent screen appeared at eye level above her desk and she paused for a moment, scrutinizing the face reflected in the opaque projection. Leaning in, she tugged backward slightly beneath each earlobe, scowling as softening along her jaw line disappeared.

"Minder," she barked to the ubiquitous information system that served the towers, "contact MedCentral and make an appointment with Dr. Lantz for tomorrow."

Having had her first cosmetic enhancement as a preventative measure long before the onslaught of middle age, Agnew was obsessed with continuing to fine tune the results now that seventy loomed on the horizon. She might have to work with younger people but she refused to be humiliated in the process. Lantz would just have to fix things—again.

And *she* would have to fix the problem with distribution of Radiance. As Overseer of Homeland Security for the Indianapolis Safe Zone there was an impressive pecking order of sycophantic lackeys below her to whom she could delegate such tasks but Agnew scoffed at the thought. She hadn't gouged her way to the top by taking the chance of others getting the upper hand through the gathering of either information or recognition and she wasn't about to risk any threat to her status at this stage of the game. Like a Gilded Age parvenu longing for the status conferred by a listing in *Debrett's*, Regina Agnew lusted after a level of power that heretofore had managed to elude her. Come the proverbial Hell or high water, her next stop would be Columbus—the seat of national power—and nothing was going to stand in her way.

All she needed to do was find the best fuel to launch the next phase of her ascent.

By the time they disembarked the Bullet train in Indianapolis it had crossed Quinn's mind that the most challenging part of the mission might simply be keeping Valaria from giving them away by looking like a gobsmacked hick as she surveyed the gleaming city. The blighted remains of St. Louis had entranced the woman from the Borders but this was amazement on a totally different level. It was Oz and Wonderland all rolled into one lustrous package and Valaria found it difficult to maintain her poker face as marvels unfolded at every turn.

The Safe Zones included only a fraction of the territory originally claimed when the extensive conurbations had been thriving concerns prior to the plague, but they nonetheless were eons ahead of the RSA's Borders settlements. Where the Borders was drab and decaying the Safe Zones were pristine and polished. Instead of a lifestyle barely in keeping with the previous century, the Zones appeared poised to make the leap into the next. Valaria had never seen such complex and modern human systems and even though the regime at their heart was mercilessly determined to mold the people into its rigid vision of Utopia, on the surface the city seemed very close to what she thought that lofty goal might actually look like.

By design, each city was surrounded by a barren mile-wide 'demilitarized zone' separating it from its own personal hinterland comprised of countless square miles of unreclaimed suburban sprawl that had been scoured for any usable resources before ultimately being abandoned to nature. Metal had been stripped from innumerable deserted buildings and any products remaining on store shelves—everything from tuna to tampons—had been appropriated by the regime for use during the lean times following The Revanche. And once Blanchard's 'Remnant' had been safely ensconced within their respective Zones, the regime not only had consolidated its power but also had mobilized the citizenry into a workforce tasked with one glorious purpose—transforming the Safe Zones into idyllic citadels, each the proverbial City on a Hill. When complete, the Zones not only would insulate their inhabitants from external threats and undesirable influences but would shine forth as beacons of state-of-the-art sophistication—a tribute to the Triumvirate's wisdom and selfless dedication to progress.

As the Bullet sped toward the beacon known as Indianapolis the magnarail tracks rose steadily until they were high above the Hoosier

City's barren DMZ, banking into a wide curve designed not only to slow the train but also intended to present the Safe Zone at dramatic advantage. It was all old hat to the dazed and dozing workers slumped around them but Valaria was enthralled, her attention temporarily distracted from the putrefying albatross killing the Guardian had shackled her to.

Although not as tall as the skeletal fingers of St. Louis's derelict skyscrapers, the cityscape before her rose to impressive heights and Valaria was captivated by its shimmering splendor. There was an extensive area of development at ground level but a significant portion of the city seemed to be concentrated into a series of five gracefully spiraling glass and metal towers. Almost more art than architecture, every elegant twist of each majestic high-rise was complimented by wide flat garden platforms that fanned outward on alternating sides. Lush with dwarf trees, flowers, and thick vines cascading over the sides, they successfully enhanced the modern skyline with therapeutic touches of green.

Striving to contain her sightseeing at a level that could still be described as surreptitious, Valaria had to hold herself in check lest she literally crawl across the workers blocking her line of sight. Silently damning them to ten minutes in Hell for the transgression of being in her way, Valaria's visual quest was further thwarted by periodic government PSA's that completely commandeered the view as the train's windows morphed into display screens at regular intervals. Christened 'GovLines' by the regime—and 'GagLines' by its detractors—the announcements extolled the Triumvirate's alleged accomplishments and always ended with a reminder of the expectation of vigilant compliance.

The bombardment became nearly constant as they drew closer to the Zone and was almost more than the rebellious exile could handle.

"Geez," Valaria murmured into Quinn's ear, slouching down in a petulant huff. "Do they ever shut up?"

She folded her arms across her chest in defiant frustration and tried to mimic the glazed-over, unreadable mug of her companion.

A smirk flitted across Quinn's face but he kept his eyes averted. "Welcome to Wonderland."

As if in response the Bullet slowed, beginning its descent to ground level en route to the station.

For convenience, the Amtrak magnarail was based in the heart of each Safe Zone. Gliding effortlessly into the glass and metal citadel's lowest level, the Bullet crossed the center of a wide expanse of pavement intended to accommodate daily foot traffic. Made from a composite of reclaimed concrete and a flexible additive, the oval-shaped expanse was weatherproof, slightly sparkly in appearance, and almost spongy to walk on. With trees and large container gardens complementing the sparkling surface it was designed to perfection and spotlessly clean.

But meticulously orchestrated purpose didn't stop with the oval expanse. In keeping with progressive city planners of the past who ordained that people both live and work within a restricted radius—an idea President Blanchard ardently embraced—multi-level housing units assigned to 'bottom-dwellers' hugged the edge of the expanse's curved perimeter perched atop the businesses that employed and served the masses. And in order to provide their more privileged tower-dwelling counterparts access to the ground level train station, stylized escalators flanking the station ascended toward automated walkways that connected the five spiraling high-rises that soared above the lowly proletariat and housed the residences and businesses of the elite.

Valaria took in the beauty and efficiency with an amazed—but increasingly jaded—eye.

Before her was clear evidence of the first lesson Quinn had sought to teach her—in the Safe Zones every citizen had a role, a job, and a clearly defined *place* in the far-from-fluid society that had developed in Naomi Blanchard's version of America.

As they left the train and passed through the station—an elegant glass-enclosed waiting area spanning both sides of the tracks—Valaria noticed an unmanned Guardian kiosk adjacent the official entry point.

"No Guardians?" she asked in quiet surprise as the disgorging factory workers quickly dispersed.

"Not necessary," Quinn explained. "Everybody was scanned before boarding and there's no way anyone could sneak onto a moving Bullet so this end's considered clean."

"Clean? Shit, half of them look stoned. Look at these people, Quinn. Are drugs allowed in the RSA?"

"Some—controlled for recreational use like alcohol."

They walked away from the station at a pace matching that of the dispersing workers—neither fast nor slow enough to draw the attention of black-clad Guardians stationed around the perimeter and wandering in pairs through the crowd. Valaria had to bite her lip to keep from repeating her oft-shared observation that black was a painfully-predictable cliché and plaid or polka dots would be a refreshing departure for government storm troopers. It made her think of the polka dot wrist-wrap Quinn had bestowed upon her months before and she wondered how its current caretaker was faring, along with his teenaged and canine charges.

Valaria's musings were interrupted by the increasing thrum of the magnarail's powerful heartbeat and she glanced back just in time to see the sleek Bullet train shoot away from the station toward the opposite end of the ground-level expanse. Once clear of the habitat area, it would gain height as well as speed, again rising above the barren DMZ that encircled the city and then continuing east to the Columbus Safe Zone.

"Holy shit," she murmured. "This place is amazing."

"Well, it's been more than thirty years in the making," Quinn observed drily. "You can accomplish a helluva lot in that much time when you're the queen bee with thousands of worker-drones at your disposal."

The words were barely out of his mouth when, as if on cue, a GovLines hologram rose up from a circular disc embedded in the spongy pavement a few steps ahead of them. The 3D images of two impeccably-groomed workers smiled warmly as they approached.

"Hello Citizens," the implausibly beautiful woman crooned. "Thank you for your contribution to our safety and prosperity today. Don't forget, we won't succeed if we don't all do our part."

"That's right," her equally-striking male counterpart interjected. "The Triumvirate's tireless dedication has set the standard and now it's our turn to contribute to Equilibrium—and to denounce malcontents who seek to pull us down!"

"So remember friends," they chirped happily in unison, "Stay alert and alert the authorities about threats to our security!"

The holographic duo evaporated into the ether, their image replaced by the phrase 'BE ALERT' that hovered for a moment before fading.

Valaria threw Quinn a mordant look. "Equilibrium?"

"More propaganda shit from the government," he explained.

An example of the regime's obsession with slogans and adroitly-crafted titles, Equilibrium was the label attached to the Triumvirate's lofty claim of having successfully balanced the post-Revanche dilemma of supply versus demand. Such programs were an essential component of the government's restructuring of the country and were lauded everywhere. Everything from GovLine PSAs like the hologram to which they had just been subjected, to broadcasts in every hallway, workplace, and residence

273

touted the accomplishments of the government's Neoteric policies—and made it abundantly clear disloyalty wouldn't be tolerated.

Quinn's words were prescient as a trio of workers passing nearby triggered a PSA praising the wisdom of the regime's 'Patriot Protocols.'

"Damn," Valaria whispered, "no wonder Otis opted for exile."

GovLines infodiscs were embedded throughout the oval expanse at twenty-foot intervals creating a honeycomb of annoying interruptions to passersby. Since they were triggered by anyone coming within range—and at this time of day the area was increasingly crowded—PSAs popped up around Quinn and Thorpe like bubbles in a pot of boiling water as they continued across the pavement. Government propaganda bombarded anyone heading for the shops and housing units at the periphery of the expanse in the same way earlier generations had been tormented by unsolicited telemarketers. It created a strange cacophony of sound as the holograms competed with the conversations of their intended audience. The letter of the law required one to stop and listen but everyone had heard them countless times and most people only paused momentarily in a gesture of compliance that seemed to suffice—and some had become adept at taking a decidedly circuitous route that avoided as many discs as possible but made them look rather disoriented as a result; their path weaving across the expanse like a drunk who has lost his moorings.

Not convinced that the GovLines dogging the heels of the citizenry sufficiently inculcated their message, the regime had frosted their propaganda cake with huge LED panels embedded in the walls between storefronts. The ultra high-definition 3-D projections alternated between displays of glamorized images of the Triumvirate—in which Naomi Blanchard always appeared larger than her two colleagues—and the myriad slogans designed to make martial law more palatable and draw attention away from the extreme price they were paying for the promise of progress and safety. Valaria noticed that a few seemed to dominate:

RESTORE stability

REBUILD the nation

RECLAIM The Wilds

The reason for rationing
is recovery!
(Report malcontents!)

DUTY
DILIGENCE
DELIVERANCE

And the ever popular…

STAY ALERT–
and ALERT AUTHORITIES
about threats to our security!

When they reached the southern side of the oval-shaped expanse, Valaria paused in front of the store they approached. She seemed almost mesmerized by the LED screen adjacent the entrance and Gideon touched her elbow before moving on.

"What's up?"

"Otis always said if pictures of a country's leaders are everywhere you look, you know the people are in seriously-deep shit. I'd totally forgotten that until right now."

"Wise man, your grandfather."

Valaria gestured to the majestic image of Naomi Blanchard and the reminder of the Triumvirate's promise of progress.

"Geez, Quinn," she scoffed quietly, "the woman can't really look like that, can she; she's been in power for almost forty years. Don't they ever see her?"

"Doesn't matter what she actually looks like; it's all smoke and mirrors—sensationalism and control." He handed her a tightly-folded reusable nylon bag. "C'mon, let's pick up today's allotment."

They entered the small store and joined a queue waiting to register for rations. At the front of the line, each person placed their hand on a scanner that immediately displayed their classification on an adjacent screen. Once registered, they continued down the counter toward a pick-up window next to the exit.

Even though Quinn appeared calm and unconcerned, as they moved up in line Valaria's heart began to pound.

When it was his turn Gideon smiled placidly at the worker behind the counter and placed his hand on the screen.

Valaria couldn't stop her sharp intake of breath and for an instant was back in the grimy factory looking into the sneering eyes of the Guardian she had killed. She hoped the scanner wasn't calibrated to detect nervousness for the hand she laid on it was clammy and cold.

Having lost every trace of an appetite, she accepted her rations almost without thinking and joined Quinn outside the shop.

"I figured you had it covered," she said quietly, "but you almost gave me heart failure when you put your hand on that scanner. How'd our handprints get into the system?"

He gave her his most beguiling smile. "Need-to-know, Valaria, need-to-know."

He turned and walked on.

"Oh my God, I hate you," she muttered to his back. "I well and truly hate you."

III.

Their first night in Indianapolis was uneventful. They accessed a small, furnished apartment on the third level of workers' housing without garnering so much as a curious glance from their neighbors and Quinn immediately hacked into the surveillance mechanism to once again register the flat as unoccupied. Confident of being unobserved, the duo settled in for a quiet evening—as quiet as possible, that is, when one has no control over the timing of government broadcasts emanating from the expansive vid-wall built into every dwelling regardless of how spartan the accommodations might otherwise be. Valaria was amazed by the scope of the 3D images. In comparison it made the eighty-inch screen back home in the pub seem like the ancient hand-held game system Otis had managed to keep from his childhood; she was almost willing to spend the evening watching the government channel just to bask in the vast display. Entertainment choices were limited and regularly interrupted by GovLines but she soon discovered numerous channels dedicated to specific sports—the regime's version of 'Bread and Circuses'—where replays of events featuring long-dead athletes playing in venues that no longer existed cycled through beginning from the mid-twentieth century. It took Valaria only a few moments to find the baseball channel and nestle into a nondescript government-issued chair with her nondescript government-issued meal.

"One good thing about the Borders," she observed during a GovLines break, "we don't have as much of this nonstop propaganda shit. Guess they've given up trying to convince us how wonderful they are. With Guardians almost literally watching you take a crap, most exiles just do their work and keep their heads down."

Quinn gave a derisive chuff. "Not much different from the Zones in that regard."

The Borders might have been spared constant governmental noise but the Safe Zones were spared the exiles' curfew and sounds of a fairly significant nightlife soon began rising from the pubs and cafes at ground level. Distracted from the game, Valaria dimmed the lights so as not to stand out as a gawker and stood at the living room window watching the patrons of an open-air club almost directly below them.

"C'mon Quinn," she urged, "let's go down for awhile—a little diversion can be a healthy thing, you know."

"Sorry," he replied without looking up from the datapad someone had left in a cleverly concealed cubby for them. "Clubbing isn't on the agenda. Low profile, remember—or have you forgotten we're not supposed to be here."

"I haven't forgotten. Hell, I couldn't feel more foreign if I'd been dropped in the middle of some remote Amazon village, if such places still exist."

She paused for a moment before deciding on a different approach. "But think of all the information out there just waiting to be overheard."

"And just think of all the plain-clothed Guardians milling through the crowd just waiting for somebody to slip up."

"Aw, come on—pleeez?"

"Bloody hell, you sound like my sister trying to wheedle privileges out of our parents."

"You never said anything about a sister."

Quinn continued studying the datapad.

"What's her name? Where is she?"

He heaved an exasperated sigh. "Go to bed, Valaria. Tomorrow's going to be a busy day."

Recognizing the unequivocal dismissal in Quinn's voice, Valaria returned to the game. She knew she should sleep but was almost desperate to stay awake and find an effective form of diversion for as long as possible.

Always prone to vivid dreams, an anticipated nocturnal reunion with the Guardian she had killed had her almost immobilized by wakeful foreboding.

IV.

Not surprisingly, Gideon rose first in the morning. He was showered and changed and eating breakfast when Valaria stumbled groggily out of the bedroom.

"God, you look terrible," he said bluntly. "You OK?"

"Of course I'm OK," she growled. "Just shut the hell up for a few minutes and let me get my sea legs."

She staggered off toward the bathroom, giving him the middle-finger salute when he informed her she had about fifteen minutes to acquire those legs.

Valaria leaned heavily against the bathroom door and looked at herself in the mirror. Quinn was right; she looked like crap.

It had been a rough night. Sleep had been elusive, the warehouse scene replaying on a continual loop in her head as she stared unseeing into the darkness. Once she finally drifted off, the specter of the dead Guardian had followed, taunting and hounding her. If she wasn't reliving the moment when she broke his neck she was plunged into the opposite scenario where Quinn lay dead with an impossibly-large, smoldering hole in the center of his forehead and the Guardian's dirty hands were on her, her nostrils choked with the foul smell of his terminal halitosis.

"For chrissake," she said to the haggard woman in the mirror, "get a grip!"

She paused for a moment before taking the wet bar of soap from the edge of the sink and scrawling the letters *WWGD* across her face on the mirror.

"What would Griffin do?" she asked her reflection.

The answer was as plain as the thick, soapy letters. Lieutenant Griffin would let it go. He would focus on the fact that she had done exactly what she had been trained to do—save her partner's life and protect the mission. She knew he was right and believed she was strong enough to eventually reach that point but the albatross of memory smelled particularly foul that morning.

278

"You sure you're OK?" Gideon asked when she rejoined him.

A noncommittal mumble was her only response.

"I mean with what happened yesterday."

She looked at him with a stoic, tight-lipped smile and shrugged slightly. "I will be."

Quinn handed her a cup of coffee as she joined him at a small built-in dinette.

"You ever kill anybody?" she asked before taking a sip.

"Yes," he said gravely. "And I've gotta tell you, Valaria, it doesn't get any easier—and it shouldn't. There really are times when there's no other choice—times when it's literally kill or be killed—but I don't ever want to get used to it."

Before continuing he sat for a moment just scrutinizing the black coffee shimmering in his cup. "I could run through all the patriotic clichés about how we're fighting for our freedom and how this is a momentous turning point in the history of the nation but I know all that flag-waving stuff just makes you want to hurl so we'll skip it. But this much we both know is true, it's time to take a stand. And standing up means there are going to be losses on both sides."

He reached across the table and clasped her free hand.

"You're strong," he assured her. "You'll find perspective…"

She nodded solemnly.

"…And anyway," he added in an irreverent effort to lighten the mood, "the guy was a total pig."

Valaria yanked her hand away.

"You are such an ass—you know that, don't you?"

"Yes," he smirked with feigned indifference. "Yes, I do."

When they had finished breakfast and repacked supplies, Quinn gave careful directions about wiping every surface of the small flat that might retain their prints or DNA. They were dressed in the uniforms required for the next stage of their mission but just before leaving he tossed Valaria the pair of coveralls she had worn the previous day.

"You ready to see how the upper class lives?" he asked while pulling his own coveralls up over his clothes.

"Can't wait," Valaria replied. "Let's go give 'em hell."

"Hold on, cowboy; no giving them hell." He handed her the ID card identifying them as janitors. "Just a good cleaning."

Wearing two layers of clothing made Valaria feel conspicuously bulky but no one paid any attention to them as they made their way downstairs and out onto the expanse. It was a beautiful morning, the sky a vivid blue with no trace of clouds but most of the people hurrying across the sparkling pavement seemed too focused or dazed to notice—what Valaria noticed was that only a fraction as many GovLines holograms were popping up around them.

"That's because it's morning," Quinn explained. "The regime wants everybody to get to work on time so saves the full bombardment for the end of the day."

"How thoughtful of them," she murmured with indignant sarcasm as they walked on.

Quickly absorbed into a sea of khaki-clad workers, they headed for the escalators at the center of the expanse, the only access point to the five spiraling towers and the suspended walkways several stories above their heads. Two beefy Guardians flanked the approach but Quinn strode forward without a trace of hesitation or concern. The thickly-muscled officers stared at the advancing duo, nearly drooling in their obvious eagerness to at least challenge if not actually find cause to detain them.

Without speaking, Quinn submitted to a scan of the tag on the back of his neck and presented his forged authorization.

Finished with her partner, the enforcers turned their attention to Valaria. "Designation?"

"Upsilon 9-3-7-9-4," she replied without missing a beat.

"Work assignment?"

"Unit seventeen, level three."

The Guardian scanned her tag and authorization before directing her onto the escalator and turning to enthusiastically intimidate the next worker.

Valaria moved up a few steps on the gliding staircase in order to join Quinn, throwing him a snarky "*See? I really was paying attention to your briefings*" look of satisfaction as she did so.

Like the current of a gently meandering stream, the escalator's smooth gradient merged seamlessly with the system of automated walkways that wove around the five towers on the next level—the realm of privileged 'mid' and 'upper' dwellers. Utilizing eddies that flowed in different directions one could efficiently travel between the high-rises with no effort beyond paying attention to entrance and exit notifications. Most tower residents chose the walkways but some actually preferred the snaking causeway's open periphery. Made of the same spongy composite as the expanse below—and augmented with lush container gardens in a park-like setting—it made walking pleasant as well as providing a route for joggers and dog-walkers.

As the escalator brought the upper level into view, Quinn nodded toward another pair of Guardians waiting at the top.

"Welcoming committee," he murmured.

The enthusiastic enforcers were almost shoving workers off the walkway in their zeal to make it abundantly clear that bottom-dwellers employed in the towers were relegated to the non-automated periphery once reaching the top.

Valaria shot Quinn an *"oh-my-God-you've-got-to-be-kidding-me"* scowl that clearly expressed her opinion as they walked away from the fortunate few. A significant number of workers commuted to the upper levels each day and the pair moved along the causeway in the company of cooks, cleaners, hair stylists, repairmen and the like along with a fair contingent of joggers and walkers.

They hadn't gone far when Quinn stopped in front of a utility room, keyed in the entry code, and led the way inside.

Valaria was about to burst.

"This place is such a God-damned *Animal Farm*," she fumed referring to a banned book Otis had smuggled into the Borders and insisted they read and discuss when she was ten. "Why do people tolerate the 'more equal' status of the bastards living up here?"

Having discovered that totalitarian allegory himself at a young age, Quinn smiled but he also offered a decidedly sympathetic shrug for those she derided. "You've got a job, you're reasonably safe, there's food on the table—it's not so surprising most of them acquiesce without much thought. And don't forget, they either survived the horror of the plague or this is all they've ever known. Either one is a pretty compelling recipe for compliance; especially with Guardians glaring at you all the time."

Valaria considered his words in silence for a moment. "I've gotta be honest, Quinn. I used to think all your 'let's form our own country' stuff was kind of stupid and that rejoining the RSA would be best for everybody in the long run. But I'm beginning to see what you mean. We should just leave these people to their perverted little Utopia and start fresh."

"Does that mean you no longer believe what Mavis Pope said about the Safe Zones thriving?"

Valaria exhaled sharply at what she now considered her friend's rose-colored memory of life prior to being exiled. "Mavis had her head up her ass much of the time. Things here may look OK but there's no way this place is thriving—not when you've got all this totalitarian shit going on and people going around looking terrified or stoned. Naw, let's go build something of our own and then maybe someday we can offer these poor sods an alternative."

"Good," he replied. "So, you ready to get started?"

"I said it before—let's go give 'em hell."

Like butterflies emerging from dull cocoons, the duo shed their worker's coveralls and stood transformed into information specialists, Quinn's documentation identifying him as an Information Technology Supervisor with Valaria cast as his personal assistant.

"You sure this is gonna work?" she asked, succumbing to a final surge of nerves.

Quinn smiled as he gave his uniform a final straightening. "Relax. Like I told you back at the Hub, I've used this identity before. And the regime's not as omnipotent as it thinks. I hide in plain sight and use their own system to transfer myself around the Zones as needed."

He looked at her and winked.

"This is where it gets interesting."

V.

The Information Technology Department for the Indianapolis Safe Zone was housed on the lowest level of Tower 2. The department was manned by twenty mid-dwelling technicians stationed at intervals around a large windowless room. Like the interconnected components of a Rube Goldberg device reacting in well-orchestrated sequence, they sat up a bit straighter in front of their terminals as awareness of Quinn and Thorpe's presence made the circuit around the room.

The lead operator hurried over to greet them, wiping instantly-sweaty palms across his thighs before reaching out to shake hands.

"It's good to see you again, Supervisor," he simpered in sycophantic recognition of the arrival of a superior. "Things have been running so much better since your last visit."

Gideon gave the underling a level stare. "Good to hear."

The man cast a nervous glance toward Valaria before cautiously venturing further. "May I ask what brings you back?"

"The system needs to be prepped for the next series of upgrades from Columbus."

"Oh, yes, of course," the man stammered with an obsequious gesture toward a door at the back of the room. "My office is yours for however long you need it."

Without introducing the woman beside him, Quinn strode purposefully past the lead technician and shut the office door almost in the man's face. Holding a finger to his lips before Valaria could speak he went to the desk, swiveled the virtual computer display around to face him, and began entering a series of rapid commands.

"OK," he said at last. "The room's secure."

"Geez, Quinn, they nearly fell at your feet."

"This is a good cover," he explained. "I'm pretty high on the food chain here." He gave a scornful huff. "In Nashville, my boss is a paranoid buffoon who hates my guts and would love to find a reason to denounce me."

"Well, McFarland was obviously wrong—you sure don't need me along."

"I wouldn't say that," he observed. "The lead tech's even more fawning than usual—bet he thinks you're some kind of government Watcher; which can definitely work to our advantage."

Without wasting time, Quinn settled in behind the desk. Although his Indianapolis persona was fairly high ranking, the data mining he needed to do necessitated digging through layers of extraneous programming and weaving his way through a minefield of encryption protocols and seductive technological traps euphemistically called 'honey pots' in order to ultimately access the information they sought.

Taking advantage of the technicians' apparent belief that Valaria was a government Watcher, Quinn periodically sent her into the outer work area where she simply walked the perimeter, giving the techies her best glower as she looked over their shoulders in a pretense of monitoring their work. It was a distraction that kept them off balance—and was a role she was born to play. Never having had patience for those she deemed "ass kissers," Valaria took no small measure of satisfaction in making the roomful of nervous technicians squirm under her disapproving gaze.

"How's it going?" she asked Quinn after completing one of her rounds.

"I'll spare you details I know you don't want. Suffice it to say this isn't easy."

He stood up, stretched broadly, and went to stand at the adjacent window.

"I keep running across references to something called the 'Radiant Cascade' or just 'Radiance,'" he commented, looking back at the translucent screen. "That's definitely new."

"What is it?"

"I'm not exactly sure yet but it keeps leading me back to MedCentral so it's gotta be some kind of medical development. God, it's probably some kind of new cosmetic procedure; the elite here are totally obsessed with their appearance."

"What about the exiles. Any luck there?"

"No. But the tech is different from the last time I was in the States."

He paused, realizing that almost a year had passed since his last incursion. "There're more layers, more encryption, more of everything. They've definitely beefed up security which makes me wonder just what they're trying to hide."

"You gonna to be able to hack it?"

"Oh, I'll get in," he assured her. "I'm just going to have to be more creative."

They had come to the end of the work day and an apprehensive rap at the office door brought the hesitant request from the lead technician for permission from the Supervisor to send the workers home. Only too happy to have the place to themselves, Quinn dismissed the techies and rather curtly refused the lead tech's offer to stay.

After an hour or two longer, he and Valaria also called it a day.

"So, where are we staying tonight?" Valaria asked as they left the office.

Quinn paused before sharing information he knew was going to be downright incendiary.

"I have a flat in Tower 4," he said without further comment.

"You have a *tower* flat? How the hell did you manage that?"

"I told you this was a good cover."

Quinn's poker face had slid smoothly into place which only made Valaria more curious about what he *wasn't* saying.

Without giving her a chance to press the issue, he walked on.

In their current incarnation they no longer were relegated to the causeway's periphery and they joined the smattering of residents on the automated sidewalk. The sun was beginning to set and the quintet of spiraling towers was alive with light and activity against a dramatic backdrop of orange and red. Off to the sides the park-like setting was pleasant and appealing in the cool spring breeze but when Valaria suggested they do the walking themselves Quinn shook his head.

"Only a few tower-dwellers opt for manual walking," he explained. "There's a garden area near my flat; we can go there later if you want."

They reached Tower 4 after making three transfers—slightly harrowing challenges to dexterity for the exile who had never been on an automated sidewalk and had no experience managing intersections that made her feel like she was tap dancing on snakes. Grateful to exit the writhing walkway, Valaria stared up at the striking glass and metal monolith in both awe and relief as Quinn placed his palm on a scanner next to the main entrance. The door slid open, triggering a disembodied computerized voice in the process.

"Welcome home, Mr. Quinn. You have a guest with you?"

"Yes, Minder," Gideon replied. He took Valaria's wrist and placed her hand on the scanner. "This is Ms. Smith."

"Welcome, Ms. Smith," the voice said pleasantly. "We hope you enjoy your stay."

Quinn's admission that he had a tower flat had been something of an understatement. The apartment they accessed on the 15th floor was spacious, well-appointed, and—as promised—adjacent one of the plate-like garden extensions fanning out from the tower's elegant twist in which the apartment sat.

As they entered, a more personalized Minder's voice greeted them. "It's good to have you home, Gideon. Environmental controls in the guest suite have been turned on for Ms. Smith."

"Thank you, Minder."

Quinn once again held a finger to his lips in an effort to forestall the comments—likely coming in the form of a disgruntled tirade—that he anticipated from Valaria.

The Minder continued. "There are thirty-seven messages from your parents, and your sister accessed the apartment four times in your absence."

"Thank you, Minder," Quinn said again.

He opened a small panel in the wall next to the door and tapped in a security sequence of his own design while Valaria glared at him openly aghast.

"OK," he said. "We're no longer being monitored, have at it."

"Your *parents*?" she sputtered. "You told me you were born in the Borders."

"So?"

"So, you *lied* to me."

"Yes, Valaria; I lied."

She chuffed derisively. "You are such a son-of-a-bitch!"

"Well, I admit Mother is a bit of a self-serving old cow," Quinn smirked, "but I don't think I'd go so far as to call her a bitch."

As had happened in the past, he was having far too much fun at her expense and Valaria slugged him on the shoulder before stalking off in a not-insignificant huff.

"C'mon, Valaria, give me a break," Gideon cajoled.

She stopped in her tracks and whirled back toward him.

"Why didn't you tell me?" she demanded. "And if you say 'need-to-know,' I swear I'm gonna rip your tongue out!" She ran a hand through her unruly hair in frustration. "Bloody hell, Quinn, you have got to redefine what you think I should know and stop leaving me out of shit."

"Noted," he replied soberly. "And you're right; I should have told you earlier. It's just that I don't go around telling people about my background. McFarland knows, but being a rebel from the Borders buys me more credibility with the Sons."

Valaria chuffed. "I don't know about that. If you ask me, being a disaffected Zoner is a damned impressive pedigree. It sure as hell's got my attention."

She plopped down onto a long, low-backed curved sectional that created a conversation area in front of an impressive fireplace. Once their presence had been sensed, the expansive heater had automatically ignited and the flickering firelight added warmth as well as atmosphere from its location in an accent wall of shiny grey granite.

"God, it's gonna take me a while to get my head around this," Valaria said, looking at Quinn through new eyes. "And just who *are* your parents anyway?"

"Nobody important."

"Well, they sure aren't 'bottom-dwellers,'" she persisted, surveying the apartment. "This has got to be an upper level flat, right?"

"Yes, but there are hundreds of upper-dwellers in each Zone, Valaria."

Quinn's evasiveness was becoming almost as troubling as it was irritating.

"Geez, don't tell me you're related to President Blanchard," she chided with undisguised derision.

"Hardly."

There was a slight crack in Quinn's poker face.

"Ah, but you've *met* her, haven't you?"

"Yes, I've met her."

Valaria pressed her advantage. "So, I take it your parents work in Columbus, right?"

"Right."

She shook her head and laughed in scoffing disbelief.

"Ho-lee shit, Quinn!"

VI.

Valaria awoke the next morning surprisingly refreshed and calm. The guest suite to which she had retreated after her dismay and disdain over Quinn's revelation had played itself out was on the opposite side of the flat from the master bedroom he occupied, the open plan living, dining, and kitchen area lying between. When she had entered the room the night before the sound of wind through Ponderosa pines whispered in the background and it had smelled faintly of lavender and vanilla. She had lingered in a bath fragrant with the same scent and crawled gratefully—if still somewhat mystified—between sheets that were softer than Yancy's silky coat after a good combing. The Minder had quietly offered an array of different fragrances and white noise backdrops but she had found herself too relaxed to even engage in conversation with the computerized valet and drifted into one of the best night's sleep she had ever experienced.

Now feeling almost perky—a word previously consigned to the scorned and musty section of her vocabulary—Valaria dressed quickly and joined Quinn on a balcony adjacent the apartment's dining area.

"Man, there might just be something to this 'more equal' shit of yours," she observed with dry condescension sitting down opposite Gideon at a small wrought iron table.

Plates of fresh fruit and pastry as well as a carafe of strong coffee sat between them. Valaria picked up a lavishly iced cinnamon roll, pulled it apart, and dangled a gooey strip over her mouth as she smirked in silent disparagement at her host.

Quinn held up his hands in surrender.

"OK, OK, guilty as charged," he said. "But don't forget, this wasn't my choice, I was born into it—and I've willingly walked away."

Valaria couldn't resist pushing the sarcasm a bit further, resting her folded arms on the edge of the table and leaning in slightly. "And what would mom and dad have to say about that?"

Gideon's face went blank and he fell silent, making Valaria belatedly realize she had crossed into uncharted territory without noticing the 'No Trespassing' sign.

"They'll have a lot to say when they find out," he stated flatly after a moment. "But since I don't plan on coming back here after we're done, it's likely I'll be spared."

Their return trip to the IT department in Tower 2 was quiet. Both were preoccupied with thoughts of the task before them as well as still wearing the residue of their uncomfortable breakfast conversation. Valaria's mood had darkened considerably and even the discovery that she had achieved rudimentary mastery of the walkway's intersections did little to lighten the load. After returning to the lead tech's office, she sat quietly off to the side while Quinn worked, periodically making the rounds of the outer office as she had the day before—today's glum countenance seeming to intensify the affect she was having on the technicians.

It was midmorning when Quinn's data-mining struck the first truly productive vein.

"Got something," he announced with quiet satisfaction.

"What is it?"

"I've been focusing on 'Radiance,'" he explained. "The trail ends at MedCentral's pharmaceutical section so it's some kind of medicine—something more significant than a cosmetic enhancement, I'd say. Give me a minute and we should know pretty much everything there is to know about their 'Radiant Cascade.'"

His fingers continued to tease the virtual screen with all the elegant dexterity of Mozart at the piano, his face alight with wonder at the intricate technological symphony playing out before him.

Valaria looked on in silence as the flurry slowed and Quinn began to scrutinize the display. "Bloody hell... You know how you said some of the workers look dazed—*stoned?*"

"Yeah."

"Well, they are," he said with disgust as his index finger scrolled through information on the virtual screen. "The 'Radiant Cascade'— 'Radiance'—is a drug... A *'repatriation pharmaceutical'* they call it. I don't understand a lot of the medical stuff I'm reading but it says it causes a 'frontal lobe cascade.'"

Valaria came to look over his shoulder. "Like some kind of chemical lobotomy?"

"Probably not a bad description," he agreed, adding with a scoffing huff, "*Repatriation*—nothing more than a feeble euphemism for mind-control all wrapped up in patriotic jargon and tied off with red-white-and-blue ribbons."

"So if they can't scare you into compliance, they've decided to drug you into a walking-dead stupor?"

"Kind of looks that way. People aren't likely to rock the boat if they can't even hold an oar. Which probably at least partly explains the drop in exiles."

"But why drug them?" Valaria asked. "Just kick their asses to the Borders like they've been doing for the last 40 years and put 'em to work out there."

"I really don't think they can afford to do that anymore," Quinn replied. "I told you months ago that the Safe Zones aren't thriving. Population and production are both down. There are empty apartments at every level in every Zone and jobs going unfilled everywhere."

"Seems like that would make the Borders even more important—we send back food and all kinds of manufactured goods."

"It makes the Borders more *dangerous*," Quinn countered. "In many ways you're stronger than the Zones. For one thing most of you still think for yourselves—and the Borders's been a slow but steady drain on the base population ever since the Triumvirate came up with the idea of gulags in the hinterland. If they can 'repatriate' dissidents and use them at reclaimed factories like we saw on our way here, they won't need the Borders anymore."

Both fell silent for a moment as they waded through more onscreen medical jargon.

"So is this it?" Valaria asked at length. "Is their *'repatriation pharmaceutical'* the answer McFarland's looking for?"

"Maybe, but I want to dig deeper. I've seen other references to repatriation and want to see where they lead."

As Valaria took her seat off to the side, Quinn resumed his data mining. With surgical precision he worked his way through layers of sophisticated encryption, muttering to himself and periodically dropping a choice expletive as he evaded numerous honey-pots along the way.

After almost two more hours of digging, he abruptly leaned back in his chair and ran a hand through his hair in frustration. "I'm getting nowhere."

"I thought you said you'd get in."

"I will—eventually—but the longer it takes the more I risk exposure. The best I've been able to do so far is access some guy's memo files that had a few references to 'Repatriation.'"

"That's better than nothing; read them."

Backtracking agilely over an abandoned pathway, Quinn accessed the memo files and began scrolling through them.

Valaria pulled a chair up beside him. "Do you know this guy?"

"No," he replied, "the name's not familiar."

"Who's he writing to?"

"Most are directed to Regina Agnew. Now that name I do know; she's the Indianapolis Zone's Overseer of Homeland Security."

In a moment, Quinn was pointing to the screen. "OK, here's something. He refers to the *'selection process for Radiance repatriation'* in a memo dated a little more than a year ago—so all this drug stuff started about the same time I left to begin looking for you."

"Search for 'Borders' and see if anything comes up."

"In a minute," he muttered. "Take a look at this. He's talking about *'expunging the seditious element in order to protect the Homeland.'*"

"The 'seditious element'—that's people like us, right?"

"Yeah."

"Holy crap; that could mean Radiance will be given to exiles too."

"Wouldn't surprise me," he murmured.

"Well that's something worth fighting."

Quinn gave her a quizzical look. "You still need convincing?"

Without waiting for a response, he continued reading.

"What the hell," he stammered after a moment. "Listen to this; it's dated about eight months ago— '*There is no question that the stubbornly recalcitrant pose a particularly vexing threat to national security. Although not yet fully implemented, the Triumvirate's plan for Ultimate Repatriation is in keeping with accepted standards of care...*'"

"...'accepted standards of care,'" Valaria repeated. "What the hell does that mean?"

"Hold on, just listen, '...*the Triumvirate's plan for Ultimate Repatriation is in keeping with accepted standards of care where age, medical condition, or cost indicate that euthanasia is in the best interest of the State.*'"

Valaria's face drained of color. "Is that really saying what it sounds like? Drug the shit out of people but if that doesn't work then the Triumvirate's decided it's OK to *kill* them? What'd they call the poor sods—the *stubbornly recalcitrant*?"

"That's how I read it."

"How can they possibly justify something like that?"

"Guess you can justify just about anything in the name of national security—especially when you hold all the cards. Naomi Blanchard's personal favorite—Woodrow Wilson—actually said no line can be drawn that the government can't cross... which brings us right back to Eugenics. Proponents called it 'the science of being well born' but I prefer 'eugenicide' because radical progressives have always gone beyond wanting to sterilize undesirables to calling for euthanasia of the old, the disabled—the outcast. One guy came right out and said if you want a certain type of society you're gonna have to exterminate people who don't fit in—Hitler loved those assholes."

Quinn began activating the dormant base memory threaded into the tech-tattoo adorning the back of his left hand.

"This is it, Valaria," he said with quiet intensity as he worked. "This is the smoking gun; we don't need to look any further. I'm gonna download these memos and then we're going to get the hell out of here."

He smiled in tight-lipped reassurance as he monitored progress of the download.

Anxious, appalled and almost certain they had to be misinterpreting what they had read Valaria began restlessly pacing the small room until a quiet exclamation from behind her nearly stopped her heart.

"Oh no you don't, you bastard!"

"What's wrong?"

"I got sloppy," Gideon explained tersely, fingers beginning to fly across the virtual screen. "Stayed submerged too long; a Wraith is on to me."

"A wraith?"

"One of their security trackers."

"Is that a person or a thing?"

"Both," he murmured. "And this one's damn good!"

Valaria stood behind Quinn's chair and watched with a mixture of fascination and white-knuckled terror as he proceeded to play a game of high tech tag with a government tracker located in a dark corner of one of the Safe Zones. His adversary was obviously talented as well as determined and the two equally-matched antagonists created a virtual technological tapestry as one chased and the other eluded capture back and forth across an elaborate network of electrical impulses.

"Hurry up... Hurry up," Valaria whispered when she could stand it no longer. She shivered involuntarily as a trickle of nervous perspiration slithered down her backbone.

"Almost there," Quinn muttered.

Beads of sweat had appeared above his upper lip and he wiped at them absently with a hand that shook slightly.

"OK," he said, pulling his hands away from the screen as if scalded. "They obviously know they've been hacked but I've managed to send my path all over the country so hopefully they won't figure out that the hack originated here. Just for fun I terminated in Nashville—I'd love to see Christopher Damon try to explain this one."

"Just for *fun*? What are you, a masochist? And who's Christopher Damon?"

"My boss-from-Hell," Gideon replied, the trace of a confident smirk washing away the intensity of the last twenty minutes. "Come on, let's get out of here."

Quickly securing the download from the lead tech's computer to his tech-tat, Quinn returned the tattoo to dormancy and led the way out of the office. It was the end of the lunch session and the staff was just beginning to filter back in, resuming their stations around the perimeter of the windowless room. After a terse wrap-up conversation with the obviously relieved lead technician, the Supervisor and government Watcher left the IT Department and made their way toward the automated walkways that would take them back to the upper-level domain of Gideon Quinn.

VII.

Lively 1940's Big Band music reverberated off the walls as the door of Gideon's flat once again opened in response to his handprint. Half eaten food was spread across the low table in front of the sectional in the living area and a trail of clothing and other detritus led toward the guest suite.

"Oh great," he muttered, leaning against the closed door behind him and looking almost as fearful as he had while doing a technological tango with the government's Wraith.

A lithe young woman suddenly emerged from the guestroom brandishing a tall glass in which bright fuchsia-colored liquid sloshed dangerously close to the lip. Her long blonde hair was pulled up in a carefree pony tail, the ends died a contrasting burgundy. She was almost flippantly cute, indulging in a few up-tempo steps in time with the music before noticing the duo at the door.

"Gideon!"

Her face wreathed in smiles, she set the glass on the corner of the dining table, ran over, and threw her arms around Quinn's neck.

Although caught off guard, there was obvious affection in his return embrace. "Hello Elise."

"Oh my God," she chirped happily, "it's been forever! Where have you been—and who is this?"

She gave Valaria a speculative glance before directing her full attention back to Quinn, arms still draped around his neck.

"I've been working," he said in response to her first question. "A concept I realize you have difficulty grasping."

Extricating himself from Elise's arms, he gestured toward Valaria. "And this is Lari."

"Larry?" Elise asked, smiling at the masculine name.

"With an 'i'," Valaria interjected.

"Well, hello, Lari with an 'i,' I'm Elise."

"My little sister," Quinn supplied when the young woman left the introduction tantalizingly open to interpretation.

Elise took Gideon by the hand and led him to the sectional by way of the dining table where she retrieved her drink. "I can't believe we're finally here at the same time!"

Valaria followed in silence and sat at the far end of the curved seating area, watching. The dynamics of siblinghood were a mystery to her and she was intrigued by the breezy interaction between brother and sister.

"That begs the question, Elise," Quinn interrupted. "Just what are you doing here? Shouldn't you be in Columbus?"

"That's my big brother," she replied pertly, looking to Valaria for support. "Does he like to boss you around, too, Lari?"

Valaria threw Quinn a thoroughly satisfied smirk. "You have no idea."

Talking over Valaria's response, Elise continued. "I'm here, brother dear, and not in Columbus because I finished my degree—which you would know if you ever bothered to check your messages! I'm celebrating before beginning my life sentence in the salt mines."

"I'd hardly call working with Father being consigned to the salt mines, but congratulations on graduating."

He took her by the shoulders and kissed her lightly on the forehead.

Elise smiled and sipped her drink, suddenly almost choking as an idea struck.

"Oh my God," she sputtered, basking in the spotlight of her own brilliance. "You guys should come with me tonight!"

"Oh no we shouldn't," Quinn replied firmly without an ounce of curiosity as to the unidentified destination.

"But it's going to be *epic*," Elise insisted. "Lari, tell him you want to come."

"Come where?" Valaria asked, mildly interested.

Elise pounced on the trace of encouragement like a kitten on a moving point of light. "It's a party—*the* party. You've just got to come!"

"And why would we want to go to one of your parties?" Gideon asked trying not to sound overly condescending.

"Because I'm telling you it's going to be *epic*. We're starting here in the Rotunda and then at midnight we're taking over the Bullet. From here the party moves to Louisville, from there to Nashville, then on to Atlanta, and then finally to Columbus. Is that not totally awesome? It's being called the 'Bullet Bash.' It's the first ever—don't you want to be there?!"

Quinn paused as an idea of his own began to germinate. His response caught Valaria totally by surprise. "That actually does sound kind of interesting."

"Interesting? It's going to be *epic!*"

Elise set her drink down with impulsive finality.

"And I've got to start getting ready. I'll meet you in two hours at the front door. If you're not there," she cautioned as if they were just salivating to be included, "I'm leaving without you."

Once Elise had retreated to the guestroom—obviously assuming Valaria was paramour rather than partner to her brother—Quinn led the way across the apartment and into the master suite.

"OK," Valaria said when they were alone, "what's with the abrupt turn-around? You nearly gave me whiplash."

She sank into one of two plush chairs adjacent sliding doors leading to another balcony while Quinn perched on the edge of the king-sized bed.

"Elise is a cute kid," she continued, "and her excitement's kind of contagious but do you really want to go partying with her and her friends?"

"My little sister's unbridled enthusiasm aside, her *epic* party might just be our best ticket out of here."

"In what way?"

"We were going to retrace our steps back to St. Louis, right?"

"Yeah…"

"Which would mean resuming our roles as workers and getting past Guardians at the escalators, at the train, at the factory—and then we'd still have to slip away and walk back to the Hub, risking detection every time we turned around."

"It worked the first time."

"Barely," Quinn scoffed, beginning to tick off the salient points. "Our cover was blown at Convergence which cost us our transport, we had to dodge TODs for days while walking, and we were almost caught at the factory. If we join Elise's troupe on their Bullet Bash we won't be scanned even once and I've got a rock-solid contact in Louisville who can help us get back to The Hub from there."

Valaria had to concede it sounded like a pretty good option.

"But improvising can cause problems of its own," she cautioned. "For example—at the risk of sounding deplorably vacuous—I don't have a thing to wear."

"Actually, that's probably not a problem."

Quinn took her wrist and led the way into a walk-in closet off the en suite bathroom. The closet was bigger than Valaria's entire bedroom back home and she stood for a moment in dumbstruck awe at the masterfully organized space and all the clothing it housed.

"As nice as all this is," she quipped sarcastically, "I really don't think your suits are going to fit me."

Gideon put his hands on her shoulders and turned her toward a section of the closet behind them where a healthy array of women's clothing stood waiting.

"I assume these have been left behind by someone other than your sister—one of your other 'Ms. *Smiths*' as the Minder calls me, right?"

Quinn ignored the obvious and Valaria began running her hand along the clothing hung with care adjacent Gideon's city wardrobe.

"Just how dressy are we talking?" she asked.

"Dressy. You can have the bathroom while I make contact with Louisville."

When they traded places a little more than an hour later, Quinn barely recognized her.

Valaria had chosen a coral-colored sheath covered in pale lace that perfectly accented the dark wavy hair that cascaded over her shoulders. The calf-length dress was augmented by a dramatic slit running from hem to thigh up the left side, tight long sleeves that tapered to a point on top of each hand, and a scalloped neckline that lay flat across her collarbones. Sleek and sophisticated, the denouement of the garment was an open back that plunged down past her slender waist, lacy fabric draping seductively along the opening.

The transformation was mildly spectacular.

The only problems were her bare feet.

"I may be about the same size as your 'friend,'" Valaria observed, "but her feet are definitely smaller."

Quinn was trying not to gawk. "Elise always says she wears the box and throws out the shoes so her feet must be big; we'll mooch something off her."

After diplomatically refraining from comparing his sister's feet to boxes when making his request, Elise happily supplied an elegant pair of high heels that proved reasonable accents to the rest of Valaria's pilfered ensemble—and made her feel like she was walking on stilts.

Just shy of his sister's two-hour mandate, they met at the front door.

Elise was dressed in a slinky, iridescent sapphire-blue tunic over shimmering black leggings. The previously-burgundy ends of her blond hair were now a matching deep blue and she had coiled her tresses into an elegant French twist from which thin sapphire-blue ribbons dangled playfully down her neck. She looked lovely and Gideon's heart constricted at the thought that these were probably their last hours together.

With Valaria in her borrowed sheath and Quinn in basic black—his signature shaggy hair and facial stubble giving him a slightly roguish air—they stood ready to leave.

"Stain not the glory of your worthy ancestors but like them resolve never to part with your birthright... Follow not the dictates of passion but enlist yourselves under the sacred banner of reason; use every method in your power to secure your rights."

~ Joseph Warren

CHAPTER FIFTEEN

I.

Valaria awoke with what could only be described as an *epic* hangover—an adjective she probably had used only once in her life prior to meeting Elise Quinn. But the descriptor certainly applied. Her head was throbbing, her throat was parched, and the light coming from above the bed felt like it was searing her optic nerves. She squeezed her eyes tightly shut and tried to get her befuddled brain to cooperate.

Just how much had she had to drink at the party last night?

Every inch of her body felt stiff and achy as she began to take inventory and she hoped to hell that Gideon kept a healthy supply of analgesics around—she was going to need a fistful!

It was with this last thought that a glimmer of clarity dawned. She should be on the Amtrak Bullet but she neither heard its pulsating thrum nor felt any trace of movement. She opened her eyes as much as she could stand.

This wasn't a train.

This wasn't even Quinn's flat.

She tried to lift her hands to shield her eyes from the piercing light only to discover that they lay like lead at her sides. Raising her head as much as she could above the thin pillow beneath her, Valaria's disoriented brain finally registered the fact that she was wearing a hospital gown and that intravenous tubing dangled from her right arm.

"Hello," she managed to croak out rather feebly. "Anybody there?"

A lurching stomach was immediately added to her growing list of physical complaints as a black-clad Guardian peered in at her from around the corner of the adjacent doorway. He appraised her as if she were an alien with two heads and then, without acknowledgement, disappeared. Never more grateful to be one-headed, Valaria dropped her throbbing cranium back onto the pillow, shut her eyes, and listened as footsteps receded down an unseen hallway.

Where the hell was she?

After a lengthy silence that served only to intensify the throbbing in her head, the brisk clicking of a confident footfall grew increasingly loud as it approached from down the hall. In a moment an official-looking woman entered the room and sat down in a chair next to the bed. She was tall and stately, beautifully dressed with a commanding air of authority and a face that was artfully ageless—and totally in control.

Even in her confused state, Valaria instantly knew she was in some deeply serious shit.

"Good morning, Miss Thorpe," the woman said with a voice that oozed superficial kindness. "I do hope you're not feeling too indisposed to have a little chat. My name is Regina Agnew—I knew your grandfather."

II.

There was a Rotunda located in Tower 1 of every Safe Zone. They were the largest upper-level public spaces, used for political rallies, civic ceremonies, and the occasional society wedding. The Indianapolis Rotunda stood almost two stories in height behind a massive retractable wall of glass that provided magnificent views of the other towers and opened onto the widest garden area along the elevated pedestrian causeway. The interior was spacious and elegantly appointed—the ideal launching point for Elise's crowd's *Bullet Bash*. Hundreds of upper-dwellers had turned out for the inaugural event and in spite of her enthusiastic insistence that Gideon and Valaria accompany her, Elise was distracted almost immediately and abandoned them just inside the door, disappearing into the shimmering throng with little more than a backward glance.

"How did your sister and her friends rate all this?" Valaria asked in quiet awe as she looked around the beautiful space.

Quinn smiled sheepishly. "You're gonna make me pay for knowing this, aren't you? Both President Blanchard and Chief Justice Maxwell have grandkids Elise's age; I would imagine they're the inspiration for this little graduation soiree."

He was surprised when she let him off the hook with a simple "Of course" and continued watching the unfolding festivities.

Elise's prediction that the party would be 'epic' was spot-on as far as Valaria could tell. Not only was the setting more opulent than anything she had ever even imagined, but those in attendance—graduates, friends, and family members—seemed to be competing with one another in their lavish attire. Equally extravagant buffet areas stood at strategic locations throughout the Rotunda where an array of sumptuous food was provided and alcohol flowed freely. There was even a live band; something almost unheard of in the post-Revanche world where entertainment consisted primarily of digitally reanimated musicians, actors, and athletes from previous eras.

For the past few years the RSA's recycled popular culture had embraced the Big Bands of World War II. Referred to simply as *Swing* by the current generation, popular ensembles led by the likes of Duke Ellington, Benny Goodman and the incomparable Glenn Miller had been given a digital resurrection and were once again in vogue. In tribute to the genre, the 12-member group ensconced on an elevated platform at the interior side of the Rotunda was led by a trumpet player doing his best to channel the magic of Louie Armstrong. Although lacking the charisma of that ancient American icon, his command of the trumpet was admirable and the dance floor soon became filled with bobby-soxer wannabes doing passable imitations of loose-jointed jitterbug dances like the Lindy Hop and the Balboa.

The band had just finished a rendition of *In the Mood* and dancers were transitioning to the slower-tempo *Begin The Beguine* when Elise reappeared at Quinn's shoulder. Looking slightly wilted from jitterbugging, she grabbed Gideon's arm and pulled him toward the music.

"Come on, Gid," she cooed, "how often do we get the chance to dance together?"

Quinn threw a plaintive look Valaria's way.

"Don't look to Lari for rescue," Elise enjoined. "Tonight you're mine, brother dear."

Gideon surrendered without much resistance and Valaria watched as the handsome pair of siblings wove a rather melancholy two-step through the crowded dance floor as the haunting melody made famous by Artie Shaw during the era of the 'Greatest Generation' once again cast its spell.

Although the entire experience was bordering on the surreal, Valaria had to admit the glitz and glamour of the party held a rather morbid fascination for her. She had always known that life in the RSA would be radically different from that in the Borders but the opulent existence enjoyed by these upper-dwellers surpassed expectations. That so few should have so much to the exclusion of so many was fundamentally appalling and she couldn't quite grasp how the American republic had slipped so far from its upwardly-mobile egalitarian moorings. Martial

Law may have been unavoidable after something as universally devastating as the plague, but how could any U.S. politician—even an over-reaching Neoteric like Naomi Blanchard—justify the strictly controlled, rigidly tiered society created in its aftermath? Valaria remembered learning how the intended 'liberation' of the Russian peasants by leftists in 1917 had devolved into unbending totalitarianism that had seen blatant favoritism of the Communist elites at the expense of the majority caught in the undertow of their *protection*. It had happened again following the Communist takeover in China after World War II, in North Korea by 1950, in Cuba ten years later and in countless other hotspots over the ensuing generations. Hell, even the original United States had experienced a period of pseudo-authoritarianism when Donald Trump and his billionaire ass-kissers temporarily ruled the roost.

Perhaps such things were inevitable when power came into the hands of zealots flawed by narcissistic demagoguery.

But in spite of her deep-rooted disdain for the 'more equal' status of the upper-dwellers she watched, Valaria also was intrigued by them. Was it rose-colored glasses, tunnel vision, or abject self-delusion that allowed them to ignore the obviously unfair advantages they had over their bottom dwelling counterparts? Believing that a truly rude awakening lay ahead, she almost felt sorry for their myopic self-absorption.

Almost.

As the highly instructive evening continued its inexorable march toward the witching hour of midnight, Elise and Gideon returned from the dance floor. The younger Quinn led the way to one of the buffet areas and the trio indulged in delicacies Valaria had never even heard of, using a variety of utensils she found somewhat baffling. If his sister noticed Lari's social lapses she attributed them to her brother's tendency to go slumming—a streak of rebellion that had always given Gideon a degree of 'cool' in her eyes. And she could see why he was attracted to his latest lover; in addition to being striking, the woman was obviously intelligent, had a biting sense of humor and a wickedly acerbic sarcastic streak. Elise had taken a liking to her and certainly wasn't going to be the one to blow the whistle that a middie—or even more verboten, a bottom-dweller—had crashed the party.

At about 11:30 the band announced that Glenn Miller's *Moonlight Serenade* would be the last song of the evening before the celebration headed for Louisville. Partygoers planning to continue on to the next venue began making their way toward the exits and Quinn was pleased to see that a majority of the crowd appeared to be heading out—such a large group would make it easier for Valaria and him to melt into the glitzy troupe and then fade away once the Bullet arrived in the Louisville Safe Zone.

The trio had just joined the excited, chattering hoard when a more than slightly inebriated gaggle of Elise's vacuous friends swarmed them and drew Quinn's sister off into a path of their own making.

"I'll find you guys on the train," she called out merrily over her shoulder as she disappeared into the sea of bobbing heads.

It was slow going across the pedestrian causeway. The automated walkways had been turned off in order to accommodate such a large, fluid group of people and the snaking line of noisy guests—many of whom were less than steady on their feet due to drink—ebbed and flowed like a tide over rocky shoals. The flow had taken on a life of its own and within minutes of waving goodbye to his sister, Quinn and Valaria found themselves gradually being separated as disparate portions of the crowd merged near the head of the escalators. Gideon quickly discovered that swimming upstream to rejoin his partner was out of the question and he was two-thirds of the way down by the time Valaria finally managed to wedge her way onto the escalator between two prattling groups of partygoers.

As the escalator deposited him at ground level, Quinn glanced back with an encouraging smile and a thumbs-up gesture which Valaria returned with only slightly less confidence. He was soon out of her line of sight and she was just beginning to grow concerned about how they would manage to reconnect once she also reached the bottom when a familiar high-pitched laugh drew her attention to the conga line of people moving toward the escalator along the ledge above her head. The shrill, halting cackle was utterly unique but its source—a slender, well-dressed woman leaning casually against the causeway's railing—in no way resembled the person with whom memory associated the laugh. The woman was just behind and above Valaria's position on the escalator and she glanced up over her shoulder as the happy partygoer laughed again, this time in open-mouthed, gum-displaying pleasure.

It was Mavis Pope! With that laugh and the display of gums it could be no one else.

But this version of Mavis Pope was trim rather than corpulent, stylishly attired rather than wearing garish homemade caftans. An obvious upper-dweller rather than a discarded Borders exile.

Valaria was utterly stunned.

And in one of life's more deviously ironic moments, time seemed to slow as the woman stopped laughing and her gaze was drawn downward like a moth to a flame, coming to rest on the startled, upturned face of her former Borders neighbor.

First bewilderment, then recognition, and finally sinister delight passed in sequence across Mavis Pope's face as the two women locked eyes in mutual disbelief before Valaria forced herself to look away.

"Officers," Mavis abruptly shouted to the honor guard at the foot of the escalator while leaning over the glass and metal railing and gesticulating toward Valaria. "Stop that woman!"

Not expecting anything more troublesome than a crowd of tipsy revelers, the two Guardians on duty were taken completely unaware and gawked at the crowd totally perplexed as to whom they should stop or under whose authority the insistent order was being issued. It gave Valaria a momentary advantage and she began pushing her way through the milling tide of partygoers as it reached ground level and spilled happily out onto the expanse.

Mavis continued shouting directives from above, shoving her way toward the escalator while Valaria—now on the shimmering oval pavement—feverishly scanned the crowd looking for Quinn. She finally caught sight of him, waving vigorously above the heads of those just outside the train station but Mavis and two official looking companions had almost reached the bottom causing Valaria to hesitate.

In an instantaneous decision to protect the mission—to protect Quinn—Valaria headed in the opposite direction.

Nighttime lighting on the expanse was muted and moody. Kicking off her borrowed shoes—and immediately grateful for the dramatic slit up the side of her dress—Valaria began to sprint away from the crowd through a virtual minefield of PSA holograms popping up all around her. Each translucent projection babbled with enthusiastic gusto as she and the Guardians now chasing her triggered the honeycomb of government claptrap embedded in the surface across which they ran.

It was an unexpected added attraction for the crowd of revelers and their progress toward the station slowed as they watched the show. They cheered and booed as inspiration struck while the unknown woman ran in serpentine fashion across the expanse, seeming to bounce between holograms like a life-sized pinball machine with an increasing number of Guardians in close pursuit.

Just as Valaria passed the midpoint—beginning to feel mildly optimistic about her chances of disappearing into the shadows ahead— five more Guardians emerged from the darkness in front of her. They trotted toward her with crackling StunStix illuminating their way like flashes of summer lightening.

Mavis Pope looked on from where she had stopped at the front of the crowd, smiling broadly in gum-displaying glee at the bagging of an irrefutably spectacular quarry as Valaria went down.

III.

"…Your grandfather and I both worked for the Telliman Institute back in the day," Regina Agnew was saying. "In fact, I took great pride in being instrumental in convincing him to join us."

Valaria opened her eyes again, squinting into the painful glare.

"Let me dim the lights for you, dear," Ms. Agnew cooed. "And let's get your bed raised a bit so we can chat."

She gestured to a heretofore unseen nurse who quickly complied without even glancing at his patient.

Once raised to a more inclined position, Valaria took stock of her surroundings. The fog was slowly lifting and thoughts were forming with greater clarity. Her right hand and arm still lay like lead at her side but the fingers of her left hand had begun to tingle as mobility returned. She shifted position as best she could but the movement brought a frisson of pain that caused her to wince involuntarily.

"Best lie still for a while yet, dear," Ms. Agnew recommended. "I'm afraid StunStix can have a lingering effect and you certainly took more than your share of volts. I'm told you put on quite the show."

Valaria remained silent, moistening her parched lips and blinking a few times as her eyes began to focus. A slender woman was visible over Regina Agnew's right shoulder, standing ramrod straight next to the door.

"You're looking well," Valaria observed hoarsely, pinning the woman with the best glare she could muster.

The response came with the trace of a dour laugh. "Thank-you. It's amazing what shedding a few pounds can do for you."

Ms. Agnew cast the slightest of glances over her shoulder. "Ah, that's right—you ladies know one another, don't you?"

"Yes, Overseer," Mavis Pope replied. "Although I freely admit I never thought I'd see you again, Valaria. How in God's name does a Borders runaway end up playing Cinderella at the *Bullet Bash*?"

Valaria's glare intensified. "Guess that'll just have to remain one of life's little mysteries— like why dogs eat their shit."

"Lovely," Ms. Agnew interjected, reclaiming the conversational reins. "Thank you, Supervisor Pope; that will be all for now. You may return to your duties."

"Yes, Overseer," Mavis replied with a glare of equal measure for the woman in the bed.

Valaria waited until the door had closed before speaking again. "What happened? Am I in a hospital?"

"What happened is quite simple. As Supervisor Pope so aptly put it, you were discovered playing Cinderella at a restricted upper-level event; consequently, you are now in one of our containment facilities."

"How long?"

"Oh, it's been a few days. As I said, StunStix can have a lingering effect—loss of consciousness, short-term paralysis and even some memory loss, which can be particularly unnerving, I'm told."

"Am I under arrest?"

Ms. Agnew raised a sardonic eyebrow. "Don't be coy, dear. That must be obvious even in your current state. You broke the law by leaving your Borders settlement. Not only that, you somehow ended up in one of our Safe Zones—the *upper-level* of one of our Safe Zones. That bears looking into, wouldn't you agree?"

When Valaria didn't respond, the Overseer continued. "I would love to have been a fly on the wall when Supervisor Pope and you recognized one another. What a delicious coincidence that your paths should cross."

"That's not exactly how I would describe it."

"No, I imagine not. So, tell me, Miss Thorpe, just what were you attempting to accomplish by infiltrating the Zone?"

"Just wanted to see how the other half lives."

Ms. Agnew sat back in her chair, crossing her arms. "My, my, such bravado."

Her voice was losing its artificial kindness and taking on a hard, cold edge.

"You have violated a plethora of our laws, Miss Thorpe; I would encourage you to take your situation a bit more seriously."

"Or you'll do what—torture me?" Valaria asked boldly, recalling distant cries she had heretofore attributed to bad dreams. Propping up her wavering bluster, she continued. "I don't know anything and have nothing to say to you people. Go ahead, do your worst."

The Overseer leaned in slightly, her voice icy and quiet. "Trust me, dear— You don't want my worst."

She paused for a moment, dialing back the menacing tone and doing a figurative adjustment of the mask she wore. When she continued her face and voice were benignly matter-of-fact.

"But that will hardly be necessary. It's only a matter of time before we find you on our security footage. There's very little that escapes observation here, my dear. We'll find you and we'll find who you're working with. There will be no need for violence. And besides that, you are Otis Thorpe's granddaughter. Having you stumble into our hands is quite the coup and we wouldn't want you to come to any harm."

"How is that a coup?" Valaria asked. "I've been in the Borders most of my life. If you wanted me all you had to do was come get me."

"True, but that was before you began playing at revolution with the Sons of Liberty."

"The sons of *who*? I don't know what you're talking about."

"Oh, of course not," Ms. Agnew replied sarcastically. "We discover evidence that the Sons of Liberty have taken an interest in Otis Thorpe, we successfully track them to your settlement, and then you—Thorpe's only living relative—just happen to go missing. But that's all just unrelated coincidence, isn't it?"

"That's right."

"And you *continue* to play," Ms. Agnew observed with a mordant smirk. "Let me make something perfectly clear. By joining the Sons you turned yourself into a rather valuable commodity—to them and to us."

"I think you both place more importance on my grandfather than he deserves."

The Overseer's eyebrows shot upward.

"Ah..." she replied with a satisfied sneer.

Valaria realized she had made a mistake, her comment being tantamount to admitting knowledge of the Sons of Liberty's interest in Otis.

"After all," she continued, trying to backpedal, "why would these Sons of Liberty of yours be interested in Otis—he's just a dead exile."

"We both know he's much more than that. As I told you, I worked with him at the Telliman Institute. I know who he was and what he did. The Guardian Star would never have been built without him, and the Star is to the current generation what the Statue of Liberty was in the past and its designers have been cast as true American heroes. That's quite a legacy; a legacy about which you obviously have been apprised."

"Lady, I don't know what you're talking about. I'm just an exile who got tired of that life and decided to take my chances here."

The Overseer rose, straightening her suit with a sweeping gesture as if ridding the garment of the unseen crumbs of her annoyance. "I grow weary of your tedious denials. We'll continue our conversation another time."

She turned her attention to a white-coated medical assistant who had entered the room in response to some unobserved signal and issued a final order before leaving.

"I believe Miss Thorpe has recovered sufficiently to begin treatment."

IV.

Farley Donovan was angry. He twisted the knotted ends of the polka dot cloth wrapped around his wrist and glared at Quinn across the table. His Texas drawl was as hot as a branding iron.

"How the hell did you get separated?" he demanded. "And how could you just leave her behind like that?"

Gideon ran a hand through his shaggy hair and glanced over at Levi Dodge who had just joined them.

"I didn't have any choice—she didn't give me any. It's like I already told you, the crowd was really big. With everybody trying to get to the escalators at the same time people just got between us. Once we were separated—and once she was made—it was her decision to distract them."

"I just don't understand how she could have been recognized," Dodger interposed.

"I don't either, but something gave her away. One minute I'm trying to get her attention and the next thing I know she's running in the opposite direction with Guardians on her tail."

Quinn had already been through all this during his official debriefing with James McFarland after making it back to The Hub the day before. He and the Speaker had gone over the mission at length, discussing and considering every detail Gideon could remember as well as studying the information he had brought back about 'Repatriation.'

After helplessly watching Valaria dodge Guardians as she sprinted across the expanse and finally seeing her go down in the midst of a fearsome StunStix lightshow, Gideon had been forced to face a very harsh reality—if the mission was to succeed he would have to go on without her. She essentially had made that decision for both of them by leading the Guardians away and—apart from feeling utterly defeated by leaving her behind—he was damn proud of her.

Once the flamboyant runner had been contained—amid a daunting StunStix spectacle and roaring approbation from the throng of enthralled onlookers—Bullet Bashers had boarded the train almost as if nothing had happened and Quinn reluctantly joined them. The party had resumed as the sleek train picked up speed, rising above the DMZ and flying through the night toward the Louisville Safe Zone while the revelers continued to eat, drink, and be merry. Quinn had done his best to become invisible, successfully evading his sister and finally leaving the train once it arrived in Louisville in the company of a group of rowdy drunks singing an off-key rendition of the monotonous chorus to Glenn Miller's *Little Brown Jug.*

But Farley Donovan was not to be diverted by details.

"So how are we going to get her back?"

"Speaker McFarland and I have already been talking about that," Quinn replied. "We've never needed to mount a rescue mission into the RSA before but he seemed to have an idea brewing. He cares about her just as much as we do, you know."

Dodger clapped a reassuring hand on Donovan's arm. "Good—so let's go get her."

Gideon paused before continuing, intentionally keeping his tone matter-of-fact. "We won't be going. McFarland's turning the mission over to another operative."

"Like hell he is," Donovan interrupted. "Valaria's one of us—and we take care of our own."

Quinn realized it was going to take more than mere orders from above to rein in Farley and Dodger's resolve and decided to share information that previously had been considered need-to-know.

"Valaria has value beyond being one of us," he explained. "And we're just gonna have to defer to Speaker McFarland on this."

"What value beyond us," Farley persisted.

"You'd never know it but she's the granddaughter of a guy who was pretty important before The Revanche. If you can believe it, her grandfather was the lead engineer on the team that designed the goddamn Guardian Star. That makes her not only our colleague but a pretty important symbol to the whole movement."

Farley obviously had more to say but Dodger edged his way back into the conversation before his friend could speak. "Wait a minute. How can she be the Star's heir? I thought her grandfather was an exiled carpenter."

"He was, but before he got his ass kicked to the Borders he was one of the geniuses behind the tower."

"Holy shit. Does the regime know who she is?"

"They know Otis Thorpe ended up in the Borders and that he had a granddaughter living with him—and they undoubtedly know she's AWOL. If they don't already know that the woman they've captured and that granddaughter are one and the same they probably will before long."

Dodger's face was grim. "Is that good or bad for her?"

"That's a really good question. Speaker McFarland seems to think they'll recognize her symbolic value as much as we do which probably will keep her reasonably safe."

"So just how is this other guy going to be better than us at going in and getting her out?" Farley challenged.

"All I know is he's a deep-cover operative. Guess that means he's already inside and can perform a surgical extraction as opposed to our smash-and-grab approach. In any case, we're just going to have to wait and see. We've been benched."

V.

Valaria's grip on reality seemed to be coming in fits and starts. Much of the time she knew where she was and that she had been detained by Overseer Agnew, but she struggled with simultaneously feeling adrift on a sea of ambiguity that seemed to radiate through her like a refreshing breeze on a stifling hot day.

It was during one of her more lucid moments that she realized Mavis Pope was sitting at her bedside.

"What do you want?" Valaria asked, acid leaching into the words.

Although not overly warm, the other woman's tone was downright conciliatory by comparison. "I wanted to see how you were doing."

"Come to gloat is more like it."

"I admit a measure of satisfaction in your capture. But what in God's name were you doing here in the first place, Valaria? And where have you been? When you disappeared, everyone in the settlement feared the worst."

Valaria paused, biting her lower lip in an effort to reel herself back from the radiating sense of ambiguous contentment that almost had the entire saga of the past ten months spilling freely from her lips. With effort she reminded herself that this wasn't the Mavis Pope with whom she had shared morning coffee on countless occasions, this was an RSA official.

"The settlement..." she said instead, words slightly slurred. "Just what the hell were *you* doing *there*?"

Now it was Mavis's turn to pause and Valaria braced herself for what she expected to be a boatload of crap.

"It's probably fairly obvious so I see no reason to lie," Mavis began. "I was sent to the settlement to keep an eye on you."

"Keep an eye on me?"

"Yes. We had information that the Sons of Liberty were interested in Otis Thorpe. Since he's dead, my superiors postulated they might find you an acceptable replacement. I'm told your grandfather was the face of the Guardian Star project for a while and it was believed the Sons hoped to exploit you in their sedition. So I was sent in—undercover—to watch you; to see if anyone showed up to recruit you."

Remembering the obese version of Mavis Pope, Valaria smiled. "Undercover? Well, you sure as Hell pulled that one off."

Mavis shuddered. "That was the hardest part—looking so disgusting all those months; that and being disloyal to our friendship."

"*Friendship*—is that what you call it?"

"Yes Valaria, friendship. I was—and am—your friend. I don't want anything bad to happen to you."

As Mavis spoke the machine next to Valaria's bed whirred to life, indicating that another cycle of treatment was beginning to course through the intravenous tubing threaded into her arm.

"Then tell me what they're doing to me?" Valaria demanded, indicating the tubing.

Again Mavis paused. "It's called 'Radiance.' It makes people more... agreeable." She moved her chair closer to the bed. "Valaria, if I can't convince you to cooperate, they'll eventually accomplish the same thing chemically and I don't want that happening to you. I want the woman I've always considered a friend to come out whole on the other side of all this."

"Is that what they do here—make people more *agreeable?*"

Mavis shrugged dismissively. "It's called a Repatriation Center. Kind of a training school designed to re-educate people who..."

"People who like to think for themselves," Valaria interrupted, remembering the intermittent cries and shouts she had heard from unseen others since regaining consciousness.

She was growing increasingly groggy and at some level realized that these seeping feelings of hazy contentment must be the result of what she and Quinn had discovered—the regime's so-called "Radiant Cascade." The unrelenting sense of comfortable vagueness washing over her was suddenly laced with fear as her own description of the process as a chemical lobotomy came to mind.

The last thing she heard before drifting away was Mavis saying "I only want to help."

As the regime's repatriation pharmaceutical, Radiance basically played a game of King-of-the-Hill with the cognitive and emotional functions of the brain's frontal lobes. Justified by the Neoterics as a humane method of treating what they called the 'anti-social psychoses' of people who opposed them—people identified as potential threats to Homeland security—the drug supplanted spontaneous thought, intellect, and self-awareness with malleable mental ambiguity.

This was the chemically induced morass into which Valaria found herself sinking. The number of treatments required varied from subject to subject and she had no idea how many she had been given thus far but increasingly struggled with feelings of inertia; her emotions blunted and her ability to think clearly becoming impaired.

But she also was determined not to succumb.

Regardless of the fact that those who were resistant to Radiance apparently found themselves slated for the Triumvirate's 'Ultimate Repatriation,' Valaria focused every ounce of her considerably obstinate core on pushing away the Cascade. She began playing mental games in order to fortify her mind against the drug's onslaught. Forcing herself to hold on to lucidity, she would recite passages from favorite books, carry on lengthy conversations with God, take mental inventory of the pub and her living quarters back home, envision in detail various chess moves Otis had taught her, and meticulously review the martial arts instruction she had received at the hands—and feet—of Lieutenant Griffin.

Whether as a result of the brain games or what Otis had always described as her "infernal stubbornness"—or a combination of the two—Valaria was at least moderately successful in holding Radiance at bay.

The extent of her victory was brought home to her a day later. It was evening and Mavis Pope's distinctive cackling laugh could be heard somewhere down the hall. Another session with her erstwhile friend was the last thing Valaria wanted at the moment and so she opted instead to feign sleep—a skill she had honed to near perfection since being taken prisoner.

Mavis entered the room and stood for a time at the foot of the bed, silently making a careful study of its occupant.

"Any progress?" she quietly asked the attendant who had entered the room with her but remained at the door.

The response was hushed and succinct. "Minimal. She's proving to be highly resistant."

"Why don't they just get rid of her and be done with it," Mavis said. "These self-proclaimed patriots are all a pain in the ass. And who cares if she's some famous guy's granddaughter? I could've told them trying to turn her would be hopeless. But we'll just have to let the Overseer come to that conclusion for herself, won't we?"

Even in her partial stupor, Valaria realized these were risky words and that Mavis must be speaking with someone she trusted. But the candid moment had betrayed the Supervisor's true colors and she was grateful. It also reinforced her long-held belief that Mavis Pope had only her own interests at heart.

So much for the fervent claims of friendship and her "I'm here to help" routine.

VI.

Several days of Radiance treatments passed before Overseer Agnew paid Valaria another visit. Having been kept apprised of their progress—

313

or lack thereof—Ms. Agnew had decided a slightly more *personal* approach might yield better results. If her strategy succeeded, she would pull the proverbial rug out from under their recalcitrant subject and see her resistance to the Cascade implode. Valaria Thorpe could prove to be just the spark needed to ignite her ascent toward the seat of power in Columbus and Regina Agnew wasn't going to let the woman's pigheadedness stand in her way.

"How are you doing today, Miss Thorpe; up to having visitors?"

A familiar white-coated medical attendant had accompanied the Overseer and came toward Valaria to administer an injection.

"Just a little something to clear your mind a bit so we can chat," Ms. Agnew explained.

Valaria appraised her adversary warily as the haziness began to subside but said nothing while the other woman dismissed the attendant with a gesture more appropriate for waving away annoying insects.

"I thought you might like to know that we found you on our security recordings."

The Overseer pulled a chair over to the side of the bed and sat down. Once again her face was a mask of calm concern.

"Gideon Quinn," she continued, shaking her head sadly. "I must say it was quite a disappointment to discover treachery at such a high level."

"Who?" Valaria asked with a veneer of innocence.

Ms. Agnew's response was slow and clearly enunciated, more to taunt than to clarify. "The man you were with."

"That was just some guy I hooked up with so I'd have a place to sleep."

"Good try, my dear," the Overseer replied, "but we've now had ample time to investigate Mr. Quinn and track his movements. What we found—and sometimes what we *didn't* find—are fairly clear indicators that Gideon has turned his rather formidable talents against his own people. I'm afraid it appears he's been seduced by the very subversives who now hope to exploit you."

"You say they want to exploit me—exploit my connection to Otis—but isn't that exactly what you hope to do?"

"We hope to *repatriate* you, dear. Your parents were loyal citizens committed to rebuilding this great nation and protecting it from its enemies; enemies from within as well as from without. If they hadn't died you never would have come under the influence of your admittedly brilliant but tragically flawed grandfather. One horrible outbreak of flu and your life's course was changed forever. We want to help you come home."

"*My 'tragically flawed' grandfather*," Valaria repeated, her voice heavy with incredulous disdain.

"Yes, dear. Like you, Otis was dreadfully strong-willed and at first he had no interest in joining the Guardian Star project. But his participation was nothing short of vital. Gratefully, he did have his Achilles Heel— your grandmother, Charlotte."

"What does she have to do with anything? She died in a terrorist attack on the D.C. tube."

Ms. Agnew's look of grief was as artificial as the cosmetically enhanced face that expressed it. "Yes, a true tragedy; so many people dead. But—sad as it was—her loss gave your grandfather a personal understanding of what we were up against and was the tipping point that finally brought him into the fold…"

The Overseer had looked off into the distance of memory as she spoke but now refocused on Valaria with eyes that were icy and impassive.

"*…as I was certain it would.*"

Valaria's heart lurched. She was sure her tenuous grip on reality must have caused her to misinterpret the Overseer's words.

"Wh… what are you saying?" she asked haltingly.

"You heard me," Miss Agnew replied, the ice water in her veins chilling a satisfying degree or two further. "I'm saying that desperate situations require desperate actions, my dear. The work being done at the Telliman Institute was absolutely essential to national security—and your grandfather's assistance was absolutely essential to that work. One does what one has to do."

Valaria stared in horrified astonishment at the older woman as the significance of her words crystallized.

"Are you saying *you* engineered the bombing? You killed my grandmother and made it look like terrorism just so Otis would come work on your damn tower?"

Rage was replacing Valaria's disbelief.

Ms. Agnew smiled in superficial sympathy. Convinced that Valaria was being led exactly where she wanted her to go, she chose her next words with particular care.

"You must look at this dispassionately, dear. What are a handful of lives lost if millions are saved as a result? And, let's be frank, it was your grandfather who resisted more traditional forms of recruitment. It was he who backed me into an untenable corner."

"You're laying this at my *grandfather's* feet?" Valaria fumed almost quaking with anger.

"One must take responsibility for what one forces others to do."

Valaria felt concussed by the Overseer's words. Her head throbbed and tremors began coursing through her that she was unable to control. "You told me when we first met that you took pride in getting my grandfather to join the Institute— This is something you're *proud* of?"

Regina Agnew smiled contemptuously, leaning in slightly and driving the dagger home. "*Why wouldn't I be proud?*"

Outrage and horror overwhelmed Valaria. Combined with the disorienting medication she had been receiving it created an emotional implosion exactly as the Overseer had intended.

"Bloody hell; wha—what kind of *monster* are you," Valaria cried, struggling to form the words and straining upward against the restraints that bound her wrists. "My grandfather never got over Charlotte's death— You... you destroyed him!"

She continued to thrash about futilely as the Overseer calmly stood, turned her back, and strolled toward the door.

"You destroyed him, you heartless bitch," Valaria screamed after her. "*You destroyed him!*"

"Resume the treatments," the Overseer said to the attendant over Valaria's increasingly hoarse shrieks. "I think we'll find her far more receptive to its influence now."

VII.

Transferring himself to the Indianapolis Safe Zone had been a fairly straightforward process and the operative stood at the main desk of the Repatriation Center with four other newcomers waiting as the night attendant checked them in. He stepped away from the retinal scanner that would verify his orders as well as his identity and stretched languidly. The transport had broken down three times while en route and the trip had taken seven hours longer than it should have. As a result, everyone was stiff and restive after sitting so long in a cramped van. Transfers between Zones were infrequent and, when necessary, traditional transportation was considered more direct than shuttling workers around via a truncated rail system. But when vehicles broke down—as they commonly did—trips became slow and painfully tedious for the passengers.

"All right ladies and gents," the attendant said pleasantly after scanning the last newbie. "Let's get you billeted for what's left of the night. Grab your gear and follow me."

He was an amiable older man who obviously welcomed this interruption to his usually boring overnight shift. With his wrinkled white lab coat sitting slightly askew over murky green scrubs, he gave an impromptu introduction to their new workplace while leading the way toward the dormitory that housed live-in personnel. The operative appreciated the unofficial tour, listening to the man's chatter and comparing what he was seeing to the building plans he had already memorized.

It was a fairly small facility with a fulltime staff of fifteen med-techs and nurses supplemented by a handful of Guardians in charge of security. In addition to the administrative area—through which they had just passed—and the dormitory to which they were headed, the working heart of the building consisted of a wing resembling a hospital where the 'repatriation' of society's malcontents began. Within that section, two long, narrow ward-like rooms lined with hospital beds were designed to treat and re-educate up to thirty subjects at a time.

Those interned at the facility were subjected to a process referred to as 'flushing' during which their system was intravenously flooded with Radiance. When the saturation level—called the Radiant Cascade—had been reached subjects were weaned from the intravenous infusion, reintroduced into the community, and placed in one of the menial service occupations for which they were best suited once the process was complete. From that point maintenance doses of Radiance would be required on a daily basis just as a diabetic would have received Insulin in the days before the Population Protocols had eliminated that chronic disease.

But at that point, it was *morning* the transfers wished could be eliminated—or at least postponed—as the sun poured through the dormitory windows before they had done little more than close their eyes. Despite their late arrival, they were expected to be alert and on duty by seven and the operative shrugged himself into wakefulness along with the others, eager to get started.

After a quick breakfast in the staff dining room, a med-tech with a dangerously overinflated sense of self-importance began their orientation.

"The work we do here is absolutely vital," she informed the newcomers proudly as she led the way toward the hospital wing. "Nothing less than the security of the Homeland is at stake…" Her litany continued nonstop as they walked. "…And it's such an honor to be involved in this groundbreaking project; you're lucky to be here. We're giving people suffering from anti-social psychoses a second chance. Their disease can finally be treated. They can be returned to productive citizenship instead of sent to the Borders. Isn't that wonderful? That's the awesome work we're doing here!"

The lecture paused sporadically while the med-tech identified various supply rooms and offices along the way before returning to the familiar theme of the importance of the facility and the contribution they were making to the health and security of the country. But the operative was no longer listening, focusing instead on confirming the Center's layout and taking note of the few strategically located Guardians posted throughout the facility.

Adjacent the first ward, they passed a medical storage area—strictly off limits without specific clearance—as well as another checkpoint just outside the treatment area.

"We have seven subjects at the moment," their guide explained as they stopped at security. "This Center serves only Indianapolis and Columbus so it's smaller than the facility in Nashville that serves the other three Zones."

The Guardian on duty opened the door and the med-tech ushered them into the ward.

Six of the fifteen beds in the first room were occupied; each subject secured by restraints around their wrists and attached intravenously to machines that were flushing their systems with timed doses of Radiance. The restraints struck the operative as overkill since the subjects lay dazed and lethargic on their beds, displaying not even a flicker of interest as the tour of new workers passed by.

"I thought you said there were currently seven subjects," he commented casually. "I only see six."

"There are four private rooms provided for special cases," their guide replied, "two in each ward. Number 7 is in one of those."

"Special cases?" one of the other newbies asked.

"From time to time we run across a particularly challenging subject who needs to be processed in isolation."

Their guide gestured toward a room they had passed just inside the door. "Subject Number 7 is in there."

When their tour of the Center was complete, the transfers were passed on to their immediate supervisors. As a computer technician, the operative was taken to the control room where a group of three Guardians monitored security feeds from around the facility; the operative becoming the fourth. The room was at the opposite end of the building from the wards and, although it might have been more convenient to be posted closer to Subject Number 7, in order for his plan to work he had to have access to the technology they obligingly were placing in front of him so he took its remote location in stride.

As was true at his previous postings, his Guardian comrades did little to acknowledge his presence, focusing with disciplined diligence on their computer screens. Their supervisor made cursory introductions around the room and the closest thing to a welcome was a nod of greeting from one of the other three officers. There was no bonhomie among Guardians while on duty and the operative was simply assigned a station and put to work.

The first lesson one learned in the control room was that monitoring security around the building was about as interesting as clipping your toenails and the operative was grateful his time there would be blissfully short-lived. Despite the fact that the purpose of the Center was to reprogram people arbitrarily labeled as dangerous by the authorities, there had never been even the smallest whiff of public dissent and monitoring security consisted of watching endlessly boring feeds from hallways and exteriors. The average citizen knew very little about Repatriation. For most it was just another among the myriad government programs cluttering their lives—and those whose friends or relatives fell victim to internment knew enough to keep silent lest they find themselves also diagnosed with anti-social psychoses and subjected to the same 're-education' protocols. As a result, officers in the control room spent countless hours observing nothing more than the routine comings and goings of fellow staff members, growing bleary-eyed from the painful monotony.

The operative couldn't help smiling a bit at their obvious complacency. If they didn't *expect* anything they'd be far less likely to *notice* anything.

Without delay he began studying the various feeds cycling across the virtual computer screen hovering in front of him. Because Repatriation was still an experimental protocol the building housed less than a third of the internees they could accommodate and required little more than a skeletal staff. Activity currently consisted mainly of a small administrative staff at the entrance, med-techs and nurses supervising treatments, and two maintenance men—who looked suspiciously like Radiance graduates and spent their time endlessly cleaning the building.

Glancing cautiously at the Guardians nearest him, the operative surreptitiously touched his temple and reactivated the dormant neural implant adjacent his right eye. Once functional, he interfaced with the building's security program and created an access portal that allowed him to tap into transmissions from the locations he was planning to breach later. When the portal was stable he began recording loops of empty hallways as targeted locations passed across his screen.

Time dragged. The operative couldn't help wondering which would be worse for those assigned here indefinitely—the sheer mind-numbing boredom or the hemorrhoids they were likely to develop as a result of sitting on their asses all day.

After twelve hours spent reviewing the monotonous sameness of the Center's hallways and exteriors, the day crew of Guardians was finally relieved and silently headed for the staff cafeteria.

"Mind if I join you?" one of his fellows asked, indicating an empty chair at the operative's table.

"Feel free," he replied with an encouraging smile.

As they tucked into their meal the other Guardian studied the operative with open curiosity.

"Something wrong?" he asked.

"Sorry, it's your implant. I noticed it this morning when you came in. Did you work with drones?"

"Yeah, for a while."

"How the hell did you end up here?"

"I developed cerebral rejection," the operative lied glibly. "Couldn't handle the interface anymore so it had to be deactivated." He tapped his temple. "Can't be removed."

The other Guardian was obviously fascinated and wanted to hear all about the implant and what it was like interfacing with drones. The conversation would have gone on indefinitely but the operative pleaded exhaustion after so little sleep the night before and was finally able to extricate himself and head for the dormitory.

By midnight the rest of the day crew had followed suit and within a few minutes the room was filled with the reassuring sounds of sleep; no one having noticed that one of their colleagues had gone to bed still clothed in his uniform.

Quietly rising to a sitting position at the edge of his bunk, the operative cautiously surveyed the sleeping crew before once again activating the neural implant in his temple. Blinking slowly, he used the portal created earlier to interface with the building's security program. It took just a few minutes to initiate the looped recordings of the hallways he would soon be using and set the 'time bomb' that would facilitate his exit. Once confident of smooth transitions he accessed the external tech necessary for the final stage of Number 7's—Valaria Thorpe's—extraction.

As planned in simulation, he now had no more than twenty minutes to complete the rescue.

Quietly strapping on his pulse pistol, the operative surveyed the room once again to make sure his fellow Guardians still slept. Nothing but a few snores and level breathing met his ears.

He left the dormitory and headed for the hospital ward.

As expected, at this time of night the halls were empty and it took less than five minutes to cross the facility. Approaching the Guardian posted outside Thorpe's room as nonchalantly as possible, the operative met his eyes with casual confidence.

"What can I do for you, sir?" the officer asked.

"I'm new; think I got the building turned around in my head. Went to take a leak and now can't find my way back to the control room."

The other Guardian was extremely young and obviously pleased to know more than an officer of higher rank. He stepped away from Valaria's door and into the hallway outside the ward in order to offer directions.

"You need to go back the way you came, sir. Turn left down the next hallway and you'll see the break room on your right; where you used the latrine. Go left from there and the next left will take you back to the control room at the end of the hall."

The operative had dropped back slightly as the young man spoke, drawing his pulse pistol and holding it at the ready.

"This doesn't have to get ugly," he said as the younger officer turned back to him. He gestured toward the door with the pistol. "Let's just step into the ward."

At first the startled young man seemed willing to comply but then appeared to have second thoughts. He suddenly lunged for the gun, grabbing the operative awkwardly as he swung the pistol out of the younger man's reach. Thrown off balance, both men went slamming down to the floor.

The two Guardians grappled for a pistol that seemed intent on eluding them. It escaped their fumbling grasps, clattering noisily to the floor and spinning across the highly polished tile. Desperate to retrieve the weapon both men dove after it, slipping helter-skelter across the slick surface in an ungainly tango of squeaking shoe leather that resembled a maladroit Ice Capades routine.

Valaria's guard got to the pistol first, sliding clumsily into a sitting position with his back against the opposite wall and raising the weapon with both hands.

The operative also slid forward. He grabbed the other man by the nearest ankle and jerked him downward before he could steady the pistol and take aim. Now flat on his back—with the pulse pistol once again up for grabs—the young Guardian began flailing about in an effort to right himself. He managed to rise up on one elbow and started to shout for help but the operative scrabbled forward and slammed the heel of his hand upward under the man's chin causing him to choke on the words and sending his head smashing down to the floor. In an instant the young Guardian lay unconscious with a stupefied look on his face.

An almost deafening silence washed over them.

The operative rocked back on his heels into a squat, listening intently for any indication that their altercation had been heard.

Encouraged by the lengthening stillness, he grabbed the unconscious guard by the ankles and dragged him just inside the ward, leaving him sprawled on the floor by Valaria's door. The six other internees lay asleep or lethargic in the semi-darkness and he paused for a moment paying silent tribute to the plight of people who under other circumstances would probably be his comrades—acutely aware that he could do nothing for them as their brains were slowly turned to sludge.

Glancing at his watch he noticed that seven precious minutes had passed.

With another glance down the silent hall outside the ward, the operative turned and entered Valaria Thorpe's room.

VIII.

Valaria opened her eyes and scowled as an all-too-familiar face swam in and out of focus.

What was Dawson Hayes doing in the pub so long after curfew?

"It's way past last-call," she slurred. "...No exceptions."

"Didn't come for a drink," Dawson replied with an indulgent smile. "I came for you. Come on Valaria, wake up. We're getting out of here."

As Valaria murmured incoherently about "damned presumptuous Guardians," Hayes carefully disconnected the intravenous tubing attached to her right arm and raised the bed to a sitting position.

He took her by the shoulders and gave her a gentle shake.

"Can you hear me, Valaria? Can you see me? It's Dawson Hayes," he said with quiet tenderness. "I'm here to help."

Even in her befuddled state, she heard the echo of Mavis Pope's words. "Yeah, sure—that's what they all say..."

Continuing to murmur reassurance—peppered with sarcastic barbs he hoped would help the reality of his presence sink in—Hayes quickly released Valaria's restraints, wrapped her in her blanket, and carried her out into the hallway.

He took a final look around, his shoulders sagging in utter frustration—there was no way even a casual passerby wouldn't notice his unconscious comrade lying supine on the tile just inside the entrance to the ward.

He couldn't just leave him there.

"Damn," he muttered, depositing Valaria in a lopsided slump on the floor.

Slightly concerned that she might rally enough to wander off, he propped the door to the ward open so he could watch her, again grabbed the young Guardian by the ankles and began dragging him into Valaria's empty room.

He had barely crossed the threshold—with the unconscious man's head and torso still easily seen through the ward's open door—when the amiable night attendant came whistling up the hall from the direction of the break room.

The man stopped dead in his tracks, hands clenched in a sudden death grip around a steaming mug of coffee.

He stared wide-eyed first at the limp security officer, then at Dawson standing frozen in the doorway clutching the man's ankles, and finally at the young woman looking confused and perturbed where she sat crumpled on the floor wrapped in a blanket.

"Go on back to your desk and enjoy your coffee," Dawson said quietly, encouraging the older man.

A mournfully sad smile creased the night attendant's lined face. "Surely you understand, son. Around here dead is world's better than derelict."

With that he dropped his coffee mug and lurched toward the alarm on the wall as Hayes leapt across the Guardian's body and dove to cut him off.

There was a brief scuffle but there was never any doubt as to the outcome. Dawson yanked the attendant backward against his chest, pinning the older man's arms and wrapping his forearm across the man's throat in a vice-like chokehold.

Death was mercifully quick and the attendant sagged against Hayes with a look of resignation etched into his weathered face.

"Shit," Dawson murmured to himself, still supporting the man. "*Shit!*"

With another glance toward Valaria, he carried the attendant to her bed and covered him with the remaining linens in what he hoped was the appearance of sleep. Turning his attention to the unconscious Guardian, he pulled him the rest of the way into the room, took medical tape from the cabinet on the wall and tightly wrapped the man's hands and feet before taping his mouth and shoving him far up under the bed. The men eventually would be missed but if anyone glanced into the room in the meantime hopefully they would assume Valaria was the bed's occupant—disguising the cause of the men's absences at least for a while.

With the same sad resignation he had seen on the attendant's dead face, Hayes quickly cleaned up the man's spilled coffee, returned to Valaria and scooped her up into his arms.

More precious minutes had passed.

They continued down the hallway and reached the stairwell leading to the roof with less than five minutes to spare.

Once again easing Valaria gently to the floor, Hayes took a few steps back down the hall, listening for sounds of pursuit. Satisfied that they were still undetected he returned and directed his attention to the nine-digit keypad next to the door.

"God, there could be thousands of combinations," he muttered.

"Just shoot the damn thing," Valaria advised groggily from her vantage point on the floor.

He couldn't help smiling at her reemerging bravado. "I'm not going to shoot it—that would tell them exactly where we are—but in about two minutes all hell's gonna break loose and then we'll have exactly fifteen seconds to get through this door, up the stairs and out onto the roof. You up to a short sprint?"

Struggling to her feet, Valaria let an acerbic glare convey the incredulity her brain couldn't yet put into words.

Stooping slightly so she could put an arm across his shoulders, Hayes braced Valaria around her waist and murmured, "Wait for it…"

A heartbeat later the entire building and surrounding perimeter was abruptly plunged into darkness as his technological time bomb brought the Center's electrical system to its knees.

There was a clearly audible click as the stairwell locks released.

With his free hand Dawson yanked open the door, half carrying, half dragging Valaria upward into pitch blackness.

"Fifteen seconds until back-up power kicks in," he explained. "And we've got another door to get through at the top before then."

Valaria's obstinate feet were refusing to cooperate as they raced the clock, repeatedly catching on the edge of the steps, and Hayes realized there was no way they were going to make it at their current pace. Shifting position in the dark, he hoisted Valaria over his shoulder and took the remaining stairs two at a time, almost plunging them both backward into the black void when he crashed headlong into the door leading onto the roof.

Struggling to retain his balance, Dawson groped blindly for the handle, flinging the door wide and literally diving out onto the hard surface of the roof still shouldering his cumbersome bundle.

The duo lay breathlessly staring up at the inky blackness of early morning while the door latched behind them and then locked a few seconds later as power was restored.

Valaria scrabbled back to the door and sagged heavily against it as lights on the ground below and along the edge of the roof around them flickered to life.

Her bemused brain was also flickering back into action. "Holy crap, Hayes," she slurred. "Why'd you bring us up here?"

Dawson didn't respond. He had risen to his knees and was concentrating again on his neural interface, switching to optical mode and scanning the sky.

Valaria followed his line of sight toward a pinpoint of pearlescent white growing larger by the second against the ebony backdrop. Her vision had cleared considerably and she blinked away the remaining blurriness.

"Is... is a plane coming for us?" she asked.

Hayes continued to work.

As Valaria watched, what she had expected to be some sort of rescue transport transmogrified into the unmistakable shape of a tactical attack drone—TOD's deadly big brother. Shimmering in the moonlight, its menacing hum grew louder as the efficient killing machine headed in their direction.

"Oh my God," Valaria slurred hoarsely. "They'll see us for sure—we're sitting ducks up here!"

Hayes joined her in the shadows of the boxlike appendage that formed the stairwell's rooftop housing and put his arm around her protectively.

"Quiet," he said in a hush. "There's nothing to worry about. We're OK; they're not going to see us."

The ominously sleek TAD circled the building in a wide flight path. Its lethal elegance was a source of reassurance for the staff of the Center as they went into lockdown below but was a source of anguish for the traumatized woman huddled in a fog of chemically-induced confusion on the roof.

"Don't worry," Hayes said again, holding Valaria close.

She was shaking like a leaf, embarrassed by her emotional response but powerless to control it.

"Don't worry? Are you nuts," she said, her words still slurring. "That thing can take us out without breaking a sweat!"

"It won't," Dawson assured her, stroking her hair. "This one's mine."

Concentrating on the optical interface that allowed him to see through the drone's high-definition lens, he slowly closed the TAD's circular flight path and brought it in for a landing.

Sprinting over to the drone, Dawson rocked it up against one long wing and opened the weapon compartment. It was empty—a gaping cavity only slightly larger than a typical casket.

"There's no time to explain," he said as he ran back to Valaria and scooped her up in his arms. "You're the drone's payload and I'm sending you back to St. Louis."

"They tell us that we are weak, unable to cope with so formidable an adversary. But when shall we be stronger? Will it be the next week, or the next year? ...Shall we gather strength by irresolution and inaction? Shall we acquire the means of effectual resistance by lying on our backs and hugging the delusive phantom of hope?"

~ Patrick Henry

CHAPTER SIXTEEN

I.

"Oh crap," Valaria moaned. "Not again." She had opened her eyes just a moment before only to squint painfully into a glare of light coming from above the hospital bed she found herself snuggly tucked into.

Closing her eyes again, she tried to shrug off the heavy vagueness that shrouded her mental acuity the same way a dense morning fog obscures everything in its path.

Thoughts were forming with agonizing sluggishness.

The last thing she remembered—or thought she remembered—was crouching on a rooftop next to a grounded TAD with *Dawson Hayes* of all people! That couldn't have been real but what a bizarre dream! Or had it been some type of hallucination brought on by the repatriation treatments she'd been undergoing since being captured at the Bullet Bash? Whatever the case, Guardian Hayes certainly was an odd choice for her subconscious to cast as hero in any rescue scenario. The only thing he was likely to rescue was an after-hours drink at the pub…

"Are you awake, Ms. Thorpe?"

An attendant had come to the side of the bed and stood scrutinizing his patient's grimacing expression and tightly shut eyes.

Too late to feign sleep, Valaria turned her head toward the voice and opened her eyes as much as she could stand.

"Sorry about the glare," he said. "Let me dim the lights a bit."

Talk about de je vu all over again—would Overseer Agnew soon be making another appearance?

Valaria braced herself for yet another round with the government's head witch, a mixture of rage and fear roiling in her belly. But the next face that swam in and out of focus a short time later didn't display the surgically perfected features of her cold-hearted antagonist.

"Valaria? Well, it's about damn time. We were beginning to think you were never going to wake up."

Still unsure on which side of reality she was standing, all Valaria could manage to croak out was a hoarse, "Where am I?"

"You're home."

"The pub?"

"No. St. Louis."

The fog lifted a bit and she realized it was Gideon Quinn who stood at her bedside. "Quinn?"

"Yeah, it's me," he assured her. "You're safe now. We got you out. Well, not me specifically—another operative."

Valaria processed his words for a moment. "There was a drone... I was *inside* it... Was that real?"

"Yeah it was real all right. The guy gave you a sedative to make sure you'd lay still, slapped an oxygen mask on your face and stuffed you into the belly of a TAD. Flew you out of the RSA right under their noses—or above their heads to be more precise. Amazing... *brilliant!*"

Valaria was silent, struggling to remember. "I thought I saw Dawson Hayes."

"Dawson Hayes? That Guardian from your settlement?"

"Yeah..."

"Geez, you really were out of it. Actually, I have it on good authority that it was none other than Sam Adams himself who got you out..." Quinn gave her a sympathetic—albeit rather patronizing—smile as he continued. "But I doubt very much that he and Dawson Hayes are one and the same."

"No, I suppose not," she agreed, scowling in frustration at the confusion that had her so muddled.

They fell silent for a moment. When Gideon spoke again his voice was full of regret. "I really thought I'd lost you."

"Sorry about that."

"You have nothing to be sorry about. What you did was damn brave! I think you're in line for a medal."

Valaria was just coherent enough to scoff at the mere suggestion before continuing. "You made it out OK?"

"Yeah—just as planned. Travelled with the Bullet Bash to Louisville, then our contact there sent me on. But what happened, Valaria? How'd you get made?"

She heaved a deep sigh, trying to pull her battered thoughts into some sort of order. In a rather jumbled narrative the story of how she and Mavis Pope crossed paths tumbled out. Now that Valaria was safe, Gideon took no small measure of satisfaction in the fact that his innate distrust of Valaria's settlement friend had been spot-on. He had always thought something was just off where Pope was concerned and was eager to hear more—especially about Valaria's experiences at the Repatriation Center. Unfortunately, the medical attendant lingering by the door had different priorities and overruled their determination to prolong this first visit, taking conspicuous pleasure in having the authority to send an officer of Quinn's rank packing.

Despite their protests, Valaria's obvious grogginess made it clear the attendant was right and she drifted off as soon as the room was quiet.

It was morning when she finally surfaced from her stupor with any degree of staying power—or at least she thought it must be morning. The windows at eye level were covered in thick blackout material but daylight streamed in from an unshielded row of narrow panes high up under the eaves providing natural brightness that balanced the harsh glare of the room's artificial lighting. She took in her surroundings with a much clearer eye and was relieved to realize that her brain no longer felt like someone had glued the neurons together with the thick white paste she had found so tasty as a child.

She also was relieved to discover that nothing more than linens secured her to the bed and that intravenous tubing no longer dangled ominously from her arm.

With a renewed sense of clarity she sat up, pushed away the linens and swung her legs over the edge of the bed.

"Stop right there, ma'am."

The attendant who had enjoyed throwing Quinn out the previous evening stood in the doorway. He was painfully young, with pale hair, pinched features and a bookish look that almost screamed 'doctor-in-training'—he already had the requisite officious manner.

"I need to take a leak," Valaria lied. What she really needed to do was get out of bed and finish shaking off the dusty cobwebs of confinement.

"Sorry, but you're not going anywhere," the attendant replied, hurrying across the room, "at least not by yourself. You've been off your feet for weeks. You stand up unassisted and you're likely to fall right back down again."

Valaria's scowl was fierce as the thunderclouds of defiance began to gather. "Well then, get me some damned assistance!"

"I have," a voice by the door interjected.

Gideon Quinn was leaning against the door jam, scruffy and handsome in jeans and a dark t-shirt covered by his ubiquitous suede duster. With arms folded casually across his chest he observed the plight of his impatient partner with a mixture of amusement and relief.

"I see you're feeling better," he said to Valaria before directing his attention to the attendant, "which means *you* need to brace yourself. Don't take anything she says too personally; she's never going to be voted Miss Congeniality."

"And *you're* never going to be able to keep me in this bed!"

"I'm afraid you have no choice in the matter," Quinn informed her. "But I promise it won't be for a minute longer than absolutely necessary. Think you can play nice for a few more days?"

The functioning portion of Valaria's brain told her it probably was best to acquiesce—at least for the time being. "I always play nice. So where's my frickin' assistance?"

Gideon smiled and stepped out into the hall. He returned a moment later with his arm across the shoulders of Kevin Eldridge as he led the teen into the room.

"Hey kid," Valaria said in casual greeting. "How's my dog?"

Kevin's shiny, pimple-speckled face was instantly wreathed in smiles. Without saying a word, the gangly teen stumbled forward and wrapped Valaria in a hug that would have made any bear proud. It took her a second to respond—being less than comfortable with such displays—but genuine affection for the insecure young man kicked in and her arms folded across his back as she held him close for several seconds.

"OK bubba, get a grip," she murmured into his ear before extricating herself from his grasp and holding him at arm's length.

"Private Eldridge has his orders," Quinn was saying. "He's to assist you during your convalescence and make sure you don't do anything spectacularly stupid during your recovery. You, Ms. Thorpe, are expected to cooperate and not be the royal pain in the ass you usually are. Are we clear?"

"Yes, sir," Kevin replied sharply, snapping to attention.

"Yes *sirrr*," Valaria added, giving Quinn an exaggerated salute and a sarcastic smirk from the edge of her bed.

"Good. Private, she's all yours—God help you."

With that Quinn turned and left the room; there was lightness to his step that had been missing for almost a month.

"So," Valaria said to her young keeper, "where's my dog?"

II.

By the end of the week Valaria was showing marked improvement. Her confusion had cleared and she was convinced her strength was completely restored. For the most part she continued to play the role of the model patient—except for coercing Kevin into smuggling in some cigarettes and taking clandestine late night walks without the wheelchair everyone seemed to think she still needed for lengthy excursions. Not one to sit idle for long, however, it was becoming increasingly difficult to play the game of recovery while waiting for her elderly doctor to give her a clean bill of health.

"Ms. Thorpe," Dr. Molly inevitably replied in response to Valaria's daily request to be released, "Rome wasn't built in a day."

Doctor Molly Colson was cadaverously thin with deeply lined skin and knobby hands peppered with age spots that made Valaria wonder if the woman might well have firsthand knowledge on the subject of Rome's construction. And in spite being blessed with a razor-sharp mind that defied her elderly appearance, every time Valaria saw the doc she was struck by the thought that the Sons better rush their medical trainees along since their primary care provider looked as if she had one foot already firmly planted in the Great Beyond. There was probably a good story behind how the ancient physician came to be involved with the Sons of Liberty but curiosity took a back seat to Valaria's focus on escaping the woman's frustratingly thorough ministrations—and Dr. Molly continued to stand firm. Several more days passed during which Valaria spent her time going to physical therapy, helping Kevin hone his chess skills, and anxiously awaiting the next visit from Quinn or Donovan.

During the unconscious hours following her rescue, Farley Donovan had kept silent vigil at Valaria's bedside until finally being ordered elsewhere. Once she had salvaged her claim on lucidity he was the first visitor following Kevin's installation as nanny and it was he who successfully smuggled Yancy into the infirmary on a fairly regular basis.

Between the three of them—Donovan, Kevin, and Yancy—Valaria was more supervised than she had been while growing up with Otis. She appreciated their dedication and concern but was beginning to find it all more than just a tad claustrophobic.

"What the hell are you doing?" Farley asked in frustration the evening before she finally got that coveted clean bill of health.

He had caught Valaria in the tiny latrine connected to her room, standing on tiptoe atop the toilet seat and blowing cigarette smoke into the air vent. "Couldn't you wait until we went for our walk?"

"Apparently not," she replied tartly.

He held out his hand to steady her but she made a point of hopping down from her perch unassisted. With a satisfied smirk, she stepped to the sink and ran the cigarette under the faucet. Donovan's ginger-colored ponytail swished slightly as he shook his head with an aggrieved smile and raised his hands toward Kevin in a *"why-don't-you-do-something-about-this"* gesture.

"Don't look at me," the teen commented. "I value my life too much."

Valaria crossed the room and plopped down on the floor next to Yancy. She pulled the dog into a hug and offered up a benign, tight-lipped smile as Kevin slipped out of the room for a little reconnaissance before their nightly escapade.

The infirmary was located in the stadium portion of The Hubbard Center in an area adjacent the home team's locker room. Originally intended for use as a triage point for players injured on the field, its state-of-the-art equipment was one of the most prized bonuses the Sons had discovered when making the convention center and arena their base of operations. It hadn't taken much to convert the emergency facility into a fairly decent small hospital and it would prove especially useful in the months ahead.

As a result of the infirmary's location, it was relatively easy for the four fugitives to evade the limited staff and slip into the domed stadium for their nocturnal adventures. The quartet would wander the dimly lit alien world of the long-defunct NFL mostly in silence, exploring abandoned concession areas, St. Louis Clydesdales souvenir stores, and VIP suites overlooking the vast field, as well as sitting in the extensive broadcast booth and climbing up to the 'nosebleed' region of upper-deck seating for a unique—and dizzying—perspective. The arena was vast, the unused portions derelict and grimy, and there seemed to be no end of interesting things to investigate—Kevin's favorite discoveries being a St. Louis Clydesdales' stuffed horse he had found in one of the team stores and presented to Valaria as a get-well token and a baseball cap emblazoned with the team's stylized Clydesdale logo. Although water stained and smelling of mildew, the cap had instantly become the crowning touch to his stylish ensemble of fraying jeans and a t-shirt and he wore it with pride during their nightly excursions.

Although technically still confined to the infirmary, Valaria rationalized defying her doctor's orders by classifying their walkabouts as an extension of her physical therapy—their exploration of the deserted stadium adding a significant dollop of interest to the otherwise repetitive routine. Farley and she had even begun doing a limited MMA workout in Lieutenant Griffin's dojo area at the far end of the field, the mental rehearsing of which had helped maintain her sanity while a guest of the RSA.

"You're doing great," Farley said in genuine admiration as the pair finished their light sparring and sat on the mat to cool down.

"I can't believe they're still keeping me in the clinic," Valaria replied, pulling her knees up to her chest and folding her arms across them.

While the two sparred, Kevin and Yancy had begun a workout of their own, dashing and dodging around the huge field in playful abandon. They looked like just a kid and his dog instead of a young rebel and the sole member of the Sons of Liberty Canine Corps; a refreshing glimpse of normalcy in an existence that was anything but.

Donovan and Valaria watched them in silence for a time.

"Are you really OK?" Farley asked at length.

"I'm fine."

"I don't mean physically; I can see your improvement every day. I mean inside. Are you OK about what happened to you?"

"I'm no crazier than before they got their hands on me, if that's what you're asking," she assured him with a smirk.

She reached across and tugged at the polka dot minion bandana still wrapped around Donovan's wrist. "I told you I'd come back."

"And it's about time I gave this back to you," he replied, holding out his arm for Valaria to untie the knot.

When she had finished, Donovan reversed the process, wrapping and knotting the prized polka dot fabric around Valaria's outstretched left wrist.

She held her forearm up proudly and smiled. "Minion Thorpe reporting for duty."

Farley pulled her into a kiss just as Kevin and Yancy passed nearby.

"Get a room," the teen called out in mock disgust.

Valaria gave him the finger as he and the dog ran off across the dimly lit field.

"I'm OK," she repeated in earnest to Donovan's earlier question. "The drug they've come up with—Radiance—is some seriously nasty stuff but apparently I never reached what they call the 'Radiant Cascade' so my brain wasn't completely fried."

She shivered involuntarily remembering the vulnerable wreck the drug had reduced her to and Regina Agnew's emotional battering that had capitalized on it. The Overseer's carefully choreographed denouement—sadistically twisting the dagger by proudly claiming responsibility for Charlotte's death—would be a specter that forever haunted the edges of memory.

Farley noticed the shiver and put his arms around her.

She didn't pull away.

III.

Valaria was finally released from the infirmary on May 25th. It felt good to be alone in her small room with Yancy and her tiny cache of personal items. No longer in need of a nanny, Kevin had returned to duty with Levi Dodge's unit which almost immediately had been dispatched on patrol. As a result, Farley Donovan—as Dodger's second in command—was also gone and Valaria found herself looking forward to being on her own for a few days.

But her solitude was short-lived. In fact, it only lasted one night.

"OK, Thorpe, no time for breakfast, Speaker McFarland wants to see you."

Gideon Quinn had come up behind Valaria as she approached the cafeteria's serving window, dashing her plan of cajoling the workers out of some coffee and toast since she had slept through their normal serving times.

Her sarcastic reply was automatic—and expected—even though they both knew she had been chomping at the bit for an official debriefing ever since she had stopped feeling like one of the pod people from *Invasion of the Body Snatchers*. She was anxious to have some time with Speaker McFarland while everything was still fresh in her mind—and had a few questions of her own she was eager to ask.

Abandoning hope of a fresh infusion of caffeine, Valaria fell into step next to Quinn as he headed for the MetroLink.

There was something steadying about the familiar train ride through the dark tunnel leading from The Hub to McFarland's headquarters far beneath the Gateway Arch. For Quinn the tunnel was the umbilicus that linked intelligence gathering to strategic action. For Valaria it was the yellow brick road that led to the Wizard in whom she had placed her trust. And after what they had learned during their time in the Indianapolis Safe Zone, both she and Quinn found the Sons' mere existence more reassuring than ever for they now realized—perhaps better than anyone—that a head-on collision with Naomi Blanchard's Neoterics had passed from likely to inevitable.

Once they were alone in his office the former Speaker of the House was effusive in his greeting. Protocols that traditionally defined encounters between government officials and the general public were a thing of the past as far as James McFarland was concerned and he pulled Valaria into a tight embrace, patting her on the back while exclaiming his pride in their accomplishment and relief in her safe return. As he held her she realized she was equally relieved and happy to see the dignified old man who was becoming something of a link to Otis and she willingly returned his unexpected hug.

Finally releasing his heroine, the Speaker indicated two chairs in front of his desk and resumed his own place behind the mahogany monstrosity which dominated his work space. As they settled in, one of the men from the outer office quietly entered carrying a tray bearing coffee and scones.

"Thank you, Edmond," the Speaker said.

The man nodded in acknowledgement, placed the tray in front of McFarland and returned to other duties.

"I thought some refreshments were in order," their elderly host explained while filling a chipped porcelain cup with the heavenly smelling brew and then holding it out to Valaria.

She reached across the desk and accepted the steaming coffee with hands she feared might tremble from withdrawal—if it hadn't been for her recent experiences in the RSA she would have been tempted to request a syringe so to inject the caffeine-rich liquid directly into her veins!

While fortifying themselves with coffee and scones they began a review of the mission's story. Quinn had already been debriefed so it was Valaria's account the Speaker was interested in and she reluctantly found herself center stage while an enrapt audience of three—Speaker McFarland, Gideon Quinn, and a small recording device—digested her words. She told the story succinctly but gave substance to the experience like a colorized version of a classic black and white film. After beginning with a quick overview of their adventure in the tunnel—taking the Speaker across the side of the overturned tram and helping him see the family of plague victims as more than just skeletal remains—Valaria then led him through their experiences at the RSA Transport Hub where suspicion that their cover had been blown turned a quick drive to the Amtrak spur into a harrowing 3-day walk. She intentionally glossed over their encounter with the Guardian she had ended up killing—one of many things now haunting her dreams—painting instead a vivid picture of the obnoxiously intrusive GovLines propaganda broadcasts, the first hints among the Bullet's commuters of what they would discover to be the effects of Radiance, and her amazement with the Safe Zone itself—both its modernity and the appalling inequities of its three distinct and disparate social levels. Gideon added clarification here and there but for the most part Valaria was in the spotlight, especially once the story was hers alone after the partners had become separated.

These were details Quinn also was eager to hear.

"Regina Agnew," the Speaker said quietly as he reflected upon Valaria's account of her time at the Repatriation Center. "I haven't heard that name since before The Revanche."

"She's been a government official as far back as I can remember," Quinn observed. "Was she involved in government even then?"

"Only indirectly. She worked for the Telliman Institute—an influential think-tank. They were the ones who designed the Guardian Star." McFarland paused and shook his head slowly. "Regina Agnew struck me as a singularly unpleasant individual even then, driven by insatiable, venomous ambition." He looked closely at Valaria. "She undoubtedly knew your grandfather."

"Yes, she mentioned knowing him," Valaria replied. She hadn't told anyone about the Overseer's proud disclosure that she had finally lured Otis into the Institute by pulling the rug out from under his reluctance by instigating the 'terrorist attack' that killed his beloved Charlotte. The emotions surrounding Agnew's declaration were just too raw and Valaria believed it had no substantive impact on her narrative.

No, she would keep that particularly painful nugget to herself.

"Did you show him the memos?" she asked Quinn instead.

"Of course."

"And do those strike you the same way they did us, sir?"

A deep, mournful sigh shuddered through the old man. "Yes, I'm afraid so."

He shook his head in grim disbelief, activating the computer screen on his desk and reading aloud the most damning memo Quinn had found.

> *'There is no question that the stubbornly recalcitrant pose*
> *a particularly vexing threat to national security. Although*
> *not yet fully implemented, the Triumvirate's plan for the*
> *Ultimate Repatriation of these subjects is in keeping with*
> *progressive standards of care where age, medical condition,*
> *or cost dictate that euthanasia is in the best interest of*
> *the State.'*

"I don't think there's any other interpretation one can place on those words," the revered statesman observed. "I suppose it really shouldn't surprise us. Dictators often employ an 'ultimate solution' in the name of national security, but I truly never dreamed Naomi would cross that line."

He ran a knobby finger down the translucent screen coming to rest on one particular phrase.

"...*euthanasia is in the best interest of the State*," he read, his voice heavy with bitterness. "The irony of those words would be laughably ridiculous if the implication wasn't so appalling."

"So what happens now?" Valaria asked bluntly after a pregnant pause. "You got your answer about why there are fewer exiles—and why there are likely to be *none* in the near future. Is that the end of it? Are you just going to abandon all those people?"

"Of course not," McFarland replied kindly. "But things have become exponentially more complicated as a result of all this."

"We don't have the manpower or the resources to go charging into the RSA blowing things up and rescuing people," Quinn said. "But we're not just sitting on our hands either."

He looked at the Speaker who indicated permission to continue with a slight nod while reaching out and turning off the recorder. "When I uploaded information about Radiance I also downloaded a 'RAT' into their system."

"A rat?"

"A 'remote access tool.' Think of it like a back door into their technology. Monitoring their transmissions is fairly easy but it's another thing entirely to actually have access. I'm working on infiltration protocols that will let me open that door and hijack their GovLines broadcasts."

"What good will listening to that crap do?"

"We're not just going to listen to them—we're going to hack into them and insert some messages of our own. We can't physically attack the Zones but we can at least tell people what's going on at the Repatriation Centers; we can tell them about Radiance and the regime's plans for Ultimate Repatriation."

"And I'm afraid that's the best we can do right now," McFarland added.

The trio fell silent and Speaker McFarland considered his guests for a moment, both pride and genuine affection in his emotive eyes.

"Well done," he said at length. "I am just so relieved that you've both come back to us safely."

"Thank you, sir," Quinn replied quietly.

The two men appeared to be drawing things to a close but Valaria had more on her mind.

"But what about your family?" she asked Gideon. "Will there be repercussions now that the government knows you're with the Sons?"

"Trust me; they can take care of themselves. My parents are government faithful; far too insulated for anything I do to impact them much. They're more than capable of talking their way out of the fact that I've been living a double life. That's one of the reasons I've kept my distance the last few years—should give them rock-solid plausible deniability."

"What about Elise?"

"Elise? Can you imagine anyone *less* subversive? There shouldn't be even the shadow of suspicion cast her way. And luckily the regime hasn't quite gotten to the level of North Korea where the entire extended family ends up in a gulag because some fourth cousin they never even met gripes about rations."

"Let's hope not," McFarland interjected sadly.

"My 'indiscretions' will be glossed over and my family will move on as if I never existed. Even Elise will get along just fine without me."

Valaria knew that was more difficult for Quinn to admit than his cavalier attitude made it seem. But that was a conversation for another time.

"OK," she continued, changing direction. "One more question."

"Go ahead," the Speaker said, slowly stirring his cold coffee and glancing furtively at her partner.

"Is Dawson Hayes 'Sam Adams'?"

Quinn stifled a laugh. "Where'd you get that idea?"

"Frankly, I got it from you."

"From *me?*"

"Yes. The first day you visited me in the infirmary I told you about seeing Dawson Hayes."

"You told me you *thought* you saw Guardian Hayes and I told you that was impossible," Quinn replied. "You were under the influence of Radiance for crying out loud. You were seeing things. The operative was dressed as a Guardian and your subconscious slapped the face of the Guardian you know best onto him."

He patted her arm sympathetically and directed his attention to Speaker McFarland. "I'm sorry sir; she's obviously still a little confused."

Valaria bridled at his words but retained her composure, quietly considering both men—especially the pensive elder statesman—as she countered Quinn's assertions. "No, I told you I had seen Hayes and you tried to distract me with the flattering news that the Sons' biggest bigwig—Sam Adams—was the one to come charging to my rescue. But the fog has lifted and I know I wasn't imagining things; I know what I saw..."

She turned to Speaker McFarland.

"I saw Dawson Hayes. I talked to him. It was Hayes who stuffed me into that empty TAD. There's not a doubt in my mind. So if Sam Adams was my rescuer, he's gotta be Dawson Hayes."

"I think *drugged* is the operative word here," Gideon interrupted, his tone softening. "I understand where you're coming from, Valaria, but this really is one of your wackier notions. They were pumping Radiance into your veins like there was no tomorrow and then the operative drugged you some more before stuffing you into the TAD. Face it, you probably wouldn't have known your own face right then—how could you possibly have recognized somebody else with any certainty. Let's not waste any more of the Speaker's time with this."

Valaria smiled sardonically.

"This is some more of that need-to-know bullshit, isn't it?" She glanced at the elderly statesman. "Excuse my language, sir."

Quinn began to respond but McFarland raised a hand to stop him. "That'll do, Gideon."

The Speaker took a sip of coffee, finally noticing that it had grown stone cold. With a scowl he set the cup aside and heaved a deep sigh while studying Thorpe's Granddaughter.

"There are many things you don't *need* to know," McFarland observed. "But this is one you perhaps *deserve* to know."

Quinn disagreed but remained silent, slipping into stoic 'poker face' mode as the Speaker continued.

"Like Gideon, Dawson Hayes was raised in the RSA—in Atlanta, I believe. His parents are mid-dwellers, the level from which Guardians are chosen, and—as Hayes tells it—he initially received his assignment with pride and enthusiasm. Luckily for us, he grew disillusioned the more aware he became of the government's repression and the role Guardians play in it. Their strong arm tactics left an increasingly bitter taste in his mouth which ultimately led him to us. Gratefully, a number of Guardians reach that same epiphany, realizing that they are not protecting the country but are, in fact, pawns of totalitarianism. As a result, we count numerous defectors among our ranks…"

Valaria impatiently nudged her way into McFarland's lengthening narrative. "So Hayes *is* Sam Adams?"

The Speaker tapped the surface of his mahogany desk with a fidgety index finger, pursing his lips slightly and pausing a beat before responding.

"Yes," he said, acquiescing to her unbending need to know. "Yes, he is."

IV.

"I knew it," Valaria crowed in satisfied delight once she and Quinn had left Speaker McFarland and boarded the tram. "I knew I wasn't imagining things!"

The dark tunnel once again swallowed them as Gideon leaned back against a seat whose cracked surface was liberally patched with grey duct tape. The tram sped forward, its slightly off-balance syncopated creaking adding bluster to Valaria's bravado. He folded his arms across his chest and his reply was delivered with disdain.

"So Dawson Hayes is Sam Adams. Why is knowing that such a victory for you?"

"It's a victory because it means I'm not crazy—and because I've finally been given a glimpse into that hallowed 'need-to-know' inner circle of yours." She glared at him from across the narrow car. "And just why was it so important to you that I be kept out of that particular loop? It's not like I'm gonna go blabbing it to the world. Who the hell would I tell anyway—Yancy?"

Gideon's look clearly expressed the *"get a clue"* he didn't find it necessary to verbalize.

"There are all sorts of reasons to keep information like that to ourselves," he said pointedly, *"safety* being the most obvious. Hell, I didn't even know his identity until recently. When I first came looking for your grandfather they never told me Hayes was Sam Adams."

Quinn leaned forward, forearms resting on his thighs. "Geez, Valaria, think about it. Sam Adams is number one on the RSA's most wanted list and he's a deep-cover operative working right under their very noses. Every time somebody new finds out who he really is the risk to his life grows exponentially. Don't you think that's a pretty damn good reason to play that particular card close to the vest?"

"But won't he have to come in now?"

"No, he used a different Guardian identity while in Indianapolis so his cover's intact."

"Won't they figure that out? Don't they have facial recognition programs that'll identify him as Dawson Hayes once the fake ID deadends?"

"They do, but I gave him a virus to download that should've totally screwed with their recordings while he was there. And if the virus is half as twitchy as I think it is they're undoubtedly still trying to unravel it—and hopefully they never will."

Quinn felt he had just scored a point in their ping-pong game of one-upmanship and he volleyed a smug smile and an arched eyebrow Valaria's way.

"I still win," she retorted. "I was right about Hayes—and Speaker McFarland told me so himself."

Gideon shook his head and laughed. "God, you are such a spoiled kid sometimes."

They fell silent until Valaria offered up an olive branch. "I'm really glad Elise will be all right."

"Yeah," Quinn replied with mournful sincerity, "me too."

Valaria wanted to talk more about his little sister but the tram pulled into The Hub's terminus a moment later and the partners emerged into an unexpected flury of chaotic activity.

"What the hell is all this?" she asked instead. "What's happening? We were only in the tunnel a few minutes."

Gideon grabbed the arm of the first officer that crossed their path.

"What's going on?" he demanded.

"Word just came in, sir—the RSA's on the move. Looks like the real deal this time!"

"They're headed here?"

"No sir," the officer replied hurriedly. "Ottumwa."

He glanced anxiously over Quinn's shoulder. "If you'll excuse me, sir, I need to get moving."

The two men exchanged hasty salutes as the other man hurried away.

"Where's Ottumwa—what's there?" Valaria asked.

"Iowa; it's our old base," Gideon replied, hurrying her through a warren of increasingly bustling corridors. "Before the plague it was a telecommunications hub and a bunch of survivors ended up there. Those who didn't hold with the RSA's reorganization plans stayed on; started broadcasting on limited frequencies and their number slowly grew. Guess you could say it's where the Sons of Liberty were born. It's only a small garrison now so if the government thinks we're headquartered there at least they're working on outdated intel."

They had reached the administration section of The Hub, an area Valaria had rarely visited and she stayed at Quinn's side as he was briefed by the officers on duty.

"...Whether or not they believe Ottumwa is the extent of our forces is unclear, sir," a middle-aged woman Valaria had never met before explained, "but we intercepted messages indicating they believe taking it will be a strategic advantage and a crippling blow to our morale."

Quinn directed his attention toward the officer sitting at the central computer terminal. "What do our numbers look like?'

The man stood so Gideon could replace him in front of the screen.

"We can only transport about a hundred," he replied, "but have contacted the outposts within reasonable distance and should be able to mobilize a total of around twice that."

Valaria pulled up a chair and sat next to Quinn as he began manipulating the screen and scrolling through maps and data related to the information they had received.

"Got any Liberty Tree agents in residence at Ottumwa?" she asked.

"As a matter of fact, one of our best—'Joseph Warren'—runs the place."

She couldn't resist a little jibe. "I suppose I don't *need to know* who he really is, huh?"

Quinn didn't respond.

"So when do we leave?" she asked, shifting gears.

"You're not going anywhere," Gideon stated flatly. "And that's an order."

"Quinn," she pleaded. "There's nothing wrong with me!"

He swiveled away from the computer and gave her a cool, uncompromising stare. "Forget it, Thorpe. In the first place you almost literally just got out of the infirmary. In the second place you're not a soldier you're an operative—a good one, I'll grant you, but this isn't some clandestine mission, it's likely to be an all-out battle and you're not trained for that."

"And your little band of misfits is," she challenged hotly.

Quinn's face was inscrutable.

"I think we're going to find out."

V.

It took about seven hours for reinforcements from St. Louis to reach the Sons of Liberty garrison in Ottumwa. After sending Valaria back to her room—in the company of a guard under orders to shoot her in the foot if she didn't stay put—Quinn supervised the loading of supplies and personnel into the Sons' meager fleet of transport vehicles. When the squad was ready to leave shortly after ten p.m. he climbed into the cab of the lead truck and they headed out under cover of darkness.

Old U.S. Highway 61 was the shortest route between the two cities and much of the two hundred sixty miles of roadway had been kept in reasonably serviceable condition after the Sons began consolidating operations in St. Louis. In order to mask their presence while en route they took a cue from World War II England and covered the vehicles' headlights in black-out shielding that emitted a limited beam of light through long, rectangular openings cut into the middle. Although

345

effective, visibility was seriously impeded, reducing the small convoy to a crawl whenever the decayed asphalt they followed gave way to sections that were little more than narrow dirt paths scratched into the gaps.

But they got there—and got there well ahead of the RSA at that. Five hulking, dilapidated trucks crammed with guns, pulse packs and nearly a hundred dissidents who were about to have their first experience as soldiers pulled into Ottumwa, Iowa's Country Day Communications Complex with about two hours of darkness to spare.

Milton Esparza—known on the Liberty Tree as Joseph Warren—was there to greet them. Standing almost a foot shorter than Gideon, he was a thickly-muscled 34-year-old dynamo with flashing brown eyes and dimples that formed canyons on either side of his mouth when he smiled. Passionately committed to the cause of freedom and the men and women with whom he served, Milton Esparza was a rising star among the Sons of Liberty.

"General Quinn," he said, saluting sharply and reaching out to shake hands.

Gideon returned the salute. "General Esparza."

The two men exchanged the greeting growing increasingly common among their colleagues—right hand grasping the opposite man's right forearm, left hand outstretched to clasp the right shoulder.

"So, my friend," Milton continued. "What have you brought us?"

Quinn indicated the men and women spilling out of the crowded transports with loud bravado. "A hundred good soldiers who are itching for a chance to show the RSA just what they think of it."

"Well, looks like they've come to the right place."

"So it would seem."

Quinn directed his attention to the squaddies stretching and milling about after their long confinement in the crowded trucks. "Hear that, you bastards? You're gonna get the chance to kick some RSA ass!"

A rowdy cheer replete with fist-pumps and raised pulse rifles swelled up from among the ranks.

Esparza and Quinn continued their confident public banter until they had passed through the groups of soldiers and closed the door of Milton's office behind them.

"Just how bad do things look?" Gideon asked, all trace of bluster gone.

"With the addition of your people, we're up to about three hundred so we'll make a strong statement. But depending on what they throw at us we could find ourselves seriously outclassed—if that happens then I'm afraid all bets are off."

Quinn nodded in tight-lipped agreement.

"You should take charge," he observed.

"No," Esparza replied with quiet finality.

"But we're of equal rank and this is your garrison."

"True but my place is with my people—I'll stand with them." He flashed the broad smile and Grand Canyon dimples for which he was famous. "Gotta get in on that ass-kicking, Quinn! And anyway, you have the superior eye so it's you who should run the show."

Gideon appreciated his friend's vote of confidence and reluctantly acquiesced to his request. He also knew it was pointless to argue with a man who could give Valaria Thorpe a run for her money when it came to being obstinate.

Joining forces, the two generals quickly set to work organizing their numbers into what they hoped would be an effective defense against the unknown that lay ahead.

Since their purpose was to protect the garrison and not to engage the enemy on the defunct farmland stretching away from the complex on three sides, about half the Sons took up positions behind a redoubt of rusted out vehicles, battered cement blocks, doors, and drywall scavenged from nearby buildings, stacks of old tires, and even long centipedes of nested shopping carts from a derelict grocery store down the road. In addition to manning that improvised barricade, about a hundred others were deployed to guard the perimeter of the complex, with a small number placed as snipers among the upper floors of adjacent buildings.

Believing they had done what they could, the dissidents settled in as the morning dew formed shimmering teardrops around them and the cacophony of stars over their heads was blotted out by the slowly brightening eastern sky.

A government force more than three times their size arrived with the sun. With brazen confidence they formed ranks at the opposite end of the field, their superior numbers and weaponry glinting in what they saw as the dawn's affirmation.

"Holy Mother of God," Gideon heard one of the Sons murmur as the reality of their situation leached into the older man's marrow.

Esparza and Quinn exchanged subtle looks that affirmed the man's observation and shook hands again before parting. Thinking as one as they headed in opposite directions, each passed the order down the lines to wait until the RSA forces were close enough to spit on before opening fire— Their fledgling troopers would have to make every shot count if they were to hold off the impending advance.

The inexperienced rebels cradled their weapons and looked out across the enemy, mouths growing dry and hearts beginning to race in anticipation of what was to come.

Their RSA opponents didn't keep them waiting long.

Unleashing a fusillade of conventional projectiles and incendiaries that shattered the morning calm, the government troops began slowly moving forward. For the rebels in the garrison it was a sobering, ear-splitting introduction and they hunkered down as comrades were felled and flaming bits and chunks of debris flew everywhere, igniting fires and inflicting heinous injury all around them.

Somewhere along the line the tension snapped and a lone squaddy opened fire. . . In a heartbeat they all joined in.

Once the shooting began, Gideon raced back into the main building and up a flight of stairs leading to the garrison's command post. Heavily fortified, it was also the site of one of their sniper nests and, when not communicating with his commanders on the ground, Quinn took satisfaction in grabbing his rifle and joining the marksman as she picked off select targets—particularly any RSA officers who obligingly came in range.

Having assumed the garrison would be easy pickings, the government troops weren't prepared for the unexpectedly heavy fire coming from behind the makeshift redoubt and along the perimeter. As comrades began falling they found their confident bravado dramatically shaken. And not only were they falling victim to the Sons' tenacity but the open fields themselves seemed to be taking sides as unseen rocks, holes, roots and debris hidden in the tangled undergrowth became additional adversaries. Stumbling across the uneven, snarled terrain and disoriented by the surprisingly successful barrage coming from the garrison, RSA troopers were going down—injured, wounded, and dead—in unanticipated numbers.

Obviously caught by surprise, *the government soldiers actually fell back!*

"Is that it?" the sniper at Quinn's shoulder asked with hopeful cockiness. "Is that all they've got?"

As if in reply, the entire building shuddered portentously and they were covered in a shower of plaster dust as an RSA incendiary rocked the command post. The young sniper wobbled on her feet like a newborn foal as the building shifted, her cockiness replaced by wide-eyed silence.

"That answer your question?" Gideon asked with a smirk.

The well-trained RSA troops had quickly re-formed their ranks and were once again advancing, supported by the constant barrage of the armaments at their rear. But in spite of heavy casualties in the garrison—and the stark reality of dwindling ammunition—the combined resolve of the rebels stationed around the complex actually managed to again repulse their better-equipped counterparts!

A derisive cheer rose from behind the battered fortification as the Sons watched their government adversaries retreat a second time.

It would be a short-lived celebration.

As enemy troops moved safely out of range, five large RSA planes appeared in the distance, their thrumming engines creating an intimidating thunder that quickly quelled the garrison's enthusiasm.

The impressive aircraft had expansive wingspans offset by oddly shaped, bulbous undercarriages that made them look like pelicans in flight with their pouches engorged with fish. They swooped in low across the horizon almost as if intending to ram the rebel stronghold now in their sights, the stunned garrison watching transfixed as the planes flew at them a scant twenty feet above the ground.

Quinn was observing the scene from the top floor of the main building and had just decided to give the order to retreat from a collision that appeared imminent when each plane suddenly belched out four small, unmanned quadrunners before arcing sharply heavenward and flying on.

Gideon stopped short, communication lines open, mouth slightly agape, eyebrows furrowed in alarmed anticipation as he looked out across the open field.

The mechanized quadrunners literally bounced as they hit the ground but oversized tires absorbed the impact and quickly stabilized them. An astonished silence descended on the garrison as the compact vehicles spread out in a line—twenty ominous machines maintaining constant speed and equal distance from one another. They sped forward while the Sons looked on in awestruck consternation.

Suddenly, like an orchestra positioning their instruments at the lifting of the maestro's baton, metal casings nestled between the four tires of each runner opened simultaneously and automated pulse canons rose up from within. The garrison's shocked alarm turned to terror as a symphony of destruction ensued, the unmanned quads beginning to strafe the terrain with waves of deadly pulses.

"*Retreat... retreat... retreat,*" Quinn shouted into the comlink looped over his right ear.

He glanced around the command post before turning his attention to the young sniper who had proven so capable over the past hour. "Grab those data sticks and then get the hell out of here!"

Bedlam broke out among the rebels. The improvised redoubt that had served them well thus far began to buckle and collapse as the pulse waves struck; fragments of all sizes being hurled helter-skelter when snagged on the edge of a warbling pulse. The buildings behind the barrier didn't fare much better. Brick and mortar already weakened by more conventional weapons—and those areas still smoldering after being struck by incendiaries—were crushed like cardboard by the canons' translucent blows. Deadly debris rained down on the men and women defending the garrison, burying many under avalanches of ruin while others were reduced to bloody husks when caught in the path of a destructive wave.

The strength of each pulse diminished as it expanded from its point of origin but—as Gideon's scarred right arm could testify—even the slightest encounter could cause grievous harm and the more focused the wave the more horrific the impact on human tissue. As the quadrunners drew closer the scope of injury and destruction increased exponentially and heart-wrenching cries from among the wounded were added to the chaos of retreat.

"Are you coming, General Quinn?"

The young sniper had finished stuffing data sticks into the small pouch she wore slung across her body and stood by the stairwell clutching her rifle.

"In a minute," Gideon replied. "You go ahead."

The young woman hesitated.

"*Now!*"

The building creaked and moaned mournfully, beginning to succumb to the throes of death. The sniper threw a concerned look over her shoulder before following orders and running down the stairs.

Quinn returned to the window and looked out across the destruction. The Iowa farmland had been transformed into a smoldering alien landscape and Milton Esparza, with a group of his men, was standing in the midst of it shooting at the tires of oncoming quads.

Gideon activated his comlink.

"Milton," he cried. "You've done all you can. Get your men out of there!"

Esparza stopped shooting and looked up at the window where he knew his friend would be standing.

"We've spit in their face," Gideon continued. "Let's go!"

"*What about the wounded?*" Milton asked, his transmission crackling in Quinn's ear.

"Being loaded onto transports as we speak... Come on—get the hell out of there!"

Esparza offered up a salute and began gesturing to his men. In a moment the small group of fighters was running for safety and scrambling over what remained of the makeshift redoubt.

Milton was the last to clamber over the barrier.

He slung his rifle strap over his shoulder and was vaulting across the hood of an old school bus when the wall in front of him gave a shuddering rumble and began to collapse.

Chunks of cement block, shards of shattered glass, and slabs of dry wall tumbled downward in an ear-splitting, deadly cascade.

Esparza dodged to his left, grabbing one of his men by the shoulders and heaving him out of harm's way as the wall crashed forward. The two men scrambled to their feet and looked back at the pile of rubble that had almost devoured them.

Milton raised his face to Quinn and laughed, famous dimples flashing.

But as he leaned down to retrieve the rifle that had slipped from his shoulder, a length of rebar sticking out from the eaves high above them snapped free of the crumbling wall that could no longer hold it.

It plummeted to the ground with the force of a warrior's spear.

In less than a heartbeat, the garrison's intrepid leader lay dead— impaled by the rebar as it slammed him face down onto the ground.

"Unhappy it is to reflect that a brother's sword has been sheathed in a brother's breast and that the once-happy plains of America are either to be drenched with blood or inhabited by slaves. Sad alternative... but can a virtuous man hesitate in his choice?"

~ George Washington

CHAPTER SEVENTEEN

I.

"Did you know him well?" Valaria asked.

She and Quinn had just left the memorial service for those lost at the Battle of Ottumwa and were slowly making their way toward the cafeteria with Dodger and Donovan. It had been an emotional ceremony. The names of each of the fallen had been solemnly announced accompanied by the somber tolling of a deeply resonate bell—which had proved mildly distracting since Valaria kept finding herself rather irreverently wondering if there really was a big bell backstage or just some electronic simulation; probably the latter. After acknowledging the dead, a man who worked in the cafeteria had performed a stirring rendition of the old funereal standby, *Amazing Grace*, and then James McFarland had given the eulogy. The Speaker's presence was a noteworthy event since the rank-and-file rarely saw 'Grandpa Jimmy' as he was called. Although the average grunt knew who McFarland was most had never heard him speak and some had never even seen him before. Many assumed that—for security—he was always on the move while others were certain he had offices hidden somewhere within the labyrinthine convention center; only a select handful knew of the separate facilities nestled beneath the nearby Gateway Arch from which the former Speaker of the House and a small group of specialists monitored the RSA. When the dignified embodiment of the former United States stepped to the front of the dais the entire auditorium had fallen silent and not an eye strayed while the energetic old man paced the length of the stage speaking of the significance of the battle and the bravery of the men and women they had lost. His message had been intense and personal, with gestures and eye contact that had drawn his audience in and made them experience his words on a deeply intimate level. As much a call to action as a tribute to the dead, by the time McFarland had finished each rebel felt like he had spoken directly to them and was honored to stand with the elderly statesman.

"Yeah, I knew him pretty well," Gideon was saying in response to Valaria's question about Milton Esparza. "It's one hell of a loss."

His voice dropped as he found himself suddenly choked by emotion.

The horrific moment of his friend's death—impaled by a length of rebar jettisoned from a collapsing building—had been running on an almost-constant loop in Quinn's brain ever since it happened. Every quiet moment flung him back to his command post vantage point and he watched in impotent shock as the scene played out in heart-wrenching slow motion over and over again. He slowly blinked the image away and mournfully shook his head as they neared the cafeteria.

"Esparza was an exile, like you," Dodger chimed in, recognizing Gideon's distress. "He was smart, outrageously courageous—a natural leader..." He smiled as the embers of memory stirred. "Had a stubborn streak wider than the Mississippi."

Walking next to Dodger, the ghost of a smirk crossed Donovan's face; he couldn't resist the opening his friend had just provided.

"Must be in the Borders's water," he jibed, throwing a sidelong glance Valaria's way.

His words earned him a glower from the woman at his side but out of respect for the dead she withheld the retaliatory strike that sprang to mind.

They had reached the cafeteria and headed for an isolated table, watching as the first shift filed in for dinner.

"I'm really sorry for your loss guys," Valaria said to her companions as they sat down. "Wish I had met him."

"Oh, you've met him," Gideon informed her.

He gestured toward the quickly filling room. "Look around you. You can see him in every one of those faces out there. You meet him every day in every person who has risked everything by coming here and taking a stand for freedom."

"Well said, my friend," Farley interjected quietly with a thoughtful nod. "Well said."

A smile creased Valaria's face but she concentrated on the milling crowd and remained silent. It had been quite a while since Quinn had had what she called a 'fife-and-drum moment'— She figured he was entitled after Ottumwa.

The four friends drifted away on eddies of thought and the table was awash in silence.

It was Dodger who finally parted the waters.

"McFarland's words were good," he observed.

The others murmured their agreement.

"Was he right in calling Ottumwa a victory?" Valaria asked. "Or was that just a dash of hyperbole to rally the troops?"

As the only member of the quartet present at the battle, Quinn was quick to reply. "You can't call it a victory in the traditional sense since we ended up retreating but it was one helluva *moral* triumph. They obviously thought we'd be scared shitless by their superior numbers; that we'd run off with our tails between our legs when they brought out the big guns. But we didn't—we held the line. Hell, they fell back *twice* before finally forcing our retreat. And if they hadn't had those damn quadrunners who knows what might have happened." He smiled fleetingly, repeating the last thing he had said to Esparza. "We spit in their face. Not bad for our first toe-to-toe with the neighborhood bully."

Having missed out on Ottumwa due to being sent south on patrol the day before the battle, Dodger and Donovan had been playing catch-up since their return and were eager to hear more.

"I'd like to have seen those runners," Farley said. "Sounds like they were pretty damn effective."

Quinn had to admit they were. "...Any time you're up against pulse cannons you're at a disadvantage," he concluded, "and those small, mobile bastards are a whole new ballgame."

He ran a hand through his shaggy hair. "But Milton and his men were making progress before our final retreat."

Gideon pulled off his half-glove, activated the tech layered into the tattoo on the back of his left hand and showed them some footage he had managed to get before the building's imminent collapse forced him to leave the top floor command post.

"Milton and his squad started targeting the big-ass tires on those things. Not easy to do with pulses coming at you; gotta come at 'em from the side to avoid the wave as it expands so it doesn't deflect your shot—or melt your face—but if you take out the tires the quads are slow and off-balance. I bet you could climb onboard from behind and immobilize the cannon without much trouble after that."

Dodger clasped his friend's shoulder. "So maybe next time, David will show Goliath a thing or two."

II.

The Battle of Ottumwa was a wake-up call for both sides.

For the Sons of Liberty it was a lesson in resolve—the energizing realization that they could stand up to the RSA and make a significant dent in the breastplate of confidence their counterparts had forged from greater numbers, better training, and superior equipment.

The regime learned this as well—what the Sons were capable of—but for them the lesson was more sobering; a shrill alarm that the dissidents' swift-flowing currents of discontent had the potential to become a vortex capable of consuming the Eden they had worked so hard to create after the plague had washed the slate clean.

These were troubling thoughts. Thoughts that were robbing Naomi Blanchard of sleep and chipping away at her well-manicured composure as tiny fissures began to appear in the façade of her 38-year-old regime.

"So, where do we stand?"

As Chief Executive of the RSA's Triumvirate, it was President Blanchard who led the cabinet briefings that began promptly at seven each morning. She took her seat between the Judicial and Legislative members of the nation's venerated governmental trio and shot an expectant look at each of the seven officials who had joined them at the table either physically or holographically.

"We were told Ottumwa would end the rebellious little charade of these self-proclaimed Sons of Liberty," she continued, the frigid edge of challenge making her voice brittle. "What happened?"

General Marcus Conway cleared his throat nervously, hoping that someone else would respond. The others around the table—the national Director of Homeland Security and the five Safe Zone governors projected from the relative shelter of their offices hundreds of miles away—remained silent, visibly relieved that this first volley from the president was thoroughly military in nature.

The silence lengthened and President Blanchard waited. She was good at waiting; had honed the skill to razor sharpness over the years and used it to unnerve those who came within her orbit and maneuver them into showing their hand or acquiescing to her point of view. Outwardly calm, she tapped the long tapering nail of her right index finger against the surface of the table and offered a bland stare toward her now fidgeting audience.

The general finally spoke. "They proved to be more... tenacious than expected, your Excellency."

"*Tenacious*," Blanchard repeated slowly, tasting the word and finding it bitter.

"They believe they have a cause," observed the Director of Homeland Security.

"James McFarland's cause," Chief Justice Karla Maxwell contributed from Blanchard's right.

The president winced inwardly.

"James McFarland," She spat out the name; just saying it brought the acrid taste of bile to her mouth. Her voice grew quiet and fierce. "God damn him to Hell. That man has been a thorn in the side of my administration ever since he left Washington almost forty years ago..." She shook her head in a rare demonstration of frustration. "Should have dealt with him when I had the chance."

"Excuse me, Excellency," the governor of Louisville ventured. "I've heard the name but can't place it. Who is James McFarland?"

Blanchard gestured curtly to Adlai Hillerman—the Triumvirate's legislative member seated at her left—indicating that he should respond.

"James McFarland was Speaker of the House in the old republic," he explained. "My predecessor. He abandoned the country at the time of The Revanche."

"Where did he go?"

"That's a very good question," the current Speaker continued. "It was hoped he would be found in Ottumwa, but our information was obviously outdated."

"And how do we know he's behind all this?" the elderly governor of Indianapolis asked with quiet skepticism. "I remember him as a mediator not an instigator."

Speaker Hillerman opened his mouth to reply but snapped it shut as President Blanchard cut him off.

"Because he *told* us so," she growled.

The Indianapolis governor was obviously taken aback. "Ma'am?"

"Director Bolton," she said, throwing a venomous smile toward her hand-picked Director of Homeland Security, "enlighten our colleague, please."

Jeremy Bolton had been a friend of the son Blanchard lost to the plague and was something of a protégé of the Triumvirate's Chief Executive. Unerringly loyal and doggedly devoted to the president's policies and goals, Bolton cut a striking figure in the uniform he had designed for those in his department and would have been equally comfortable among a gang of jackbooted thugs as he was seated in a Cabinet briefing.

He was a rising star and the governors all knew it.

Standing slowly, Bolton smoothed the somber grey tunic that fell to mid-thigh over the razor-sharp creases of his trousers. He moved to the end of the table opposite the Triumvirate and remotely triggered an unseen projector. A large translucent 3D screen coalesced as his audience directed their attention his way.

"Someone among the Sons of Liberty has been hacking into our GovLines broadcasts—we're assuming it's Gideon Quinn since it falls within his skill set."

The governor of the Indianapolis Safe Zone once again was skeptical. "Hacking in? I've seen no evidence of that."

"That's because so far our Wraiths have been able to cut them off before the signal dispersed. Unfortunately, they have yet to succeed in tracing the hacks back to their source."

Without further comment, Director Bolton turned toward the screen and opened one of the messages they had managed to block before it played nationwide.

The 20-second vignette had been filmed in James McFarland's sitting room where nothing could betray his location. The former Speaker of the House sat in his favorite chair with the stars and stripes of a faded American flag as a backdrop. Looking more like someone's favorite old uncle than a revolutionary, his message for the unseen populace of the RSA was succinct and sincere.

> *"My name is James McFarland and I was Speaker of the House of Representatives in the United States Congress prior to The Revanche. President Blanchard wants you to believe that the RSA is alone in North America and that her government has your best interests at heart. Neither claim could be further from the truth. Thousands of your fellow Americans are living west of the Mississippi and are eager to rebuild the old Republic. You don't have to settle for a life of fear and deprivation... Keep listening—the Sons of Liberty are among you."*

The room was as quiet as a tomb, all eyes slowly and cautiously turning back toward Naomi Blanchard who could barely contain an apoplectic fury.

"Isn't that just lovely," she snarled.

III.

Gideon Quinn's fingers were flying across the computer screen projected in front of him while his two most promising apprentices looked on with the enthusiasm of RTS gamers, almost salivating in near-pathological eagerness to get their hands on a screen.

"Bloody hell," he muttered. "This one's good—think I've met him before."

Quinn and his protégés were in the command center underneath the Gateway Arch, once again attempting to exploit the Remote Access Tool Sam Adams had implanted in the RSA's computer system while rescuing Valaria Thorpe the month before. The RAT was Gideon's baby, designed as a back door that would allow them to infiltrate the regime's GovLines propaganda broadcasts and inject their own brief messages. Unfortunately, Quinn's ingenious portal had yet to prove vigorous enough to withstand the government technicians with whom he and his techies now parried. Known as Wraiths, their opponents were equally skilled and highly motivated to keep technological intruders at bay—since failure could mean far more to them than merely losing a job. Gideon was almost certain he and his current antagonist had crossed technological swords the last time he was in the States.

Still focused on the screen in front of him and tapping and dragging his way through the invasive labyrinth he was creating, Gideon stood.

"Rayne," he said to the young woman on his left, "you take over here and keep this bastard occupied while Carter and I create a little havoc elsewhere."

The woman slid eagerly into the seat Quinn had vacated, flipping her long jet-black French braid over her shoulder as she zeroed in on the task her mentor was entrusting to her. The braid swished across her back like the tail of a frisky colt as she settled in.

Gideon couldn't help thinking of his sister Elise whenever he was around Rayne Padgett—except for the fact that she was serious where Elise was flighty, meticulously organized where Elise gave new meaning to the word haphazard, and determined to make a contribution to the cause of freedom where Elise was only determined to have a good time. He smiled in spite of his current frustration with the Wraith; Rayne and his sister really weren't anything alike but there was just something about her that always triggered a homesick longing.

While Rayne continued to play tag with her government counterpart, Gideon and his other favored techie, Reuben Carter, accessed the portal from another station and began weaving their way through layers of encryption and skillfully evading honey pot traps along the way as they sought to outwit the Wraiths and worm their own path to pay dirt.

Carter glanced Rayne's way as he joined Quinn. She appeared calm and focused while he was so excited to be working next to his idol he was afraid he might actually wet himself. They weren't exactly rivals but he sure envied her composure.

Not only were Gideon's favorite assistants poles apart in terms of demeanor, they also anchored opposite ends of the spectrum when it came to appearance. Where Padgett was tall and willowy with the flawless porcelain skin of her Asian-American mother and a face one would expect to see illuminated by a spotlight rather than the reflected glow of a computer screen, Carter looked exactly as one would imagine someone who spent their life submerged in the bowels of technology. With unkempt hair and wrinkled clothes—and a round-shouldered, portly build that betrayed a sedentary life spent hunched over a computer. Reuben Carter was the epitome of a tech junkie and quite literally would be first in line to have his consciousness uploaded into a cosmic mainframe should the opportunity ever present itself. But whatever their differences, both tyros were excited to be assisting their hero in tormenting the regime in Columbus, with personal back stories that more than provided the proverbial ax to grind. Their skills had grown exponentially under the tutelage of their mentor and to say they were eager to prove themselves would have been an understatement.

"I... I think I'm in," Rayne suddenly stammered in excited wonder.

"Is the breach stable?" Quinn asked as he and Carter continued to forge a separate branch of the RAT's pathway.

"I think so... *yes*," she almost shouted, the triumph in her voice garnering the attention of everyone else in the room.

Gideon shot a glance at the clock. It was 6:37 p.m.—*perfect!* One of the government's four main broadcasts ran during the dinner hour and watching was mandatory. Every viewing screen in the country would be tuned in; every home, every public place, every government billboard would soon be resting in the palm of their hand—at least for a few seconds.

"Outstanding," he crowed. "Deliver the package!"

With a few additional strokes across the screen—and beaming with the delight of a child on Christmas morning—Rayne completed the final electronic link that connected their transmission to that of the RSA.

Everyone in the command center held their breath. All eyes rose to the large viewing screen centered on the wall above their work stations on which GovLines broadcasts played in pantomime 24/7. While they waited in a collective emotional limbo, one of the technicians slipped away and knocked on James McFarland's adjacent office door.

The former Speaker of the House didn't have to be told what the pervasive hush indicated as he emerged from his inner sanctum; the silence almost crackled with anticipation.

"Turn up the volume, please," the elderly leader murmured into the electrified stillness.

"...And in related news," a perfectly coiffed newswoman was saying, "in light of an increased threat of terrorist activity, the Office of Homeland Security has announced they are raising the protection level from orange to red. Citizens are reminded that—with a red level advisory—a daily curfew will now run from 6 p.m. until work transports resume at 6 in the morning..."

Suddenly, her voice was sliced by static and the picture on the screen distorted slightly, her bright red lipstick momentarily a crimson smear across the viewing panel. The transmission appeared to be struggling to maintain its stranglehold on the airwaves as the woman's carefully scripted monologue and highly polished delivery were pummeled by Quinn's technological battering rams.

In a moment she was gone, her distorted image supplanted by the kindly face of James McFarland sitting in front of an old American flag.

> *"My name is James McFarland and I was Speaker*
> *of the House of Representatives in the United States*
> *Congress prior to The Revanche..."*

Like a politician's campaign headquarters receiving news of victory on election night, the Sons in the control center erupted in cheers, jumping to their feet and hugging and slapping one another on the back as McFarland's first message to the people of the RSA played above them.

The elderly statesman gestured Quinn toward his office over the shoulders of the other celebrants and closed the door behind him.

"Well done, Gideon," he began, wrapping gnarled fingers around the younger man's hand in a congratulatory grasp. "This is a huge accomplishment."

"Thank you, sir."

Something in the old man's tone sounded like there was a 'however' hovering in the background and Quinn braced himself.

"However, I'll be even more proud of you if you can accomplish the next task I have in mind."

IV.

"*No*," Valaria sputtered unequivocally. "No way in hell. Not even if you embed a bunch of nude pictures of the president."

Quinn balked inwardly at the bawdy image her suggestion conjured up but couldn't help smiling a little in spite of himself.

"And don't even try playing your '*but McFarland wants you to*' trump card," she warned.

"But he does—it was his idea."

Valaria sighed heavily, shaking her head. "Jesus, Mary, and Joseph..."

"I think even the Holy Family would weigh in on McFarland's side on this one," Quinn observed with a lopsided grin. "Think about it, Valaria, your grandfather is still something of a folk hero in the RSA— kind of like Henry Ford or Thomas Edison in the Old Republic. Combine that with the fact that you've experienced Radiance firsthand and you've got yourself one helluva a good reason why it's only logical for you to do a 'LibertyLine.'"

"*LibertyLine?*" Valaria asked, her incredulity punctuated by an arched eyebrow and a mordant smirk.

"Yeah, one of my assistants thought they needed a name."

"Let me guess—*Rayne Padgett*, right?"

Valaria's comment dripped with the suggestion of romantic interest in the young technician on Gideon's part. It was a conversation they had had before but this time he didn't take the bait.

"That's not gonna work. You're not changing the subject."

Something resembling the sound a cat makes just before expelling a hairball escaped Valaria's throat as Quinn continued.

"Speaker McFarland may be the face of the Old Republic but he wants younger faces to represent the Sons of Liberty. And he thinks one of those faces should be yours."

"Let 'Sam Adams' do it—he was there, too; Hayes saw firsthand what Repatriation is all about."

"Oh, that would make a lot of sense, wouldn't it? Have one of our deep-cover operatives stand in front of a camera and talk to the RSA."

"Well shit, better him than me."

"Face it Valaria, you're the one who's been saying we need to do something for those people," Quinn continued, playing what he felt was his real trump card. "It's time to ante up; gotta put your money where your mouth is."

Valaria had to admit he had a point—although she wasn't likely to say so out loud. And the more she thought about it, the idea of speaking her mind to the whole damn country was more than a little appealing; it'd also probably be as close as she'd ever get to being able to give Mavis Pope and Overseer Agnew the crude gesture she'd like to throw their way.

She glared at him with quiet skepticism that almost bordered on acquiescence. "Just what does McFarland have in mind?"

"He'd like you to do two spots," Gideon ventured tentatively, not wanting to spook her. "One as kind of an introduction—like the one he made—and then another specifically about Repatriation."

There was a long—*long*—silence during which Quinn barely drew a breath lest his quarry take flight and disappear into the underbrush.

Much to his amazement, she didn't bolt.

"OK," Valaria said at last. "I'll do it."

The new star attached one caveat to her unwritten LibertyLine contract—that Yancy be at her side for moral support. It wasn't much to ask—in fact, Speaker McFarland thought the dog's presence might add to her appeal—and so the following morning the three traveling companions took their shortest and most pleasant trip together, piling into a MetroLink tram and heading for the Gateway Arch.

Recording a vignette was a fairly straightforward proposition. Valaria knelt down on one knee with her arm around Yancy in front of the same battered American flag that had served as the backdrop for Speaker McFarland's LibertyLine; an anonymous—yet highly symbolic—setting.

It took a few tries but before long Thorpe's Granddaughter—and her grinning black-and-white dog—brought a smile of affirmation to McFarland's face when everyone present at the filming agreed she had nailed it. Since Valaria had always cast herself in the role of outlier, the elderly statesman was particularly pleased with her opening line…

> *"My name is Valaria Thorpe and I'm a member of the*
> *Sons of Liberty."*

She glanced at the dog and waggled his alert ears with her free hand before looking confidently back into the camera.

> *"…And he is too. If my last name sounds familiar it's*
> *because my grandfather designed the Guardian Star.*
> *President Blanchard calls Otis Thorpe a national hero*
> *and believe me, he was—but not the way she claims.*
> *My grandfather never would have supported a regime*
> *that stands up only by holding its people down; he*
> *spoke out for freedom and he died a Borders exile…"*

Pausing for effect, Valaria nodded soberly and pulled Yancy in a bit tighter.

> *"Yeah, that's right, he died an exile! Keep*
> *listening—the Sons of Liberty are among you.*

V.

In the weeks following their first LibertyLine incursion, Gideon and his staff were fairly successful injecting their anti-government snippets into RSA broadcasts. Speaker McFarland's introduction and Valaria's first foray into life on camera were included in a series of vignettes that incorporated other testimonials as well as quick visuals and printed messages warning about the deadly reality of the regime's 'Repatriation Protocols.'

"…Don't be fooled," Valaria's warning about Radiance had concluded, *"there's nothing patriotic about the government's Repatriation plans. It's just another way to subdue and control you. Their drugs almost stole everything from me—my memories, my personality, my ability to think for myself…"*

The video cut away to a shot Dawson Hayes had taken of Valaria huddled on the floor in a confused stupor the night of her rescue. She shuddered involuntarily at the gaunt face and haunted, dark-rimmed eyes that stared vacantly up at the camera as nervous fingers plucked at unseen fuzz on the blanket she clutched about her.

"Don't let that happen to someone you love! Be smart—be careful—and keep listening… The Sons of Liberty are fighting for you."

Despite the best attempts of the regime's Wraiths, once embedded Gideon's constantly reconfiguring portal tunneled its way in and out of the RSA's electronic core like a tenacious colony of ants evading the exterminator. The messages didn't always get through and sometimes were cut off mid-run but the Sons' voice was definitely being heard—and Naomi Blanchard was almost literally foaming at the mouth with rage.

Unfortunately, the rebels' online success wasn't being paired with success in the field.

The Battle of Ottumwa—coupled with LibertyLine incursions—had been the proverbial throwing down of the gauntlet as far as the regime in Columbus was concerned and the president was determined to respond with the full force and authority she had at her command.

"I want them *dead*," Blanchard quietly hissed. "I want them all dead."

As was often the case, the seven Cabinet members fell silent in the face of the president's quiet rage and tried to become invisible lest some fault be found specifically with them.

"How is it possible," the Chief Executive demanded, "that a group of *outcasts* has been able to repeatedly breach our firewalls?"

She glared at the people and the holographic projections seated around the table, her voice increasing in intensity while remaining icy and quiet. "Someone needs to explain this to me because it damn sure shouldn't be happening!"

In his capacity as Director of Homeland Security—and feeling fairly safe due to his status as Blanchard's surrogate son—Jeremy Bolton broke the frigid silence.

"Gideon Quinn obviously has a fairly competent cohort of programmers working with him, your Excellency," he began. "But the countermeasures our Wraiths deploy successfully cut them off more often than not. Our goal, of course, is to turn their RAT against them and use it to hunt them down—and we're almost there. In the meantime we continue to saturate the media with new anti-terrorism messages that specifically target the Sons."

Blanchard glanced left and right toward Speaker Hillerman and Chief Justice Maxwell, the largely symbolic members of the Triumvirate. They averted their eyes and remained silent—knowing from long experience when it was best to let the Chief Executive command the room.

"...*More often than not...we're almost there...in the meantime...*" she repeated testily. "Enough rhetoric, Jeremy, I want results! The masses will believe what we tell them to believe. I don't care if we have to force-feed Radiance to the whole damn country; it's the Sons of Liberty we need to focus on. I want more—more drones in the sky, more boots on the ground."

She slowly turned her steely glare on General Conway.

"Did you hear me, Conway?" she asked with quiet malevolence. "Get your lazy ass out of that chair and get me some results in the field!"

He knew better than to disappoint her.

Government propaganda already was amped up like an athlete with 'roid-rage,' and under the nearly panic-stricken leadership of General Conway the military arm of the regime quickly followed suit. As a result, autumn was marked by a series of campaigns that saw the RSA extend its powerful tentacles into the Borders in a quest to annihilate the smaller, more agile Sons of Liberty. It was the first time in over a generation that the country had mobilized its Guardians for more than internal policing and intimidation and there was a distinct shift in atmosphere as ordinary folks and government yes-men alike hunkered down to see what would happen next.

What happened was a succession of demoralizing defeats for the Sons of Liberty.

On September 19th, a company of rebels was ambushed in a narrow ravine while heading south from St. Louis to reinforce an outpost near the border of Arkansas. Draped in moss and alive with countless rivulets of spring water seeping down the steep, rocky walls, the gorge was called the Black Hole—and should have proven a shadowy respite from the drone flyovers that had dogged the squaddie's heels all day, slowing their progress and causing them to scatter into the trees and underbrush with tedious regularity. Their efforts to avoid detection appeared successful, however, and they had approached the pass with confidence knowing they would be shielded from view once within its dank, shady recesses.

But they had, in fact, been seen.

Unbeknownst to them, one of the drones with which they had played hide-and-seek had detected their presence, its pilot back in the RSA extrapolating their route and relaying the information to government forces on the ground. Moments after entering the gorge, the squad had been trapped like fish in a barrel, targeted by a group of Freebooters firing at them from behind the trees and rocky outcroppings lining the narrow path—accompanied for the first time by RSA liaison officers. The terrain of the steep pass allowed for neither counterattack nor retreat as the Freebooters closed in behind them and the Sons were forced to forge ahead, ultimately fighting hand to hand as the 'booters abandoned their newly-acquired RSA weapons in favor of the close-in fighting to which they were virtually addicted. Icy tendrils of fear gripped the less-experienced dissidents as the ravine reverberated with the Freebooter's eerie, ululating cry—to which the screams of their hapless victims were quickly added.

Less than an hour later more than half the rebel squad lay mutilated and dying on the muddy, blood-soaked floor of the gorge.

Back in the RSA, the routing of the Sons at the Black Hole was a highly-touted—and highly sensationalized—victory. It galvanized Naomi Blanchard's belief that the Freebooters would prove a valuable asset in the drama to come and she directed a reluctant General Conway to expand use of the pathologically unpredictable mercenaries as Guardian forces were deployed throughout the Borders.

As September gave way to October and brilliant autumn hues were splashed atop the virtually uninterrupted leafy canopy stretching across the continent, the schizophrenic Guardian-Freebooter alliance inflicted another demoralizing blow on the Sons of Liberty when a mixed force of nearly five hundred laid siege to a strategic stronghold called Fort Washington. Successfully corralling two hundred Sons within their fortification inside a defunct utility plant, the Guardian in charge had bombarded the fort with incendiaries and pulse cannons. The response was stiff resistance from the marksmen inside and for much of the day the rebels held their ground. But with all his forces pinned within the fort—with no hope of victory and no help for the wounded—the Sons' commander finally conceded defeat and ultimately raised the universally-recognized white flag.

Unfortunately, no policy for the taking of prisoners had been established and the lead Guardian was faced with an impossible dilemma. Unprepared to take the captives with them but unwilling to simply let them go the Guardians turned the prisoners over to their Freebooter comrades and moved on, abandoning them to an unspeakable fate.

What followed was nothing short of slaughter.

When news of the butchery at Fort Washington reached St. Louis, demoralized outrage coursed through the exhausted rebels. Recoiling from the stories of carnage that came straggling in with the handful of battered and filthy survivors, the Sons hunkered down to lick their wounds and reconsider a strategy that, up to that point, seemed good for nothing more than emboldening the enemy. The conclusion they drew was almost unanimous; their loosely organized system of outposts should be consolidated as quickly as possible in order to allow them to regroup, recuperate, and re-evaluate their options.

In an icy late-October rain, while preparing to follow orders to evacuate and regroup farther north, word reached the men and women stationed at a derelict high school in Cape Girardeau, Missouri that a Guardian force equipped with missile launchers and quadrunners had crossed the Mississippi River by way of the nearby Shawnee Parkway. Officers in charge of the outpost continued the evacuation but, hampered by the bone-chilling rain and barren ground that was quickly turning into a muddy quagmire, progress was excruciatingly slow. Even before spotters could be posted, government forces began the long range bombardment that was the overture to the quadrunners' destructive percussion solo to come. Within minutes, the unmanned runners' oversized tires were digging through the wet, mucky terrain with disdainful confidence as they turned their pulse cannons on the rebel fortification and opened fire.

Although most of the Sons escaped, the outpost was obliterated—claiming the lives of thirty-nine in the process and destroying the precious cache of munitions stored there.

It was another devastating loss.

"I don't know how much more of this we can take," Gideon admitted somewhat ruefully.

He once again was meeting in closed session with Speaker McFarland and five other officers, including Levi Dodge. A disheartening pall had settled over the group as they analyzed the lengthening list of defeats and mounting loss of life that haunted them.

James McFarland considered Quinn's words thoughtfully.

"I understand," he replied. "We knew there would be losses but the past weeks have proven almost beyond endurance. The only direction consistently open to us appears to be retreat—something as demoralizing as it is undeniable."

"And that has got to change," Quinn said emphatically. "There's increasing dissention in the ranks and who can blame them? They're bone weary. We're *all* bone weary."

The faces of his fellow officers were lined with fatigue and he ran a tired hand through his shaggy hair as he took their measure.

"Hell, we can barely keep our troops fed and supplied anymore," he continued. "At this rate, we'll be little more than scavengers by the time winter sets in. And let's be blunt, this isn't a real army with binding enlistments. There's nothing but dedication holding any of us here—and for many that dedication's beginning to wear thin. Every time we post another defeat—and every time we have to cut rations—we take another step toward a level of attrition we won't be able to survive."

Quinn's eyes met the expectant gaze of Levi Dodge who thus far had been keeping his own counsel.

"Bottom line," Gideon said pointedly, "if we can't prove ourselves a viable alternative to the current regime, we're going to see our numbers dwindle as people simply begin to drift away."

The officer on Dodger's left nodded soberly. "So what do we do about it?"

"Up to this point we've only been playing defense," Quinn replied. "And no points are ever scored if the other team always has the ball."

"Interesting metaphor," Dodger interposed skeptically. "Just what do you have in mind?"

"I propose we go on *offense*."

Almost as one, the other officers shifted uncomfortably.

"Hear me out," Gideon continued before anyone could object. "Jeffers, you just reported that your last patrol barely made it back because you stumbled across a well-equipped Freebooter encampment on the other side of the Missouri near St. Charles, right?"

T'Neesha Jeffers was an intense African-American woman no one could ever accuse of lacking courage—or bravado—and she openly balked at the higher-ranking officer's words.

"Right… but there was no way in hell we could've taken those bastards on. It was all we could do to stay under their radar and get our asses back across the river."

"Don't get me wrong," Quinn assured her. "You and your squaddies did exactly the right thing—you got back here in one piece and brought some damn-important information back with you."

"I agree it's helpful to know that a bunch of 'booters are holed up almost in our backyard," Dodger chimed in. "But we sure-as-hell aren't prepared to do anything more than avoid them… You can't be suggesting we attack the bastards."

Quinn paused for a moment, assessing his friend with a raised eyebrow and a cheeky, thin-lipped half smile.

"But that's *exactly* what I'm proposing," he replied. "I think we should throw everything we've got at that Freebooter camp and take it down."

"That's insane," Jeffers blurted. "Sorry general," she added hurriedly, acknowledging her insubordinate tone, "but do you realize just what you're suggesting?"

"I'm suggesting," Gideon continued firmly, "that we seize an opportunity to stem the tide of the tsunami that threatens to engulf us. I'm suggesting that we take advantage of the element of surprise and take the fight to the 'booters instead of continuing to give them the satisfaction of seeing us retreat every time we meet up."

"But just how do we do that, sir," another officer ventured. "Now that they're aligned with the government they've got more of *everything*—more people, more weapons…"

"That's right," Quinn replied. "And if we succeed we'll not only put them down and put the regime on notice, we'll have access to everything we need to resupply for the winter and re-energize our cause."

"It's an interesting proposition," Speaker McFarland observed quietly.

The six officers fell silent as they waited for the revered statesman to continue.

"I'm assuming you have thoughts regarding how to proceed."

"Yes sir, I do," Quinn assured him.

VI.

When Freebooters weren't busy pillaging the regions they defended as tenaciously as any predator might guard their urine-marked territory, they spent their time eating, drinking, fornicating and fighting among themselves. It was a brutally violent subculture that made for a significantly abbreviated lifespan and left its members scarred both physically and emotionally—as Gideon and Valaria had witnessed firsthand when attacked by two psychotic young 'booters during their original journey to St. Louis. Aligning themselves with the RSA, however, meant that Freebooters now were well-stocked with food and drink—particularly drink—and pillaging had largely been supplanted by the game of cat-and-mouse they currently engaged in with crazed abandon against the Sons of Liberty.

It was knowledge of the RSA's munificence—keeping their 'booter allies well-supplied (and well-lubricated!)—that inspired Gideon Quinn.

"We know where they are," he explained the following day while meeting with Valaria Thorpe, Farley Donovan, and Levi Dodge, "but we'll need more intel before we commit to a full-on attack."

"Are you really serious about this?" Dodger asked.

"Damn right I'm serious."

Donovan shared Levi's skepticism and was glad his friend—who had more currency with the general—had broached the subject first. "You really think we can pull it off?"

"I not only think we can pull it off," Quinn replied. "I think we've *got* to pull it off—if we have any hope of being a viable player in all this, that is."

Valaria looked at him expectantly. "So when do we leave?"

Gideon couldn't help smiling. Once McFarland had given his hesitant blessing to what many of the other officers continued to believe was an outlandishly brash plan, bringing Thorpe and Donovan onboard had been as natural as taking his next breath.

"We're not going," Quinn replied gesturing toward Dodger, "you and Donovan are."

This was news to Levi Dodge. "*What?*"

"We're needed here," Gideon continued, ignoring his friend's outburst. "If this is going to work we've got to be more organized than we've ever been before. We also can't risk McFarland's approval being withdrawn;

it's tenuous enough as it is. If Dodger and I are gone for even a couple days I'm afraid those who still object might gain the upper hand."

"You mean they might get McFarland to see reason," Dodger added with a more than half-serious smirk.

Farley Donovan acknowledged what he believed to be his friend's understatement of the situation with a subtle nod and a raised eyebrow but chose a more diplomatic route.

"So what do you need from us?"

"We need the two of you to retrace the route T'Neesha Jeffers' patrol took and do some basic recon—numbers, layout, routines…"

"If we're not going with them, we should at least send Jeffers along," Dodger interjected forcefully. "She's a hothead but she knows what's out there and is one helluva good fighter."

"If they do their job right, there won't be any fighting but, yeah, sending Jeffers makes sense."

"And I'm taking my dog," Valaria informed them.

Gideon seemed ready to object but she didn't give him an opening.

"Kevin and I have been working with Yancy for months now. He's obedient, he's responsive—he's got better instincts than any of us—and I'd trust him in a fight just as much as you trust Jeffers."

"Take the damn dog," Quinn acquiesced. "God knows he's proven himself an asset on more than one occasion. Just understand you could be putting him in harm's way."

Valaria was convinced that Yancy's presence would help keep them *out* of harm's way but managed not to take a verbal victory lap.

They left the next morning, a cold and damp November dawn that chilled them to the bone and turned their breath into foggy vapor. Jeffers wasn't pleased to have a dog along but, since the team had been hand-picked by General Quinn, she kept her opinion to herself—for the most part.

"If that mutt can't keep its damn mouth shut—if it becomes a liability," she informed Valaria bluntly as the trio shouldered lightweight backpacks before heading out, "I'll slit its throat."

Valaria's glower was malignant. "You lay a hand on my dog and you're dead. You hear me?"

"Children…" Farley interrupted, placing a calming hand on Valaria's shoulder, "let's play nice."

His companions' version of 'playing nice' was a fragile ceasefire marked by hostile silence and simmering animosity.

"Yancy won't be a problem," Donovan assured Jeffers as they set out. "He's the smartest dog I've ever known."

"You better hope so," T'Neesha muttered sullenly.

In spite of the tension between Valaria and Jeffers—or perhaps because of it—the quartet made good time. St. Charles was just over twenty miles west of St. Louis, part of the metropolitan delta that fanned out westward for more than thirty miles from the city center. Lieutenant Jeffers and her patrol had been returning from a routine scouting assignment in the fan's northwestern sector when they almost literally walked into a Freebooter camp in a defunct park called Fountain Lakes. 'Booters always dug in near a source of fresh water and the clan controlling that region had taken advantage of the four small lakes comprising the park and were squatting in a deserted resort hugging the northern shoreline of the largest body of water. Nothing but dumb luck had kept the Sons' patrol from being discovered by the spotters their adversaries routinely posted throughout their territory and when the five-man squad had approached the lakes only Jeffers' innate wariness had prevented them from openly walking down the dirt road leading to the dilapidated cottages the Freebooters currently called home and into the unwelcoming arms of their nemeses.

"We headed north through Florissant then west to scout between the Missouri and the Mississippi," Jeffers told Donovan and Thorpe during a fleetingly loquacious moment as they walked. "Circled around and came in from the northwest, planning to cross the Missouri at St. Charles and come back in along Old 270, almost screwing up royally at the lakes."

It was one of the Sons' standard patrol routes. Each time a squad went out they scouted a specific quadrant of the greater St. Louis basin. This time, however, scouting wasn't the purpose so the quartet took a more or less direct route toward the lake area currently occupied by Freebooters. They crossed the Missouri River at Interstate 70 but otherwise eschewed the highways that had served St. Charles during better days. Instead, the quartet took a more circuitous path through overgrown city streets lined with the omnipresent shells of deserted homes and businesses that watched them through the haunted eyes and dumbstruck maws of countless gaping windows and doors.

Jeffers was walking point down one such nameless street, her senses keenly attuned to any change in the ambient noises around them but it was Yancy whose canine instincts suddenly alerted to an unseen presence in the near-distance.

"T'Neesha," Farley called out quietly, indicating that the dog at his partner's side now stood rooted to the spot almost literally on point.

Accepting the dog's tell—or simply acceding to caution—Jeffers dropped to a crouch by the nearest tree. The others followed suit. The lakes were still about five miles away but they knew from experience that Freebooter spotters could be posted anywhere—a reality that made the hair on the back of Valaria's neck stand up as she pulled Yancy close.

In a moment the human components of their motionless tableau heard what their canine colleague had already picked up on—the unmistakable sounds of a pack of feral dogs on the prowl.

"Shit," T'Neesha hissed as barks and snarls from the unseen animals grew louder.

Donovan stood, pulled Valaria to her feet and began sprinting toward an adjacent two-story house.

"This way," he shouted over his shoulder.

By the time they reached the second floor—up an unsteady flight of stairs weakened and partially destroyed by wood rot—the roiling pack had torn through the tangle of weeds and brush that formed the ubiquitous backdrop of their world. It careened to a halt halfway up the street, a dozen mangy snouts lifting almost as one as they caught the scent of a new and interesting quarry.

"Quiet," Jeffers commanded fiercely as a low growl began to rumble deep in Yancy's throat.

Valaria hushed the dog and ordered him into a 'down' at her side. She knelt beside him, wrapping her hand securely around his muzzle and murmuring calming assurances into his ear while Donovan smoothed the ruff of fur bristling with vigilance down the dog's spine.

T'Neesha was on the other side of Farley, watching the feral pack from the edge of a shattered window still partially covered by the tattered fragments of grimy lace curtains.

"So what do you think of Yancy now," Donovan whispered. "We'd still be out there if it wasn't for him."

Jeffers replied with the glancing blow of a stony glare.

Outside the pack had begun to amble down the street on rangy legs, pausing occasionally to snap and snarl belligerently at one another while continuing to sniff the air as they tracked their new prey.

Most of the millions of domestic dogs across the planet had died off in the chaotic morass created by the plague but the strongest, most resilient had returned to the wild, interbreeding with coyotes and creating a hardy, aggressive, and fearless mongrel that was every bit as much of a scourge to survivors as were the human ferals known as Freebooters.

As they watched the dogs from their upper floor vantage point—barely daring to breathe—a large brindled male emerged at the head of the pack. Clearly the Alpha, he sniped angrily at those on either side, his prominent shoulder blades rising visibly on either side of his powerful neck as he skulked aggressively forward.

In a moment the dogs were in front of the house, noses aloft while still butting, biting, and snarling at one another in a nonstop reassertion of the canine pecking order. Just as the milling pack seemed ready to move on, a fleeting whisper of wind caught the tattered curtains next to Jeffers, brushing them gently against her cheek—and drawing the eyes of the Alpha inexorably upward.

The feral locked eyes with his quarry, his scarred and battered face seeming to sneer in satisfaction, a long trail of drool dripping from his mouth as he bared his yellowed teeth in a savage grin.

"Block the door," Jeffers cried as the Alpha broke eye contact and snarled a command to the rest of the pack.

In a heartbeat the ferals were galloping madly into the house and up the stairs, barking and growling fiercely—as much at one another as at the prospect of a hearty meal.

Donovan threw himself against the bedroom's blistered wooden door while Valaria and T'Neesha assessed their options. Several pieces of furniture remained in the room and the two women moved as one toward a large armoire standing in moldering grandeur against the opposite wall.

As Farley braced the door the dogs began to hurl themselves against it, screeching in fierce desperation while jagged nails clawed at the brittle exterior.

The sound of splintering wood was quickly added to the unnerving feral howl.

It took a few minutes for Valaria and Jeffers to move the armoire. As cumbersome as it was heavy, the piece kept snagging on holes in the worn carpet and it seemed an eternity before they were able to wedge the piece against the door and allow Donovan to move away.

After long minutes with nothing but a weathered door standing between him and a pack of ravenous mongrels, he appeared more than a little distressed.

"What do we do now?" Valaria asked as he slouched to the floor. "Looks to me like we are well and truly trapped in here."

For the first time, T'Neesha sounded a tad rattled. "They'll give up eventually, won't they?"

"One can hope," Donovan replied. "Probably depends on how hungry they are and what else catches their attention... *Shit*, this royally screws with our timeline."

Jeffers fell silent, brooding over his words.

Without further comment, she suddenly shrugged off her backpack, crossed the room and vaulted out the open window behind them onto the off-kilter porch roof below.

"Complete the mission," she shouted as she dropped to the ground.

Before the startled trio in the bedroom could even process what had just happened, Jeffers came around to the front of the house, stuck her pinky fingers in her mouth and cut loose with a loud, shrill whistle.

"Come on, you mangy prats," she yelled, waving her arms in the direction of the dogs that remained in view. "What are you waiting for?"

The remnant of the pack skulking outside began to howl as Jeffers sprinted into the tangle of weeds and woodsy undergrowth that once had been the lush backyards of a desirable middleclass neighborhood.

In a moment the alpha emerged from the house. Pausing only long enough to raise his pulsating nostrils to catch her scent, he added his deep wail to the mounting cacophony and took lead as the growing number of ferals milling around outside the house galloped off in the direction Jeffers had taken.

"Bloody hell," Valaria breathed as their howls faded. "What did she just do?"

"She just saved our asses," Donovan replied in a stunned hush.

"Will she make it? Does she even have a chance of outrunning them?"

"I honestly don't know," he stammered, trying to regain his composure. "She's fast—and she's got her pistol and a StunStik—she might be okay."

He paused almost reverently. "We should do what she said and keep going."

Valaria shook her head in disbelief. "I don't know if she's the bravest person I've ever met or a complete lunatic."

"A little of both," Farley observed soberly, adjusting his pack more comfortably between his shoulders. "Come on, let's get going."

Out of a residual sense of caution, they left the armoire firmly braced against the bedroom door and Donovan led the way to the window through which T'Neesha had just vaulted. Dropping to the ground from the lopsided porch roof, he gestured for Valaria to wait while he checked the perimeter of the house.

He was barely out of sight when Yancy, standing on hind legs with his paws on the cracked and blistered windowsill, once again went on the alert.

"*Farley...*" Valaria called from the open window. "*Something's still out there!*"

Donovan didn't need her warning. He came around the side of the house just as three scrawny ferals loped languidly out the front door and down the wide concrete steps. Four startled pairs of eyes locked as man and beast stopped in their tracks in mutual surprise.

The dogs lowered their heads and began to growl; a throaty rumble accompanied by curled lips and ears flattened in warning.

Farley took a long, slow breath.

"Easy fellas," he said to the trio in quiet, even tones. "No need to get all excited... I like dogs, just ask Yancy."

He started to back away, slowly drawing his pistol and trying to keep each feral in view as they spread out in unspoken yet decidedly calculated formation—one directly in front of him, the others moving to his right and left.

What followed was almost more of a nightmare for Valaria—who could only hear it—than it was for the man who lived it.

In the few seconds available to choose a target, Donovan needed to decide which dog was the ad hoc leader of this fragment of the pack. As adrenaline surged through his system, his sharpened senses told him that if he killed the new Alpha the others might choose *flight* rather than *fight*.

...He shot the larger, center dog between the eyes just as the feral on his right sprang at him with claws and fangs bared.

"Donovan," Valaria shouted from the front upstairs window. "Are you all right? ...Farley?"

She leaned out of the unprotected opening as far as she dared but the sharply slanted roofline of the lower level of the house still blocked her view.

"*Farley!*"

Several pistol shots in quick succession and the snarls and pathetic cries of an unseen dog were the only replies.

Turning from the window, Valaria dashed across the room and threw her weight angrily against the armoire that trapped her in the bedroom. At first it refused to budge but a second determined shove convinced the heavy piece to angle forward about a foot—just enough for woman and dog to wriggle through. Without hesitating, they ran down the stairs and out the front door.

Donovan lay on the ground next to what had been a driveway. One of the ferals was sprawled across him, another lay a few feet in front; the top of its skull a bloody mass of bone and brain.

Valaria grabbed the front legs of the dog that pinned her partner and heaved its dead weight aside.

"Are you all right?" she asked, sagging to her knees beside him.

Farley raised himself up on his elbows as Yancy edged in and offered him slobbery affirmation of a job well done.

"I think so," he stammered, pulling away from the loyal mutt. "Where's the third dog?"

"*Third* dog," Valaria repeated, a jolt of fear coursing through her as she looked around in alarm.

Yancy seemed calm enough and her thudding heart slowed. "Must've run off."

A shudder ran through Donovan but he managed a laugh as he sat up.

"Well, that was certainly a stunning miscalculation," he drawled with a shaky grin.

"Miscalculation?"

"Yeah... Thought I was shooting the trio's Alpha; seemed logical it would be the big male in the center."

He paused and gestured toward the carcass Valaria had heaved aside. "But the smaller female off to the right was clearly in charge... And she let me know it in no uncertain terms."

"Gotta watch out for us Alpha females," Valaria observed in a half-hearted attempt to lighten the moment.

She grabbed his hand to help him stand, realizing as she did so that the blood on his arm was his own. "Geez, she really nailed you, didn't she? How bad is it?"

"Not too bad," he replied, wincing in pain when Valaria pulled the torn sleeve away in order to better see the wound on his forearm.

"We've gotta clean this. What if she had rabies or some kind of shit like that?"

"She didn't have rabies," Farley assured her testily.

"Bloody hell," Valaria sputtered over his reply. "The first aid pack is on Jeffers' belt."

Donovan reached out to her with his good hand.

"I'll be fine until we get back to The Hub," he said as he stood. "We need to keep moving. Who knows what's up with the rest of that pack—or with the Freebooters for that matter."

Valaria insisted on at least rinsing his wound with water from the bottle she carried in her rucksack and wrapping it in cloth she tore from the hem of her shirt. He accepted her ministrations noting for good measure that if she really loved him she would dress his wound with the omnipresent polka-dot 'Minion' wrap she wore tied around her left wrist—a comment she deftly deflected with the simple observation that it was too soiled at the moment to be useful as a bandage.

Allowing Yancy to take point, they set out at a brisk pace down the street. Jeffers had mapped out their route when the trio first met so the two remaining members knew that Huster Road would lead them to the park's entrance. Dilapidated and overgrown roadside signage was soon advertising the recreational opportunities available at Fountain Lakes and it wasn't long before they came upon a chipped and dented sign indicating the street they sought.

The recreation area surrounding the lakes was approached by a wide entryway lined with long brick planters and wrought iron lampposts—all of which now were overgrown and mournfully decrepit. They stayed well off to the side, cautiously making their way into the overgrown woods while avoiding the last of the spotter locations Jeffers' squad had previously identified.

Their orders were to watch the Freebooter encampment for twenty-four hours in an effort to gauge the size and preparedness of the clan and get a general feel for the 'booters's routine—if there was one. After some careful scouting—evading two more spotters in the process—they found a well-placed lookout just inside the tree line on the opposite shore from the cottages currently serving as Freebooter Central. Nestled into a rocky outcropping surrounded by pine trees and thick undergrowth, the small moss-covered hollow gave them a clear line of sight across the lake while at the same time allowing them to blend in with the rocks and trees.

Shrugging free of their lightweight backpacks, each extracted a pair of old fashioned binoculars. While Yancy curled up in contented alertness beside them, they settled in to watch.

Their observations proved fruitful. As unpredictable as Freebooters were, the chaotic disorder of their lives held a certain offbeat rhythm. Hunting packs came and went with some degree of regularity and spotters were clearly being rotated throughout the day. But the majority of the 'booters—those remaining in camp—spent their time cheering and jeering one another on in spontaneous and brutal sparring while simultaneously indulging in a great deal of drinking.

By nightfall, the camp was alight with bonfires and alive with the sounds of bawdy and violent revelry.

By dawn it lay cloaked in deep, inebriated slumber.

"I can't believe I'm saying this," Valaria observed as they watched the pattern begin to repeat itself the following day, "but if these bastards are really this predictable we might actually be able to pull this off."

Her partner agreed. If the Sons could successfully approach the camp at night, an early morning raid should catch the 'booters unaware—as unaware as they were ever likely to be, that is.

When the encampment once again devolved into drunken debauchery with the setting of the sun, the two spies quietly prepared to leave.

"What's up with your arm?" Valaria asked, taking note of the fact that Farley was having difficulty repacking his gear.

"Nothing," he assured her.

"Lying prat; let me see it."

Donovan surrendered his arm with obvious reluctance, wincing in pain as Valaria removed the impromptu bandage. The wound on his forearm was oozing and the surrounding tissue was deeply inflamed.

"Holy crap, Donovan, this thing's infected already."

"Yeah, maybe a little but it'll be fine once we get back to St. Louis."

"Fine my ass; you can barely use your arm."

"That's why I brought you and Yancy along," he drawled with intentional cheerfulness. "You guys can protect me."

"Yeah, right," Valaria chuffed as she once again rinsed the wound with water from her pack and wrapped another length of reasonably clean cloth around it.

Making their way back through the park was fairly easy. The moon was high and bright and they were able to identify and avoid spotters posted along the route they retraced. Despite feeling reasonably confident, however, their progress was slow and cautious. When a battered sign hanging askew from its metal moorings loomed out of the reflected moonlight and directed them back to Huster Road, their relief was as tangible as their growing concern had been.

They skirted the park's official entrance, walking along the overgrown verge in order to avoid the moon's prying eyes but had gone only a few yards farther when a young woman in her late teens strode directly into their path.

Dressed in soiled, over-large blue jeans and a faded St. Louis Clydesdales sweatshirt, the teen evaluated the trio before her with stolid curiosity while absently tucking grimy dishwater blond hair behind her ears. She tilted her head slightly and began twisting a lank strand of hair around her right index finger.

"Hi there," Valaria said into a lengthening silence.

"Hi there..." the girl parroted.

Her quiet mimicry sent a cold chill down Valaria's spine.

"What are you doing out here all by yourself?" Donovan asked.

"I live here," she replied. "...Over there—across the lake."

"Oh yeah? We live around here too," Farley lied. "Back in St. Charles."

"There are people in town?"

"You bet; you should come visit some time."

"Yeah," she said with a vacant smile. "I'll tell my folks."

"No doubt," Valaria muttered to Donovan.

The filthy young woman's gaze shifted toward Valaria when she spoke and then slithered down to the black-and-white dog at her side.

"I like your dog..." she said without inflection.

In a flash of déjà vu, Valaria found herself back on the road to St. Louis facing off with a pathetically-rabid ten-year-old 'booter who had said the same thing.

"Geez, what's with you people and dogs," she murmured.

The girl stared at her blankly as a tense silence settled between them.

"Well," Farley said into the awkwardness, "we better get going."

"Don't go yet," the girl replied, her eyes locking on Donovan's bloody shirt sleeve. "You should meet my brothers."

"You have brothers out here with you?" Valaria asked, senses tingling.

"They're kinda my brothers," the teen explained, again twisting a lank strand of hair around her index finger. "We hunt together."

The girl's demeanor was beginning to undergo a subtle change and her posture shifted from benign to something more… intentional.

"I'm afraid we don't have time to wait," Donovan said with a knowing glance in his partner's direction. "We need to get home."

The grimy teen took a decisive step toward Farley but Valaria stepped between them.

"Don't go yet," the young 'booter purred, tilting her head almost coquettishly.

Valaria's response left no room for debate. "Sorry. We're leaving."

As Valaria motioned Yancy forward, the girl darted between them and grabbed her by the wrist.

"I said don't go," she hissed, tightening her grip.

In response, Valaria wrenched the teen's arm sharply down, breaking the girl's hold on her. The younger woman lurched forward but Valaria stood her ground, slamming the heels of her palms against the girl's ears in a powerful strike to the mastoid bone. Staggering clumsily backward, the young 'booter pulled a short knife from the pocket of her jeans. Shaking her head in pain, she struggled to regain her balance.

"Kid, don't make me hurt you," Valaria said as she assumed the opening stance Lieutenant Griffin had drilled into their heads. "Just let us go."

The girl lunged at Valaria, swiping out with her knife. It moved in an ineffectual arc that was easily avoided but Yancy took the threat more than seriously. Snarling in defense of his humans, he threw himself between Valaria and the teen, grabbed the girl by the pant leg and jerked her to the ground, coming away with a length of torn denim in his teeth for good measure.

"Just stay down and let us leave," Donovan advised.

She had lost a shoe when Yancy pulled her down and he now held the frayed canvas slip-on proudly in his mouth, shaking it vigorously.

"Who are you people," the girl snarled.

"We're nobody," Farley assured her.

The young 'booter was once again on her feet. She had managed to hold onto the knife when Yancy had taken her down and held it outstretched in front of her, slowly moving it back and forth between her targets.

Emitting a guttural shriek, the teen suddenly lunged at Donovan but Valaria got there first. In a heartbeat she had the girl in a headlock. Resisting the instinct to apply a death-hold to her neck, she again flung the youngster to the ground.

"Scavenger bitch," the girl growled.

As she struggled to stand, Valaria and Donovan caught a glimpse of movement in the shadows that formed the backdrop to their impromptu drama. Anticipating the arrival of the girl's 'brothers,' both took a few steps back.

The young 'booter was still brandishing the knife when a figure emerged from the dark tree line, grabbed her from behind and in one effortless movement yanked the girl's head back and slit her throat from ear to ear.

A sickening gurgle escaped the crimson gash as the teen slid to the ground in a lifeless heap at the feet of T'Neesha Jeffers.

Swiping the bloody knife across the dead girl's sweatshirt, Jeffers casually replaced it in its sheath while using the back of her free hand to wipe a spatter of red off the side of her face.

She glared at her shocked colleagues.

"You hold back like that again," she hissed angrily at Valaria, "and you'll get us all killed!"

"On you depends the fortunes of America. You are to decide the important questions upon which rests the happiness and liberty of millions yet unborn. Act worthy of yourselves."

~ Joseph Warren

CHAPTER EIGHTEEN

I.

Unfamiliar faces stared at Valaria from around the perimeter of the oblong table. She shifted uncomfortably under the scrutiny. It was the day after their return from the field and she and T'Neesha Jeffers were meeting with the small cadre of officers who were privy to the planned attack on the Freebooters at Fountain Lakes.

"They've got spotters stationed about every mile for a good ten miles around the lake," Valaria began in response to the expectant looks directed her way when Quinn had handed over the meeting's reins a moment before. "So you'll need to send a prep squad through ahead of the troops to clear them out..."

Irked that the General had deferred to the exile rather than a fellow officer, Jeffers interrupted.

"The spotters are arranged in multiple zigzags so once your preppers find one, the next will be farther ahead at either the 10 or 2 o'clock position—the tricky part will be finding their first lookouts as the prep squad fans out. I recommend you dispatch them in twos, that way they can split up after their first kill and head toward 10 and 2 in order to find the next spotter. Once located the two can regroup to take him out; after that the pattern will be a consistent zigzag and they can move forward together."

"They'll have to work fast," Valaria added, leapfrogging over her nemesis before she could continue, "since spotters are rotated about every eight hours. But with preppers clearing the way you should be able to move your troops across the river and all the way to the lakes without any trouble."

"*Should* be able to," Levi Dodge repeated pointedly. "If we miss even one spotter the entire mission could come crashing down on our heads. We'll be moving a helluva lot of people through St. Charles—and it all has to be done on foot since we currently don't have even one fully charged transport."

"And eight hours doesn't give us much of a window," another officer observed.

"It'll be enough," Gideon replied with quiet confidence. "You didn't come across signs of spotters this side of the Missouri?"

"No," the two women assured him in stereo, each punctuating her response with an icy glance toward the other.

"Good."

Quinn swiveled his chair away from the table and referenced the detailed map projected behind him.

"We'll send the preppers in about three hours ahead of the main assault group. That should give them time to clear the way for us. The two northern bridges present the best flanking approach so we'll divide our forces, deploy from there, and approach the lakes from two sides."

He turned back to Valaria.

"If the prep teams head out at midnight and we deploy at 3 a.m. we should be ready to attack before dawn. And based on what you and Donovan learned from watching their camp, the 'booters will still be sleeping off the previous night's binge, which should go a long way toward preserving the element of surprise."

Gideon's gaze shifted from Valaria to his fellow officers. Although some remained skeptical, most appeared to be coming around—or at least acquiescing—to what, admittedly, was an audacious plan. But hell, what choice did they have? They were running short of everything—especially morale—and the noxious Freebooter/RSA alliance meant that all the supplies they needed to make it through the winter and re-energize the troops lay just across the Missouri River. Once their bellies were full and they had a significant victory under their belt, Quinn was convinced the attrition the Sons were currently experiencing would taper off.

Hopefully it would also help with recruitment.

"Permission to join the preppers, sir?" T'Neesha Jeffers asked. "I know what's out there and feel I'll be an asset in the field."

"Agreed," Gideon replied. "Pair up with Thorpe."

The lieutenant visibly bristled.

"With all due respect, sir," she said in a voice that was just barely on the acceptable side of civil, "since Thorpe and I have both been over the route, wouldn't it be better to have us take two others in?"

"No; you work well together. I'm not breaking up a winning team."

The two women locked eyes in a stony glare but since the tone of the meeting was decidedly military even Valaria held her tongue; she would set Quinn straight once they were alone. She got her chance a short time later when the meeting adjourned and she and Gideon headed for the infirmary to check on Donovan.

"Geez, Quinn, do you ever listen to anything I tell you?"

"What are you talking about?"

"I'm talking about me and T'Neesha Jeffers."

Quinn looked mildly perplexed.

"And?" he coaxed with an almost imperceptible shrug.

"I told you Jeffers threatened to *kill* Yancy..."

"Yeah—did she hurt him?"

"No."

"So what's the problem?"

"The problem is the woman's a complete bitch. I've never known anyone so bossy and cocksure of themselves. She never has a good word to say and never listens to anybody else's opinion."

Quinn couldn't help smiling. "Now who does that remind me of? What's the old saying... *That's the pot calling the kettle black?*"

"You're saying we're alike?"

An arched eyebrow was his only response.

"Bloody hell, Quinn, I'm nothing like her. The woman's a lunatic. She jumped out a window into a pack of feral dogs, for Christ's sake."

"And running headlong into a 'pack' of StunStik-wielding Guardians at the Bullet Bash was sane?"

"That was totally different."

"No it wasn't. Both were impossible situations and you guys did something damn brave in order to protect your mission and your partners."

Valaria fell silent but he could tell she had more to say.

"I just don't trust her," she admitted quietly after a moment. "She's really out there. You should've seen her face when she killed that 'booter. The woman's got ice in her veins."

For a moment Valaria was back at Fountain Lakes, dragging the body of a teenaged Freebooter into the reedy shallows. They had had Yancy pace the muddy shoreline in order to leave evidence implying the girl had fallen victim to a pack of ferals, and hoped that the water—and animals drawn to the body by the scent of blood—would obscure the real cause of death by the time she was found.

Gideon reached out and lightly touched Valaria on the back as they walked on.

"Jeffers did what had to be done," he replied with hushed sincerity. "And as far as having ice in her veins, try to cut the woman some slack; she's seen a lot of ugly shit in her life. She may be a humorless prat but I trust her. I trust her with your life."

They walked in silence for a few minutes.

"Speaking of the 'booter she killed," Gideon began with measured caution, "what happened there? Jeffers' report said you held back in a situation she portrayed as clearly requiring lethal force."

"The 'booter was just a kid," Valaria replied. "But if I hadn't been able to subdue her I would've done whatever it took to silence her."

"I know you mean that but I can't help wondering if you held back not only because she was young but because you still carry that dead Guardian on your conscience."

Valaria inwardly winced. "So what if I still think about that guy? Bloody hell, Quinn, you're the one who said we should never get used to killing. But he's not gonna keep me from being effective in the field. I can do what has to be done."

The Guardian she had killed the day she and Gideon infiltrated the Indianapolis Safe Zone had stopped haunting her dreams and she hoped Quinn's resurrecting him wouldn't inspire an encore in the nights ahead; her sleep was brittle enough as it was.

"So if I send you out with Jeffers you're gonna be able to take down the spotters you find? I've gotta ask because we can't take the chance of those bastards sounding the alarm."

"I won't let you down," she assured him.

They had reached the infirmary. Conversation died away as they entered and their eyes fell on the Sons' elderly doctor, Molly Colson. The ancient physician was making morning rounds with a quartet of medicos-in-training following in her wake like a flock of downy ducklings. She acknowledged Quinn and Valaria with a nod as the newcomers crossed the room toward the hospital bed at the far end where Farley Donovan lay unconscious and riddled with fever, his freckles standing out in sharp relief against pale skin, his ginger-colored ponytail lank from perspiration.

"He looks like death," Valaria observed bluntly while gently taking his hand.

Quinn didn't even try to soften her words. "You guys did what you had to do. Being attacked by a feral so far from base was pretty much a worst-case scenario. There was no way you could know the wound would get infected and going ahead with the mission meant we got the intel we needed."

"Small consolation if he doesn't make it."

Dr. Molly's troupe had arrived at Donovan's bed and the two visitors stepped aside in order to accommodate the physician and the group of students who hung on her every word and busily entered information into the data pads they carried.

"This final patient was admitted due to an animal bite," the doctor was saying, "and I'm afraid you're going to see this problem with some degree of regularity since we have an animal population that is beyond our control and no way to vaccinate them even if we did have access."

With a gesture, she directed the young woman on her right to begin changing Farley's bandages as she continued.

"The microbiology of bite infections is usually polymicrobial—which means multiple species of bacteria are involved—and a broad mixture of aerobic and anaerobic microorganisms will be present, those that require oxygen in order to proliferate and those that don't."

Her students stepped closer to the bed as the wound was exposed. Even from where she stood off to the side, Valaria could easily see the angry red tissue.

"The most common symptoms of infection from bites are inflammation, pain, and swelling. These manifested in this patient within the first 24 hours. By the time he arrived here he demonstrated further signs: extreme fatigue, fever, and swollen lymph nodes."

The doctor moved in and pushed her glasses up onto her forehead in order to better scrutinize the exposed wound.

"Since being admitted, Patient Donovan has developed additional problems. He began having difficulty swallowing as well as stiffness in the jaw, neck and abdomen. He's been unconscious for the last twelve hours or so."

Jerking her head slightly so the glasses lodged in the furrows of her forehead plopped back down to the bridge of her nose, Dr. Molly turned to her students and addressed a young man who stood at the edge of the group.

"Michael, what would your diagnosis be?"

The intern swallowed hard before answering. "It isn't rabies... tetanus?"

"Why the hesitation?"

"The fever and stiffness fit but you didn't say anything about muscle spasms—and can you even get tetanus from an animal bite?"

"Tetanus usually presents in a descending pattern," the doctor replied, "so the symptoms exhibited thus far could be a first sign, particularly trismus of the jaw. And, yes, Michael, you can get tetanus from an animal bite. The *Clostridium tentani* bacterium is commonly found in soil, manure—and saliva—so any open wound is a potential entry point if the source of the injury has been contaminated. If this is tetanus we can expect the patient to develop rigidity of the pectoral and calf muscles followed by powerful contractions of the major muscle groups, which is called 'tetany.' But that could take days or even weeks to manifest."

The group of clinicians lingered around the bed, tapping notes into their data pads as Dr. Molly continued the ad hoc seminar.

"Unfortunately, there is no blood test for diagnosing tetanus so we have to rely on symptoms. Since they don't occur simultaneously it can be problematic to say the least."

She pulled a simple kitchen spatula out of her lab coat pocket and held it out. "*This* is the most reliable test I know of."

"A *spatula?*" one of the women asked, her skeptical tone implying that faith in her aged instructor had just taken a hit.

"That's right," Dr. Molly replied, holding the narrow kitchen implement aloft with a flourish. "I know it sounds bizarre but the 'spatula test' is actually an accepted clinical diagnostic for tetanus. You simply touch the posterior pharyngeal wall—the back of the throat—with a soft-tipped instrument and observe the result. If tetanus is present there will be an involuntary contraction of the jaw—the patient will bite down on the spatula. A negative test result would be a normal gag reflex as instinct kicks in and the patient tries to expel the foreign object."

As she finished speaking the doctor gently opened Donovan's mouth and inserted the wooden handled kitchen tool. The reaction was instantaneous—and not the gag reflex Valaria had begun silently praying for.

Farley's jaw snapped shut on the spatula.

"In my experience," Dr. Molly concluded as she massaged Donovan's jaw until it relaxed enough to extract the spatula, "this test has had zero false positives and the overwhelming majority of infected patients produced the results we just saw."

"So this is tetanus," Michael said, obviously pleased that his hesitant diagnosis had been confirmed.

"With little doubt."

"How do we treat it?" another trainee asked.

"*That* is part of the problem," the elderly doctor replied solemnly, glancing toward Thorpe and Quinn. "If I had tetanus immunoglobulin I could inject it intravenously and its antibodies would kill the clostridium tetani but I haven't seen any of that for more than a decade. If I had penicillin or some other antibiotic I could prevent the bacterium from multiplying and producing the neurotoxin that causes muscle spasms but our supply of antibiotics was exhausted months ago. Magnesium or drugs such as diazepam could be given to control the muscle spasms that are bound to develop but..."

"Is the prognosis really that bleak?" Quinn interrupted from the sideline.

"There are homeopathic remedies we can utilize but unless we are resupplied—soon—the condition of all the patients you see here will deteriorate rapidly."

"Another reason for Fountain Lakes," Gideon whispered to Valaria as the doctor and her students moved on.

II.

The Battle of Fountain Lakes took place in two strategic waves. Based on the information provided by Jeffers and Thorpe, a squad of preppers was sent in three hours ahead of the main assault group. Selected from among the graduates of Marcus Griffin's elite 'Kinetic-Kills' martial arts training, they were the best of the best—all of them eager to show their Sensei and the officers above him that they had what it took to silence the 'booter lookouts scattered among the trees and deserted buildings along the Sons' planned approach.

When they reached St. Charles the prep squad split into eight two-person teams. Four crossed the Missouri River at the I-70 bridge and fanned out to scour the northwest approach to the lake while the other four crossed via old highway 370 to come in from the north.

Jeffers and Thorpe were among the teams crossing at the northern bridge. Because of their knowledge of the route, they had briefed the others about the type of locations favored by spotters before the sixteen agents had split up and headed for their respective crossings. Moving as silently as the clouds that flowed in thick grey waves across the new moon, they set about flushing out and taking down their quarry while an icy mist added a frigid counterpoint to the importance of their quest.

As expected, the first sighting proved to be the most challenging. Valaria was just about ready to insist that they backtrack and try a different approach through the weed-tangled darkness when Jeffers stopped short, palm shooting upward a fraction of an inch in front of her partner's nose—the abruptness of the gesture stoking the fires of animus that smoldered between the two women.

Rooted to the spot, they stood and listened to the ominous stillness that shrouded the trees and undergrowth ahead of them.

Valaria cocked her head in concentration and blew on her ice-cold hands. Nestled at the heart of the calm was the barely audible sound of something large moving somewhere above them.

Was someone shifting position in a nearby tree?

The two preppers dropped into a crouch, listening intently and scanning the dark silhouette of tangled branches arching over their heads.

As Valaria peered into the frigid darkness, Jeffers suddenly grasped her shoulder and pointed toward the upper reaches of a majestic oak that proudly asserted itself amidst the weedy rabble. At first Valaria saw nothing—fortifying her belief that T'Neesha wasn't as sharp as she claimed—until a fleeting break in the cloud cover allowed the sliver of moon to assist their search for a moment.

Caught in sharp relief against the moon's murky pallet were the dangling legs and feet of someone sitting astride a large upper branch of the nearby oak.

The two women stayed down, Jeffers crossing her arms and tucking her cold hands under her armpits as she directed a questioning look toward her partner. Any Freebooter vantage point was going to be a challenge but tree-spotters were particularly problematic since it was especially difficult to dislodge them before they could sound the alarm—and a silent hands-on kill was much preferred to the use of weapons since stealth was their top priority. T'Neesha pointed toward an adjacent tree whose branches intertwined with those of the oak and raised an expectant eyebrow. Knowing that Jeffers still harbored doubts as to her competence, Valaria had assumed she would throw the gauntlet of their first kill at her feet and she didn't hesitate to take up the challenge.

Although she wasn't an experienced climber, Griffin's MMA training had produced a strength and agility that gave Valaria a degree of confidence as she began the slow process of trying to scale the tree without alerting her quarry in the adjacent oak. Pulling herself onto a low-hanging branch, she quietly worked her way upward, pausing on each progressively higher perch to listen for signs of movement from her Freebooter target as he slowly came within range. The man appeared to have settled comfortably into the crotch of the tree where the branch he straddled joined the main trunk and Valaria noticed that his head was tilted off to one side suggesting he might actually have fallen asleep. Thanking God for that particular stroke of largesse, she began crossing over to the booter's oak. Silently swinging down from an upper intersection of branches, she steadied herself on a stunted limb protruding from her side of the tree trunk's impressive Y but before she could spring the glint of a knife blade suddenly shot past her from out of the darkness below the tree. It missed its mark, lodging in ridges of bark just to the right of the Freebooter's head and abruptly yanking him back to wakefulness.

"What the f—" he sputtered.

In seconds the man had scrabbled into an alert frog-like squat on the thick branch he had been straddling.

The element of surprise having been wrenched away, Valaria had nowhere to go but forward. She vaulted through the Y of the tree trunk and landed almost on top of the 'booter. He was lithe and agile and the two adversaries grappled nimbly on the balance beam of the branch, neither able to secure the purchase needed to produce an advantage— Valaria's intention to silence the lookout with a clean and relatively impersonal kill effectively shot to hell.

The anonymous 'booter pulled back and paused for a moment, taking stock of his situation as well as his opponent. He lurched forward a second later but Valaria had anticipated the movement and was able to land a decisive fingertip jab into his left shoulder joint as he lunged toward her. In an instant the arm hung numb and useless at the man's side. He staggered a bit and she aimed a second jab at his larynx to silence him, then pulled her fingers back into a fist at her waist and in a quick one-two strike thrust the knuckles of both hands into the soft tissue of his abdomen. Reeling back completely off balance, the Freebooter crashed gracelessly through the lower branches of the tree, landing with what seemed like a deafening thud on the hard ground below.

Jeffers was quick to move in and finish him off.

"What the hell were you thinking," Valaria snarled in a hush after dropping to the ground.

Her partner's response was equally disdainful and delivered with a withering scowl. "What are you talking about?"

"Why in God's name did you throw that knife? I was just about ready to take the bastard out—"

"You sure as hell didn't look ready," T'Neesha hissed. "I was saving your ass—again."

"*Saving my ass*—you woke the guy up and nearly got me killed!"

"I finished him off!"

"Only after I knocked him out of the tree…"

With herculean effort Valaria stopped short and reined herself in.

"This is lunacy," she said. "We don't have time for this shit."

"That's for damn sure," Jeffers agreed. "Don't know what you're whining about; the guy's dead and you're back on the ground all safe and sound."

"Right," Valaria seethed. "The guy's dead."

As the two women glared at each other, the cold mist began turning to frigid sleet— a gesture from Nature that perfectly punctuated the icy quality of their partnership.

Relieved to split up a moment later in order to find the next lookout and establish the zigzag pattern of the spotters they tracked, Valaria cinched the black hood of her borrowed jacket more tightly around her face and headed toward the 2 o'clock position from the oak tree's high noon while Jeffers stalked off in the direction of 10.

It was Valaria who discovered the next 'booter about a mile farther on but she didn't trigger the short-range signal that would call Jeffers to her side until after subduing and silencing the man.

Let the arrogant lunatic think what she wanted, Valaria would prove she was more than able to hold her own in the field.

III.

Uncooperative weather having slowed their quick-march to little more than a crawl, it was more than four hours after the preppers had been dispatched across the Missouri River when the Sons of Liberty finally converged on the two bridges. Temperatures had dropped precipitously overnight and the cold rain that had dogged their heels and transformed their path into a quagmire of slick mud had now turned to sleet that sliced at them with countless icy shards as they marched.

Gideon Quinn walked many times farther than his troops that day, striding up and down the long column, his ubiquitous suede duster flapping out behind him in the wind as he encouraged the men and women under his command to press forward through the frigid rain. Three miles away, Levi Dodge likewise encouraged the other half of the two-front assault force as it, too, struggled to maintain a reasonable pace.

By the time the two groups had finally slogged their way through the woods the preppers had cleared and stood in wet, shivering silence near their respective entrances to Fountain Lakes, the sun had already washed the eastern sky with vivid streaks of color.

"Well, that settles it," Dodger observed, speaking to his counterpart through the wireless communicator looped over his right ear. "We sure as hell can't attack the 'booters in broad daylight."

Quinn's incredulity crackled through the wireless receiver. *"You're suggesting retreat?"*

"What else can we do?"

"We can move forward as planned—and that's exactly what we're going to do!"

"General—*Gideon*—it's nothing short of reckless to attack a gang of Freebooters without the advantage of surprise."

"We move forward as planned," came the forceful response in Dodger's ear.

Thus committed, shortly after sunrise the Sons of Liberty began their assault on the Freebooter encampment—more than two hours later than planned. The sleet had turned to snow by then and was accumulating quickly, covering the natural area that had once been Fountain Lakes Park in a thick, wet blanket of white and effectively muffling the sounds of myriad rushing feet. The assault force entered the camp from two directions; Levi Dodge approaching from the northwest with nearly 75 under his command, and Gideon Quinn leading 100 more through the area cleared by the teams led by Valaria and T'Neesha Jeffers.

When they converged—essentially surrounding the perimeter of the camp—both men were astonished to discover that through nothing short of Divine Intervention the element of surprise had miraculously been preserved—

The camp was silent and the Freebooters still slept!

Before any stragglers or early risers had a chance to realize what was about to happen, Quinn gave the order to begin a preliminary bombardment using two incendiary shoulder-launchers they had brought along.

The ensuing barrage ruptured the morning calm and disoriented 'booters were soon staggering out of the ramshackle cottages and makeshift shelters comprising the encampment—most still clothed (or unclothed!) for sleep, virtually all of them running barefoot and unarmed into the snow. The cacophonous melee that followed was a chaotic pageant of confusion as the Sons surged forward and the momentarily witless Freebooters struggled to organize a counterattack.

The white mantle of thick, wet snow was soon tinged with red and the cries and smells of battle quickly filled the air.

Occupying the high ground, Quinn's forces had a clear view of the Freebooters' movements and each time their quarry attempted to outflank the rebels Gideon countered with another wave of troops, finally joining the last of his reserves as they swept down the northeastern slope and into the fray. To his grateful amazement, the Sons appeared to be maintaining the upper hand, cutting down the notoriously well-disciplined, infamously unyielding Freebooters as they rushed around in bewilderment and disarray, totally disoriented by the surprise assault and hampered by their still somewhat inebriated condition.

Moving downfield with his troops, Gideon dodged an oncoming 'booter, glancing over his shoulder as the snarling woman slipped in the wet slush and fell in an ungainly sprawl onto the bloody corpse of a dead comrade. Bracing herself against the chest of the lifeless man, she scrabbled to her feet and whirled back toward the adversary who had felled her. Sneering at Quinn, she pulled a knife from the belt cinched around her waist and stooped slightly into a menacing half-crouch.

As she took a moment to blink away the blur of her intoxicated vision, Gideon leveled his pulse pistol at the woman and smiled benignly.

"There's no need to die today," he said with calm assurance.

The 'booter's response was really never in doubt. With another snarling shriek, she raised the knife over her head and lunged forward in a pitifully hopeless attack.

The shriek and her hapless assault were stopped short by a single blast from Quinn's pistol.

Gideon leaned against a nearby tree and closed his eyes for just a second, shaking his head at the futility of the woman's fury. Pausing there a moment longer, he assessed the scene before him.

What was once a bucolic get-away for generations of Missourians was being transmogrified into a panorama of bloody carnage that would sear the memories of the inexperienced Sons of Liberty forces and haunt their dreams for a long time to come.

The beleaguered mercenaries' attempts to counter the rebel attack continued—and continued to be thwarted. Although they screamed and shouted at one another—and attempted to rally with their eerie, ululating battle cry—the Freebooters remained in disarray. Suddenly, and without warning, they broke ranks and began running helter skelter away from the fighting through an old orchard at the far end of the park.

The battle—which had been going on for less than an hour—was suddenly over.

Once the din of combat began to subside, a cheer of elation erupted from the rebel forces, sparked as much by the wonder of their accomplishment as by the victory itself. Hours of marching through rain, sleet, and snow had left them exhausted even before taking on their notoriously-vicious enemy causing the euphoria of triumph to quickly recede into a fatigued fugue as the conquerors began huddling together for warmth and rest or wandering aimlessly among the corpses littering the camp.

"What do we do with the survivors?" a captain, filthy and wet from the fighting, asked Quinn once the officers had gathered in one of the cottages to debrief.

"They're mostly noncombatants," another chimed in. "Mostly women and kids. And what about the wounded? Are we going to take them all with us? Are we going to take them prisoner?"

Quinn's reply was filled with contempt for their adversaries. "Do nothing with them. Leave them here. Leave them to bury their dead— it's what the bastards' comrades just did."

The first officer scoffed in derisive agreement. "Yeah, the invincible Freebooters ran off with their tails between their legs. Let the government come to their aid; we owe these people nothing."

Acknowledging the officer's comment with a nod, Gideon shifted his attention to Dodger and asked the logical next question, bracing himself for the answer. "How many did *we* lose?"

Dodger paused a beat, not knowing quite how to respond.

"None," he said simply.

A profound silence engulfed the room and the general sagged into a nearby chair.

"What did you say?"

"None," Dodger repeated. "We've suffered injuries but not one fatality."

"Jesus, Mary, and Joseph," Gideon breathed, a look of dumfounded awe on his face. He sat in silence for a moment before continuing. "What about supplies?"

"As we suspected," another officer responded, "the States are definitely paying the 'booters off in provisions. We've found a stockpile of pulse rifles, ammunition and even shoulder-mounted rocket launchers—far better than anything we've got."

"Any non-military supplies?" Quinn asked.

"Lots of food—and plenty of booze."

"What about meds?"

"We haven't been able to do much of an inventory, but at first glance it looks like there's a significant cache of pharmaceuticals; lots of coats and boots, too."

"Take it," Quinn ordered.

"What about the 'booters still in camp?"

Gideon ran a thoughtful hand through his shaggy hair and paused before replying.

"I'm tempted to leave them as empty-handed as they leave the people they victimize," he admitted. "Give them enough food to last a couple of weeks and take the rest."

Conversations were quiet as his officers set to work and preparations were made for the march back to St. Louis. Everyone was still stunned by their success and Gideon shook his head in quiet amazement as he reviewed the relative ease of their victory. *The 'booters had actually turned tail and run—and he'd lost no one in the process!* What an unbelievable outcome and an incredible windfall.

He prayed it would be enough.

It is the duty of every American to save their civil and religious rights from the outstretched arm of tyranny.

~ Mercy Otis Warren

CHAPTER NINETEEN

I.

In spite of the astonishing reversal of fortune bestowed on them by the victory at Fountain Lakes, the winter it ushered in brought the Sons of Liberty crashing back to reality. Feeling like the dark horse winners of some old athletic championship, they returned to The Hubbard Center re-energized by their feat and laden down with the spoils of war. But the storm that had muffled them in white and transformed the battlefield into a slippery red quagmire was only the first act in a long, bitterly cold seasonal melodrama that would offer no intermission until mid-March—and was critiqued by an increasingly unappreciative audience whose restlessness was amplified by every blustery day and every additional inch of snow.

But it wasn't the weather that would chill Valaria Thorpe to the bone—Farley Donovan was dead.

After merging their companies for the march back to St. Louis, Gideon Quinn and his officers led the troops across the I-70 bridge in the wake of the sixteen preppers who had retraced their steps in order to scout for signs of trouble. Since depleted batteries had kept their transport vehicles grounded in St. Louis, squaddies paired up to share the burden of carrying their booty back to base; military decorum gradually eroding as the victorious caravan slowly became more of a celebratory conga-line that hardly noticed the cold, blowing snow that covered their tracks almost as soon as they'd marched through it.

As they moved through the city's slowly narrowing fan-shaped delta, Quinn ordered the troops broken into small groups and dispatched them along different routes in order to melt back into The Hub as surreptitiously as possible. One victory hardly made their ragtag army an equal to the RSA—or even to the Freebooter mercenaries they had just caught off-guard, for that matter—and the general believed keeping their presence in St. Louis undetected was currently their greatest asset; one that must be preserved for as long as possible.

So they had split up and moved on.

Dodging numerous drone flyovers as they wormed their way through the snow-congested city, it was well after dark when the last of the squads once again was safely under the dome. Upon arrival each group added the supplies they carried to the previously bare shelves of the Sons' reserves and waited to be dismissed for chow and some much-deserved rack time.

Food and sleep were the last things on Valaria Thorpe's mind, however, and as soon as the Hub's door latched behind her she made a b-line for the infirmary to check on Donovan.

All she found was an empty bed.

"Where's Farley Donovan?" she asked of Molly Colson when she located the doctor working in a nearby office.

The elderly physician stood, pushing her glasses up to her hairline and gesturing Valaria into a chair on the opposite side of the desk standing between them.

The younger woman lowered herself almost gingerly; her fingers clutching the arm rests in a white-knuckle combination of hopefulness and anguish. Her voice wavered slightly.

"Is Donovan still here?"

"Miss Thorpe," the doctor replied as she resumed her seat at the desk, "the most difficult challenge any physician faces is the loss of a patient... I'm sorry but your friend didn't make it."

"No," Valaria stammered. "No, that can't be right."

Despite her years of experience, years that served to insulate most doctors, the aged caregiver looked genuinely stricken.

"There's no easy way to share or to receive that news. I'm so sorry we couldn't save him."

"*Couldn't save him*," Valaria murmured, closing her eyes and shaking her head in disbelief. "What happened?"

Molly Colson considered the woman across from her for a moment before answering.

"Even in the best of circumstances," she explained slowly, "full blown tetanus is fatal about ten percent of the time. In our situation—where we have neither the means to prevent nor to adequately treat the disease and its complications—we're faced with the stark reality of a much higher fatality rate."

"Complications?"

"Pneumonia if muscle spasms cause the patient to aspirate material into the lungs; seizures if infection spreads to the brain; pulmonary embolisms, kidney failure. In Mr. Donovan's case it was an embolism. He went very quickly; very quietly."

At Donovan's memorial service two days later, Valaria sat stone faced and detached. She was having a hard time sorting through the emotions churning within—anger, loss, regret... and an over-powering sense of guilt because she wasn't sure she had even loved him. Not the way he loved her, anyway. She had loved his strength, his sense of humor—his touch—but knew she had never crossed the line of truly belonging with him. It was a subtle form of betrayal that haunted her since she would never have the chance to make it right.

"You didn't do anything wrong, you know," Gideon Quinn tried to assure his partner when the two returned to his quarters after the service. "It's not your fault you weren't here when he died."

Valaria sagged into one of two overstuffed chairs conferred on the room's occupant by virtue of rank. Resting her elbows on the upholstered arms, she interlaced her fingers in front of her and considered his words.

"In my head I know that's true, but in my heart it's a whole different story."

"Listen," Quinn pressed, "Farley wouldn't have wanted you to do anything differently. He would have been totally pissed if you had stayed behind in order to sit by his bed."

"But nobody should die alone."

"We all die alone, Valaria."

She sat forward slightly with just the trace of a wry smirk. "Is that the best you can do—*we all die alone*? Bloody hell, Quinn, you really suck at this condolence shit!"

He returned her smile and offered her whiskey from a bottle he had snagged from the Freebooter cache. She'd be all right; it would just take time.

II.

As Quinn had hoped, success at Fountain Lakes—and the supplies it brought with it—proved to be a potent antidote to the attrition the Sons of Liberty had been experiencing before the raid. The rank and file might be bitching about the weather—hell, the officers were, too!—but at least they were doing it on their own time. Now that their bellies were full and they had a victory over the Freebooters to brag about in exaggerated detail, the average yob had returned to the routine of work duties and physical training with the same low-grade insolence typical of soldiers for millennia before them.

Emboldened by the uptick in morale, Gideon and his closest colleagues began discussing the viability of their most audacious idea yet, the scheme that had taken Quinn to Settlement #4 in the first place and introduced him to Valaria Thorpe—

An attack on the Guardian Star.

"It's what we've always said has to happen if we're ever going to get the RSA to let us go."

Gideon, Levi Dodge, and three other officers had joined James McFarland in his office under the Gateway Arch and were gathering around a small conference table adjacent the Speaker's desk.

"That's true, General," the woman sitting down at Quinn's left said, "but—with all due respect, sir—I'm not convinced this is the right time."

"We're not suggesting day after tomorrow," Dodger interjected. "Talking about it is just the first step—a step I think it's time to take."

The former Speaker of the House smiled beneficently at the men and women around the table. Still adroit at the give-and-take of politics, the elderly statesman offered up an olive branch.

"I understand your concerns, Major Collins," he said to the woman, "but I encourage you to set them aside for the time being so the conversation might benefit from your expertise."

She responded to the compliment with a tight-lipped smile and a gesture indicating at least temporary acquiescence to the proceedings.

"No one denies that the Guardian Star is the government's linchpin when it comes to controlling the Borders," Quinn observed. "Its mere presence is intimidating and when you add drone flyovers and the Guardians themselves that's a pretty wicked one-two punch. *But...*" he added with emphasis, leaning in and making eye contact with his colleagues, "the RSA's Safe Zones are so far away and so bogged down by their tangled bureaucracy, if the Star can be compromised I truly believe the States will have one hell of a hard time holding on to the Borders buffer."

He paused to let his words sink in.

"Remember, I've lived in the Zones," he added. "I've experienced that bureaucracy firsthand; worked within it. Believe me, the RSA is already on life-support and Naomi Blanchard's Neoterics aren't nearly as omnipotent as she'd like everyone to believe. Why the hell do you think they're resorting to something like Radiance—drugging their own citizens into a submissive stupor? That's probably the best evidence we've got that the regime is weakening from within. We just need to give it a push."

"But you're being naïve, Gideon, if you think Blanchard will give us what we want just because we take down the Guardian Star," one of the other officers observed.

"I'm not saying it'll happen automatically," Quinn assured him. "We'll still have a fight on our hands. The Star is only the first domino— but it's the one that has to fall in order to get things started."

"And don't forget Texas," Dodger contributed from his friend's right. "We all know we've got one helluva fight ahead of us. We also know Texas is watching; Farley Donovan made that clear. They may not be directly threatened by the RSA but they've definitely got a horse in this race—The Wilds. Donovan agreed with us that a major statement like taking down the Guardian Star would go a long way toward getting his country to recognize our existence and maybe even support our fight."

"OK," Major Collins said, asserting herself once again. "So let's say for the sake of argument that we're all on the same page when it comes to targeting the Star. Just what does that mean? Where do we go from here? We've all assumed you brought back more than Valaria Thorpe from your trip to the Borders, General. For this conversation to be anything more than academic you must have discovered information out there about the tower. Am I right?"

Quinn smiled as he surveyed the expectant faces of his colleagues and activated the 3D panel embedded in the conference room table.

"Let me to take you on a little tour."

III.

Grayson Talbot, the elderly governor of the Indianapolis Safe Zone, was thinking about his high school science teacher as he sat down at the desk in his office and triggered the transmitter that would insert him holographically into the Cabinet Room 175 miles away in Columbus. It was one of the fundamental principle of physics Mr. Parkinson had hammered into their heads some sixty years ago that was niggling at his brain that morning; Newton's third law—*For every action there is an equal and opposite reaction.*

The Governor shuddered. He was certain that he and his fellow cabinet members were about to see that law played out in dramatic fashion.

Holographic projectors in each of the five Safe Zones whirred to life and, after a few flickering hiccups, interactive 3D images of the duly appointed Zone governors soon joined their flesh and blood colleagues in a room that bore a chill beyond what was warranted by the wintry weather outside.

The RSA's Chief Executive—ever lethally-poised—was the source of the cold.

"Good morning, ladies and gentlemen," Naomi Blanchard began, her words brittle with frigid vitriol. "We have but one item on our agenda this morning—the debacle at Fountain Lakes."

Even from the safety of his office, Talbot's holographic image winced; here came Newton's third. He certainly wouldn't want to be in General Conway's shoes today!

"General Conway won't be joining us today," the president was saying with undisguised disdain for the absent officer dripping from every word.

She gestured behind her at a woman standing ramrod straight by the door. "This is General Sylvia Burke, our new military liaison. General, why don't you start things off for us? I'm certain we'd all be interested in hearing your take on what happened in Missouri a few days ago."

The general stepped forward—a more self-assured presence than Talbot had ever seen in a face-off with Naomi Blanchard. Her tenure would undoubtedly be even shorter than Conway's.

"Your Excellency, there's no denying that Fountain Lakes was a disappointment..."

Before she could continue, the president's icy calm interrupted her. "Excuse me— a *disappointment?* Is that what you just called it?"

"Yes ma'am."

Since Blanchard had characterized the event as a 'debacle,' Talbot braced himself for the verbal vivisection to come—and figured Conway was about to get a cellmate, wherever that poor sod had ended up! But the general continued with unexpected confidence and the president surprised the elderly politician by bestowing at least a temporary stay of execution.

"If you'll allow me, Excellency," the general said, moving forward and activating the computer screen at the front of the room. "It obviously was disturbing to learn of the Freebooters' collapse during the Sons' raid but we've known from the beginning that 'booters are bound to be a useful—albeit unpredictable—variable in our efforts to control the insurgents."

She turned toward the translucent screen behind her and began tapping and dragging into view the files that were pertinent to the point at which she was driving.

"That being said, I believe it would be throwing the proverbial baby out with the bath water to conclude that our use of Freebooters was ill-advised and should be discontinued as some have suggested. I assure you, Excellency, we can use them to our advantage despite their admittedly self-serving unpredictability."

The president's largesse was obviously waning and the general's pace increased accordingly.

"So, yes ma'am, I call Fountain Lakes a disappointment rather than a catastrophe—the Freebooters ran away and the Sons' bravado was momentarily inflated."

"*Momentarily*," the president repeated, the menace in her voice intensifying.

"Yes, ma'am," the general replied, pausing only long enough to open the file that was intended to be her denouement.

Footage from a drone flyover began playing behind her.

"Surveillance footage captured the rebels withdrawal from Fountain Lakes," she pointed out as images of the Sons crossing the I-70 bridge played out in a loop on the screen. "They dispersed on the other side of this bridge and the snow storm increased shortly thereafter which forced the recall of our drones but we now know they must have at least one major base somewhere within marching distance of St. Charles. I've already ordered more TOD flights in a twenty-five mile arc of the I-70 bridge. It's only a matter of time, Excellency, before we know where the bastards are holed up."

Rising from her seat, Naomi Blanchard bestowed the rarest of gifts upon General Burke—a sly and approving smile.

IV.

It fell to Dodger to pack up Farley Donovan's belongings. Valaria had walked the path of grief before and knew that—although painful—the memories stirred by sorting through the minutiae of the life just ended was at least a partial anodyne to the sorrow. When she offered to help, Levi was openly relieved. She brought Yancy along for moral support and the dog stayed close, seeming to sense the solemn nature of what his two human friends were doing and keenly aware of the scent of the one who was missing.

"Farley didn't have much family, did he?" Dodger asked as he and Valaria sat down on opposite bunks in the men's dormitory and pulled Donovan's large duffle bag into the space between them.

"No; his parents are dead. He's got cousins and an uncle in Texas but I have no idea where."

"Don't know how we'd get anything back to them anyway," Levi mused quietly as he unzipped the duffle.

None of the Sons of Liberty had many possessions. A decidedly motley collection of wayward scavengers, Borders escapees, and Safe Zone defectors, they usually found their way to the Sons with little more than the shirt on their back and many didn't even need the crates, cardboard boxes, and empty drawers that had been scrounged from around The Hub in order to provide each with a modicum of personal space in the dormitory. Since Farley Donovan had come from the relative security of Texas, he had had more than the typical squaddie but there still was precious little inside the duffle he had brought with him.

"There are some newbies who could use the clothes," Dodger said as they folded Donovan's extra garments and set them aside.

Valaria held up a faded 'Lone Star State' sweatshirt. Farley's swaggering pride in his country's tenacious survival filled the room for a moment; she could almost see his broad smile and hear his sexy drawl.

"You should keep this," she said, holding out the sweatshirt. "Farley would want someone he knows to have it."

Dodger nodded in grateful acknowledgement, set the sweatshirt off by itself and reached into the pocket of his shirt.

"And you should have this," he observed, holding out a simple gold cross on a chain. "The doc gave it to me when I made arrangements for the burial."

"I wondered what happened to that," Valaria replied, remembering that it never left Donovan's neck. "You can keep it if you'd like; you knew him a lot longer than I did."

"I'm not much for religion," Dodger admitted. "Farley was, and I think he'd be pleased to know you have it. You're a believer, aren't you?"

"Yes," she said simply, taking the necklace and putting it on. "Thanks."

There wasn't much else. Farley had kept a slender, old-fashioned leather wallet that had belonged to some relative from a previous generation and inside was a printout of his Texas citizenship ID and a dog-eared photograph of a young couple holding a baby. Dodger handed these to Valaria as well.

"You guys about done?"

Focused on their task and thoughts of Donovan, neither had realized Gideon Quinn had joined them and was standing observantly at the foot of the bunks.

"Yeah," Dodger replied, sliding the now-empty duffle toward Quinn who moved it into place at the end of Farley's vacated bed.

"Excellent," he said. "We've got work to do."

Valaria stood as Yancy trotted over to welcome Quinn. "That include us?"

"You might as well come along," Gideon smirked. "It's too damn hard to keep you away."

"Ooo, does that mean I 'need-to-know'?"

"Don't press your luck," the general chuffed, even though it had been his intention all along to offer both friends a diversion from the heavy loss they shouldered.

The three rebels—and their canine shadow—headed for Gideon's quarters. Although also an officer, Levi Dodge's lower rank meant that he shared space with two others and, since it literally was an emptied storage closet, Valaria's cubbyhole barely accommodated her and the dog let alone guests. As a result, Quinn's larger accommodations were their usual destination anytime the group wanted to have a private conversation—or an uninterrupted game night.

The room assigned to the general had been someone's office in a previous life. A reasonably serviceable desk still remained under the windows at the far end as did a small table with four straight-backed chairs standing adjacent a narrow bed that had been added to the room from those in the dormitory. Two overstuffed chairs liberated from a lobby somewhere in the complex rounded out the room's accoutrements. Although a luxury, the chairs had a persistent musty odor which made them a less than stellar attraction as far as Valaria was concerned. To her, the best thing about the place was the small private bathroom accessible through a side door—now *that* was luxury.

"So what's up?" she asked, flopping onto one of the chairs.

"This is about the Star, isn't it," Levi said, taking a seat at the table.

Valaria's ears perked up—as did her posture. "What about the Star? What's going on?"

"Relax, woman," Quinn said with a satisfied smile at her brightening. "We'll bring you up to speed."

It didn't take long to share the gist of the meeting held a few days earlier in Speaker McFarland's office. Valaria devoured every morsel of information, growing increasingly intense when they discussed reactions to her grandfather's schematics of the tower's design.

"I'm in," she said during a lull, all trace of flippancy gone. "You know how important this is to me—it's why I'm still here."

Gideon didn't believe for a minute that that was the only reason Valaria still hung around but she continued before he could toss her an adequate comeback.

"And face it, you wouldn't have the information you need about the Star if it wasn't for Otis and you wouldn't have access to *him* without *me* so I'm part of whatever happens next—got that?"

"Down girl," Quinn chided. "You don't have to bully us."

"Gideon says you've been studying the Star," Dodger interjected, "that you probably know it as well as he does by now."

"I have— I do. Well, rudimentary knowledge, anyhow; couldn't dissect the damn thing like him but can undoubtedly help throw a shoe into the works."

Her veiled reference to the Luddite genius who had raised her brought another smile to Quinn's face.

"We've got a few techies who could undoubtedly be brought up to speed on your grandfather's intel," he said, "but I think it's best to keep that knowledge—and our plan—within a very small circle. Speaker McFarland agrees, so the three of us are pretty much it when it comes to planning."

Valaria smiled hungrily. "Excellent. So where do we start?"

"Well, there's going to have to be a full-on ground assault at some point," Dodger began. "There are about three hundred Guardians garrisoned at the Star and they're not going to walk away without a fight. We're gonna need the biggest force we can muster in order to face them.

That'll mean consolidating all our outposts and leaving only a skeletal defense here." He looked at Quinn before continuing. "I've been thinking about that a lot. We'll need to move our forces toward the Star slowly and in small groups if we don't want to show our hand prematurely. That's going to take some careful strategizing."

"I agree..." Quinn nodded, glancing Valaria's way with another reference to Otis, "it'll be quite the chess game."

"We thought the raid on Fountain Lakes was a logistical nightmare," Levi added. "That was barely a dress rehearsal in comparison to what we've got planned for the Star."

"And that's why you're taking lead on the ground," Gideon said. "You're the tactician and you've got the trust of the people involved. I'll handle the internal assault."

"*We'll* handle it," Valaria corrected forcefully.

"Yes, I suppose we will. But that means you're going to have to do some damn-serious studying between now and then and some additional physical training. We won't be able to get more than two operatives inside the tower. If you're determined to be one of them you've got to be willing to take it to the next level."

"That tower is as much Otis's legacy as the pub," she assured them. "I have no intention of letting him down—or being left behind."

V.

Training for the assault on the Guardian Star was what helped everyone survive that long, stubborn winter. Although the rank-and-file didn't know exactly what they were preparing to do, it was obvious that something big was in the works and there was electricity in the cold winter air. Speculation among the squaddies ran rampant. One day the scuttlebutt would have them getting ready to attack the capital itself while the next day's gossip would identify the plan as a full-blown exodus into The Wilds. Every new rumor brought a smile to Gideon Quinn's face for it meant that the real target was still a mystery and if there were any turncoats among them they were as much in the dark as the dedicated rebel standing next to them.

As her gossiping counterparts prepared for battle Valaria Thorpe also began training, but her regimen was taking place after the rest of the squaddies had cycled through the calisthenics, martial arts, and gunnery practice that filled their days. Well after the typical yob had finished their work duties and training, Valaria and Quinn headed for a closed-off section of the complex for some specialized instruction.

"Better not be squeamish about heights," Gideon cautioned as they set out for their first session. He opened a set of double doors with a flourish and they were greeted by a wall of warm, humid air. "...and I bloody-well hope you can swim!"

They had entered a natatorium and an Olympic-sized swimming pool shimmered before them in the low lighting.

"OK, you've got my attention," Valaria said with no small measure of incredulity. "What's swimming got to do with taking down the Guardian Star? It sure-as-hell doesn't have a moat."

"Not swimming," came a voice from behind them, "...*diving*."

A woman had just entered the natatorium through another set of doors. Well past middle-age—with the post-menopausal spread to prove it—she walked toward them carrying some odd-looking bodysuits draped over her arm.

"Valaria," Quinn said, "this is Carolyn Sumner. We need some training that she's uniquely qualified to help us with."

"Olympic diving?"

"Well, not the stylized dives the old pros had to master but trust me, knowing how to dive is gonna make our time at the Star a lot easier."

"OK, now that definitely needs more explanation."

"Getting us *into* the Star is the easy part," Quinn said, adding "kind of," with a shrug before continuing. "But the challenge of getting us *out* again is why Carolyn's here... 'cuz we're gonna have to jump."

"*Jump*—" Valaria sputtered. "Out of a mile-high tower?"

Quinn was unmoved by his partner's outburst.

"Well, we'll only be about half way up," he pointed out.

"Oh, only half way."

"Come on, it'll be fun. Carolyn's gonna teach us how to dive into water and then we'll transfer that skill into body-sailing."

Valaria managed to quash a barbed response to the idea of body-sailing down from the Guardian Star—a suggestion she found about as appealing as bungee-jumping into the Grand Canyon—and almost drew blood as she reined herself in by biting down on her lower lip.

Quinn ignored his partner's incredulity and gestured toward the diving tower. "We've got four levels of jumps here at the pool to help us get started and then we'll head into the dome to practice sailing from some loftier heights."

Carolyn Sumner held out the suits she carried—garments designed for sailing rather than swimming. Made from a material she identified as 'InsulSkin,' the formfitting bodysuits had an invisible zipper on each side that ran from the wrist up along the inside of the arm and then down the outside of the torso to the hip. Concealed within were lightweight, roughly triangular 'wings' ingeniously folded so they barely added any bulk to the sleek garments. Once extended from outstretched arms, it was the wings that would enable Quinn and Thorpe to sail safely to the ground from the Guardian Star's midpoint.

"Hey, you volunteered," Gideon reminded his partner when she didn't immediately share his enthusiasm.

"That I did," Valaria muttered to herself with a *"what-the-hell-have-I-gotten-myself-into-now?"* heavenward glance as they headed into the locker room to change.

Luckily, she did know how to swim. Otis had seen to that since one of their few recreational opportunities had been a tiny lake just within the 5-mile limit of their Borders world. In spite of being a competent swimmer, however, Valaria's *approach* to a body of water could best be likened to that of an enthusiastic Golden Retriever. As a result, she was inordinately relieved when Ms. Sumner ordained that their introduction to more elegant means of entry should begin at the pool's edge rather than the diving tower.

As Quinn had pointed out, the sophisticated intricacies of competitive diving weren't on the agenda—something else for which Valaria was duly grateful! But she had a lackluster start nonetheless; one that found her flailing about in her own uniquely awkward and painful version of a belly flop and had her partner growing concerned that she might not be up to the challenge after all. Valaria was undaunted, however—as well a tad mortified—and between her own determination and patient instruction on the part of their accomplished teacher, she soon was entering the water in a relatively smooth, if not actually graceful, arc. Within three weeks both students were producing reasonably successful leaps from the highest platform and their confidence was growing.

When they had proven their newfound prowess on a consistent basis, they said goodbye to Carolyn Sumner and headed back to the dome for the next level of training—

Literally the next level.

"The dome's perfect for body-sailing," Quinn said as they entered the huge arena one night in mid-March. "We can work our way up at a gradual pace and eventually come pretty damn close to the height we'll actually be jumping from."

Valaria surveyed the maintenance scaffolding that had been brought out from some remote storage area and assembled near midfield.

"What?" Gideon asked with a satisfied smirk as he followed her gaze. "No old movie reference?"

The two flight students began working through a series of stretches in anticipation of their first jump while Levi Dodge and two other officers distributed the dome's old wrestling mats around the intended drop zone. Although Quinn seemed to be approaching the transition from pool to pads with a 'diving is diving' nonchalance, the obvious difference in landing technique had Valaria passing from mere pause to near panic.

"By the time we're done," Gideon said, directing Valaria's eyes upward to the permanent network of scaffolding at the arena's highest point, "we're gonna be jumping from the dome's catwalk. How cool is that?"

VI.

By the beginning of April the Sons of Liberty were ready for their assault on the Guardian Star—as were the two operatives whose job it would be to facilitate that attack from inside the tower. While training progressed, Levi Dodge had been working tirelessly to prepare an advance on the Star that would get their troops into position without alerting the opposition. It was a daunting task—one that made the loss of Farley Donovan painfully fresh as he missed his friend's sharp mind as well as the man's presence. Not only did Dodger have to work through the complicated logistics of transferring troops and supplies in small groups from disparate locations but he had to do so while taking into account the regime's intrusive 'eyes-in-the-sky' and their ability to mount an aerial attack in response to anything their drones might observe. Encountering TADs while en route to the tower—or the unmanned quadrunners equipped with pulse canons that were their counterparts on the ground—would put a serious damper on any chance of success the Sons might have.

And Dodger had to concede that the odds were already pretty much stacked against them when the threat of Freebooters was added into the mix.

"Bring us up to speed," Gideon said to his friend when he, Dodger, and Valaria gathered for another late-night strategy session in Quinn's quarters.

"I think I've worked out most of the kinks," Levi began as he activated the computer embedded in Gideon's table and accessed a 3D holographic map of the region. Tapping on various Sons of Liberty outpost locations, he brought to life the avatars he had created representing about twenty small groups of rebels. With the finesse of an experienced RPG participant, Dodger manipulated them around the map as he explained his plan for surreptitiously moving the groups toward the Guardian Star.

"Looks good," Quinn said when he was finished.

"We'll be moving troops mostly at night in order to reduce the risk of being detected by drone flyovers," Dodger continued. "If we can manage to elude them—and their Freebooter lackeys—once we get our troops distributed throughout the undergrowth around the Star we'll be good to go... After you guys take care of things on your end, that is."

Gideon reached out and triggered a replay of the troop movements Dodger had just walked them through.

"We won't even approach the tower until you send word that the troops are in position," he said while studying the screen.

"That's gonna be a logistical challenge all its own," Valaria pitched in from her side of the table.

"But manageable," Quinn replied.

Dodger wanted to hear more but Gideon was focused on their purpose, not the logistics of their approach.

"Once inside the Star," he continued, sweeping Dodger's display off-screen and accessing the tower's schematic, "we'll split up. I'll take out their ability to launch drones and then open the main doors for your troops while Valaria blows the elevator controls to keep as many Guardians as possible stranded in the upper levels."

"Sounds straightforward enough," Dodger said.

"It is," Valaria assured him. "Quinn's made me go over the procedure so many times I think I could do it in my sleep."

"You guys have the hard part," Gideon said. "We may be able to open the doors and minimize the number of Guardians who pour out but once you breach the tower they're gonna throw everything they've got at you."

"We'll be ready for them," Dodger replied with quiet certainty.

The trio fell silent and Valaria shifted purposefully in her chair, throwing a determined look toward her two colleagues.

"There's one more thing I want to talk about... I think Kevin should stay behind with the reserves here at The Hub."

"Why?" Dodger asked. "He's been training with all the others. He's a good soldier."

"He's only fifteen," Valaria replied. "He's just a kid."

"There are lots of teenagers among us," Gideon pointed out.

"Yeah, and personally I don't think any of them should be going. Listen, Kevin doesn't talk about it much but he's lost a helluva a lot in his few short years."

"So has everybody else."

"I know that, but the kid's still grieving for Donovan and I just don't think he's up to the task."

Another silence fell as the two men considered her words.

"Please guys," she said at last, her voice gentling. "Let him stay back and take care of Yancy." Her eyes became almost pleading as she added a startling confession. "I don't want to lose the kid."

As much as he loved Yancy—and as much as he felt obligated to take care of the dog for Valaria—Kevin wasn't at all happy when his orders to stay at The Hub came through. Although unsure of himself in myriad ways and definitely still grieving, the teen had approached training for the hush-hush op with vigor and dedication; not only did he want to prove himself to his adult friends but he yearned to avenge all the losses he blamed on the repressive regime in Columbus.

"This is your idea, isn't it," he accused Valaria, his voice raw. She could be totally clueless sometimes—and had all the finesse of a T-Rex—but this was the first time he felt truly angry with her.

"What do you mean? I don't have anything to do with troop assignments."

"Bullshit," Kevin sputtered. "You're best friends with the guy in charge. Quinn's always gonna listen to what you want."

"He may listen," she argued, "but nine times out of ten it goes in one ear and out the other or he tells me outright to go to hell."

"Well, I'm the one telling you to go to hell this time," the teen said hotly. "I'm gonna be part of this deployment."

"Face it, kid, we've all got our role to play in this thing. Those staying behind are just as important as anybody else. Protecting the dome is crucial; Speaker McFarland's here, as well as all our supplies and computer crap."

"You really expect me to believe you didn't tell them to leave me behind?"

"Kevin, I don't have that kind of influence."

"Yeah, sure."

"Cross my heart," Valaria said, stretching the truth to molecular thinness. "I won't deny being relieved that somebody I trust is gonna be here to take care of Yancy, but I didn't make the decision to have you stay behind."

Kevin seemed marginally mollified if not entirely convinced but on the day of her deployment—when Valaria delivered not only Yancy but also Otis's chessboard, crucifix and dog-eared Bible into his care—he considered anew the strong possibility that she was, indeed, the puppet-master pulling the strings behind his reserve posting at The Hub. In light of her gesture of trust, however, his anger and longing for vengeance on the RSA ebbed somewhat and he was left with mostly gratitude—and deep concern—for the prickly, unpredictable, foul-mouthed woman who had become his surrogate family.

VII.

Sons of Liberty from across the region began their slow, nocturnal deployments toward the Guardian Star during the second week of April. Following Dodger's instructions, larger groups were broken down into teams of no more than twenty-five as everyone spread out and worked their way through the ubiquitous tangle of nature that had reasserted itself across the country following the plague.

As their counterparts moved stealthily toward the Star in slow and staggered increments, Gideon and Valaria began their final walkabout together—retracing their steps to Settlement #4.

"You realize you can't just go walking back into town bold as brass when we get there, right?" Quinn asked when they were still about a day away.

Valaria wished she had kept track of how many times he had brought that subject up over the past few weeks; felt like at least fifty. "Of course I realize it. Do you think I'm a complete moron?"

Under ordinary circumstances, the question would have been too tempting to resist, but Gideon's focus was elsewhere. "I understand your eagerness to check on Jasper and the others, but we'll have to scope things out first and make connections with our contact before doing anything else."

"Our *contact*," Valaria muttered, rolling her eyes. Why couldn't he just use the guy's name? It wasn't as if she didn't know who they were meeting.

Their 'contact' approached them the evening of their seventh day out. They had made camp in a wooded area just east of the settlement, the cluster of warning lights at the tip of the distant Guardian Star forming the dominant constellation in the clear night sky. It had been an easy crossing. The weather had been forbearing and there were no signs of Freebooters, only benign encounters with two different groups of scavengers who were as wary of them as they were of the ragtag nomads scuttling away like cockroaches caught in the glare of an unexpected light.

"So, 'General Washington', we finally meet," Dawson Hayes said to Gideon as he stepped out of the shadows into the glow of the solar camp stove warming the two travelers. "Hello, Valaria."

Quinn stood and reached out to shake hands.

"Guardian Hayes," he said, "or should I call you 'Sam?' Join us."

"Dawson will do just fine," Hayes replied, taking up Quinn's offer of a place by the camp stove and folding his lanky frame to sit cross-legged opposite Valaria.

She openly gawked at him, mildly flummoxed... *Dawson Hayes was a member of the Sons of Liberty*—their so-called 'Sam Adams.' It still boggled her brain. Why had she never picked up on his subversive leanings? He had spent almost as much time at the pub as Pete and Jasper. It was nothing short of surreal to see the man sitting casually at their campsite talking with Quinn.

"This is bizarre to the point of being surreal," she said.

"So, not much different from the last time you saw me, huh?" Dawson quipped with a wink. "You're looking much better, by the way. No lasting ill effects?"

"No," she replied. "Fit as the proverbial fiddle."

"And as delightful as ever," Gideon added from his side of the camp stove, raising his cup of coffee in tribute.

"Glad to hear it," Hayes said, "because you've got quite the adventure ahead of you; beginning with a redux of our last encounter. You're both going to need all your wits about you if we're to succeed."

"About that redux," Valaria said. "That's the first thing I'd like to talk about."

"That can wait," Quinn interjected, his attention focused on Hayes. "Give us an update on the status of the tower and the settlement."

"Things at the tower are status quo; nothing out of the ordinary, no indication that anyone's aware of our plans. I'm afraid the settlement's a different story."

"What's happened?" Valaria asked.

"They're still under a full Guardian occupation. No big surprise there, but the regime has begun using Radiance on the exiles. Anybody who steps out of line—or even mildly pisses off the powers-that-be—finds themselves 'in treatment' as they call it. From what I hear, every settlement's the same. They're calling them 'Quells'—those who have reached the Radiant Cascade; because their so-called antisocial psychosis has been quelled, I suppose."

Valaria wasn't surprised to learn the government had expanded its use of Radiance into the Borders but her anger boiled nonetheless.

"What about Jasper and Pete? Are they all right?"

"Yes," Dawson assured her with a smile. "They took over the pub after you left; ran it until just recently."

"Why don't they still run it?"

"Some bureaucrat from the Zones has been stationed in town to monitor Radiance treatments; moved into the pub and promptly shut it down. I haven't met her. She's just referred to as 'the Supervisor.' Between her entourage and the Guardian occupation force, I wouldn't advise going near the settlement."

"Hear that?" Quinn asked Valaria. "The town's off limits."

Valaria responded with an insincere nod. There was no way in hell she was going to be this close to the settlement and not go check on Jasper and Pete.

What Quinn didn't know wouldn't hurt him.

Her chance came at dusk the following day when Dawson and Gideon went on a scouting mission to the Star. This was Valaria's home territory and she felt confident in her ability to slip in and out of the settlement without being noticed. She'd be back in no time at all with the two men none the wiser.

Grabbing Quinn's suede duster for a little extra protection against the sunset's falling temperatures—and a StunStik just in case—Valaria headed out.

Their camp was less than a mile from the settlement and within just a few minutes the domes came into view, a cluster of mottled husks receding into the twilight and looking like the discarded shells of gigantic bugs as dim lights glowed beneath the curves of their dingy translucent panels.

Valaria left the shelter of the nearby tree line and moved toward the farm area just south of town; the day's work would be over and she'd be able to get a decent view of the settlement from the shadows cast by the northernmost agricultural dome. Once crouched in the dark at the edge of the curved foundation the familiar smell of fish and rich loam filled her nostrils and triggered fragments of memory that tugged at her heart.

In the near distance she could see the dome that she and Otis had shared. A resolute vanguard on the settlement's western edge, her grandfather's squat home had always been the figurative center of town since it housed his pub, *The Shoe and Gear*. Sooner or later virtually everyone was drawn to the pub's promise of distraction from the monotony of routine and the pall of oppression that painted their lives a cloying, hopeless grey.

Now even that respite was gone.

Without realizing it, Valaria's crouch had become more of a mournful sag as she leaned heavily against the dome's foundation overwhelmed for a moment by all the suffering brought about by one barbaric act of terrorism that had knocked the world's dominoes down. Shaking herself free from an increasingly dark reverie, she sat up straighter.

In addition to the StunStik, she had snagged a small night scope from the stash of supplies they had brought along and she raised it to her eyes for a better view of the settlement. As expected, there weren't many people about. She recognized Miss Baxter's arthritic gait as the old woman slowly crossed the commons. As she watched, two Guardians loomed into view directly ahead of the elderly exile and Valaria could see her pull up short as they obviously had something to say about where she had been or where she was going.

"Leave her alone, you bastards," Valaria muttered.

As if obeying her command, one of the Guardians gestured the frail woman on her way and the two men resumed their purposeful strut across the compound.

When they were out of her line-of-sight, Valaria put the scope back in her pocket and ventured out of the relative safety offered by the shadows cast by the farm's curved rooflines. Darting across the open area beyond, she plastered herself against the base of the next dome, grateful for sunset's lengthening gloom.

Her heart was racing and her pulse pounded in her ears. She hadn't expected seeing the settlement to inspire this level of emotion and she closed her eyes for a moment to steady herself.

"You better go home," a quiet voice behind her said.

She whirled around to find her former neighbor, Carlos Rivera, shambling toward her in small, measured steps.

"You better go home," he said again.

"Yeah... I better," Valaria stammered, recognizing the stupefying effects of Radiance in the face and demeanor of one of the settlement's previously-stalwart defenders.

"You been at work?" he asked, obviously struggling to make sense of what he was seeing.

"Yes," she lied. "I've been at the farm."

He looked over her shoulder rather dubiously at the oblong domes of the farm but the frisson of doubt tickling his brain never made it past the layers co-opted by Radiance.

"You better go home," he said once again.

"Yes, yes I know," she assured him with a mixture of sympathy and anger—God, how she wished she could get her hands on the bastards who had done this to him!

"Tell me, Carlos," she said, realizing that a zombified exile might be her best source of information—someone who would never be believed if he happened to mention seeing her. "How are Jasper and Pete? Have you seen them today?"

"They're good," he said with a placid half-smile. "They take care of us since the soldiers came. They make supper."

Valaria started to ask just who 'us' referred to but stopped short—she wasn't at all sure she wanted to know just how many of her former neighbors had been chemically lobotomized.

"You better go home," Carlos repeated, returning to a familiar theme.

She smiled at him, almost overcome by emotion. As much as she wanted to see and talk to Jasper, knowing he was 'good' was probably the best she could realistically hope for.

"We both better go home, don't you think," she said after a moment.

Carlos seemed to take Valaria's words as an imperative and began shuffling away. She died a little as she watched the previously proud, strong man's slow, deliberate steps as he rounded the dome and headed for home.

Quinn was right—she shouldn't have come. Not only was it dangerous, there was nothing for her to accomplish here and the tragedy of the place was heart-wrenching. She turned to melt into the darkness that had fallen but a loud voice on the other side of the dome stopped her in her tracks.

"What the hell are you doing outside?"

The two Guardians who had accosted Miss Baxter had completed their circuit of the settlement and were starting again—and Carlos Rivera had had the misfortune of literally crossing their path.

"We're talking to you, you moron," a second hard, ridiculing voice barked.

Valaria slithered around the base of the dome in the opposite direction from the voices. She didn't know just what she could do but there was no way in Hell she was going to let them rain further abuse down on a man who already had been reduced to a virtually empty shell.

As she watched the Guardians, a slender woman crossed the commons with long, confident strides.

"They have a tendency to wander," the woman informed the officers as she drew near.

An icy shudder ran down Valaria's spine and she pulled herself deeper into shadow. It wasn't just the woman's brutally nonchalant observation that chilled her; it was the crisp, authoritative voice. It was a voice she knew all too well.

Mavis Pope had just come on the scene.

"He's harmless," she was saying as she tucked a strand of her stylish bob behind her ear. "Aren't you, Carlos?"

Even in the dim light, Valaria could see the woman's condescending smirk as she addressed the Guardians. "Take him back to his dome and put him to bed with the other Quells."

"Yes Supervisor," one of the officers replied, shoving Carlos in the direction of a nearby dome.

A man stood in silhouette watching from the open doorway of the residence. He jogged forward to help Rivera rise from where he had stumbled to the ground after being pushed.

It was Jasper Hahn.

Valaria felt like she was watching a poorly written melodrama. It was all she could do to keep from calling out to her grandfather's friend and creating a role for herself in the sensationalized scene playing out on the settlement's stage.

And hadn't the Guardian just cast Mavis Pope as *Supervisor* in the evening's performance?

...Dawson Hayes had said a supervisor had been sent to the settlement to monitor administration of Radiance.

...That meant Mavis was actually in *charge* of the place; she was the director of the little melodramatic freak show unfolding beneath the new moon's wan spotlight!

Valaria's breath snagged as she remembered Hayes also had said the supervisor had moved into Otis's dome.

...Which meant Mavis Pope was living in her former home!

The thought of the regime's spy living among and using Otis's things brought a putrid taste to Valaria's mouth. Her breath became jagged as she considered following her nemesis back to the pub and confronting her. The idea of unleashing Marcus Griffin's 'Kinetic-Kills' on her so-called friend was an almost overpowering temptation—justice for herself and for the settlement—and loathing for all that Mavis represented roiled within her like the waves of an angry sea.

When Jasper and Carlos had disappeared into the residence, she crouched in the darkness that had swallowed the settlement, quietly seething as Mavis Pope switched on a flashlight and walked confidently away. Closing her eyes, Valaria once again leaned heavily against the dome. The only thing keeping her from indulging the almost-primal urge to follow was the reality that hundreds of people were relying on her to do her part at the Guardian Star.

No act of vengeance was worth the risk of screwing that mission.

She turned and trotted back toward the shelter of the tree line. As difficult as it was to accept, there were times when discretion truly was the better part of valor.

VIII.

"I'd like to believe you've just been out in the bushes taking a leak," Quinn said quietly from where he sat sipping coffee in front of the solar stove. "But I've been sitting here for at least twenty minutes so don't even try that lie."

Valaria stood at the edge of their campsite and considered her options. They were few.

"I see no reason to lie," she responded defiantly. "I've been to the settlement."

"Obviously."

"No one saw me," she informed him hotly—choosing not to mention the lobotomized zombie that had been Carlos Rivera in a former life.

"Will I ever be able to trust you to follow orders?" Gideon asked, her flippancy chipping away at his self-control. "Don't you realize what could have happened if you'd been seen or worse yet, captured?"

"Of course I realize it; that's why I made sure nobody saw me. Did you hear me? *Nobody saw me.* There was no harm done."

She lowered herself into a squat opposite him. "Bloody hell, Quinn, there was no way I was going to be this close to the settlement and not make sure Jasper and Pete are OK."

"And are they?"

"Yeah; I saw Jasper from a distance. They're all right."

Gideon studied his partner as she stared into the glow of the solar stove.

"What else?" he asked, picking up on her tension.

"I also saw Mavis Pope."

"*Mavis Pope*," he repeated. "Are you sure?"

"Oh yeah, I'm sure. She's the 'supervisor' Hayes talked about."

"Well, that's what I'd call some damn-sweet poetic justice."

Valaria didn't follow his logic. "How so?"

"She *hated* the settlement, right? And she gets sent back here? That's better revenge than wringing her scrawny little neck would be; the satisfaction sure lasts a helluva lot longer."

He turned to the rucksack at his side, extracted a nutrition bar and tossed it to his partner.

"Oh, that's perfect..." he continued, on the dawn of an epiphany.

"What?"

"I bet she's being punished for your escape. Somebody would have to pay for that screw-up and Regina Agnew would make damn sure it wasn't her. She's the consummate manipulator—always the reason for success but never at fault if something goes wrong. Hell, she could get sprayed by a skunk and convince you it was roses."

Still not happy about Valaria's insubordination—although in reality her refusal to toe the soldierly line was hardly a surprise—Quinn was glad to have her reassured about the status of her grandfather's friends and had to admit he found it personally gratifying to know that Mavis Pope had received at least a dollop of justice by being posted to the Borders she loathed.

When Dodger signaled them the following morning that the troops were finally in position, Gideon smiled broadly. He had moved past Valaria's impulsive lapse and was eager to get underway. His partner's resolve, on the other hand, was beginning to waver.

"Gotta tell you," Valaria said, adjusting the polka dot 'minion' wrap that still adorned her left wrist, "I'm less than enthusiastic about this part of our little adventure."

Quinn couldn't help smiling at her trepidation—and at the care she took of his fraying token.

"You're about to attempt one of the boldest acts of sabotage in the history of the country and *this*..." he said, gesturing into the clearing they had just entered, "this is what you're nervous about?"

A gleaming Tactical Attack Drone sat in solitary elegance at the center of the clearing, leaning toward them on one long, graceful wing.

As they came within range, Quinn addressed its pilot twelve miles away in the Guardian Star. "Hey Dawson, you out there?"

"*I'm here,*" came the disembodied replied through the com links tucked in their ears. "*Ready to get this show on the road?*"

"Ready as I'll ever be," Valaria volunteered. "I still don't know how we're both gonna fit inside that thing. As I recall from the last time I played stowaway, there was barely room for one."

Dawson remotely opened the payload compartment on the TAD's belly and the duo stood looking into an opening just slightly larger than an average-sized coffin.

"*It'll be cramped,*" he admitted, "*but you won't be inside very long.*"

"Here's your chance to finally get your hands on me," Quinn taunted.

Valaria pinned him with a sneer. "In your dreams, you egotistical prat."

"*Valaria,*" Hayes continued, ignoring their banter, "*I think you should get in first.*"

In addition to their InsulSkin flightsuits, both wore worker's coveralls and shouldered a small backpack carrying the items each would need. As Valaria climbed into TAD's dark maw she pulled the pack off her shoulder and hugged it to her chest in order to press herself flat against the back of the compartment.

Following her example, Gideon shrugged off his own pack and climbed aboard, pulling it tightly into his abdomen and shifting close to his partner so Hayes could remotely secure the hatch.

"Is that your tool pouch or are you just happy to see me?" Valaria quipped.

"Now who's being a prat?" he asked.

"Just a little gallows humor," she smirked as the darkness enveloped them.

All of the RSA's drones were designed to take off and land more to the vertical than the horizontal and required very little in terms of a runway as a result. From his work station in the Guardian Star, Dawson engaged the TAD's electric engine and brought the drone home.

We fight to set a country free and to make room

upon the earth for honest men to live.

~ Thomas Paine

CHAPTER TWENTY

I.

A solitary maintenance technician stood at the mouth of the shallow flight deck that fanned outward from the Guardian Star just above the midpoint of the mile-high tower. He looked westward across the expansive horizon where thunderclouds gathered.

A storm was coming.

The air grew humid with the threat of rain and he let it wash over him; even its humidity was refreshing after hours inside the environmentally-controlled behemoth that dominated the barren landscape.

Stepping out of range of the docking bay's cameras, the officer stretched languidly and watched the wide arc of an incoming TAD making its final approach. He was still in awe of TOD's big brother—both its size and the destruction it could wreak. Giving the drone a wide berth as it banked gracefully and glided onto the shallow flight deck, he jogged back into the bay, grabbed the umbilical tether that would recharge the TAD, and secured it for the night—totally unaware that stuffed inside was a truly one-of-a-kind payload.

"Sit tight 'til you hear the maintenance officer hook up the charging umbilicus," Dawson told the drone's passengers through the communicators tucked in their ears. *"There'll be a clunk and then a gentle hum similar to the sound they make flying overhead."*

Quinn and Thorpe lay face-to-face in the pitch black payload compartment, the other person's breathing their only point of reference. It was stiflingly hot and oxygen would soon be in very short supply so both were relieved when the external sounds played out just as Hayes described.

"I'll switch over to the docking bay cameras," Dawson continued, *"and release the hatch when it's clear."*

Long moments passed, their dark coffin growing increasingly stuffy as they lay as still as possible listening to the muffled sounds of workers scurrying around the landing bay hangar. Finally, Dawson's voice once again crackled in their ears.

"We got lucky; the drone's been tethered at the end of the line so there's nothing to your right but a wall."

After another lengthy silence—both in their ears and outside the drone—Hayes spoke again.

"OK, I'm gonna release the hatch, but brace yourselves—you're facing straight down so be careful or you'll drop right to the floor."

"I'll go first," Quinn whispered.

Valaria braced her feet against the end of the TAD's belly and turned slightly in order to grab the mechanism above her head that normally secured a more deadly payload and had been poking into the back of her neck for the entire flight. From his station far above them, Dawson triggered the pneumatic gear securing the hatch and it opened downward, bringing with it a rush of fresh air that filled the small compartment—and the grateful lungs of its occupants.

As Valaria hung in ungainly fashion inside the drone, Quinn dropped into a defensive squat beneath the pearlescent drone. When he gestured the all-clear, she released her hold and fell with admirable grace into a squat at his side.

The two operatives shielded themselves behind the widest part of the drone's fuselage and surveyed the landing bay. It was an impressive sight. About 200 feet across and almost that tall, the hangar was roughly octagonal in shape due to the angles of the tower and could accommodate at least a dozen TODs or about half that many TADs. Although spotlessly clean and meticulously organized, Quinn and Thorpe were surprised to see unexpected signs of wear virtually everywhere. As long as it was functional, apparently the RSA didn't care about the appearance of something so far away since they could always use stock footage of the tower from its prime if needed for their propaganda.

"Looks like we're good," Gideon murmured to their Guardian mole. "You get started shutting down systems at your end and we'll get going down here."

While Hayes worked to sabotage the tower's communication and scanning capabilities, Quinn's job was to shut down logistical systems in order to prevent the launching of drones. Valaria would complete their trifecta by accessing the primary maintenance shaft and crippling the elevator that traveled at amazing speeds up and down her grandfather's mile-high brainchild thus stranding as many Guardians as possible inside.

"Remember," Gideon reminded his partner before they parted company, "once you breach the junction box and plant the charges you'll only have five minutes to get back up here before the shaft blows. This is where running the stadium stairs pays off, kid, because you're really gonna have to haul ass."

"Yes sir, General sir," Valaria scoffed with a smirk and a mock salute. "Fifty e-creds says I'm back before you're even half finished."

"Fifty credits? Where the hell would you get your hands on fifty e-creds?"

Without replying, Valaria served up a final flippant salute and slipped away, moving unobtrusively among the resting drones toward an access panel on the back wall.

So far, so good, Quinn thought as he watched her go. If their luck held, within an hour he should be able to give Dodger the go-ahead.

But unfortunately, their luck had just run out.

Straightening the coveralls Dawson had supplied, Quinn stepped around the end of the glistening TAD just as a real technician emerged from underneath the wing of an adjacent drone.

The man looked at Quinn like a cow looking at a new gate.

"What the hell are you doing over there?" he demanded.

Gideon gestured toward the open TAD. "Just noticed this hatch has come open," he lied. "Looks as if something's wrong with the latching mechanism."

The technician's expression grew quizzical—and maybe even mildly suspicious—but he followed Quinn to the far side of the large drone in order to check it out. Just as they reached the open compartment, the landing bay was filled with noise and activity caused by the fortuitous arrival of an incoming TOD. Distracted for a moment, the Guardian glanced fatefully toward it.

That momentary lapse was all Quinn needed.

Grabbing the technician's head with his left hand, Gideon pulled the startled man flat against his chest by wrapping his right arm around his neck. As the man struggled to breathe and cry out, Quinn squeezed, applying pressure to both carotid arteries. Loss of consciousness came quickly and it was easy to finish him off with a sharp and silent left hand twist of his neck.

Before he could sag to the floor, Gideon hoisted the technician onto the curved cover of the TAD's gaping payload compartment. Grateful for the pneumatic connection that required little more than a tap in order to close, he watched the man's body rock slowly away from him as the curved hatch smoothly rose into place and dumped the dead technician into the belly of the drone.

Straightening his coveralls, Quinn moved on.

II.

Valaria glanced over her shoulder one last time as she reached the maintenance shaft's access panel at the back of the hangar. She could no longer see Quinn and the landing bay had just become a welcome beehive of noisy distraction as the approach of an observation drone focused the attention of the flight crew. Sporting an air of purposeful nonchalance, Valaria removed the panel, ducked through the three-foot-high opening, and secured the cover behind her. Nothing but a few anemic shards of light managed to shimmy through the ventilation slits at her back and she stood still for a moment letting her eyes adjust to the gloom as she paused on a narrow walkway that circled the perimeter of the open shaft.

"Geez Otis," she muttered, taking stock of her surroundings, "you couldn't have designed this thing with some built-in lights?"

Somewhere deep within the belly of the beast, the Guardian Star's heart pulsated with an ominous, rhythmic thrumming. It was accompanied by a constant rush of cold air that was funneled chaotically upward and made standing in the shaft like braving a windstorm on the prairie.

Three levels of that vortex stood between Valaria and the junction box that was her target.

Shedding her coveralls, she activated lighting panels incorporated into her flightsuit just below her collarbones and headed for the network of stairs some fifty feet away that would take her down into the wind and dark. The stairs were steep but rough in texture and, encouraged by the small oasis of light that accompanied her, Valaria began her descent with sure-footed confidence—but as she reached the landing of the level housing the junction box that confidence was suddenly up-ended as the lighting panels at her collarbones inexplicably began to flicker.

"Holy crap," she muttered as they gradually faded out.

In a moment the darkness that had been held at bay by the light of her flightsuit became absolute and the cold air rushing up from out of the inky blackness assaulted her with haughty bravado. It caused her to squint as she struggled to see into the abyss, shivering involuntarily before groping behind her and pressing herself against the reassuring wall of the shaft her fingers finally encountered. Clenching her fists in the encroaching dark, Valaria's focus snagged on the rhythmic thrumming of the mechanized heartbeat that pulsated from deep within the black and reverberated through the icy metal wall against which she now braced herself.

"Shit," she muttered angrily as the stark reality of being completely alone in an unknown dark momentarily overwhelmed her.

Taking stock of her situation as time in the dark lengthened, being alone slowly became as much an emotion as a physical reality and it pushed her thoughts in unintended directions.

Geez, her whole damn life had been pretty much defined by 'aloneness.' Even with Otis there were times when she'd felt solitary and apart, and despite her valued Minion status, aligning herself with Quinn and his Sons of Liberty had brought only a nascent sense of belonging— Hell, even her relationship with Farley Donovan had been a lopsided affair that would probably have satisfied neither of them had it continued.

She wondered if belonging was what she even wanted.

"Get a grip, woman," she murmured with a sardonic smirk at her lapse into philosophizing about the meaning of life.

Standing in the dark, glued against the wall of icy metal, Valaria realized that what she *really* wanted right then—what she needed as much as a flashlight—was the calming effects of a goddamn cigarette.

What a time—and what a place—for a nicotine attack!

Cautiously shifting her weight so as not to relinquish the rather precarious hold she maintained on her balance, Valaria once again peered into the black abyss below the narrow walkway on which she stood. It returned her stare with insolent confidence that its victory over her was now certain.

Her own confidence continued to wane as she found herself in the dark figuratively as well as literally; self-doubt slithering its way into her brain as the cold air chilled her thoughts as well as her flesh.

What had made her think she could do this? Had it been vainglory that induced her to break into this maintenance shaft with only a few tools and her meager understanding of the technology she was sent to sabotage?

Seeking a moment's refuge, Valaria crouched down, leaned back against the cold metal and absently fingered the cross that hadn't left her neck since Farley died.

As she struggled to decide what to do, thoughts of her grandfather rushed in. Everything she had undertaken to this point had been inspired by the embittered Luddite who had always taken a rather perverse pleasure in throwing a metaphorical shoe into the well-oiled machinery of society.

Well, unfortunately, it was going to take more than a *shoe* to accomplish the task entrusted to her!

Far below, close to three hundred resistance fighters were poised and waiting to begin their assault on the Guardian Star. She had to help them! If she couldn't—if she failed to find a way to disable the elevator, the tower would spew forth destruction and the patriots would be easily overrun!

"All right, Thorpe," she murmured, channeling her Son's of Liberty drill instructor, "move your scrawny ass!"

Rising slowly to her feet, Valaria slapped in frustration at the now lifeless light panels on her suit. They crackled with false encouragement but remained inert.

Carefully turning around so the rushing air no longer slapped her in the face, she stretched her arms out to essentially hug the angle of the wall she now faced. She moved slowly along the shallow walkway, the fingertips of her outstretched right hand leading the way with the heightened sensitivity of a blind person adeptly reading a text in Braille while her extended left hand provided support as she inched her way forward.

If she could find the junction box, she'd still have a shot at accomplishing her mission.

In her mind, Valaria could clearly see the schematics she had committed to memory and knew she had to be close. Her grandfather had entrusted those plans to her and it was as much for him as for the cause of liberty that she mustered the dregs of her confidence and determined not to fail.

Continuing to edge slowly to her right, right-hand cheek to the wall with arms extended, Valaria was beginning to feel encouraged about finding the box—but unfortunately the tremulous fingers of her outstretched right *hand* couldn't alert her to a broken panel and an impending gap in the walkway just inches away from her *feet!*

Without warning, Valaria suddenly stepped into nothingness.

Thrown off balance, she plunged into the unexpected gap, hands flailing for purchase and adrenaline shooting through her system with such force it felt like her internal organs were being shoved into her throat.

As she thrashed about, arms and legs akimbo, her chin struck the walkway's edge, clamping her jaws violently shut and momentarily forestalling her plunge into darkness. In the instant she dangled there, supported only by her chin and jaw line, her hands instinctively shot upward and grabbed the walkway's edge.

For a moment she hung limply above what felt like the vastness of time and space itself—with the uncompromising rush of cold air and the ever-constant heartbeat of the Guardian Star jeering contemptuously at her from deep within the dark.

Hands now clammy with fright and muscles straining, Valaria hauled herself back onto the narrow walkway, slid into a sitting position and pushed herself as far away from the edge as the depth of the ledge would allow. She sat motionless for a moment, frozen by terror and trembling with relief. Slowly her heart rate returned to a reasonable pace and she leaned her head back against the cold metal in an attempt to calm her mind as well as her body.

Which side of the gap had she ended up on? Stretching out gingerly to lie flat on her belly, she explored the walkway, closing her eyes in silent celebration with the discovery that the gap was now *behind* her.

She hurt all over—especially her head which had been violently jarred when her chin slammed onto the ledge. Rolling back to a sitting position, she concentrated on relaxing her breathing. Something was loose in her mouth and she realized she was bleeding. Assuming she had broken a tooth she worked it forward but as the rush of adrenaline receded searing pain was taking its place and she discovered she had bitten off the tip of her tongue!

"Oh great," she muttered, spitting the useless piece of flesh into the dark and forcing herself to stand. "This just keeps getting better and better."

Pausing every few moments to slap angrily at the bodysuit's light panels and spit out the blood that continued to ooze from the end of her throbbing tongue, Valaria resumed her blind examination of the periphery of the elevator's maintenance shaft in search of the junction box that was her goal. As irony would ordain, the box was only a few feet beyond the gap that had very nearly brought her quest to a seriously abrupt end.

Intensely aware of the fact that time was passing and the patriots on the ground would be overrun if she didn't disable the elevator, Valaria again slapped angrily at the uncooperative light panels below her collarbones. The one on her left flickered mournfully to life emitting an anemic glow.

"Better than nothing," she murmured.

Spitting out the blood that pooled under her tongue and threatened to dribble down her chin, Valaria turned to examine the utility box.

As expected it was state of the art, composed of the same lightweight alloy from which the Guardian Star itself was constructed and accessible by way of an eye scanner she couldn't possibly fool. In order to attach the explosives to the convergence of technology inside, she would have to cut through the row of smooth hinges along the edge of the cover using the miniature laser in her pack. The laser would only last about ten minutes but that should be enough. It also would provide additional light once activated so she could finally stop swatting the panels at her shoulders as if accosted by mosquitoes in search of a free lunch.

Small favors.

Focusing the laser's intense, narrow beam, Valaria had just begun the painstaking task of cutting through the formidable alloy hinges when a subtle but distinct shudder ran through the ledge—

The elevator was moving!

She switched off the laser and braced herself against the wall of the maintenance shaft. The shudder passed but as it did so the echo of an alarm added its plaintive wail to the ever-present torrent of cold air.

Somewhere out there, something was happening—but why the hell hadn't Quinn updated her?

Reaching up to activate the com link in her ear she discovered the reason for Gideon's silence; the link was missing—undoubtedly dislodged when she fell through the gap!

"Bloody hell," she sputtered in frustration, realizing her connection to the others was lost.

Reactivating the laser, Valaria assessed her progress—which was almost nil.

"God, this is going to take forever," she lamented.

Directing her gaze heavenward, her lament became a cry of desperation that echoed mournfully in the darkness.

"This is going to take *forever!!*"

She slumped down on the ledge in a defeated squat and turned off the laser. Because the junction box was made from the same alloy as the tower, attaching the explosive charge to the cover would do little damage; she had to get inside.

"Oh Otis, I can't *do* this," she admitted to her grandfather in anguished defeat. "They're going to be slaughtered and it's all my fault."

She moved from squatting to a sitting position, pulled her legs up to her chest and lowered her forehead onto her knees.

"Why didn't you pass on some of your technological expertise instead of just preaching your damned Luddite philosophy? Throwing a *shoe* into the works isn't going to make any difference here!"

Another shudder ran through the shaft and with it came the slow realization that, although a shoe wouldn't be sufficient, there actually was one thing she could do that might cripple the Star's elevator and keep the Guardians from sending squads to the surface. For a moment she thrust the idea aside but within seconds the decision was made.

There simply was no other option, and the thought of the brave patriots so far below fortified her growing sense of resolve.

As did the polka dot cloth still wrapped around her wrist.

Sliding up the cold wall so to stand erect, Valaria slowly opened the pliable zippers on each side of her flightsuit. With a graceful, almost reverent gesture she extended her arms and shook loose the lightweight wings they concealed, peered once again into the throbbing heart of the tower, and smiled sardonically at the uncompromising icy black below her.

"All this for a damn cigarette."

She heaved a long, cathartic sigh and brought Farley's cross to her lips before tucking it into the flightsuit's tight neckline.

Crossing herself slowly in deference to the archaic faith that had become her own, Valaria activated the explosive charge in her pack, spread her InsulSkin wings and embraced the icy darkness.

EPILOGUE

Garrett Spivey strolled slowly along one of the pedestrian walkways that meandered around Gateway Park and ultimately led to the mammoth Arch on the banks of the Mississippi. He hadn't been here since covering its rededication for FirstNet News when it was still one of the fledgling newsies on the re-crafted InfoWeb. His twelve-year-old grandson had never been here and he had decided the time was right for a pilgrimage to the historic site. It was late autumn and the influx of tourists had dwindled to a trickle so the duo had the place almost to themselves—the perfect setting for the walk through history the grandfather hoped to share with the beloved youngster.

Spivey paused and leaned against the railing to wait for Tyson. The boy had crouched down a few hundred feet back in order to get a better angle on the Arch he scanned with the multimedia tech that was a ubiquitous addendum to modern fashion. As he waited, the retired reporter's eyes moved from the main resident of the park to its dramatically smaller cousin centered in the grassy approach in front of it.

The meticulously crafted bronze statue was of a woman staring defiantly westward. Her sculpted hair was blowing away from her face in a nonexistent wind and she had one hand on her hip while the other reached down toward a dog at her side. Spivey's eyes grew misty as he read the dedication:

> "For Valaria Thorpe and all the Patriots of The Restoration
> who took the ultimate stand against tyranny."

Although less commanding than the riverbank's arch, this tribute to valor and self-sacrifice held more significance for Garrett Spivey than the gigantic monument that dwarfed it. He was especially moved by the ancient quote at its base:

> "May our land be a land of liberty, the seat of virtue, the
> asylum of the oppressed, a name and praise in the whole
> earth until the last shock of time shall bury the empires of
> the world in one common undistinguished ruin."

> Joseph Warren – 1772

Tyson joined his grandfather at the rail just as two other visitors approached who, unbeknownst to the Spiveys, were on a pilgrimage of their own. When his young companion started to move toward the statue, Garrett held him back with a light touch on the shoulder.

"Wait a second, Ty," he said. "Let's give those folks a moment or two alone."

Tyson shifted his attention to the opposite walkway where a middle-aged woman strolled alongside an elderly man in a autochair. He couldn't see the old man's face but the woman glanced their way, pushing her long, black braid over her shoulder as she smiled in gratitude at the pair of tourists waiting respectfully off to the side.

"Do you know them?" the boy asked.

"Not personally," his grandfather replied, "but I'm almost certain that's Senator Padgett-Quinn and her father."

"Quinn? You mean the guy who took down the Guardian Star? Wow, is that who that old man is?"

"Well, he had some help—like the woman in that statue—but, yeah, I'm pretty sure that's him."

As Spivey and his grandson watched, the other pair of pilgrims paused in obvious reverence before the smaller monument. Taking something from the hand of her father, the woman stepped closer to the statue to begin an annual ritual.

"What's she doing?" Spivey asked his grandson who was using his tech to surreptitiously zoom in on the duo.

"Looks like she's tying a polka dot cloth around the statue's wrist."

THE POLITICS OF "GUARDIAN STAR"

Readers undoubtedly will notice that the tyrannical government of *Guardian Star* rises from the ashes of the Neoteric Party, which is an off-shoot of modern progressivism. Creating a new political party was intentional on my part—as was the decision to place it decidedly to the *left* of America's political center. Virtually all dystopian fiction depicts a regime that emerges from the opposite political stance from what I've chosen, falling prey to the assumption that right-leaning governments might slither into totalitarianism whereas their liberal counterparts surely would stand firm against it. But I contend that *both* ends of the political spectrum reflect mirror images of extremism and, as a result, both run the risk of crossing the line into fascist tyranny.

To illustrate my point, consider the traditional political continuum as simplified below. It moves right and left from a moderate center with government control increasing the further you go in either direction—but only the *right* is traditionally tainted by the final label "fascist."

Democrats   **Republicans**

COMMUNIST   LIBERAL   MODERATE   CONSERVATIVE   FASCIST

⇐   ⇐   ⇐   ⇒   ⇒   ⇒

But I don't think the straight-line continuum works. Like many political scientists, I see politics as a *circle* where extremes of right and left *both* end in fascism:

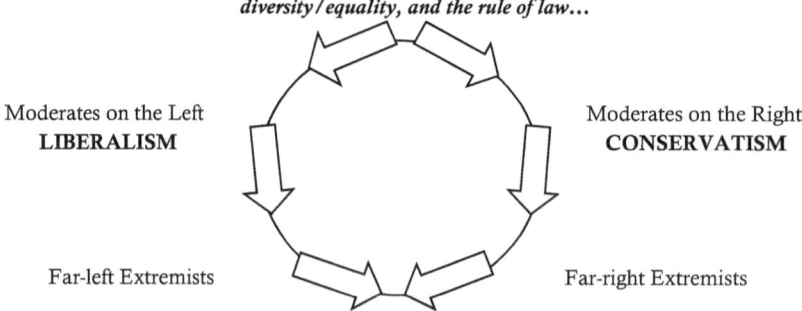

FREEDOM

From representative government, open elections, diversity/equality, and the rule of law...

Moderates on the Left
LIBERALISM

Moderates on the Right
CONSERVATISM

Far-left Extremists

Far-right Extremists

...to rule by few (or one!), strict government control/regulation, hyper-nationalism, and prejudice/discrimination against 'outsiders.'

FASCISM

As a result of seeing politics as circular, my vision of American fascism as portrayed in *Guardian Star* springs from the *left* side of the circle for two reasons. First and foremost because—under the wrong set of circumstances—I believe a liberal like Naomi Blanchard would be just as likely to embrace absolutism as any over-reaching politician on the right. Secondly, since they typically are given a 'bye' when dystopia is portrayed, I felt it was time to explore the potential for the development of *liberal* fascism.

Firmly believing that extremism on either end of the political spectrum has the potential to morph into authoritarianism, in closing I urge readers to listen to *every* political voice with a critical ear—and to challenge them when needed. Americans have always walked a tightrope between Left and Right since politics often boils down to deciding which side will create fewer problems. As a result, I place my hope in the average citizen, believing that they—as Thomas Jefferson said—should "decide for themselves what will preserve or endanger their freedom."

Guardian Star
and
The American Revolution...
Did you spot the connections?

I freely admit to having a fascination for the "what if" of futuristic fiction—particularly dystopia. As a lifelong student of history, I've also always been especially intrigued by the American Revolution.

So, as a fan of both dystopia and America's colonial period, when *Guardian Star* first began taking shape in my imagination, I found myself reflecting on the downward authoritarian spiral that developed between England and her American colonies. As a result, when it came time to put pen to paper – or fingers to keyboard, as the case may be – I had great fun slipping events from colonial times into the story of Valaria Thorpe and Gideon Quinn—as hinted at by the thematic quotes from famous American patriots that mark the beginning of each chapter.

In light of the above, I hope you'll indulge me a bit and check out the following "quiz" to see if you can identify the connections that have pulled my two fascinations together. Your forbearance is appreciated since I also must confess to spending almost 30 years teaching U.S. History and political science which makes throwing a quiz your way as natural to me as instincts honed in the classroom that have me inclined to try my hand at herding the neighborhood squirrels!

Let's start with some of the more basic parallels between the novel and the colonial rebellion, circa 1775...

1. The novel's Reorganized States of America (the RSA) correspond to which of the following real-life entities?
   a. France
   b. The American colonies
   c. England
   d. Spain

2. During America's fight for independence, which of the following would most closely have paralleled the Borders?
   a. France
   b. The American colonies
   c. England
   d. Spain

3. In the novel, the rebels hope the Republic of Texas will eventually support them against the RSA. This casts Texas as
   a. France
   b. The American colonies
   c. England
   d. Spain
   e. The Native Americans

4. Farley Donovan is an "import" from the Republic of Texas. As a result, which of the following heroes from the American Revolution does he most resemble?
   a. Lafayette
   b. Sam Adams
   c. Paul Revere
   d. Charles Cornwallis

5. During the American Revolution, England hired Hessian soldiers. What group plays a similar role in the novel?
   a. The scavengers
   b. The Freebooters
   c. The Sons of Liberty
   d. The RSA's "wraiths"

Now for a few questions that may be a bit more challenging…

6. In the novel, former Speaker of the House James McFarland's "Liberty Tree" nom de plume is never given. Who would he have chosen?
   a. Thomas Jefferson
   b. Patrick Henry
   c. Thomas Paine
   d. Benjamin Franklin

7. Banastre Tarleton had a reputation for brutality during the War for Independence and was often referred to as "The Butcher." Which character from Guardian Star most resembles Tarleton?
   a. Mavis Pope
   b. T'Neesha Jeffers
   c. Regina Agnew
   d. Kevin Eldridge

8. When the RSA institutes a Guardian occupation in Settlement #4, their action reflects a law that was absolutely *loathed* prior to the American Revolution. That law was known as
   a. The Quartering Act
   b. The Stamp Act
   c. The Intolerable Acts
   d. The Townshend Acts

9. While discussing the Guardian occupation at the pub, Jasper Hahn refers to the "Settlement Council." Which colonial era entity would be a close comparison to the function of that group?
   a. The English Parliament
   b. The Town Meetings
   c. The Continental Congress
   d. The U.S. Congress

10. Near the end of the novel Mavis Pope is sent into the Borders to supervise the residents and oversee implementation of "Radiance" among those identified as troublemakers. This casts her in the role of what colonial entity?
    a. A member of Parliament
    b. A colonial Governor
    c. A member of the Sons of Liberty
    d. A Hessian soldier

Finally, let's check your recall of Revolutionary War battles...

11. When Gideon takes a small team to warn "Sam Adams" and the garrison at Six Flags of an impending RSA raid, a comparison can be made to
    a. The Battle of Saratoga
    b. Bunker Hill
    c. The Battle of Trenton
    d. Lexington and Concord

12. Which of the following battles does the rebels' short-lived success at Ottumwa parallel? (The death of Milton Esparza, aka "Joseph Warren," is a great clue 'cuz the good doctor died at that battle just like Milton died at Ottumwa!).
    a. The Battle of Saratoga
    b. Bunker Hill
    c. The Battle of Trenton
    d. Lexington and Concord

13. This one's hopefully a give-away. At the Battle of Ottumwa, it's noted that Quinn and Esparza pass the order down the lines to *"wait until the RSA forces are close enough to spit on before opening fire."* What famous line from #12's battle does that parallel?
    a. "No taxation without representation."
    b. "We have only begun to fight."
    c. "One if by land, two if by sea."
    d. "Don't fire until you see the whites of their eyes."

14. Gideon Quinn's audacious plan to attack the Freebooters at Fountain Lakes is similar to what daring battle carried out by George Washington?
    a. The Battle of Saratoga
    b. Bunker Hill
    c. The Battle of Trenton
    d. Lexington and Concord

15. When they attack the Guardian Star, the Sons of Liberty hope to inspire the Republic of Texas to support them. Which of the following battles from the American Revolution does that parallel? (HINT: Remember what *country* Texas can be compared to.)
    a. The Battle of Saratoga
    b. Bunker Hill
    c. The Battle of Trenton
    d. Lexington and Concord

"KEY" to the Quiz...

At this point another caveat is appropriate. Because of my years as an educator, please be patient as my "teacher hat" slips back into place here and you get a little more than just the answers...

1. In the novel, the RSA (the Reorganized States of America) corresponds to (c) **ENGLAND**. Just as Great Britain controlled and, in many ways, took advantage of the American colonies (despite a certain level of colonial autonomy since 3,000 miles of ocean separated them!!), the Borders is being exploited and seriously oppressed by the RSA (in spite of experiencing their own dash of autonomy due to their distance from the Safe Zones).

2. OK, if the RSA can be compared to England then it's probably pretty obvious that the Borders parallel (b) **THE AMERICAN COLONIES.** The colonies were under England's thumb and

443

were considered *subjects* of the realm rather than bona fide *citizens*. Guardian Star's Pioneers find themselves in exactly the same position (with even more dire consequences in light of the regime's plans for "Ultimate Repatriation"!!!).

3. The fictitious Sons of Liberty's hope that the Republic of Texas will eventually support them against the RSA casts Texas as (a) **FRANCE**. By the time the American Revolution rolled around, France and England had sparred numerous times. Both were dominate players on the world stage and drooled over the prospect of expanding their influence into "The New World." The colonists knew that if they could get France to recognize and support them, they'd have a much better chance of gaining independence from England— just as the Pioneers' chances of success would grow exponentially if the Republic of Texas came in on their side.

4. As an "import" from the Republic of Texas – *the novel's version of France* – Farley Donovan most resembles (a) **LAFAYETTE**. The Marquis de Lafayette was a young French aristocrat—he was only *19!! Doesn't* that blow your hair back?!? As impressive as his age is, Lafayette's trip to the colonies was even more noteworthy. After being ordered by the French king not to join a fight in which France wasn't involved (and even after meeting England's George III), the young Frenchman was undeterred. Traveling to Spain, and *disguised as a woman* so as not to be recognized (or a courier, according to some sources), he finally set sail for America in 1777. And if that isn't a tribute to the teenager's determination to join our struggle for freedom, Lafayette's final act is the icing on the proverbial patriotic cake... To avoid delays that might lead to his discovery and arrest, *he bought a ship he named 'La Victoire'* so he and his small group could leave as quickly as possible! Farley Donovan likewise leaves the relative safety of Texas to align himself with the Sons and join a fight his country isn't involved in but that he – like Lafayette – sees as essential to the broader cause of liberty. And, like the young Frenchman, Donovan is willing to risk everything in order to make a bold and daring statement. Let's hear it for heroes!!

5. England's hiring of Hessian mercenaries from Germany during the American Revolution is similar to the RSA recruiting (b) **THE FREEBOOTERS**. Hessians were the "Terminators" of the 18th century— brilliant but brutal soldiers feared the world over. Where Guardian Star's Freebooters may lack the military polish with which the Hessians virtually gleamed, they undeniably are brilliant and brutal "foreigners" who are for sale to the highest bidder!

6. In the novel, former Speaker of the House James McFarland's "Liberty Tree" nom de plume would have been (d) **BENJAMIN FRANKLIN**. McFarland is an elderly politician who is in many ways the novel's patriarch. He has strong connections to the RSA but finds himself leading and inspiring the Borders's rebellion— without directly entering the fray due to his age. The comparison to 70-year-old Benjamin Franklin is probably fairly obvious. Franklin was one of the revolution's philosophers as well as being the colonists' envoy to England, America's first Ambassador to France, one of the writers of the Declaration of Independence, and a member of the Continental Congress. Both men were essential to the dramas in which they found themselves!

7. Banastre Tarleton was a scourge of the War for Independence with a well-deserved reputation for brutality. Referred to as "The Butcher," Tarleton most resembles (c) **REGINA AGNEW**. General Tarleton's influence within the British military was potent— just as Regina Agnew is a powerful presence in the RSA's opposition to their own "colonial uprising" and one seriously-scary lady! Like the General, Agnew is eager for recognition and status (she's determined to ultimately claim a position of authority in the capital city) and ruthless in her dealings with anyone who gets in her way (as seen most vividly in her engineering of the "terrorist attack" that claimed the life of Otis Thorpe's wife, a strategy designed to get him to join the Telliman Institute for which Agnew worked at the time and which she saw as a stepping stone to greater things!!).

8. When the RSA institutes a Guardian occupation in Settlement #4, they resurrect a colonial-era law that the American colonists found particularly odious. That law was (a) **THE QUARTERING ACT**. Under the Quartering Act (actually two laws passed by Parliament in 1765 and 1774), local colonial governments were forced to provide provisions and housing for British soldiers stationed in the colonies. That meant *the colonists themselves* had to provide living quarters and supplies for British soldiers they basically considered an occupational force, being obligated to give up space in their barns and even in their *homes*. When the Guardians are stationed in Settlement #4, the Pioneers living there are likewise expected to provide food and shelter for the occupiers regardless of the hardship such a requirement represents.

9. The residents of Settlement #4 definitely are NOT jumping up and down for joy at the prospect of a Guardian occupation. When they meet to discuss what – if anything – they can do about it, Jasper's reference to the "Settlement Council" most closely compares to (b) **THE TOWN MEETINGS** of colonial times. Before the revolution, colonists did enjoy a *dash* of autonomy BUT they undeniably were at the *bottom* of the English pecking order since the King and Parliament were still making the big decisions 3,000 miles away in England!!! Nonetheless, each colonial era community (comparable to the novel's Settlements) held town meetings where small-scale local problems were debated and resolved— just like the "Settlement Council" referred to by Jasper.

10. When Mavis Pope is sent back to the Borders to supervise the residents and oversee implementation of "Radiance" among troublemakers, she can be compared to (b) **A COLONIAL GOVERNOR**. As explained in #9, colonists did have *some* local authority but each colony also had a *Governor*— a loyal appointee shipped over from England who basically served as the King's eyes and ears, vetoing anything to which he felt the Monarch and Parliament would object and making it clear that the *real* power remained in the hands of the Brits. This is the role Mavis Pope

plays when she's sent back to the Borders to oversee the use of "Radiance."

11. In the novel, when news is received of an impending RSA raid on the weapons garrison at Six Flags, the small team sent to warn them can be compared to the skirmish at (d) **LEXINGTON AND CONCORD** which is identified by historians as the unofficial beginning of the American Revolution. The parallel is probably pretty obvious when you think about it— the Brits were absolutely salivating at the prospect of capturing Sam Adams and John Hancock who were reported to be in Lexington as well as confiscating the stash of weapons said to be stored in nearby Concord. Luckily, Paul Revere's and William Dawes's "Midnight Ride" successfully warned Adams and Hancock, and resistance at Lexington from the now-famous "Minutemen" bought the time needed to move the guns and ammunition stored in Concord. Guardian Star's version of events has Quinn and his group encountering Freebooters in the woods (their "Lexington") but then little drama at Six Flags (aka "Concord") since their Sam Adams has taken off and the contraband supplies have been relocated.

12. The fictitious Sons of Liberty's short-lived success at the defunct power plant in Ottumwa, Iowa (where I gave you the clue that the death of Milton Esparza – aka "Joseph Warren" – was key!) is similar to (b) **BUNKER HILL**. At the battle of Bunker Hill the original Sons gave a remarkably strong showing that put the British on notice and even had the larger, better trained and equipped force retreating several times before they finally gained the upper hand and overwhelmed the patriots. Unfortunately, in the process one of the Sons' rising stars – Dr. Joseph Warren – was killed; a leader who many historians say would have been as important as Sam Adams and George Washington had he lived! Guardian Star's "Joseph Warren" (Milton Esparza – one of the *Borders's* rising stars!) also is lost when the RSA finally overpowers the rebels at Ottumwa— but not before the heroic amateurs force the RSA into retreat twice!

13. When Quinn and Esparza pass the order down the lines at the Battle of Ottumwa to "wait until the RSA forces are close enough to spit on" before opening fire it parallels the famous line from Bunker Hill (d) **"DON'T FIRE UNTIL YOU SEE THE WHITES OF THEIR EYES"** extolling the Minutemen not to use any of their precious ammunition until the Brits were really, *really* close. It'll always be debatable which American officer said this— if *anyone* did. Some sources attribute the words to Gen. Israel Putnam while others claim the credit belongs to Col. William Prescott. Who said it, or whether or not it was said at all, is essentially moot since the patriotic bravado of the statement became firmly entrenched in American folklore regardless— and the same need for restraint and self-control it conveys is clearly present at our Battle of Ottumwa where the inexperienced Sons of Liberty volunteers are dramatically out-numbered and out-classed by RSA forces!

14. In the novel Gideon Quinn holds firm to his plan to attack the Freebooters holed up at Fountain Lakes despite their greater numbers and seriously-scary reputation— as well as the doubts of his colleagues and their advice against such a risky raid. Remembering that the novel's Freebooters can be compared to Hessian mercenaries, this incident is intended to resemble (c) **THE BATTLE OF TRENTON** in the actual War for Independence. After being chased out of New York in the fall of 1776, George Washington's exhausted, ragtag troops (about **90%** were gone at that point!!) settled in for the winter in New Jersey. Morale was super-low and Washington even wrote in a letter that he thought "the game is pretty near up." When Hessians were discovered nearby in Trenton, however, he decided to make a bold, kind of last-ditch statement by raiding them. Gideon Quinn's ill-advised raid on the Freebooters is equally audacious and – just like his 1776 counterparts – in spite of the odds being *dramatically* stacked against them the novel's rebels also are successful. Can you see the "Trenton-esque" aspects in the following quote from the novel: "*To his grateful amazement, the Sons appeared to be maintaining the upper hand, cutting down the notoriously well-disciplined, infamously unyielding Freebooters as they rushed around in bewilderment and disarray, totally*

disoriented by the surprise assault – and hampered by their still somewhat inebriated condition." The Hessians were sleeping off an "intoxicating" Christmas celebration when Washington's forces attacked. Just like our Freebooters, they attempted to rally but ended up literally running away— and just like in the novel, the original patriots suffered injuries but, miraculously, no one died! And one final comparison should stand out... both the fictitious and actual victories re-energized the causes for which our respective Sons of Liberty fought and re-supplied their dwindling resources.

15. The novel's climactic event – the attack on the Guardian Star – is the trigger that inspires the Republic of Texas to support my fictitious Sons of Liberty. If you remember that *Texas* represents *France* in the book, you'll see a parallel between this battle and (a) **THE BATTLE OF SARATOGA** because after the colonists' victory there the French began to openly support them against Great Britain. Most historians identify Saratoga as a pivotal event since the struggling Americans probably would have been forced to capitulate had they not received the help from England's longtime nemesis which came on the heels of that victory. The same can be said of the Pioneer's situation in the novel. Without Texas entering the fray on their side – an event *foreshadowed* rather than directly depicted in the book – the RSA almost certainly would have triumphed.

So how'd you do?
...And how did I do in terms of incorporating into "Guardian Star" a few comparisons between the Pioneers' plight and that of the original Sons of Liberty? If you're like me, dystopia is always thought-provoking and I hope this connection to U.S. history will make this particular dystopia even more so.

FROM THE AUTHOR...

Thanks so much for reading my book! There's nothing more gratifying than sharing the product of one's imagination with someone who enjoys the same kind of stories! I'm truly honored that you took the time and sincerely hope the characters—and what they experienced—spoke to you. If you'd be willing to review the book on Amazon and Goodreads I'd really appreciate it. Not only is your feedback invaluable to me as a writer but the more reviews a book gets the more likely it is to be discovered by readers with similar interests. So trust me, any social media thumbs-up you give to the books you're reading definitely puts a grateful smile on the face of whoever wielded the creative pen.

If you'd like to spend a little more time with Martha, Jacob, and the others, please visit my website at *www.lbrockwaylieske.com*. The site is a work-in-progress but I hope you'll enjoy the additional insights you'll find there about the story and the characters. The website also has information regarding my other novels, what I'm currently working on, and general areas of interest we might have in common. It's been fun putting it all together; please visit from time to time!

ABOUT THE AUTHOR...

Lorna Brockway Lieske is an award-winning educator who taught
American History and U.S. Government for more than 25 years.
Although she'll tell you she found her calling in the classroom, Lorna has
been a storyteller from childhood—spending summer evenings with
friends in Tucson, Arizona weaving tales with her sister for neighborhood
adventures they billed as "Story-Come-True." Lorna's love of story-
telling followed her into the classroom where her original curriculum
materials include "Hands-on-History" activities, educational short stories,
and simulations on topics ranging from the French and Indian War
through Westward Expansion to the Bill of Rights,
the U.S. legal system, and basic economics.
Lorna lives in Michigan with her husband Richard and their dog, a
loveable, loyal—and irrepressible—Shiba Inu named Riley.